Death Sentence

Jacki Bishop

Death Sentence – Jacki Bishop

©2014 Jacki Bishop. All rights reserved.

ISBN: 978-0-9905315-0-0

Early Riser Publishing
P.O. Box 711
101 E. Baltimore Ave.
Media, PA 19063
www.JackiBishop.com
jaxstir@comcast.net

Disclaimer:
The town of Media, Pennsylvania, in which Death Sentence takes place, is an actual town. All places mentioned in the novel are accurately portrayed. The characters and situations, however, are fictitious, a product of the writer's imagination.

Cover Artwork: © Nejron | Dreamstime.com

Cover Design: Rik Feeney / www.RickFeeney.com

Dedication

In Loving Memory of

Rose Marie Yost

Marilyn Osbourn

Iris Devens

Gone too soon....

Death Sentence

Acknowledgements

First and foremost, I would like to express gratitude to my family. My husband, Hank, patiently listened to each chapter as it came "hot off the press." More importantly, he took over as "tech guy" in the face of my technology deficit. My sons, Andrew and Eric (and his wife, Emily) were encouraging and helpful. Love and support from the rest of my family, Joyce, DJ, Marcia and Paul, was appreciated.

My "first reader," Mary Donaldson-Evans (and her husband, Lance) gave me sound suggestions for improving my novel. Mary was especially helpful at instructing me as to the nature of "real teen-aged girls." These wonderful friends were always encouraging and supportive.

My gratitude also goes to the many people in the justice system, my colleagues and friends. Leah Greene, my wise mentor and friend, taught me to navigate the system.

The "Chester Old School" intensive probation officers, whom I had the privilege of supervising: Rob, Dave, Derrick, Sarah, Heather, Karen—I love you guys!

Other important friends and colleagues include: Don, Dina, Ingrid, Meghan, Anthony, Deb, Mel, Jerry, Larry, Patty, Pete, and Diane. Please forgive any unintentional omissions.

Much appreciation goes to Tom and Kris, my writing instructors, who are very knowledgeable and were supportive and encouraging.

Huge thanks goes to my friend (since first grade!) Dorothea, who led me to Diane Harper, who encouraged me and introduced me to this process of publishing.

Last, but hardly least, thanks to Rik Feeney, my editor, publishing mentor, the "midnight writer" and comedian. He has helped me navigate the perilous shoals of the publishing world.

Chapter 1

"I didn't kill my wife, honest to God! You've got to believe me!"

Tears streaming, his face a mask of grief, words tumbling over one another, Jeff Korbin was a pathetic sight.

Sitting on the other side of the cold, stainless steel table, flanked by a burly prison guard, Rory Chandler sighed audibly. She looked around the bleak cell, pushing down her uneasiness and trying to concentrate on her client. His refrain was typical, but his intensity rang true; there was something compelling about it.

Now he was sobbing. That brought Rory out of her head and into the moment.

"Mr. Korbin, I want you to understand just what your options are. The DA has agreed to drop the Murder 1 charge if you plead, that is admit, to the lesser charge of manslaughter, and frankly…"

"No! Never!" He jumped up, a hulking figure towering over Rory. The guard stepped quickly to Korbin's side and gripped his arm.

"Hey, Korbin, you either keep it together, or go back to your cell. This lady's here to help you!" He nodded in Rory's direction.

Korbin sat down, head in hands. When he'd regained his composure he raised his head and looked directly into Rory's eyes, speaking quietly but forcefully.

"I didn't kill my wife. I will *never* admit to that. I loved Kathie."

"Mr. Korbin." Rory held his gaze and spoke calmly. "I don't doubt you loved your wife—in your own way. But the facts remain; if we go to trial, the jury will hear that Kathie had taken out a Protection from Abuse order against you. You must know that's powerful evidence toward motive, and very damaging."

"But that was *six months* ago! I hit her once and have never regretted anything so much in my life! We were in counseling together—did you know that? We were working things out— she was gonna ask the judge to rescind the order. Talk to our therapist!" He fumbled in the pockets of his jump-suit, handing Rory a rumpled business card.

It was indeed the card of a psychologist, with an appointment date that had already passed.

"Talk to her," he entreated. "She'll tell you!"

"I will, Mr. Korbin. In the meantime, I wish you would at least consider the DA's offer; I'll be back in a few days."

The anguished sound of his sobbing was audible as the guard ushered Rory out and the door clanged shut behind her. Her heart went out to Jeff Korbin; he wouldn't fare well in prison because he was emotional, and vulnerable. The other inmates would label him a "punk" or worse—she shuddered to think what could happen to him.

Rory consciously focused on Jeff Korbin and not her own fears as she was buzzed through another set of doors; with each second between locked doors she descended further into her own private hell.

She'd learned that it was important not only to know the guards' names, but to be friendly and not condescending. She'd heard stories of arrogant attorneys being "detained" between doors for overly long periods of time; this was part of the prison mentality, and she'd learned to play the game. It was especially important for her as a woman to strike the right balance— appearing confident and courteous.

As the last door closed behind her, Rory breathed in the fresh, though somewhat humid air and heaved a huge sigh of relief. It was always like this when she left the prison—a personal victory.

She looked back at the imposing grey stone edifice, its outer fence topped with barbed wire. The yard was dusty and bleak; several prisoners, clad in orange jump-suits, sat in groups doing nothing in particular. She guessed that even on this hot, humid, June day they preferred to be outside with at least a glimpse of freedom.

Rory strode quickly to her car before her presence could provoke comments from the inmates. She started the car's engine and cranked up the air, taking deep breaths.

She felt like she was thirteen years old again, visiting her brother, Sean in prison. After the visit, Rory had somehow gotten separated from her parents. Lost in her own thoughts and misery, she'd failed to step through the doors when they were buzzed open by the guards. When she came to her senses in the tiny, locked space, the terror had prevented her from calling out and she'd crumpled to the floor, where she remained until her distraught parents rescued her. They'd told her it'd been only five minutes, but to Rory it was an eternity…

A tap on her window brought Rory sharply to the present. Despite the air conditioning she'd broken out in a cold sweat. It was Gus, one of the guards she knew well and liked. She lowered the window. "Hi,Gus."

"Just checking on you Miz Chandler. I saw you sittin' out here for a while. You look a little pale; are you ok?"

"Oh, thanks for asking, I guess I was just lost in thought. I have a tough case…."

"Oh yeah," Gus replied, "Korbin seems a nice enough guy, respectful, not like some of 'em, you know? I'll keep an eye out for him, okay?"

"Thanks, Gus, I really appreciate that. See you next time."

"Bye, Miz Chandler, you take care now." Gus waved as she left.

He was a good guy, Rory thought, wondering how anyone could manage to stay cheerful and pleasant while working at the prison. But it did buoy her spirits that Korbin had at least one person to look out for him; he would need it. She was not particularly optimistic about her chances of getting him off.

She glanced at the clock on the dashboard. Oh shit! Late again.

Her twin daughters, Kate and Alex, played on a softball team. With any luck, if she gunned it, she might make the last few innings.

She was often torn with guilt over her commitment to her clients and her family; it was tough to find a balance. She'd done better when the girls were small and she worked only part-time. But now they were in high school and she felt they needed her less, and she enjoyed the challenges of her job. She knew she was a sucker for a tough case, and she knew why. If only Sean had had a competent attorney all those years ago, things would've been so different for him. She'd long since forgiven her parents for not paying for an attorney. And she realized that public defenders were, like other attorneys, varied in their abilities; Sean had drawn a particularly indifferent one who'd put no effort into the case. He was ok now; the substance abuse which had made his and his family's life hell for so many years had been under control for a while, as far as she knew, but still the emotional scars and depression remained. And Rory still worried.

The beautiful Pennsylvania landscape was rolling by pretty quickly, but she took a moment to appreciate its beauty, in full abundance this June afternoon. Looking again at the clock, Rory was pleased that she might see more of the game than she'd anticipated. That was before she saw the flashing lights coming up fast behind her.

"Fuck!" she blurted. "Now I'm done!" It was a Pennsylvania State cop and they could be pricks. She pulled over to the shoulder, grabbed her wallet and began looking for the necessary documents.

She saw the trooper in her side mirror approaching her vehicle, so she opened the window. She looked up, the resignation on her face changing to a smile, as she recognized her friend, Roland.

"Girlfriend, you were tearing up the asphalt. Where's the fire?" the trooper asked with a grin.

"Oh, Roland, my girls' softball game started 2 hours ago and I was hoping…"

"Be on your way, but consider this a stern warning! Oh, and watch out for those local cops; they can be treacherous! Keep in touch, you hear?" And he waved her on.

Whew! That was a close one. With any luck, she might still make the game.

Rory was smiling as she thought of her encounter with Roland. They'd been friends for a few years now. Though there were many African-Americans on the force these days, Roland was the only gay trooper she knew of, and he kept pretty buttoned-up. She knew only because he'd taken her into his confidence when he'd asked her to defend a friend of his, a teacher, who was in jeopardy of losing his job, solely because he was gay. She'd accompanied his friend, Ted, to the hearing before the board after reviewing his file, which bore witness to the fact that he was an excellent teacher. She "reminded" the school board of the consequences of firing a teacher on the basis of sexual orientation. The litigation could go on for years and would be costly; moreover, they would no doubt lose. Ted had kept his job, and in fact, was her daughter, Kate's chemistry teacher now. A damn fine one too, Rory thought with satisfaction.

Pulling into the parking lot next to the field, Rory could see the scoreboard. Good, the Panthers were ahead by 3 runs. Oops! It was the last inning.

Leaving the car, she quickly scanned the bleachers for her husband, Marc. There he was, her rock, standing up cheering the team on. Another wave of guilt hit her as she climbed up and put a hand on his arm.

"Hi Honey!" He gave her a quick kiss. "It's a pretty exciting game and I think the Panthers have it in the bag!"

"I'm sorry I missed it; I had to visit my new client at the prison, and then I got stopped for speeding, but fortunately it was Roland and he let me off..." Rory stopped, realizing that Marc was "back in the game" and hadn't heard a word.

She tried to concentrate on the game but was still wallowing in her own guilt for letting her daughters down, again. How was it that Marc could put his equally demanding job, as a forensic psychologist, on the backburner when it came to family? She had to admit that, lately, he'd been a better father than she'd been a mother.

The roar of the crowd signaled the game was over and Rory stole a glance at the scoreboard to reassure herself that the Panthers had won. She had no idea what role, if any, her girls had played in the win, but they were both good athletes so she assumed they'd done their parts.

Rory followed Marc to the field and joined in embracing Alex and Kate. Marc was lavish with praise. "Way to go, Alex, a home run to start off the game! WOW! And that double-play, Kate, that saved the day!" He ruffled their hair and kissed their shining, sweaty faces. Rory kissed her girls and beamed at them.

The girls were clearly too pumped to notice their mom had been late for the game. Kate spoke for both of them, "Hey guys, the coach is taking us all out for pizza after the team meeting, so we'll see you later at home!" And they ran off.

Rory looked at her watch, then looked at Marc. "It's nearly six, should we get take-out? What do you feel like?"

"Well," Marc grinned, "I feel like pizza, but I know that's anathema to you, so..."

"No, no, we can compromise. I'll get your favorite pizza and a Caesar salad for myself; done! By the way, 'Mr. Mensa,' thanks for giving me credit for knowing what 'anathema' means; it was your 'word of the week' awhile back. See you later." She smiled at the reference to his obsession with enhancing the family's vocabulary.

Rory called in the order and then drove to pick it up. She was only too happy to accommodate Marc's taste, especially since he was the one who showed up punctually at every game.

When she arrived home Marc had changed into sweats and was watching the news on the kitchen TV. She excused herself to change and left the food on the table.

Upon her return, Marc was halfway through his pizza and totally engrossed in the news of the day. Did she really want to hear the Dow-Jones had plunged again? Or that the youth all over the world were rioting in the streets? Financial chaos reigned; she knew that, she just got tired of having it hammered into her head. Besides, she really needed Marc's undivided attention right now.

When the news was over, Rory took the remote and turned off the TV.

"Hey!" Marc exclaimed. "What about Jeopardy?"

"I hope you don't mind skipping it tonight, I'm sort of preoccupied with my new case and I'd like your opinion on it. It always helps me to talk it out with you."

"Okay, shoot, I'm all ears," he looked up expectantly.

"I agreed to take on a reduced-fee client, and he's facing a Murder 1 charge. You may have heard about it; Jeff Korbin is charged with his wife's murder."

Marc did a double-take and his jaw dropped. "Are you kidding me? The D.A's slam-dunk murder case? That's the guy you went to see in prison?" His voice registered disbelief.

"Yes, and I'm taking the case," Rory answered quietly, beginning to panic. "And I could really use your help and support…"

"You can't be serious!" Marc was getting red-faced. "You're *really* taking on another difficult, time-consuming case? Are you going to keep fighting Sean's battle forever? Just because he got a lousy deal in court, you have to save everyone?

"That's not fair, Marc!"

"Not fair? What's not fair is that your family doesn't come first anymore. We are supposed to go on vacation together in a month—a long delayed vacation—together, as a family, or had you forgotten when you stepped in to play 'savior'?"

Maybe it was the mention of Sean, always a sore subject. Rory stormed from the room, emotions in turmoil.

In a fury, she went up to her office, where she paced the floor, her mind reeling. This was not her husband talking. This wasn't the patient, supportive husband who'd encouraged her to pursue her career. She knew she'd been absent more than usual lately, but Marc had given no sign that he objected; he just took up the slack. She suddenly felt weak and alone without his support and guidance.

Rory continued to think as she took a long, hot shower. Like her heroine, Scarlett O'Hara, she decided to deal with it tomorrow. But, she would do this with or without Marc's support; a man's life depended on her. She believed him to be innocent and she would *prove* that he was.

Chapter 2

Rory awoke as bright sunlight from the window at the top of the vaulted ceiling filled the room, bouncing off white walls covered with dancing rainbows reflected from hanging crystals. The leaves of a rubber plant glowed a bright green.

Still groggy from the pills she'd taken to sleep, Rory instinctively reached for Marc. His side of the bed was empty, although apparently slept in. She sniffed the air for coffee—Marc always made it—and smelled only the faint scent of lavender issuing from the sheets. She closed her eyes and listened; there was no sound, save bird song and the lilting chorus of wind chimes, filtering in from the partially open windows.

Gradually she remembered the awful argument with Marc the previous night. Too upset to sleep, she'd taken two Ativan, which she rarely did, and had fallen into a deep, dreamless sleep. She'd missed seeing her daughters last night, and, evidently, judging from the silence, this morning also. Despite last night's resolve to win this case on her own, she felt abandoned without Marc's support.

Rousing herself with some effort, Rory glanced at the bedside clock—8:30. She never slept this late, was normally in the office by 8, and she'd scheduled a meeting with her summer interns for 9:30.

Flinging her covers off, she stumbled to the bathroom with the hope that a hot shower would revive her. She let the water course over her body as she studied the patterns in the marble shower stall. Her brother Sean had redone the bathroom, matching artfully the veins of white and pink running through the gray stone; it always touched her that he'd taken such care to transform a mundane room into a work of art.

Rory had to stop this thought process, knowing she would inevitably start worrying about her brother. She finished the shower with a cool spray and stepped out to face the day.

Quickly she dried her mane of shoulder-length auburn hair, applied some mascara to accent her green eyes, and dressed casually. Since she'd scheduled no court appearances for today, she could dispense with her "lawyer uniform", a dark suit and heels.

Rory glanced at the bed—an antique double, with a tall carved oak headboard—it had been their first wedding gift from a college friend. Today, atypically, she left it unmade, and descended the back stairs to the kitchen.

The kitchen was spotless, which explained why she'd slept so late; there had been none of the usual morning noises, and Marc had undoubtedly taken the girls out for breakfast, she reasoned, with a stab of jealousy.

Peaches, the family cat, sat expectantly by her empty bowl, silently imploring Rory to feed her.

"Good morning, sweetie," Rory murmured, happy to find some life in this empty house. "Mommie will feed you." Peaches purred her thanks and rubbed her silky fur against Rory's legs. She was a gray Persian with orange flecks in her fur, and was as sweet as she was beautiful.

Conscious of time constraints, Rory put on coffee and toast. As she waited for her breakfast she looked appreciatively at her sun-drenched, spacious kitchen, feeling somehow comforted. The pale yellow walls and white wainscoting had a cheery effect, offsetting the rich cherry cabinets and dark granite counter tops; the kitchen of this old house had also been rehabbed by Sean.

She took her toast and coffee to the built-in breakfast nook. From her snug seat in the booth she had a clear view of the back yard. Her pale pink tea roses were in bloom, no thanks to her.

These hardy roses were found all over her neighborhood in abundance, no doubt influencing the name of her little borough—Rose Valley.

Hardly touching her toast—it tasted like sawdust—she knew it was time to head out. Checking that everything was turned off, she grabbed her bulging briefcase and went through to the attached garage. As her Prius glided soundlessly down the drive and into the street, she wondered idly whether Marc had taken the train or driven into Philadelphia; or, was he working locally today? It was odd not knowing where he was spending the day. She could've called him, but wasn't prepared for another rebuff.

Though his office was in Philly, and most of his testimony was given in their court, he also worked with local police and private attorneys giving his expert opinion on forensics—his specialty was profiling. Rory had used his expertise often, and hoped he might be helpful with the current case. She sighed, fearing this might not happen.

It occurred to her, in a flash, that her interns might be just the ticket. She'd been pondering how to use them, and this case seemed tailor-made. They would get the experience of working on a murder case, and she would have extra help.

Rory remembered interviewing the interns on a few occasions. Sarah Justice, a petite blonde, was at the top of her class at Widener. She had a trendy way of speaking, in which all of her sentences sounded like questions. Beneath that façade, Rory detected a fierce intellect. Sarah's father was a judge, so she probably knew her way around a court room, though she didn't seem the type to use his influence. Sarah had, Rory knew from one of Sarah's references, chosen to attend Widener Law School, when she would likely have been welcomed at her father's alma mater, Yale.

Sam Logan, while equal to Sarah in the brains department, appeared less confident. He was in the top third of his class at the University of Pennsylvania. That was Rory's school, and she knew how competitive it was. She'd not been in the top third—she'd worked her ass off to be in the top half.

Parking anywhere close to the court house at this hour was an impossibility, not to mention expensive, so she drove a few blocks down from her office to find street parking.

Leaving her car parked under a tree, she headed to her office. She actually loved walking the streets of Media, a small town, with an abundance of Victorian-era homes, tall street trees and perhaps one of the last trolleys running down the main street; it was charming and prosperous. Rory tried to stay in the moment as she took in the quiet splendor of the streets—walking was a meditation for her.

She approached the huge court house—a stone, columned edifice—taking up two blocks. The towering trees surrounding it were here in August of 1851, when the first session of court convened.

Crossing Front Street, Rory arrived at her office a few minutes ahead of schedule. Good, she thought, she'd have a few moments to collect herself. Blake Ford, her receptionist/man-Friday, also a part-time law student, bade her "Good Morning," and announced that her interns were waiting in her office.

"Thanks, Blake, did you...."

"Yes, Rory, I offered coffee—Sarah preferred tea, and they've been here...mmm, about ten minutes, I'd guess. You're later than usual, are you okay?" Blake seemed concerned.

"Didn't sleep well, Blake—tough case, you know?"

"Oh, yeah, I heard about it; maybe your interns...?"

"You're reading my mind, as usual. I'm counting on them. And now I'd best not keep them waiting any longer—please hold all calls, unless they're really important—thanks, Blake. And by the way, I really appreciate you!"

"Aw, shucks, Rory."

Blake hid his obvious pleasure in humor, as was his way.

"Good Morning Sarah and Sam!" Rory closed the heavy door behind her. "I'm really happy you're here, and I'm also glad that you're punctual. On the way over I gave some thought about your internship. And, believe me, you're coming at a good time, since I need all the extra brain-power I can get. What would each of you would like to learn during this internship?"

Not surprisingly, Sarah went first. "Well, I'm really excited to be here—I'm happy I got my first choice. I've sat in on plenty of hearings, trials, whatever, and I've done a ton of research for cases, but, I think, I'm ready to try out my book learning in the real world and get a feel for what it's like. That's about it." She glanced at Sam, as if giving him permission to begin.

Sam looked at Rory intently. He didn't speak immediately, seeming to first gather his thoughts. "I'm really not that comfortable in a court room—I find it somewhat overwhelming. I'd like to gain some confidence, specifically in the area of presenting cases before judges, DA's and even jurors. Like Sarah, I feel I've crammed lots of facts into my brain, and I'm eager to apply it. And, I'm happy to have you as a teacher, Ms. Chandler. You've a good record not only for winning tough cases, but also for being scrupulously ethical. I've had some of your former professors at Penn, and they give you high marks."

"Wow, I'm flattered! Thank you both for your candid answers. And please, call me Rory." Sam's praise lifted Rory's spirits, and she found herself momentarily at a loss for words.

Sarah chimed in, "Rory, I really like your name—don't know any women by that name—is it a nick-name? How'd you get it?"

Rory smiled. "You know, I get asked that all the time, especially by clients who'd assumed I was a man. My mother has never given me a straight answer, but my best guess is, that since she was getting her PhD in psychology during her pregnancy with me, she named me after the Rorschach. Who knows? She just says she liked the name, and saw no reason why a female couldn't have it. Oh, and one of the less famous Kennedy women is named Rory. And speaking of names, Sarah Justice, I bet you get a lot of flak about that."

"Touché—sure do get lots of comments." Sarah shrugged. "And honestly, there are many lawyers and some judges in our family history, so I don't know which came first—the profession or the name. I mean, you know, back in the day, that's how people got their last names."

"Well, I guess I'm glad my name isn't Sam Hill," Sam joined in with a laugh.

"It's good to get to know each other a bit; we'll surely know each other better by summer's end," Rory said. "Oh, and as I assume you already know from law school, always ask questions. That's how we all learn, and if I don't know the answer I'll at least point you in the right direction."

Both interns nodded.

"Okay, then let's get started. I'm representing a man charged with murder one, without an alibi, and against whom a Protection From Abuse order, PFA, for short, was taken by his late wife. He's in jail—couldn't put up the bail—and I believe he's innocent. I'm pretty good at spotting BS, and either he's an Oscar-worthy actor, or he's truthful; I know it won't be an easy case to try, he's the only suspect they're pursuing. The police seem to have a knee-jerk reaction, looking first at the spouse/partner and no one else; sometimes investigators get lazy. We can't afford to be—we'll have to work twice as hard. The DA sent me the discovery files—police reports, forensics—and there isn't much. So, what do you think?"

Silence reigned as the interns pondered their weighty assignment. Rory sat expectantly, suddenly fearing she was asking too much; after all, they each had another year of law school.

Sam broke the silence with a surprising enthusiasm. "Wow! What an opportunity—to just jump right in with a Murder 1 case. I'm really pleased that you have faith in us."

"Ah, yeah, I'm still taking it in—I'm kind of, like, flabbergasted? I thought maybe we'd be gofers, not doing much of substance, but this…." Sarah ran out of words.

Rory was surprised at their reactions—opposite from what she'd expected. Sam was showing real guts, and Sarah was, perhaps, less confident than she'd first appeared.

"OK, good. I do think you're up to this, and, honestly, I don't think I could do it without you. Now, I'm giving you copies of what I've received from the DA and I thought we could all pour over this until lunch-time and then discuss it at lunch."

As she handed out the papers, Sam waited eagerly and Sarah somewhat reluctantly.

The interns started reading the material immediately. Rory had read through it—and would do so again—many times. But for now she took a moment to observe her students. Sarah's brow was furrowed and she was chewing on her bottom lip. She played with her mid-length blonde hair, twisting it around her finger. She was undeniably beautiful, in a classical sense; however, it was revealing that she had nervous mannerisms, not initially apparent.

Sam was actually smiling as he studied the briefs. He briskly turned pages, jotted notes in the margins and was totally absorbed in the process. His longish brown hair flopped over his brow as he worked. He wasn't what Rory would call handsome—his nose was too long, his lips too full—but his warm amber eyes and sincerity gave him a real charm.

Rory relaxed, feeling she had allies here, intelligent, conscientious colleagues, who would be an asset in this difficult case.

*****

Rory tried to go over the same, raw facts with a fresh eye. The victim, Kathie Korbin, w/f or white female, age 39, had been strangled, apparently with brute force , and left in a heap in the middle of her living room. There were no signs of forced entry. The medical examiner estimated time of death at 2 p.m. on 5/15/14. Forensics found no skin under her fingernails, indicating she didn't put up a fight, and/or was taken completely by surprise. There were no fingerprints found in the home other than hers and her husband's (the defendant).

The pictures were hard to look at; it was difficult for Rory to be detached when confronted with a truly gruesome death.

The bruising on Kathie's neck was extensive and horrific; her eyes were open in what could only be construed as a mask of terror.

There really wasn't much to go on; the police were pursuing the obvious, a crime of passion perpetrated by someone who knew the victim. The spouse or partner of the victim was nearly always the primary person of interest. Add to that a recent PFA against the suspect, and for the police, it was a foregone conclusion. Was the case as straight-forward as the DA believed? She and her interns would have to dig around and think outside the box to solve this one.

Rory noticed Sarah looking around the office, and saw Sam look up. It appeared they had finished reading the discovery.

"Hold any questions until lunch, unless there's anything you need to know right now."

Sarah commented, "This isn't a question, but I was just admiring your office, especially that old desk."

"Good eye, Sarah," Rory smiled. "My former partner and mentor, Charlie Laws, left the desk for me, since he knew I loved it. It's a library table, actually, that's why there aren't any drawers; it forces me to be more organized." She smiled again as she thought of Charlie, and decided to call him soon.

"OK, I'm taking you to the Towne House, arguably the oldest restaurant in town and at one time the only one. It's a notorious lawyer hang-out; it even has an exclusive club within, where one must have a card to be admitted. Judges and elite attorneys dine there. I don't have a card—I'm a bit of a reverse snob. Even if I were offered a membership, I wouldn't join. Why don't you take a break, and I'll meet you in the reception area after I've checked my messages—say ten minutes?"

When they had left Rory took out her cell phone to check for any personal messages. Her heart leapt, and as quickly, her stomach knotted; there was a voicemail from Marc. She hoped they could resolve the nasty argument of the night before; their arguments were rare, and last night's was particularly nasty. And they'd never gone to bed angry with each other.

"Rory, I'm sorry I blew up last night—I know I over-reacted. It's just that, well, I know some background about this case. Can't really discuss it on the phone—we'll talk when I get home."

Chapter 3

Having dismissed her interns after lunch, Rory stopped back at her office.

Blake was at lunch; she checked her box for messages and found a few that she took to her office. Nothing pressing, except a call from the DA, which she would return first.

Secretly hoping Stan Como was still at lunch, she'd seen him holding court for a group of interns when they passed the exclusive "Lions' Den" club at the restaurant, she planned to leave a short message and continue the game of phone tag. His receptionist answered. "Hi Janet, it's Rory, is Stan in?"

"Sure thing, Rory, he just came in. I'll put you right through."

"Rory, hello, thanks for getting back to me. It's about the Korbin case," the DA offered briskly.

"Hi Stan, I assumed it was. I met Korbin for the first time yesterday."

"And I assume you offered our terms in the plea agreement?"

"I did, but he wasn't having it; he claims he didn't kill his wife and won't go for a plea. He hopes to be exonerated."

Stan's response was somewhere between a snort and a snarl. "You're kidding, right? It was a generous offer and won't stay on the table long! Did you remind Korbin that the death penalty is an option?"

Rory replied calmly. "I explained the plea bargain to him and urged him to consider it; he was emphatically opposed to it and very emotional. I felt little was to be gained by pressing the issue."

"Do you think you have a snowball's chance in hell of winning this?"

"That remains to be seen, Stan, but I have to honor my client's wishes and won't cram the plea agreement down his throat." She struggled to keep her anger at bay.

"How noble of you, Rory, not to mention naïve. So, I guess I'll see you in court."

"Unless Mr. Korbin changes his mind," Rory replied.

The line went dead.

"Shit! Shit! Shit!" Rory cursed, pounding her fists on the desk.

Back from lunch, Blake rushed into her office. "What happened? You okay?"

"That goddamn, pompous-assed, son-of-a-bitch DA! Sorry, I didn't hear you come back."

"Oh, you returned Stan Como's call; that's never fun."

"Sorry about the outburst…"

"It wasn't the first and won't be the last, but it's my favorite part of the job!"

"Tell you what, Blake, I'll need help to win this one. Thank goodness the new interns seem sharp. They could be a huge help to me."

"So, Sarah's smart as well as pretty…"

"And I think you know where I stand on office romances?" Rory tried to sound stern.

"Yes, Ma'am," Blake replied in mock solemnity. "I guess that's why we've never hooked up." He leered dramatically before making a quick exit.

That and twenty years, she thought, but it did make her smile.

She was finishing the last of her calls, when Rory remembered the conversation with Korbin and the card he'd given her. Finding it in her purse, she dialed the number of his therapist, Dr. Adele Grant. Rory was surprised when Dr. Grant answered in person. Explaining who she was and acknowledging doctor-patient confidentiality, Rory asked if the doctor could simply confirm that Jeff Korbin and his late wife had been in counseling together. Sensing the doctor's reticence, she added, "Look, you can phone Jeff at the prison, or I can get him to sign a waiver."

After a moment's hesitation, Dr. Grant answered. "Considering the gravity of his circumstances, I can tell you they were in therapy." She added "I'll be happy to testify for the defense in court if it comes to that."

"Thank you so much Dr. Grant—it may come to that. I do appreciate your help."

Rory thought this could well be her first stroke of luck A witness for the defense; that was a start.

Satisfied with her accomplishments, she noted it was only 3:30 and decided to head home. She'd missed so many family dinners, not to mention her girls' games with her long hours.

She told Blake she was leaving for the day.

"Didn't mean to scare you off," he grinned. "Seriously, it's good to see you go home early for a change."

Rory pulled out her phone and listened again to Marc's voicemail as she walked to the car. She was alert for any clue as to his mood; she heard only contrition in his voice, and breathed a sigh of relief.

Her next thought was, what could he know about this case that she didn't already know? And would it help or hurt her client? She would simply have to wait. She turned her attention to planning a special dinner for Marc—it would be just the two of them, because the girls had a late practice.

Arriving home after buying groceries for dinner, Rory felt unbelievably lucky, especially considering how she'd felt this morning. Often too busy to appreciate that her home was her sanctuary, she dumped the sack of food, and made herself a cup of tea.

She took her tea outside to the wrap-around porch, putting her feet up. She was hidden from her neighbors, her rambling, turn-of-the century stone and frame house was tucked back from the road behind high hedges that lent privacy. She recalled spending many evenings on this porch in nice weather. Towering oaks, tulip poplars and ashes stood like sentinels around the perimeter of their almost two acre property. She smiled and breathed in the fresh air.

Her tea finished, Rory unpacked the groceries and started preparing their special dinner. She rinsed the scallops and fresh lettuce from her garden separately. Slicing a loaf of crusty multi-grain bread , she coated both sides with fresh garlic and olive oil, then wrapped it in foil. Home-made pesto from the fridge completed her ingredients. Glancing at the kitchen clock she noticed it was nearly five. She wondered what time Marc would be home; she decided to call him.

"Hi, Hon," he answered on the first ring. "You got my cryptic message?"

"Yes, I did—I know we can't discuss it on the phone. Just wondered when can I expect you for dinner?"

"For dinner? Great! How about I pick up some wine? Let me check the train schedule; hmmm, looks like if I catch the 5:28, I'll be home by 6:15—ok? Better run—love you."

"Love you, too," Rory replied quietly. But he'd already hung up.

Later, Marc strolled in; laden with wine and daisies—her favorite flowers—just as Rory was putting the final touches to the salad.

Sniffing the air and taking in the table setting, he exclaimed "What have I done to deserve this? I smell scallops and pesto, right?"

"Yep, and one apology deserves another. I owe you one, too, for storming off. Let's enjoy our feast and then talk."

*****

After the dishes were rinsed and stowed in the dishwasher, Rory and Marc sat down in the breakfast nook.

Rory was on pins and needles, but knew better than to rush Marc, who was taking his time, collecting his thoughts.

Finally he spoke. "Where to begin? O.K., I know Jeff Korbin, went to high school with him and we played football together. Kathie was a few grades below us; he fell in love with her the first time he saw her—she was a knock-out—sweet girl, too." He stopped to sip his wine and then continued.

"Jeff was lucky to catch her eye and they dated. He was the star quarterback—counted on getting a full ride to college. There were lots of scouts and we all thought he'd get into a Division-I school, maybe Penn State or Michigan. Problem was he never got an offer. Rumor had it that he may have been taking steroids. Anyway, his folks couldn't put him through school, and no more scouts came. Kathie dropped him like a hot potato. He went nuts in the locker room that day, throwing stuff around, kicking lockers…"

"Hold it; you're not saying that he killed her over that, all these years later!"

"There's more," Marc continued calmly. "Kathie started dating other guys in our class, they were all college-bound. And it soon became obvious to me that she was looking to move up in the world. Couldn't blame her; her parents owned a little grocery store and they expected her to help out once she finished school. College wasn't in her future either. She ended up with Brandon King, the captain of the team, who was headed to Dartmouth. They dated until graduation. Meanwhile, Jeff did not take it well. One day in the locker room, Brandon was bragging about how far he'd gotten with Kathie, when Jeff took a swing at him and hit the locker instead. Then he kicked it and warned Brandon that if he ever so much as heard him say Kathie's name he'd kill him."

"And, from that scenario—what? over 20 years ago, you deduce that he's capable of murder? Raging hormones and huge disappointments not withstanding? Look, you've told me nothing that would hold up in court!"

"I know that! But I'll never forget the look on his face when he was protecting Kathie's honor, (Marc used finger quotes). It was naked rage, fueled by jealousy. Look, I'm not trying to build a case here, I just wanted you to have some background, and as a profiler, we do take history into account. I thought you should know who you're dealing with"

"And I appreciate that, I do. I just wonder what relevance it has today. I guess I need to know if he's kept a steady job, had any run-ins with employers, or any major blow-ups. I certainly don't want to be blind-sided by that asshole DA."

"Let me guess, Stan-the-man—and your fave!"

"You guessed it. Now, getting back to the past, after all that drama, somehow Kathie and Jeff got back together."

"Well, we graduated, my friends and I all went off to different colleges. Brandon never called Kathie or kept in touch at all after he left. She, like the dutiful daughter, went to work at her parents' grocery."

"And Jeff was more than happy to step into the void."

"Not right away. But eventually, I think, Kathie realized that her chances were limited. To her credit she did get an associate degree in paralegal studies. Jeff had a decent job at UPS. They started dating and…"

"So, you're saying she 'settled', that she was opportunistic and didn't love him?"

"I'm not saying all that. But the word around town had it that she got knocked up, so they got married. Supposedly she miscarried and couldn't have kids after that."

"Actually, I'm surprised at how much stock you put in the local rumor mill—I had no idea. "

"Look, Rory, in a nutshell, here's what I know of Jeff: he's strong, athletic, and can be prone to violence, especially where Kathie's concerned. We already know that he hit Kathie. Do you know why? I think it would behoove you to find out. Believe it or not, I'm looking out for your best interests here."

"I know that, Marc, and I appreciate it. It's just that I'm desperate to find a way to win this case."

"What if it's not winnable? I mean, maybe you should persuade him to cop a plea?"

"Oh, God, now you're sounding like Stan!"

"Take that back!" He leaned across the table and playfully swatted her hand.

They were chasing each other around the house in what looked like a game of tag, when the girls came in.

"So, this is what you do when we're not home? Run around like first-graders at recess?" Kate gave voice to her thoughts, while Alex rolled her eyes.

"More importantly," Alex added, "got any dinner left for hardworking, serious girls who worked their butts off at practice? It sure smells good in here!"

Rory, doubled over from laughter and exertion, nodded to the kitchen. "Of course, we saved some of your dad's favorite meal for you—you'd best get to it before he does!"

"Oh man!" Marc complained in mock horror. "I was sure that whole thing was for me! How often do I get this meal? How often does your mother *cook*, for that matter?"

The girls were unmoved as they filled their plates with what was left of the meal. They sat in the breakfast nook and their parents joined them.

Conversation centered on their practice and the likelihood of their getting into the playoffs.

Katie, who had finished eating first, said "We have a pretty good chance of beating Conestoga, but it's not a shoe-in—we'll have a grueling practice tomorrow."

Rory listened appreciatively as she watched her animated daughters. They were fraternal twins, each with her own personality and with features from both parents. Katie had her father's dark hair and bright blue eyes, while Alex had strawberry blond hair and Rory's green eyes. They were attractive, athletic and bright. Katie was a few minutes older than Alex, and often took the role of big sister; she could be bossy, Alex often complained. They had a strong bond, but also had lives and friends of their own.

Marc was in on the discussion of the team's chances and had some ideas of his own, since he hadn't missed a game. "I agree that Conestoga will be a tough one—is their ace pitcher still out of commission?"

Kate and Alex looked at each other and grimaced. "Sources report she may be recovered enough to play," Kate said.

Just then, Rory's cell trilled and she left the table to find it and take the call. As she answered, she noticed it was Ginny's number. Her stomach knotted, as she hoped Sean's wife didn't have bad news. "Hey, Ginny, good to hear from you," she lied. Ginny usually called when there were problems with Sean. And from the tone of her voice, it sounded like this was no exception.

Rory glanced over to the nook, where the girls were still conversing, but Marc seemed to have left the discussion to listen to Rory's conversation.

"Well, to be truthful, things aren't going so well for Sean right now. He's depressed, has missed several days of work, and….." she burst into tears.

Rory lowered her voice; she knew Marc was listening, and didn't approve of her "meddling," as he called it, in Sean's life. "I'm sorry to hear that, Ginny. Is he still taking anti-depressants?"

"No," Ginny replied forlornly. "That's a huge part of the problem, as soon as he feels better he stops taking his meds. And he won't listen to me, won't see the shrink. I was hoping maybe you could talk to him. You seem to be the one person he always listens to. "

"Of course I'll talk to him, can you put him on the phone?"

"Well, he won't leave his room, he'd be angry if he knew I called you. I was wondering if you could possibly come down to see him, I really hate to ask, I know you're busy..."

Rory felt backed into a corner, but could she turn her back on her brother? She never had. "Uh, well, if the girls get into the soft-ball playoffs, there will be a game Saturday. I could leave after that, and be in Baltimore by early evening, if that works."

"Thanks so much Rory—that would be wonderful. I just can't tell you..."

"You know I'm always there for Sean—see you soon. Bye."

Rory couldn't help noticing that Marc had left the room. The girls looked at each other quizzically, and then at Rory.

Chapter 4

Resisting her first impulse to rush after Marc and plead her case, Rory decided to let him stew for a while. Instead, she sat down with her daughters to answer the question on their faces.

"That was your Aunt Ginny—apparently Uncle Sean isn't doing well. She's asked me to come down and talk with him."

"Can't you talk to him on the phone?" Kate asked.

"If only it were that simple." Rory sighed. "Ginny hasn't been able to get him to leave his room and he's missed several days of work. He's that depressed, and off his meds."

"Well, duh, no wonder..." Kate's lips were pursed.

Alex cut her off. "Sounds like he's in bad shape, Mom, you look upset."

Fighting tears, Rory choked out "Yeah, it's tough for him and Ginny needs support. Sean's my big brother, he always took care of me. It's my turn now; you two know how close siblings can be."

"Mom." Alex bit her lip. "Why did Daddy leave the room like that?"

"I can't speak for him," Rory said carefully. "But in the past he's been critical of my involvement in Sean's life."

Kate jumped in. "He hates it when you leave—he's such a grouch!"

"Well, I'm sure you two can cheer him up. Besides, I'm not going down until after what I assume will be your first play-off game on Saturday."

"Don't jinx us, Mom!" Alex wailed. "Tomorrow night's game will be really tough! Coach says 'One game at a time'."

"Okay," Rory soothed. "From what I've seen, my prediction is that you'll come out on top; just my unbiased opinion. It's getting late, girls; you must have homework." She kissed them both and went to look for Marc.

As expected she found him on the computer in his study, staring fixedly at the screen. He didn't look up when she entered. She sat in a chair across from him and prepared for a long wait; he surprised her with a quick response.

"So, I guess you want my blessing." He glared at her.

"I know better than to expect that, Marc." Rory's voice was a whisper. "I've only ever hoped that you could understand."

"It's tough, Rory, for me to understand how you can miss your daughters' games and then rush to Sean's side the minute he calls for help."

"He didn't call—it was Ginny. He's too depressed to get out of bed, hasn't been to work…"

"Then he needs to man-up—take control of his life, stop asking his sister to manage it!"

Marc's recalcitrant stance silenced Rory. "I don't have the energy to argue with you—let's just agree to disagree." Rory left the room before Marc could see the tears coursing down her face.

*****

After another night of drug-aided sleep, Rory awoke early. Glancing over at Marc, it looked as though he was still asleep.

The girls were up and dressed and met her in the kitchen. "I'll drive you to school," she offered. "That way we can have breakfast together."

"Great, Mom!" Alex gave her a hug.

"Do we have time for waffles?" Kate asked. Then, looking around, "Where's Dad?"

"Still sleeping—we'll leave him some waffles if he doesn't make it down in time. Kate, Alex, look alive! Help me get this show on the road."

The girls scrambled to get the ingredients and implements while Rory, despite her queasy stomach, hurried through preparations.

Breakfast over, without an appearance from Marc, they put their dishes in the sink. Rory left a covered plate of waffles for Marc with a note: "Missed you, enjoy the waffles. And please feed Peaches. Xo- R"

On the way to school, radio blaring, Alex turned the volume down to ask Rory, "Mom—are you coming to the game tonight?"

"Of course!" The question was a punch to her gut.

"OK, great, I just wanted to remind you that—win or lose—there's a tailgate after the game."

"Oh, right—I'll stop by Planet Hoagie and get a tray of assorted hoagies—ok?"

"That would be perfect—thanks mom!"

Arriving at the school, Rory pulled over to let the girls out.

"Thanks for breakfast!" they chorused.

"Good Luck! See you later." She spoke to their backs as they raced each other to the building.

Rory was early for work—not only did she find a parking space close to her office, she soon found she was the first to arrive. It was just 7:30.

She happily unlocked the front door, turned on the lights and went straight through to her office. *Bless him,* thought Rory; Blake had tidied the desk she'd left in disarray in her haste to leave yesterday.

Getting right to work on a list of activities for the interns, she wrote: Investigate crime scene/observe hearings in Adult and Juvenile Courts, visit the prison , visit law library.

And her list included: call Charlie for lunch, check Jeff's employment record, do police check (Roland).

That was enough for the moment she decided as Blake came in with her coffee. She looked up, surprised—she hadn't heard him come in.

"Good Morning, Sunshine! Jeez—I thought we'd had a break-in; when's the last time you beat me to work? What gives?"

"Good morning, Blake—thanks for the coffee, and for straightening up my messy desk. To answer your question—I got to bed early, got up and had breakfast with my girls and took them to school. It was nice." Rory beamed.

"It seems to have done you a world of good." Blake smiled. "What's on today's agenda, Boss? Anything you need me to do?"

"I've jotted a list of activities for Sam and Sarah—do you mind having a look?" She handed him the list. "And if it looks ok, please make copies for the interns."

Blake read it, nodding. "Looks good—if you want I can take them to the courts, introduce them, maybe sit in and answer their questions."

"I think today we'll focus on having them visit the crime scene, and later we'll go to the prison. Would you like to go?"

Blake didn't answer immediately; Rory looked up, cocked her head.

"Nah—really don't want to. I know I'll have to eventually, but, it creeps me out," he admitted with a rueful grin.

"Believe me, I feel your pain. Let me know when you're ready; it's better to go with someone who knows the ropes. Oh, please call the prison and make sure the warden knows I'm bringing interns. It's no big deal, but they like to know."

"Sure thing." Blake answered. The sound of the front door opening ended further discussion and Blake rose to greet the interns.

Blake handed Rory the copies, as Sam and Sarah came in with their coffee and tea . They appeared full of anticipation. Rory stood, smiling her welcome and handed them each a copy of the list she had made as she motioned for them to sit.

"So, here's the list for the next couple of days, have a look at it and I'll answer any questions."

Sam responded first. "It's pretty straight-forward, except I'm not sure about the crime scene investigation? What's that about?"

Sarah looked up and nodded. "Yeah, is that something we can even do?"

"I think as students you have a lot of latitude. You can do it on the down low—you know, ask questions, ask the cop on duty to show you around. Cops get kind of bored staking out a crime scene, so they might welcome the break. Just see what you think. We seem to agree that the police didn't collect much evidence from the scene. Actually, I'd like you to do it this morning, and then we'll go visit Korbin this afternoon."

"Okay, jumping right in—I like that!" Sam grinned.

"So, we just, like go there and see what we can see?" Sarah was biting her lip.

"That's about it—let's not over think this. Just trust your instincts."

Rory gave them the address and they agreed to be back by lunch if not sooner.

Then she settled down to her list, calling the HR department of UPS. She was pleased to reach someone fairly quickly. At first somewhat guarded, the woman who answered was persuaded to talk after Rory explained that she could have Korbin's employment records subpoenaed if necessary.

As it turned out, Jeff's employment at UPS was without incident—he'd received good evaluations regularly in his 20-odd years with the company.

Relieved, Rory was beginning to have some hope. So far, the two phone calls she'd made on his behalf had yielded positive results. The next was to Roland—she left a message on his cell asking that he check for a criminal record on Korbin.

She'd saved the best call for last—now she phoned her old partner, Charlie, to plan a lunch meeting soon. He answered on the second ring and seemed delighted to hear from her. "So good to hear your voice, Rory, I've missed working with you."

"Ditto—I've missed you terribly, when can I take you to lunch?"

"Let me check my appointment book, it seems I'm busier now than when I worked. OK, I've got Wednesday or Thursday open next week; what's your preference?"

"Can you pencil in both days, and I'll call you next week?"

"Sounds good—'til then, take care."

"You, too—say Hi to your wife for me. Look forward to seeing you."

Rory hung up with a nostalgic smile on her face. It would be great to see him again.

Busying herself with overdue paperwork she'd put on the back burner since taking Korbin's case, Rory wrapped up a good deal of the important work, and created a pile of minutia for Blake. She was distracted when a call came in.

"Hello, Rory here," she answered crisply.

"Well, hey, Sugar, with the lead foot—you called?"

Rory's faced creased into a smile as she recognized the trooper's voice.

"Hey, Roland, how're you doing?"

"Just fine, thanks. Got your record check done..." He was being coy.

Rory prepared herself for the worst. "And?"

"It was boring, frankly—your man is clean, we got nuthin' on him. I had no idea you were in on such a high-profile case."

38

"Nice way to put it, Roland—you mean how did I get mixed up in a loser case? The DA is pretty confident, and threatening the death penalty since Korbin won't cop a plea, but it's beginning to look up."

"I have confidence in you, Rory."

"Thanks, Roland, I appreciate that; how about lunch when this is over?"

"You bet; I never turn down a free lunch. Bye now."

Perhaps my luck is turning around, she thought, but, realistically, she knew there was a long road ahead.

Just then, Sarah and Sam burst through the door, obviously revved up.

Rory looked up expectantly. "Well, go ahead, what did you find out?"

Sarah started. "We found something...at least, Sam did—don't know if it's good or bad."

Sam continued, "I found Kathie's appointment book wedged between the headboard and mattress of her bed. I looked through it quickly, but did find a 2PM appointment with a 'JK' on the day before she died."

"Good work finding it! It at least proves that the CSI team didn't bust their asses finding evidence. You did put it back, right?"

"Of course! And I picked it up with a tissue," Sam confirmed. "It made me nervous just looking at it!" he shuddered involuntarily.

"Good instincts, both of you—that was pretty gutsy; you did well your first time out! Well, now we have more questions for Korbin—ready to go to the prison?"

Grabbing lunch on the way, Rory updated her interns on the information she'd received during the morning, emphasizing the positives.

Rory drove while Sam and Sarah kept up a constant chatter, lapsing into silence when the prison loomed before them.

"I know it's creepy," Rory empathized, "but just follow my lead; you'll be fine. The warden has sanctioned your visit."

Having been buzzed through several doors into the bowels of the prison, the trio waited in the small, stark interview room.

"I'll be taping this interview as I've done with our discussions—it helps later when we can be more objective."

Korbin was ushered in by the guard and sat across from Rory at the table. She introduced the interns and got straight to business.

"Mr. Korbin—we've been investigating and have some good news and some not so good—which first?"

"Might as well hear the worst first." The muscles of his face tightened, as if he were bracing himself.

"We've found Kathie's appointment book. The day before her death she had 'JK' marked in for a 2 p.m. meeting—was that with you?"

Jeff looked puzzled, not immediately replying. "No, I'd seen her a few days before that, at our counseling session." His face grew dark as he continued. "But she called me that night before she died and left a message—my phone was off. She sounded upset, maybe scared, and asked me to get back to her. I didn't even hear the message 'til the next day, and by then…, if only I'd had the chance to talk to her…" He put his head in his hands.

"I guess the message is still on your phone?" Rory had to ask.

He raised his head. "Don't know, the cops took it."

"If the appointment wasn't with you, who else? Is there anyone else she might've seen with the same initials?"

"Thing is," he mused, "she never referred to me as JK—only Jeff. Have another look at that book; there should be plenty of notations for 'Jeff' since we went to therapy every week."

"But, who else could it have been?" Rory persisted.

Korbin's brow furrowed. "Jeremy Katz was her attorney for the PFA hearing; she was working for him. That would make sense since she said she wanted to have the order rescinded."

"OK, good, I know Jeremy; I'll check it out."

"And the good news?" Korbin began to look hopeful.

"The good news is that your therapist confirmed that you and Kathie were in counseling, *and* she offered to be a witness for the defense, if needed."

"Wow," Jeff marveled "she is a very compassionate lady, and she was fair, never took sides. She really helped us...." He choked up.

Rory gave him a moment, then said, "The other good news is that you have no criminal record, that really helps, and you've a good work history at UPS. Taken together, I couldn't have hoped for better news."

Korbin sighed—his face relaxed visibly, a much younger and more handsome man emerged.

"But..." Rory hated to have to say this, "we do have an alibi problem; the 20-minute lapse when the dispatcher couldn't reach you. Did anyone see or talk with you during that time?"

"You know I've been thinking about that, and... well, I don't know if this will pan out, but I talked to a guy on the sewer crew—up on Hidden Hollow Road and asked him how long the road would be closed. He said 'few hours,' so I made the delivery on foot. It was a bit of a hike, could've taken twenty minutes."

"Well, that's something to go on—we'll check it out. Meanwhile, I'm optimistic about what we've learned in just a few days, so don't lose hope. Do you have any questions?"

Korbin shook his head, looked at Rory with a mixture of relief and admiration, and said, "Just thanks, thanks for believing in me." He nodded towards the interns to include them.

Arriving back in Media, Rory dropped the interns off. "Let's call it a day—actually, a very productive day—thanks! I'll stop by Katz's office on the way home and see you two in the morning."

On her way to Jeremy's office, Rory phoned to make sure he was in. She spoke with Helen Yates, Jeremy's administrative assistant, who sounded depressed, unlike her usual bubbly self. She told Rory that Katz would see her.

Entering the offices of Klein and Katz, Rory noticed that Helen's face appeared pinched; she was on the phone and motioned for Rory to go through.

Rory and Jeremy had always enjoyed an easy working relationship and she liked him; he could be quite charming. She asked how his partner, Joe Klein, was doing; she'd heard through the grapevine that he'd been battling cancer.

"Thanks for asking," Jeremy replied. "He's in remission at the moment; don't know what his long-term chances are. He's pretty close-mouthed about it but he seems pretty fragile; he's lost a ton of weight, but tries to come in two to three days a week."

After some small talk, Rory got down to business, saying, "As you may know, I'm representing Jeff Korbin. I was just wondering if you'd spoken with Kathie before her death, and if she mentioned her desire to have the PFA order rescinded?"

Jeremy looked startled, then recovered quickly. "Jeff must've told you that; she never mentioned it to me, and she was working here. "

Jeremy stood up, looking at his watch. Rory took this as a dismissal, but had another question. "And, just out of curiosity, who heard the case?"

"Oh, the President Judge himself—Keller," he replied.

As Rory passed through the outer office, Helen was still on the phone. She looked up to mouth a quick "Bye," and offered a wan smile.

Rory was struck by what she considered an unusual encounter. Helen was her friend, had been for years, and though her daughter Alicia was older than the twins, they'd played together often when they were younger.

And her relationship with Jeremy had always been easy. But as soon as she'd mentioned Korbin, Jeremy had changed. Perhaps they were both affected by Kathie's death—after all, she had worked there. Still, Rory thought, it was curious.

Chapter 5

Rory congratulated herself as she arrived at the girls' game ahead of time, and, more importantly, before Marc. She went to the fence and called to Kate and Alex, wishing them luck again and admitting to herself that her real motive was that they knew she was there.

She took a seat in the bleachers and reserved one for Marc with the cooler of hoagies. The seats were filling up fast and she began to get caught up in the excitement of the game, realizing it would probably be the first game she'd seen in its entirety this season.

Spotting Marc scanning the crowd, she waved and motioned him up. "Hey, glad you could make it" he said as he joined her. She didn't detect any sarcasm, so she said, "Me too! This is your seat; the hoagies for the tailgate are in there."

"Glad you remembered—I'd forgotten. By the way, thanks for saving me breakfast—it was a nice surprise."

"Well, I was up early, so…..it was nice spending time with the girls before school. And they reminded me of the tailgate—I hadn't remembered either."

Further discussion was impossible as the teams took the field and the crowd stood and cheered loudly.

The game proved to be fast-moving, and the teams were well matched. Still, it looked to Rory as though the Panthers had an edge. In the second inning, Alex hit one out of the park and the crowd roared, sending Rory and Marc to their feet, cheering and fist-pumping. Kate's forte seemed to be at fielding—she played first base and was quick to get players out.

By the fifth inning the Panthers were ahead by 5, a nice, comfortable lead. They were still going strong, while it looked as though Conestoga was running out of steam. Fingers crossed, Rory allowed herself to think they would win, and sharing the victory with her girls promised to be sweet.

After another run by the Panthers, when the crowd noise had subsided, Rory heard the subdued, but distinct buzz of her cell. She saw it was from Ginny, and reluctantly left the bleachers, mouthing to Marc "Ginny."

Away from the noise, Rory took the call, as her anxiety rose.

"Rory, thank God you answered! Can you come right away? Sean's in the hospital, an overdose they think. I don't know what to do; I found him unconscious when I came home from work. Oh *please*, can you come? I'm *so scared*!" Ginny's words came out in a rush of emotion.

Rory was riveted to the spot, stunned, but of course she *knew* she had to go, and she promised Ginny she'd be there as soon as she could pack a few things and let Marc know.

Rather than hiking back up the bleachers, Rory decided to call Marc's cell. It went to voice mail, so Rory left a hurried, urgent message, hoping he would understand why she had to leave. She couldn't worry about Marc or even the outcome of the game—she had to be with Sean. God, she hoped he'd make it.

Speeding home, she packed a few essentials for the trip, not knowing how long she'd be there or even what was awaiting her. The thought occurred to her that she might need a black dress, and, fighting tears, she pushed that idea away. She tried to still her mind to permit rational thought. She left a message for Blake, telling him she'd be away for a few days on a family emergency, and reminding him of the list of things that she'd planned to do with the interns.

She promised to be in touch as soon as she knew anything. She tried Marc's cell again but had the same results as before, so left no message.

She knew this trip well and had plenty of time to think . She thought about Sean's troubled life in his late teens, when he'd started using and hanging with the druggie crowd. Her parents had practiced "tough love," which often meant long absences from home, when he was either in rehab or living on the streets. It was an incredibly stressful time for everyone as Sean missed holidays and milestones in Rory's life. She'd been disappointed, but never angry with Sean.

But the worst, the *very* worst, was when he'd been convicted of felony Breaking and Entering, and imprisoned for six months. Rory believed his story that his friend, Josh, had said they could sleep at a neighbor's house; they were out of town and Josh had told Sean he had their permission to stay there because he was taking care of their pets. Sean had been kicked out of his home again and needed a place to stay. There were lights on when Sean arrived, so he assumed that Josh was already there. He shoved the door and it opened; the terrified neighbors were at home and called the police. Since Sean was high at the time, he was basically incoherent when the police arrived and arrested him; he was jailed until his hearing, because his parents refused to put up bail money.

The hearing was over quickly because Sean refused to plea bargain, knowing he was innocent and naively believing he'd be exonerated. Josh had apparently lied on the stand and denied planning to meet at the neighbors' house and even went so far as to say they were only *acquaintances*. That was the final blow, *the Judas kiss*, she thought; she'd seen Josh at the house often.

She'd understood, even at 13, that Josh was covering his own ass, and to Hell with the friendship. To her, it was unforgivable.

As for Sean's testimony, the DA had shredded him on cross-examination and his public defender offered no rebuttal.

He was found guilty of felony breaking and entering and later sentenced to six months in jail.

Rory had left the court room feeling bereft, but with a kernel of rage pushing up and feeding her desire, her *need* to study law. She knew she could do better and bring compassion and ethics to the legal system, to right some of the wrongs she'd seen perpetrated against her brother.

She smiled at her innocence, but knew she still held on to some of that idealism. *Had she made a difference?* She hoped so.

Sean's life had been no walk in the park since then. He'd had more stays in rehab. There'd been many holidays not shared with the family. It had taken Sean a long time to come back to a semi-regular kind of life. He'd gotten an Associate degree, he'd met and married Ginny, and for a few years now, he'd had a job as a drug counselor at a rehab he'd been in. Rory stopped worrying so much, and now, *this*.

Coming back to the present, Rory noted that she'd made good time and would soon be at the hospital. She hadn't called her parents, and she might not, even though they lived nearby. They didn't need old wounds reopened.

And, although the game must've been long over, Marc hadn't called. Rory didn't have the time or energy to process what that might mean.

Arriving at Johns Hopkins, Rory parked and rushed into the building. The information desk provided her with the floor number of the O R. She went to the elevators, and pressed #3. As the doors opened, she spotted Ginny, huddled in a corner, looking drawn and haggard. She went to her and enfolded Ginny in her arms.

Reacting woodenly at first, Ginny soon burst into tears.

"Oh, Rory, thank God you're here! I think I'm still in shock. He was doing so *well*, I just wasn't prepared."

"How could you have anticipated this? We all want to believe that he's ok now, that the addiction and depression are over, but ...you just never know." Rory was at a loss.

"Now that I think of it, he started to decline after his high school reunion. I was surprised that he wanted to go, but thought it was a good sign..."

"Did he talk to you about it when he got home?"

"Not really, just in generalities, but then he got quiet. Soon he started missing work, saying he was sick. He missed a week, and then another. It scared me and I pleaded with him to see his doctor; he'd stopped taking his meds..." Ginny ran out of words, overwhelmed by the enormity of her grief.

They were still clutching each other when the doors to surgery opened and a distinguished looking, middle-aged man in green scrubs came out. He came over to Rory and Ginny, the only people in the waiting room.

"I'm Dr. Graham," he said, offering his hand. "I assume you're Mr. Morris's family."

Ginny offered her hand, "I'm his wife, Ginny, and this is his sister, Rory—How is he?"

"He'll pull through. Then once he's stabilized, he'll be assessed to determine the next steps in treatment. The toxicology reports haven't come back yet, so that will give us more information. Do you have any questions?"

Rory's mind was reeling with questions, but Ginny spoke first.

"When can we see him?"

"He'll be in the recovery room for an hour or so, depends how quickly he wakes up. And when Mr. Morris is in his room, I'll be around to see him. Give it at least an hour."

"That's fine, thank you Dr. Graham." Ginny was looking more hopeful.

"OK, Ginny, you heard the doctor's orders, let me take you out for dinner. Let's just get out of the hospital for a while. In fact, before we leave let's get the phone number of the head nurse so we can call."

Ginny seemed happy for someone to make decisions for her and leaned against Rory for support as they left the hospital.

*****

It was hours before they finally saw Sean; they'd been sitting in the waiting room for a very long time before Dr. Graham came out of his room and gave them the go-ahead, cautioning them that Sean was still very tired and might nod off at any time.

They entered Sean's room together, Ginny going to his side to give him a kiss; Rory observing his deathly pale face, the bruises under his eyes and his almost skeletal thinness.

Rory walked over to stand next to Ginny, saying, "Hey, bro, you gave us a little scare there, but doc says you'll be okay; you know we love you and need you in our lives..." She stopped before the tears came.

"You didn't need to come, I'm sorry. I've just been so confused... nothing makes sense..." His speech was slurred and his eyes started to close.

Rory nodded towards the door and went out, leaving Ginny some privacy with Sean. She knew there was no way to have a discussion with him tonight.

As she left the room her phone buzzed; there was a message—she hadn't checked since she'd left home—it was a text from Marc. It read: "Figured it was serious when you didn't come back and then was afraid to call since you'd be at the hospital. I'm really sorry about Sean and hope he's okay. BTW, the girls' team won and they'll have the first playoff on Saturday. Their glee was somewhat dampened by the news about Sean. And we all miss you and hope you'll be home soon. Love you."

Tears formed in Rory's eyes. She felt proud and regretful at the same time, having missed out on another opportunity to share the thrill of victory.

But she had to be here, that she knew; Sean had suffered for so many years. It was past midnight, she noticed—too late to call Marc. But she could dash off a quick text so that he knew she was thinking of him and that she'd be staying with Ginny for a few days.

*****

When Rory awoke the next day, she discovered that Ginny had left for the hospital; there was a note, promising to call as soon as she knew anything.

In the meantime, Ginny suggested she get some rest.

As if on cue, Rory's cell trilled. It was Ginny. "Hi Rory, hope you got enough sleep—I didn't have the heart to wake you. As it is, there's not much I can do here. He's about to be evaluated, that is, if he stays awake long enough; he's been in and out all morning, not very coherent. And the tox report isn't back yet, so I'll probably head home for lunch—OK? "

Relieved to hear Ginny sounding so much better, Rory suggested, "Why don't we meet for lunch at Inner Harbor, maybe Philips's?"

"Oh, that would be good. See you there about 12:30?"

"Fine by me—see you then." Rory noticed another call coming in; it was from Marc.

"Hey, thanks for calling and thanks for the text last night. It was too late to call when I finally saw it, and I was a bit strung out by then. But I slept like a rock—just woke up and saw that Ginny had gone to the hospital without me."

"So, what's the story on Sean?"

"Don't know for sure, yet. He had his stomach pumped last night; we saw him after the procedure, but he was far from coherent—looks awful. The doc says he'll be fine, but we haven't gotten the toxicology report back yet, so don't really know what he took. He's being evaluated today. That's about it; Ginny says he's still in and out of consciousness today, so it may be awhile before we can really talk to him. I'm meeting Ginny for lunch, and then we'll go back to the hospital."

"Well, you'll let me know once you hear something? The girls and I miss you and want you home soon."

"Oh, please tell them I'm so proud of them, and I'm sure to be home for the first playoff game. I have to talk with Sean first and find out what the *hell* he was thinking—I'm sad and pissed at the same time."

"I hear you. But he must've been in a very dark place to contemplate, you know, killing himself."

Rory was beyond gratified at the first hint of empathy Marc had shown toward Sean; she was breathless. "He's been in dark places for a large part of his life, Marc. We don't know really what triggered it this time, but before I leave, I'll get answers."

"Oh, I know you will, counselor. Just keep me in the loop. Have to go now—love you!"

"Love you, too, and I will keep in touch. Hugs for the girls—at least they have the playoffs to keep them occupied. Bye."

After meeting for lunch, Ginny and Rory sat outside by the harbor, enjoying the lovely June day. Rory was pleased to see that Ginny had regained her composure. She looked so much better, and she'd had an appetite for lunch.

Ginny phoned the hospital to find out whether it would be possible to see Sean today. He was scheduled to be evaluated at 2:00 p.m., and that would take about 2 hours, at the least. The nurse promised to call when Sean got back to room.

They decided to stay by the harbor and stroll around, maybe find some reading material for Sean while they awaited the call.

Shortly after 4:00, the head nurse called. They could meet with Dr. Graham that night at 7:00 and then spend some time with Sean, who was apparently much more alert.

*****

At seven sharp, they were waiting outside his office when Dr. Graham arrived. Ushering them in, he motioned for them to take seats.

"OK, let's get down to business. Toxicology reports show high levels of both Valium and Klonepin in his system. As you probably know, they are strong tranquilizers and both drugs suppress the central nervous system. Fortunately, he didn't take enough to kill himself. The psychiatrist who evaluated him believes he is not currently suicidal and has recommended a day-hospital program for him. He'll be assigned a therapist to see both at the day program and on follow-up when he leaves. He'll remain here for a few days, under observation, but should be out by the weekend. Do you have any questions?"

Ginny looked stricken. "The Valium was mine; I took it occasionally when I had trouble sleeping. I didn't know he was even aware of it, it was hidden."

"You're not responsible for this—if he was feeling desperate, he would have found something, regardless. He'll be fine and now maybe he will get the help he needs."

They thanked the doctor and walked to Sean's room. Rory asked, "Do you mind if I see him first? Then you can have the rest of the time with him. I really need some answers from him."

Ginny looked puzzled and uneasy, but nodded in the affirmative.

Rory went into the room, closing the door. Sean looked much better and was sitting up. "Rory, I didn't want you mixed up in this—I'm sorry you came all the way down here…"

"It was a matter of life and death," Rory said briskly. "Did you really believe I wouldn't come, under the circumstances? Let's not minimize this."

"Look, I was feeling hopeless, I was confused—I just wanted the pain to go away…"

"Of course I understand that, but to consider taking your *life*? Please help me understand what triggered this. I mean, you were doing so well..."

"I was, I was. Where to start? Well, I'd been teaching some classes at the rehab, and the boss encouraged me to go back to school and get my degree. That made me feel really good, so I looked into it. One of the first things I found out was, since I have a felony conviction, I can't be a teacher."

"Yeah," Rory said, nodding, "that must've been disappointing; when did this happen?"

"Oh, a few months back..."

"And what, you've been brooding since?"

"No, I kind of put it out of my mind, until..."

"Until your recent high school reunion, right?" Rory answered for him, suddenly understanding.

"Yeah, how'd you know?"

"Your wife noticed your behavior changing after that. What happened?"

"Josh was there, and I really didn't want to even *see* the MF-er. But he sought me out—took me aside, and was really apologetic, like, 'if I can ever make it up to you....' *As if*! I just felt sick, and it all came back. I was civil to him, but it made me crazy, and I haven't been able to get it out of my mind since; it's been eating away at me—what *could* have been!" Sean flopped down on his pillow, tears in his eyes.

Rory looked thoughtful. She didn't speak at once. Then, as if a light bulb went on, she looked at Sean and smiled. "So Josh is remorseful—that's a good thing! And I think we'll take him up on his offer to help—I have a plan!"

Chapter 6

Sarah listened to Blake explain that Rory would be out of town for a few days with a family emergency. Sarah was surprised at her strong reaction to Rory's troubles; she'd somehow seen Rory as invincible and had formed an attachment in the short time she'd known her. Realizing her view was naive, she acknowledged her disappointment and concern over Rory's absence.

She'd totally missed most of what Blake had said since his mention of Rory; she tried to be slick as she glanced at the sparse notes Sam had taken. She was the compulsive note taker, but not today. Apparently, they'd be observing court—first adult and then juvenile. Boring! She'd been there—done that. Court hearings weren't especially riveting.

Blake was asking for questions and, since she hadn't paid attention, she didn't have any. But she was betting that Sam would and he didn't disappoint.

Scanning his notes, Sam asked, "What's the difference between adult and juvenile court?"

"Good question, Sam. Without going into too much history, I'll just say that Juvenile Court grew out of the concept that children should not be held as culpable as adults and should be rehabilitated rather than jailed with adults, as was historically the case. At the present time, however, you might not see much difference in the hearings. Plea bargaining is as prevalent in juvenile as it is in adult court. Juveniles can be sent to prison directly, if they are charged with a serious felony, usually involving a firearm and/or violence, and if they are fifteen or older. In Pennsylvania, the charge of murder is automatically heard in adult court, regardless of age. The detention center, a locked facility, is where juveniles charged with serious offenses are housed until disposition of the case. There's more, but does that answer your question, Sam?"

Sam nodded.

"OK, then we should head over to adult court. You'll probably have questions as you observe the hearings, so jot them down and we'll go over them later. Ready?"

As I'll ever be, thought Sarah, as she preceded the men out of the office.

The Court House was directly across the street so they didn't have far to walk. There was already a line on the steps waiting to go through security.

After essentially being waved through upon showing their county ID, a practice Sarah viewed as sloppy, the trio proceeded up the wide and ornate marble steps to the second floor.

They would be observing the hearings presided over by Judge Lisa Calder. She was on the bench reviewing files and Blake took them up to meet her. Certainly no older than Rory, the judge was attractive enough to wear her jet-black hair in a severe bun at the nape of her neck. She welcomed Sam and Sarah warmly and told them a bit about the kinds of cases that were on the day's docket. They took their seats in the back of the courtroom on benches that reminded Sarah of church, and worse yet, of her many years in Catholic school, but she skipped the genuflect.

Opening her notebook, she prepared to take notes, or at least to give that impression.

The first case was a bail hearing for a forty-ish man charged with rape. The apparent victim was a young, twenty-something woman, who appeared to be terrified and unwilling even to look in the direction of the defendant. Bail was set high enough to prevent the accused from being on the street, at least until the trial. Sarah surmised that it would be a trial rather than a plea bargain due to the serious, felony charges. She also sympathized with the victim, who would, in all likelihood, have to take the stand and thus be humiliated by the DA on cross. Sarah had volunteered as a rape counselor and had learned that many women viewed the cross examination by the DA to be nearly as painful as the rape. Many women failed to report rape, because of the stigma attached to it and the implication that they'd done something to encourage it.

The rest of the hearings weren't particularly interesting and Sarah found her mind wandering. She wondered if attorneys got bored with the monotony of the same cases day in and day out. However, she didn't think Rory was bored; she still seemed to enjoy her job, and in fact, seemed to be on a mission. That intrigued Sarah, who'd gone into law because it was a family tradition. But, she could choose to approach the law as Rory had and possibly make a difference.

Before she knew it, the gavel banged and court was recessed until after lunch. They filed out of the court room following Blake.

"Why don't we stop by the cafeteria, food's not bad, and get some lunch to take back to the office; then we can discuss your questions as we eat. If you've had enough of adult, the plan is to go to juvenile after lunch. They'll resume at 2:00 p.m.. That work?"

"Sounds good to me," Sam replied. Sarah nodded in agreement.

Sam hadn't taken notes, but he sure had lots of questions.

Sarah found it amusing that Blake had little time to consume his lunch as Sam peppered him with questions. They were good questions, to be sure, and Sarah found the discussion interesting. But, finally Sarah put out her hand and said, "Whoa, Sam, let's give Blake a chance to finish his lunch."

Blake looked up gratefully and Sam apologized.

"No need to apologize—your questions are legit, and I think we'll have time to answer the rest of them before we go over to juvenile court."

The time went quickly, Sam had all of his questions answered, and Sarah found that she, too, had some.

They headed over to Juvenile Court, housed in a separate and newer brick building behind the main courthouse. Security here, interestingly, was more thorough. Sarah was required to send her purse through a scanner much like the devices at airports. The men had to empty their pockets and put the contents into baskets. Some were pulled out of line and subjected to a more intense search, with a wand. *Were juveniles more dangerous?* Sarah wondered.

As soon as the three had been cleared, Sarah asked Blake: "Why do you think the security is more thorough in juvenile court?"

"Hmmm," Blake mused. "I hadn't thought about it, but my guess is that since there are seven or eight court hearings going on at once in adult court, the volume is much greater. There's usually only one juvenile courtroom in use —two at most."

"So, it's more about convenience than security?"

"I guess you're right. It doesn't make much sense, but I'm guessing it's the main reason. If you like, we can talk with the director of courthouse security."

"No…that would probably make the person defensive… I was just wondering."

"It's interesting to have interns who see everything from a fresh perspective. So, thanks for all the questions. By the way, if Rory hasn't weighed in on this already, it's not a perfect system—and not only in this county. We think the justice system as a whole needs an overhaul, but change happens slowly, and crime seems to be on the rise. Anyway, we need to go meet the judge before court starts."

They entered the courtroom, which Sarah noticed was much less formal than the one in adult court. There was also a jury box, although she was almost certain there was no jury in Juvenile Court. Judge Mason, a stern looking older man with rimless glasses, barely looked up as Blake introduced the interns. He had nothing to say by way of introduction, merely uttering an insincere sounding, "Good luck with your internship," before looking back at his paperwork.

Blake led the way to the back row and the three seated themselves, Blake sitting between Sarah and Sam to make it easier for them to ask questions between hearings. He gave each of them a court docket so they could distinguish the different types of hearings and jot notes.

The first several hearings were dispositional in nature. In each case, the juvenile sat next to his/her probation officer. The PO had conducted a study, written a report with recommendations, of which the judge had a copy. In only one of the hearings was an attorney present, and in that case the juvenile disagreed with the disposition. The PO had asked that the juvenile, formerly adjudicated on the charge of robbery, be placed in a juvenile institution. The probation officer did so based on the serious nature of the offense and because the juvenile was not particularly cooperative during the period of study on which her report was based. Additionally, the juvenile had tested positive for illegal substances on two occasions. The attorney representing the juvenile, argued that the youth was an "A" student and came from a good family (meaning *rich,* Sarah thought cynically), claimed that he adhered to family rules. After a brief sidebar, a compromise was reached whereby the youth was placed on an electronic home monitor; the case was continued for a period of three months. The PO did not look especially happy with the outcome, while the juvenile, dressed in a three-piece suit, smirked as he left the courtroom. The parents appeared both relieved and apprehensive.

Sarah sided with the PO and believed that the juvenile would continue to bend the probation rules. She made a note in the margin of docket next to his name: *He'll be back before the three months are up.*

The next case was a juvenile who had obviously come from the detention center. He was dressed in a khaki jumpsuit and shackled hand and foot. His offense was selling prescription drugs in school. His PO had done the study while he was in detention. The recommendation by probation was that he be released from detention, placed on a monitor, and return to court for disposition in one month. The DA argued adamantly and at length against releasing the youth. The Judge, after the debate, and after giving a stern warning, agreed to release the juvenile.

The sheriff was in the process of removing the shackles when the defendant looked towards the DA and muttered, "Prick."

The DA wheeled on him and shouted, "Did you just call me a prick?"

Whereupon the sheriff confirmed, "Yes, he called you a prick."

The Judge entered the fray demanding, "Did you just call the district attorney a prick?"

The youth, appearing unmoved, agreed. "Yes, Your Honor, I called him a prick. I don't think he was being fair with me," he whined.

"Young man!" the judge roared, nearly jumping from his seat, "You seem to forget that you are in a court of law and have egregiously disrespected the DA and the court! Bailiff, take the young man back to detention where he can reflect upon his utter contempt of the court! Case continued for two weeks."

Sarah, whose face had turned bright red with suppressed mirth, left the courtroom immediately, Blake following behind her.

When they reached a secluded spot in the lobby, Sarah exploded: "Oh my God, Blake, have you ever...?" She was soon overcome by a fit of giggles.

Blake, too, appeared more than amused as he answered, "I've seen lots of courtroom antics, but this one definitely beats them all!"

Looking around, Sarah asked, "By the way, where's Sam?"

"He was still sitting in the courtroom when I left, looking seriously pissed off. I don't think he found the incident funny."

Chapter 7

Sam was angry—angrier than he remembered having been in a long time. He'd barely spoken to Sarah and Blake after court, and had tossed and turned all night, hardly sleeping. He was still pondering the reasons for this extreme, for him, eruption of rage.

He knew, but didn't want to face, that in a short period of time, he'd been attracted to Sarah; she was so different from him, so full of life, so much a creature of the moment. He was sure she could never have feelings for him, so he'd made no overt gestures toward her. Sam was certain that Sarah could have her pick of anyone whom she chose.

He was troubled, though, at her reaction to the juvenile hearing; it seemed that she and Blake had aligned against him. He'd been outraged by the juvenile's disrespect towards the justice system; he found nothing funny in that, and was pleased by the judge's swift, unequivocal response.

That Sarah and Blake had found it funny was an affront to his beliefs. Sam got up and dressed, not particularly looking forward to seeing Blake or Sarah. He wondered, as he made his way towards the office, how this would affect their working relationship. He arrived at the office just as Blake did, and entered after the door had been unlocked. As soon as Sam took a seat, Blake asked, "Coffee, same as usual?"

Sam nodded in response.

As the coffee was brewing, Blake addressed Sam, " I know you're upset about yesterday. And I can understand your reaction was different from mine. I won't try to justify my reaction—it just happened. Frankly, I found the whole thing surreal. The youth was certainly out of line, but, he's a juvenile. What I found more astounding, and yes, amusing, was the response of the other court officials. It could have been handled differently, without playing into the youth's hands. As it turned out, they all conspired to make it a travesty. That's my take— you're entitled to whatever feelings you have."

Sam didn't answer immediately. He was mulling over what Blake had said. Finally, Sam answered. "I appreciate your explanation—it's obvious now that you weren't sanctioning the defendant's behavior."

"Absolutely not—he was way out of line, but he got the reaction he wanted. He orchestrated a theater of the absurd. And actually, the funny part, for me, was adults behaving badly. You expect the kids to have a chip on their shoulders, but we adults need to rein in our reactions, especially in the courtroom. The kid got what he deserved, but also what he wanted, an audience. I would've expected more professional behavior from the adults. Then again, I've seen egos run amok in the courtroom many times, and more often than not, the representatives of the court are the ones who make asses of themselves, but of course they don't see it that way."

Sam nodded thoughtfully. "So how do you think it should've been handled?" Sam was curious.

The coffee had finished brewing and Blake handed Sam a cup. Then he answered. "In hindsight, I think the DA should not have reacted in open court, but instead, should've asked for a sidebar, and gone up to the bench and told the judge quietly what the kid had said. The juvenile would've been detained, without the circus atmosphere."

Sam was nodding approvingly when Sarah entered.

"Hi Guys, sorry I'm late, any word on Rory, and how she's doing?"

"Yes," Blake answered. "I heard from her last night. Her brother is doing better—I'll let her fill in whatever she chooses in that regard. She would like it if the two of you could check out Korbin's alibi witness. It may be a tough assignment, but she wants you to try and find out where the sewer project is currently operating. Then, see if you can find the man Korbin spoke with about how long the road would be closed. That's basically it for today. I would suggest that you first contact the borough office to find out where the sewer crew will be. If you can find the guy, that would be fantastic, and I'd say you can call it a day. By the way, Rory should be back Monday for work. Are we good?"

"Yeah, we're good." Sam replied and Sarah agreed.

Sam had decided to say nothing to Sarah about the previous day's incident. He considered Blake's response a good one and had a greater appreciation of his perspective. He wasn't so sure what Sarah would say, so he felt it best to leave it alone.

"So, Blake, if you could direct us to the borough office, I think we can take it from there." Sam was eager to get straight to work.

"Sure thing—here's a map of the county. The office is here, and they should be able to show you on the map where the crew is working today. Call me if you run into any snags."

"OK, then, I guess we're off!" Sam said briskly. And to Sarah: "I'll drive—my car is close by."

"Slow down," Sarah whined as they headed for Sam's car. "I didn't even get tea this morning."

Sam bit back a sarcastic remark about her tardiness and said instead—"I'll stop at Starbucks, it's on the way." And glancing at her heels, he added, "Not sure that foot gear will work with our assignment today."

"I thought we were doing more court watching or something."

"No, I think we're done with that." Sam spoke in an acerbic tone that was unintended, but slipped out nonetheless.

"Yeah, I had enough of that—boring! Well, except for that juvenile hearing which was hilarious....oh, sorry, you didn't find it funny."

"No, I really *didn't*," Sam said tightly.

Silence reigned until they reached Sam's car. He opened the door for Sarah and got in himself.

"Oh, Sam, if you don't mind stopping by my car—it's down on 5th—I just remembered I left my running shoes in there. That should make it easier for me to keep up with you."

"OK, just direct me," Sam replied.

After getting the shoes Sam drove to Starbucks so that Sarah could get her tea.

"Can I get you anything Sam?" Sarah inquired as she left the car.

"Nah" Sam replied curtly. He was fuming again and not looking forward to being with Sarah alone for the remainder of the day. Unlike Blake, she seemed unrepentant about her reaction to the hearing. Moreover, she was being insensitive to his feelings. He realized he was having a tough time putting this behind him, despite his intentions to let it drop. He'd just have to find a way to get through today. But, damn! He wasn't accustomed to being in such turmoil; he relied on structure and order.

He was deep in thought as Sarah slipped into the car.

"Sorry for all the delays, Sam, I know you're anxious to get going on this. Do you know the way to Borough Hall?"

"Yeah, it's up the road a ways, pretty sure I know which building it is."

Arriving at Borough Hall, Sam grabbed the map and got out of the car. "You might as well stay here and finish your tea," he said over his shoulder.

He came back in a few minutes and handed Sarah the map, which had the route highlighted. "Can you follow a map?" he asked brusquely.

"Yeah, I'm pretty good at it, I'll do my best not to get us lost." She tried for humor but Sam just grunted.

After driving for about fifteen minutes, Sarah's brow furrowed. "Ummm, I ah, don't really know where we are, the streets aren't marked, like on the map."

Sam abruptly pulled onto the shoulder. He snatched the map from Sarah, and cursed, "Shit—why didn't you tell me sooner? Show me the last point where we were on course—can you do that?"

Sarah fumbled with the map and glared at Sam—"It's not my fault the roads aren't marked out here in the boonies!" She pointed—"Here, that's the last street sign I remember." She folded her arms and pouted as Sam looked at the map.

"Maybe we should call Blake..."

"No way! I'll figure it out myself. At least *one* of us has a sense of direction."

Sarah continued to stare straight ahead. She looked angry, but Sam noticed a few tears starting to leak out as he looked over. *Oh jeez, now I've done it,* he thought.

"I'm sorry, Sarah, I shouldn't have been so harsh."

That was all he needed to say before the floodgates opened and Sarah was sobbing. She wiped furiously at her eyes, as if to make it stop. Then, she gave up and started talking in choking sobs—"I can tell you've been mad at me all morning— and I don't know why and I can't make it better! And my dad always yelled at me for getting us lost..." she tried for a laugh and got a hiccup. "Sorry, don't know how my dad got into all of this..."

"Well my guess is that sometimes your dad was a dick to you, just like I was..."

This time she did laugh, all out. "You got that right, Sam! I just haven't seen this side of you, it happened so unexpectedly. I didn't know you cursed—you're just so... proper, and professional. And I feel immature next to you."

"I'm serious about law, and I guess I must come off as stiff sometimes. It takes me awhile to open up. Actually, I admire your spunk and wish I could be more spontaneous."

"Huh," Sarah replied, "just goes to show ya...people are multi-layered, to quote Shrek, and complicated..."

"I agree, and just so you know, I was still smarting about that hearing yesterday. I talked with Blake about it, and he helped me to look at it differently. But I was feeling that you just weren't taking court seriously."

"You're right. This is not an excuse, by the way, but I've been around lawyers and judges my whole life, my career was decided for me probably at birth, so I guess I am a bit jaded. What struck me as funny yesterday was that these professionals let that kid push their buttons. And they helped to make a mockery of the whole thing. Sure, the kid will pay the price by spending more time in detention, but his creds went sky-high with the other juvies, and you can be sure the story has spread like wildfire, and not just among the kids."

"Wow, I'm impressed—you really thought it through. Blake said the same thing, in a different way. I think I do understand now and I guess I had this unrealistic notion of the court as infallible. But, the egos of those guys—the DA and the judge—got in the way, and they forgot that they were in charge. They stooped to his level...."

"Exactly! And kids are so good at manipulation; we really have to keep in mind that we're the adults. If I'd been either of them, I'd be so embarrassed, but I bet they're just feeling a sense of moral indignation."

"Wow, I'm sorry. I guess I overreacted."

"Accepted, and I'm sorry I screwed up the directions. Let's see if we can find our way out of this mess."

Together they looked at the map, then backtracked until they found the street sign, obscured by deep foliage.

They heard the drone of heavy equipment before they actually found the crew.

Sarah asked for permission to question the workers, giving the crew foreman as little information as possible regarding their mission.

They divided up the crew of eight men and Sam and Sarah set out.

Sam looked up; having had no satisfaction with his interviews, and saw Sarah waving wildly at him, motioning him over. Sarah had questioned three of the four men and then approached the last and asked if he remembered seeing a UPS delivery man when they were working on Hidden Hollow Rd. The man's answer got Sarah's heart beating overtime.

Chapter 8

Rory was happy to be headed back to work. Her visit with Sean and Ginny ended on a positive note and she was planning how she would undo the wrong that had been done to Sean. In short, if Josh really meant what he'd said, he should be willing to testify at an expungement hearing and admit that he'd lied at Sean's hearing. The statute of limitations should protect him from being charged with perjury. And with the charges erased, Sean would be free to pursue his dream of teaching. She prayed it would work out as she hoped.

As she drove to work she thought about the wonderful weekend with her family. She'd gotten back Friday night and was at the twins' playoff game on Saturday. The girls had won that game and were over-the-moon happy. She and Marc were communicating much better than they had been recently and had celebrated as much with the best sex they'd had in years. Recently there'd been a long dry spell, which had served to heighten the tension between them. And Marc's newfound empathy for Sean amazed Rory. Of course, she hadn't told Marc of her plan to return to Baltimore and initiate an expungement hearing. One step at a time.

As she neared her office, Rory's thoughts turned to work and she replayed Blake's phone call in her mind. She'd laughed at the courtroom incident, but was concerned that their differing reactions might've driven a wedge between Sam and Sarah. She certainly couldn't afford tension on her team. She pondered how to best deal with it.

Rory entered the office and stopped short. Sarah, Blake and Sam stood next to a basket of what looked like homemade muffins. Sarah came forward first and gave Rory a hug, whispering in her ear, "I really missed you—we all did! And Sam baked you these." She offered the basket.

"Jeez," Rory smiled, "I should've stayed longer; thanks so much! Sam, you bake?"

Sam blushed, and shrugged—"My mom insisted that I learn my way around the kitchen; I've found that I really like it."

"Good for you! And thanks." Rory grinned her appreciation.

Sarah seemed to be bursting with excitement, and said, "We're also celebrating some very good news!"

"Out with it!" Rory commanded.

"OK, here goes, not to be overly dramatic or anything, but... Sam and I found the guy on the sewer crew; he remembered Korbin, and basically corroborated his story. We found an alibi witness! So, of course, Sam remembered to get the guy's name and address—I was so pumped, I would've probably forgotten."

"Sarah deserves the credit on this—she didn't give up." Sam insisted.

"You both deserve credit, I can't tell you how pleased I am with what you've accomplished so far. Korbin will certainly be relieved when we tell him.

In the meantime, Blake, can you take Sam and Sarah to the law library after I've had a few moments to chat and catch up with them?"

"Sure thing, Boss, I'll be ready."

Settling in Rory's office, Sam and Sarah told Rory what had happened during the last few days.

Sam talked about how much he'd learned about court procedure, and how fully Blake had answered his questions. He looked at Sarah and grinned as he told Rory about their 'difference of opinion' on a juvenile hearing.

Rory told them Blake had mentioned the incident to her and she'd been worried there might be tension.

"Oh, you could say that!" Sarah laughed. "It almost came to fisticuffs before we both calmed down enough to be rational. But," she glanced at Sam for agreement, "I think we've worked it out, and hopefully we'll be more open with our feelings before it gets explosive in the future."

Sam nodded, "It was a real eye opener for me. I had to look at myself and realize that everyone doesn't have the same reaction to events."

"Right," Rory agreed. "So, what did you learn?"

Sarah burst out with, "I don't ever want to make an ass of myself in court like that! And I think you have to try to leave your ego at the door. Oh, and kids are manipulative."

"I have to agree with Sarah. One aspect that I didn't see at all was that the kid was actually trying to get a reaction, and to him that show was worth his extra days in detention. It's hard to believe, but he virtually strutted his way out of court. "

"We want to believe our clients and give them the best possible defense. I believed Korbin was innocent even before we started to get corroboration of his story. It could've been the opposite, but, having accepted his case, it's imperative for me to do my best. There are many tough situations, but it's important for us to be professional in all of our dealings. Sounds as though you learned a lot."

"How are you doing, Rory? We did miss you and hope you're ok." Sarah's brow was furrowed.

Rory took a deep breath, then decided to trust them. She told them, in as few words as possible about Sean's past and current situation. She ended on a positive note with her belief that his record could be expunged so that he could go on with his life.

Sam and Sarah nodded somberly. Sarah said, "I hope it works out; sounds like a good idea."

"Thanks, I think it will," Rory said brightly. "Now, Blake is ready to take you to the Law Library; so I'll see you later."

After they left, Rory looked at her appointment book. She had a few phone messages to return and she needed to call the DA to alert him to her request for a review of the bail hearing for Korbin, based on new evidence provided by an alibi witness. And although she didn't like Como, she did respect his knowledge and wanted to pick his brain regarding the expungement hearing. Swallowing her pride, she dialed Como's number.

"Hi Janet, it's Rory—is Stan in?"

"He is, Rory, I'll put you right through."

"Rory—good to hear from you! Let me guess, Korbin wants to cop a plea?"

"Sorry to disappoint, Stan. Actually, we've found an alibi witness; just wanted you to know what was going on. We'll be requesting a review of bail." Rory tried to keep the annoyance out of her voice.

Stan sighed loudly, "It will just serve to delay the inevitable, you know."

"Look, Stan, I have to represent the best interests of my client. I don't expect you to agree. Anyway, I respect your knowledge of the law and have a question on another matter. Do you have a minute?"

"Sure... I guess." He sounded dubious, as if anticipating a snare.

"I have a client who was found guilty of felony B&E about 30 years ago. He was convicted based on testimony of his presumed friend and later sentenced to six months in jail. He recently saw his friend at a HS reunion and the guy was remorseful, seems ready to recant. They were both barely adults, eighteen, when it happened. What are the chances of an expungement being granted?"

"Hmmm, I doubt the DA would want to go after the friend for perjury, what with the statute of limitations. It pretty much rests on whether they believe him, but it's worth a try."

"OK, thanks, Stan. I really appreciate this."

"Sure, Rory, bye."

Rory felt a bit disoriented; Stan had been cooperative and helpful, leaving her with the uncomfortable task of reassessing her opinion of him. She hated being judgmental, but accepted that she wasn't immune to that defect.

Next on her list was to schedule a definite lunch date with Charlie, her former law partner. She reached him and set up lunch for Wednesday.

Having finished her paperwork, and having some time before her interns returned, Rory decided to sit in on some Protection From Abuse (PFA) hearings.

Crossing the street to the Court House, Rory found the docket posted and went to the designated courtroom. She slipped in the back door and took a seat. President Judge Keller was presiding. She wondered why he would concern himself with such low-level hearings; they were mundane enough that she would expect the newer judges to pay their dues by sitting at these hearings. He was the presiding judge at Kathie Korbin's hearing, she remembered, so maybe this wasn't random.

The President Judge was not one of her favorites. She rarely went before him, avoiding him at all costs. In her opinion, he was not that bright, was extremely political, and was slimy, with a proclivity toward inappropriately touching women. She forced herself to pay attention to the hearing that was unfolding.

The plaintiff, a young woman named Moira Kelly, appeared to be in her twenties and was quite beautiful. She was requesting protection form her former boyfriend, who, she claimed, was stalking her.

The defense attorney was requesting to submit evidence to the contrary, when the judge ruled in Ms. Kelly's favor.

"But, Your Honor..." the attorney began, as the gavel banged. Then the attorney announced loudly, "This will be appealed!"

The judge shrugged and replied, "Recess for lunch."

So much for justice, thought Rory as she rose to leave. She was eager to get back to the office and have lunch.

Going back to court after lunch, Rory remembered that she'd left a pile of briefs in the courtroom. Court had not resumed so she went in the back door to retrieve them. She was shocked to see the judge conversing—intimately it appeared— with the plaintiff she'd seen earlier in the day. The woman was standing in front of the bench. Rory grabbed her things quickly and retreated to the lobby

It was most unusual for a plaintiff to have an informal discussion with a judge outside of a hearing. The regular protocol was for the attorney to arrange a meeting.

As she was taking a seat in the lobby, the courtroom door was flung open and Ms. Kelly hurried into the lobby, rushed through it, and out of the Court House with a look of utter disgust on her face.

Chapter 9

Very early the next morning Rory set out to put into action her carefully crafted, though very risky, plan. She had replayed the courtroom scene where Judge Keller was talking with Ms. Kelly. In her mind, she could see the blue recording light on. Judges were so accustomed to the light being on they rarely thought of it, which meant every word the judge said was on tape. Court personnel routinely played back these tapes in lieu of requesting a transcript, which would take much longer. She had to get permission to listen to the tape from the supervisor of Court Recording, Marilyn Hanson, whom she knew well.

"Mornin' Marilyn, thought you might like this." Rory offered a cup of Starbucks coffee.

"You're an angel, the cafeteria coffee sucks! What can I do you for at this hour?" She looked at the clock. "I'm usually the only one insane enough to be around these hallowed halls at the crack of dawn."

"Oh, I'm up against it in a murder case and don't have time to wait for a transcript, so I just want to take a quick listen to a tape, if you can give me the keys to Courtroom 8—I know what to do—I'll just take some notes and be on my way."

"Sure, Rory, you know the drill, I'm not supposed to, but you also know everyone does it. Honestly we'd never get all the transcripts done if we had to do one for every hearing."

"I do know, that's why everyone turns a blind eye. Thanks, Marilyn!"

Rory hurried to the courtroom, wanting to put this behind her as soon as possible. She found yesterday's tape easily enough. Skipping through it was another matter entirely. She fast-forwarded and rewound endlessly hoping to find the hearing she was looking for. Finally, her patience was rewarded. She heard the gavel bang down for lunch recess, and the recording machine remained on, as she'd suspected. She heard bits of conversation as people left the courtroom. The defense attorney was ranting to a colleague. Then a relative quiet settled in. She fast-forwarded frequently, stopping to see if there was any noise. At one point, she heard what sounded like static but kept listening. It was possibly the scraping of a chair—it was as if someone was near the recording apparatus and arranging things on the desk. Was it her imagination or was there a low humming of... what was that? Sinatra's "I Did It My Way"—how appropriate, thought Rory. In mid-hum, a door opened and the humming stopped. Tentative footsteps grew louder. A voice, clearly the judge's, dripping in honey, encouraged the visitor, presumably Moira, to come closer.

"Hello, my dear, I'm so glad you got my note. You know I see so many of you unfortunate young girls, taken in and abused by your boyfriends—it's a sin—God knows I do my best to stop it. But I can only do so much! But I could do more, much more, if only you'd let me." His words were cloying.

"I... I'm not sure I understand your meaning Judge...," she sounded confused.

"Oh, I think you do, Moira, may I call you Moira? I think you know where this is going. So if we could just get past preliminaries and agree to meet for dinner tonight? I can promise to keep you very safe..."

"Nooo," came the strangled reply.

Heavy, quick footfalls receded into the background followed by the sound of a door being flung open.

"Fucking bitches!" muttered the judge. "Think they own the world—beautiful fucking bitches, all of them!" She heard loud noises like objects being thrown.

Holy shit! thought Rory, *what have we got here*? Her hands were shaking as she rewound the tape back to exactly where it was when she'd started. This was huge, but what could she do with it—who would believe her? The idea of pitting herself against a powerful, political, not to mention, The President Judge, was laughable, to say the least. But it really wasn't funny, it was abuse of power at its worst.

She returned the key to Marilyn and thanked her, scanning the lobby furtively as she quickly made her exit.

A few blocks from her office, she wandered into Seven Stones Café and took her coffee outside to a table. She sipped the liquid, breathed in the cool morning air and tried to recover her equilibrium.

Surprised to see someone she knew at this hour, she waved to her friend Don Mandel, as he came out with a large coffee. He was a lawyer who worked in adult probation, and was a real rabble-rouser, always trying to change the system and known to deluge the local paper with editorials. She liked Don, found him refreshing, in what was too often a desert of corruption. As soon as he sat down he asked: "So, what's up with you? And don't tell me 'nothing,' because I can read distress a mile away!"

Don was nothing if not direct. Rory decided to trust him, if for no other reason than that she had to get it off her chest. "Well," she began, "you probably won't believe this but, here's what just happened..." And she told it all.

"He's a piece of shit," Don said without preamble. "He hits on the female PO's all the time. Most of them won't go in front of him. Neither will I if I can avoid it. And he's the President Judge—can you believe it? What a joke! I believe every word of what you told me, Rory."

"Yeah, and now what? Can't do anything!"

"Oh, I wouldn't be so sure of that, I'll put my thinking cap on, there's always something you can do! Anyway, thanks for the insider info; time to go take on the system! Bye!"

"Bye, and thanks for listening."

Realistically, Rory thought, what could she hope to do? She thought back; he was the judge in Kathie's PFA case, and in Moira Kelly's case. She'd already wondered why he bothered to do these low-level cases. Now she wondered how many he actually heard. This was something her students could fact check. She could take them to the archives today. Now she was eager to get to the office. She gathered her things and walked double-time to the office.

Blake was arriving just as she got there and did a comic double-take.

"OK, boss, give me a few moments to get your coffee!"

"No thanks," she held up her hand, "I'm over my quota for the day already, anymore and I'll get squirrelly on you!"

"And that would be different, how?

Her response was to swat at him.

"I rest my case, ladies and gentlemen of the jury," he said with a bow.

"No, seriously, Blake—I have a lot on my mind, which at this point, is going ninety miles an hour and I need some time to slow it down. I just need a half hour or so, 'til the kids arrive to get my shit together and get on with the day."

"OK, you got it. I'll corral them until you're ready, and I'll take messages."

"Thanks, Blake."

Rory sat at her desk gathering her thoughts and waiting for her pulse to slow. It had helped to talk to Don, who gave her some support and affirmation. What to do about it was another matter. She needed to record what was on the tape and what she'd actually seen in the courtroom. She'd been routinely taping interviews with Korbin, discussions with her interns, as well as any insights, or thoughts that came to her. A finger of fear ran up her spine, as she began recording this incredibly damning evidence. The only real proof that it'd happened was on the original tape. Only she and Don knew about it. Rory had no idea where this could lead. She hoped Don had some ideas;

he seemed comfortable with going against the system. Sighing with relief when she'd finished, she turned the recorder off and put the tape in her safe.

Blake tapped on her door and she was glad to put the situation that was weighing on her mind to rest for the moment.

"Sorry Boss, but the kids are here and rarin' to go, and Stan called to say the bail hearing is on for 9:30 tomorrow with Judge Campbell in Courtroom Seven—OK?"

"Great—that means I need to go out to see Korbin today, and I have something for S&S to do, so you get to go to the prison with me."

"But, I, ahh…"

"No buts, believe me, I know what I'm talking about. No one hates going more than me. You just have to get over it— I'm helping you!"

Blake left unhappy and unconvinced.

Sam and Sarah came in and took their customary seats. " I have another assignment for you. I'd like you to look through the archives, in the courthouse basement. Let's go."

Rory escorted her students to the archives in the basement of the court house, with the directive to research PFA hearings over the past few years, noting who the hearing judge was, then Rory returned to the office.

She found an unusually reluctant Blake and tried to humor him. "You deserve the afternoon off, so as soon as we're finished, you can leave. That is, unless you let me take you to lunch first."

"My God, Rory, I'm shocked at the lengths you are willing to go just to get me into the prison—what are you, a sadist?"

It was Rory's turn to look shocked. "Is that what you think? Have I ever told you why I hate to go to the prison? Why I had to force myself? Why I sometimes feel physically sick? Do you want to know?" Rory's voice was shrill, her face pale. She collapsed into a chair.

Blake brought her a glass of water.

"I'm sorry, Rory. Do you feel like talking about it?"

Rory accepted the water and the apology. "It's time I told you—God knows, it hasn't done me any good keeping it inside all these years."

So she told Blake the story of being locked in between prison doors when she was thirteen when she and her parents were visiting Sean.

Blake was sympathetic, and then he shared the origins of his claustrophobia. His father had locked him in the closet from a very early age for any infraction of rules, minor or major. His father was a drunk.

As they left, Rory promised Blake that she would help him through the prison visit.

Rory taped her session with Korbin. He was pleased an alibi witness had been found and that a new bail hearing was set for the next day. She cautioned him, as she did all of her clients, not to be overly optimistic about the bail being lowered. She believed the hearing would go in his favor, but she knew better than to give false hope.

She and Blake left the prison in a good mood. They had high hopes for Korbin and both were happy to be on the outside of the prison.

"Whew! That was pretty scary, but thanks for making me go in. Telling me your story made it easier."

Blake left, thanking Rory for the afternoon off, while Rory headed back to the office. She spent the remainder of the afternoon preparing for the up-coming bail hearing. She had spoken on the phone with the sewer worker, Roy Thomas, and would meet with him in person first thing the following morning. It should be a fairly routine hearing, and God-willing Korbin should be a free man by noon.

She decided to call Helen, Jeremy Katz's secretary. She'd been on Rory's mind since their last meeting. She wondered if she was upset over Kathie's death or if she had any knowledge of Kathie's last days. The phone rang a few times and then was answered by Jeremy. "Oh, Hi, Jeremy, it's Rory. I was calling to speak with Helen—is she in?"

"No, she's not, Rory."

"Well, could you please ask her to call me—I'd like to take her to lunch. I have some questions to ask her about Kathie, since she worked with her."

After a pause Jeremy asked, "What questions? Maybe I can answer them—I worked with her, too."

Feeling awkward, Rory answered, "Well, just her state of mind, what was going on with her. I just wondered if she'd confided in Helen, if they were close."

"No, I didn't notice that she and Helen were particularly close. Sorry I can't be of more help. But, I'll tell Helen you called. Bye now."

That was a wasted call, thought Rory—hopefully Helen could shed more light than Jeremy had. The call left her feeling uneasy.

To get her mind off the call she decided to record her thoughts on the interview with Korbin. Putting the tape player on her desk, she hit play. Just then, the outer door burst open and she could hear loud footsteps marching in her direction. Instinctively, she covered the recorder with papers, leaving it on.

Her worst nightmare, Judge Keller, stood in the doorway, having flung open the door. She was shocked, but not surprised, to see him. She tried to hide her fear.

Red-faced, he spewed rage. "How dare you spy on me? What do you think you're doing? What I do is none of your business! Do you have any idea I can end your career like this?" The judge indicated with a snap of his fingers. "Stop Snooping!" He turned abruptly on his heel and headed out, almost colliding with the interns, frozen like statues in the doorway.

Chapter 10

Sarah was the first to recover and ran to Rory, checking to make sure was all right.

"My God, Rory, you're trembling—what the Hell just happened? Who was that asshole?"

"That asshole, is none other than, the president judge."

"You're kidding, right?" Sarah smiled at the joke.

"Wish I were—have a seat, kids—this might take a while."

Sam, registering shock, slid into a seat next to Sarah as instructed.

Rory wished Blake had been there for support, but she had to do this one solo. She told them she'd been observing PFA hearings, and what she'd seen. Then she played them the brief, but smoldering, tape of the judge's recent visit.

"I've had my suspicions about the judge, which is why I sent you two to the archives, and now I'm even more suspicious as to what his connection is to Kathie and perhaps other women who've filed PFA's. It puts us all in vulnerable positions. So I want you to stay together and be especially observant. He's got my number; hopefully he doesn't get yours as well, now that he's seen you. He's ruthless, powerful and well-connected, if not particularly bright, in my humble opinion."

"Wow," Sam said, "I had no idea how corrupt the 'Halls of Justice' could be!"

"It is shocking," Rory conceded, "but you have to remember that corruption is everywhere. Any place you find power, even in the church, you will find abuse of power. I'm not condoning it, by the way—I abhor it—and the excuse that 'everyone does it' is a poor excuse. We're all responsible for how we choose to conduct ourselves, and, at the end of the day, we have to believe in what we're doing."

"I'm glad you guys came back—why did you come back, anyway?"

Sam and Sarah looked at each other, and Sarah clapped a hand to her mouth.

"Oh my God!" Sarah exclaimed, "We came back to tell you that by far the most PFA cases were heard by one judge—and it was Judge Keller," they emphasized, in unison.

"Bingo!" said Rory. "Now what?" she wondered out loud.

"Well," Sam added, "we could start looking at the outcomes of the cases that the judge heard. For instance, did he always grant the PFA's, did any harm come to the plaintiffs? Those kinds of things would be of interest, I think."

"That's a lot of digging for you guys, but I do think that's the direction we need to go, as discreetly as possible, because, he's not a person you'd want as an enemy, or a friend for that matter."

"You're amazing, Rory—the judge comes in and scares the bejesus out of you and you still keep your sense of humor." Sarah was smiling and shaking her head.

"Oh, I'm still scared plenty. I'm just trying to cope; something I've learned to get through rough times. This can be a tough business, like life; you can't take yourself too seriously."

Looking at the clock Rory groaned, "Where has the time gone? Why don't you guys go home—I still have some work to do on Korbin's bail hearing for tomorrow."

"No way!" Sarah said.

"We're staying here until you leave—don't want any replays of the recent past!" Sam added.

"Ok, thanks, I'll explain what the hearing is about as I write my memo to the judge; it's a fairly uncomplicated motion, and it should go in Korbin's favor. Judge Campbell is a fair jurist. We will interview our alibi witness first thing in the morning before we go over to the courthouse; you should be here for that, since he's met you. I told him to come at 8:15."

Rory continued, "The alibi witness will take the stand and be questioned first by me, and then the DA, Basically, I will help him tell about his meeting with Korbin and then the DA will cross-examine. The Judge will rule on my motion to reconsider bail."

Rory was ready to leave. "Let's get outta here—it's been a long day! Hope I didn't ruin anyone's plans."

"Not at all," Sarah assured her. "Sam and I were going out for pizza—do you want to join us?"

"Thanks, but my family's waiting for me—see you in the morning."

*****

Rory was anxious to get home—it had been a long day, filled with emotion and uncertainty. She was glad to have talked with Sam and Sarah about what was going on; she hadn't liked the subterfuge involved with having them do research without knowing the reason behind it. She didn't think she'd discuss it with Marc, since he felt the case was interfering with their vacation plans. And he also seemed to think Jeff Korbin was guilty, or at least, dangerous.

Despite their truce, he hadn't wavered in his disapproval of her working on this case. And the idea of her tangling with the president judge would make him nuts. Not that she liked it, but damn, she wouldn't back down either.

Finally home, Rory was not happy to see the garage door open and an empty spot where Marc's Honda usually was. Entering the house, silence greeted her and she could see that no one was home, with the exception of an unfed Peaches, who rubbed against her legs, purring and looking plaintively at her empty bowl.

"Oh, Peaches—you poor baby, it's just you and me, I guess." She rubbed the cat's head and then went to get the food. On the way, she noticed a piece of paper on the table. Marc had scrawled: 'Couldn't reach you—we got hungry, so went out— M'. *Oh shit*, she thought, we're back to the cold war. She checked her cell and noticed that it was still off—there were two messages from Marc. She listened to the first, when he explained that they were dining at Fellini; it didn't sound like an explanation as much as an accusation, so she passed on the second message. Besides, it had been sent nearly forty-five minutes ago.

Peaches' pacing and mewling brought her back to the present and she fed her. Not hungry herself, she decided it would be good to go for a jog, release some of today's pent up frustration.

Thankful for the long June day, she was soon jogging down her road, a winding residential street with little traffic. She hadn't bothered to leave Marc a note, she thought with a twinge of guilt; he'd left her one, however inadequate. It felt good to be out in the cool night air. She'd been working too much lately to keep up her fitness regimen.

She noticed a dark blue BMW coming toward her slowly. She didn't know of anyone in her neighborhood who had one, so she tried to get a glimpse of the driver. The windows were tinted, making it impossible to see inside. Intriguing, she thought. Perhaps we have a celebrity among us.

She continued jogging, enjoying the sensations and getting into what runners called "the zone." Enjoying it, she didn't notice other matters consuming her had receded in her awareness. Finishing her loop, she started home, feeling the weeks of inactivity in her aching muscles. Her breathing was coming in gasps and she wished she'd brought water.

She noticed that same Beemer come towards her, slowly, as before. Maybe the person was looking to move here, she thought, though she knew of no homes for sale. *Strange*.

She was happy to see her front porch light on and relieved to be almost home. Slowing almost to a walk, she checked her pulse and wasn't paying much attention when, suddenly, she heard a car speed up behind her. She turned and was literally forced off the road. The impact from the car grazed her hip and she tumbled to the side of the road. She looked up as the car sped off—it was the Beemer. In the gathering dusk she couldn't manage to see the plate.

Chapter 11

She'd been soaking in the tub when Marc and her daughters had arrived home that night, trying to ease the pain of her injury. She'd been scared, terrified, actually; she couldn't make sense of this apparently intentional and random violence. *Or perhaps it wasn't random.* Could it be the judge? She could think of no one else who bore her ill will. He had, in fact, just threatened her. Possibly she was getting a little close to the truth? For now, she'd decided to be wary, but keep it to herself until she sorted it out. She wanted to tell Marc, but knew he'd insist she get off the case immediately. It was her stubborn streak, she knew, but she needed to stay with this case.

Now, she got quietly out of bed and dressed quickly. She could manage only a piece of toast with her coffee—she took some pain pills; her hip was already starting to throb. Peaches, always in tune with Rory's moods, jumped up onto her lap and started purring.

"Hello, you sweet thing," Rory crooned, petting her. It always made Rory feel better to have the cat on her lap. And she hadn't even begged for food. Cats were underrated, in Rory's opinion.

Finishing her breakfast, Rory apologized to Peaches as she moved her, and winced as she got up. She filled Peaches' bowl, and gathered up her things.

A sleepy Kate poked her head around the door jamb and asked, "Hey, Mom, why're you leaving so early?"

"Oh, hi sweetie," she went over to give her a kiss, "I have a bail hearing and an early interview. I'm hoping my client gets out on bail, then I'll be a lot less involved at work."

"That would be great Mom—we miss you. Why are you limping?"

"Oh, I didn't realize I was—I went out jogging last night—guess I overdid it."

"Please take care of yourself, Mom—I love you. Bye."

"Bye, sweetie, love you, too."

She hadn't realized she'd been limping, but it did hurt. It would probably take a while for the meds to take hold. It would be a reminder to her to be cautious. It occurred to Rory, somewhat belatedly, maybe she was onto something, or someone.

Blake had the coffee on when she got to the office. Of course he noticed her limp and commented on it. Rory told him the same lie she'd told her daughter, at the same time wondering why she was keeping it secret.

"Oh, I forgot—Wonder Woman rides again! How was your afternoon?"

"You go first, Blake—you had the time off—I'm sure it was more exciting."

He looked skeptical, but answered, "Well, I said 'screw the law library,' and went to the movies, which is something I virtually never do. Saw *Hunger Games on Fire*—pretty good."

"Good for you—you actually did take time for yourself. I'll let the interns tell you about our afternoon/evening," Rory said, smiling innocently.

"I hate when you do that—now I have to wait to hear the juicy stuff!"

"They'll be here soon enough."

As if on cue, the outer door opened and Sam and Sarah entered. Rory noticed they were almost always coming in at the same time. And she was sensing something between them. She smiled.

Blake immediately demanded to know what happened yesterday afternoon and they were only too happy to fill him in.

Roy Thomas, the alibi witness, arrived on time, so the animated discussion ceased. Rory introduced herself and led him into her office, followed by Sam and Sarah. He greeted them and took the seat Rory offered.

Rory tried to put him at ease, asking him to tell her exactly what had transpired when he had seen Mr. Korbin at the work site. She showed him three pictures of men about Korbin's age to see if he could pick out Korbin; he chose correctly. She explained to him that the DA would cross examine him and try to get him to change his testimony. It was important for him to stay with the simple truth and to answer just the question asked. Finally, she asked if he had any questions. He looked nervous, but had no questions.

Believing they were as prepared as they could be, the four crossed the street to the courthouse. They were a bit early, so the security line wasn't very long. When they reached the appointed courtroom, it was empty. This gave Rory time to familiarize her witness and students with the courtroom and their places in it.

The sheriffs brought in Korbin. Shackled and wearing an orange jumpsuit, he was led to the defense table and took a seat. Rory smiled at him.

Stan Como soon entered and Rory spoke briefly with him, saying that she'd shown the witness three different pictures and he'd picked out Korbin. He shrugged as if that was of no consequence.

Before long, the door behind the bench opened and the court crier announced, "Court is now in session, The Honorable President Judge Norman H. Keller presiding."

Horrified, Rory looked daggers at Como, who raised his brows and shrugged, as if to say, *I didn't know, either.*

The satisfied smirk on the judge's face said it all. "Good Morning, Ms. Chandler, Mr. Como. I understand this is a Review of Bail hearing for Mr. Korbin, who is being held on a Murder 1 charge. And the reason for the review? Please advise, counsel."

Rory, still in a state of shock, hoped that her voice did not betray her.

"Your Honor, directing your attention to the memo, we are requesting from the Court a reduction of bail, based on a witness who has come forward prepared to testify as to the whereabouts of the defendant at the approximate time of his wife's death. We request the Court's permission to put Mr. Roy Thomas on the stand."

"Mr. Como—do you have any objection to this?"

"No, Your Honor, Ms. Chandler gave me due notice."

"Very well, then," Judge Keller sounded put upon, "let the witness take the stand and be sworn in."

Roy Thomas took the stand and was sworn in, then questioned by Rory, much as he had been earlier in her office. He spoke confidently and gave a credible impression, Rory thought. She then turned it over to Como for cross-examination.

Rory had to admit that Stan was straightforward and didn't try to intimidate or trip up the witness. Again, Roy did well with the questioning.

When the prosecution rested, Rory requested that consideration be given to lowering bail for Mr. Korbin, based on the testimony of Mr. Thomas, who had proven to be a credible alibi witness.

Judge Keller banged the gavel and announced: "Bail remains at the original amount of one million dollars. I've heard nothing today to change that order."

"But, your Honor....." Rory protested.

Judge Keller looked at Rory and banged the gavel again. "I've ruled on this case...Next case!"

Rory was so angry she was literally shaking. Sam put his arm around her and led her from the court room. Stan came up to her in the lobby.

"Hey, I'm really sorry—I had no idea he was hearing the case. I mean, I want to win, but not like that!"

"Thanks, Stan, really, that means a lot." She heard no trace of insincerity in his voice.

Turning to Sam, who was closest to her, she said, "We've got to go and see Korbin in the holding cell."

The three of them walked solemnly to the holding cell, where they were buzzed through a set of doors. They had to speak with Korbin through the bars. They could see him seated on a bench, head in hands. He came to the bars, eyes red, tears streaking his face.

Rory had no words to ease his pain, but spoke anyway. "I'm so sorry—I really thought we had this one. I know you must feel dreadful, I do. But, please don't give up. We haven't given up—we believe in you and we're going to keep at it."

"Look, I know you're doing your best— I'll be ok. It's just better not to hope, I guess." His words sounded hollow.

"No, you need hope; patience helps, too. I know that's a tall order. We're looking out for you and determined to find out who really killed Kathie."

As they walked back through the main lobby, Rory spotted Roy Thomas, looking a bit lost. She went up to him.

"Roy, you did a great job on the stand—it was in no way your fault that bail wasn't reduced. This judge is... well, he's very...strict. We really appreciate you coming in. And once we go to trial, we'll need you again. You're very important to the case; we just have to hope we don't get the same judge."

"Thanks Ms. Chandler, I was afraid I didn't do a good enough job, since it's my first time and all..."

"No, no, you were perfect. Why don't you come back to the office with us, and maybe have some coffee. We can answer any questions you may have, other than the obvious one, of why bail wasn't reduced."

The four crossed the street to Rory's office.

When Roy Thomas had left, Rory excused herself to meet her former partner, Charlie, for lunch. And to Sam and Sarah she said, "Why don't you take the afternoon off—you've been working hard, and you're probably as bummed as I am right now. I'm not coming back after lunch. We'll hit it hard again tomorrow."

Rory decided to walk to the restaurant; her hip was feeling better, and she needed to blow off steam right about now before she exploded with rage. She'd kept it at bay all morning for the sake of others, but she was beyond infuriated. In her mind 's eye, she kept seeing that smirking face and those hard eyes, knowing that he had gotten to her, had hit her in her most vulnerable spot. He was in a position to preside over all of her cases and virtually nullify her. This was an intolerable position to be in.

He could so easily intrude on her professional life without recourse. And the bastard seemed to be enjoying it. She remembered what her friend, Don, had said. He *was* a piece of shit. *Well, God damn him*, she thought, I will not go down easily or cower in the face of his arrogance.

What sprang to her mind was a balm; she had something on him that he would hate to have made public. And she was prepared to use it.

Chapter 12

Rory was feeling better by the time she reached the Court Diner, an eatery chosen because there would be few lawyer types there, despite its name. This place was strictly blue collar, but the food was wholesome, and some of it even healthy.

Charlie was already seated in a corner and waved Rory over.

"Don't get up," she said as she reached down to give him a hug. "It's so good to see you! How long has it been?"

"Hard to say," Charlie replied, "time flies when you're retired; don't know how everything got done before. I've missed you, my girl. You're a sight for sore, old eyes—how are you?"

"No point in lying to you Charlie, I never could get away with that. I've been better."

Before Rory could expand on that, the waitress came over, pad in hand.

"Can I get you folks anything, or do you need more time?"

Rory looked briefly at the menu as Charlie ordered a turkey burger.

"And I'll have the Cobb salad with balsamic vinaigrette, without the ham and no roll. And iced tea, please." Rory replied.

"I see you're still eating healthy. My wife's on my case, so I'm trying to do the same. I do feel better, so that makes it easier, just like you always told me. Anyway, what's up kiddo?"

"Let's say, I'm feeling overwhelmed, but I'll start with the most recent event which has me really upset." She went on to recount the murder case which led her to observe PFA cases, which led to the scene between the judge and the plaintiff, and finally, listening to the incriminating tape. She was still unsure how the judge had got gotten wind of her interest, but he had, and now definitely had it in for her. She related how he'd stormed into her office to threaten her and then intervened to preside over her court case. Leaving out the part about being forced off the road—knowing he'd insist she go to the authorities—she told him that she'd been followed by a navy blue Beemer. She believed the judge was stalking her, trying to intimidate her, and might possibly be involved with Kathie Korbin's death.

"Wow! You sure do have a lot going on. Let's try to break it down a bit. The President Judge is a womanizer—no question about it—to what depths he would descend is anyone's guess. What you heard on the tape is disgusting, but I believe he's capable of it. Murder, that's another kettle of fish; I just don't see that. Using his power to intimidate you in court—again, that's up his alley. What to do about it is a sticky matter. He's the President Judge, so how do you get around it? You can't go to the CID—he's got them in his pocket. The only agency I can see taking this on is the State Attorney General's office. I say that because of the highly publicized case in Lucerne County where two judges were taking money from juvenile rehab centers in exchange for ordering juveniles into those facilities. Since then, the AG's office is much more attuned to issues of local officials involved in misconduct. If the AG's office has valid info, they form a Grand Jury which hears evidence and decides whether or not to proceed with prosecution. That also happened with the Penn State/Sandusky case—bad business, that was. So, they've been very busy."

"I just feel as if I have to do something, not only because what he did is reprehensible, but because he could easily ruin my career; he's already threatened to!"

"Yeah, I hear you, he is scum. But, I don't think he's a murderer, nor do I think he's stalking you. For one thing, I think he drives a big, garish Caddy, with a vanity plate that says something like PRES JUDG—can't really see him in a Beemer—doubt he would fit, for another!" Charlie laughed at his joke.

That brought a smile to Rory's face as well.

Lunch arrived and they spent time catching up on their lives outside of work, as they ate. After lunch, they vowed to meet more regularly, and Rory promised to keep him current as events unfolded.

As she left the diner, she called Don Mandel. "Hey, it's Rory—do you have time to talk today regarding our conversation of the other day? Stuff has happened and it's scary."

"Sure, Rory, sure—give me fifteen minutes—same place?"

"Great, Don, thanks so much!"

Rory was sitting outside of Seven Stones Cafe with an iced tea when Don appeared, ahead of schedule.

"Thanks, Don I'm really a bit unglued about what's been going on." She went on to tell him about the judge's angry visit to her office, being run off the road by an unknown driver of a BMW, and finally Judge Keller's appearance at her review of bail hearing, which she knew had been assigned to Judge Campbell.

"Whoa, I'd say he has it in for you in spades. What a fuckin' creep he is. But, I doubt it was him in the BMW. If I recall—and I try to remember what kind of car each of the judges drives—I think our Pres. drives a big clunky Cadillac—that would suit him, wouldn't it?"

"Funny, that's what Charlie said, too—just had lunch with my former partner."

"Charlie Laws—how is the old guy? Always liked him!"

"He's fine, and he keeps very busy. Anyway, I discussed this whole situation with him and he thinks the only way to get to the President Judge is to alert the State AG. He said, and I agree, that the AG is very sensitive to local issues of judicial misconduct since that whole brouhaha up-state and of course the cover-up at Penn State. So, they're more likely to take any tips seriously, even anonymous ones."

"Well, then, I'm glad I was able to copy that tape before the judge got smart and erased it. At least, I assume he may have," Don said smugly, smirking.

"Oh my God! You actually did it?" Rory lowered her voice to almost a whisper.

"Yep, it needed to be done before he suspected. He obviously thinks you know something, but he's not sure of what yet. He wants to make sure you know the full weight of his position. Obviously, you don't care!"

"Well, we have the ammunition, now we have to decide when and how to use it. This is really huge, Don—I guess you know that. I'm really glad to have your backing. I still can't believe it..."

"Rory, you know I thrive on this shit. This is enough to get him disbarred and maybe more—at least, out of our lives. When this breaks, his power base will dissolve like fog in the sun."

"Nice metaphor—guess that comes from writing all those editorials."

Don chuckled, "Yeah, one of the perks. But getting back on point, Charlie's advice was on target. I think we need to get this tape out to a major newspaper at the same time as the AG gets it. That will give the state a bit of an impetus to get going on it. And it will turn the tables on El Presidente. It should at least get him off your case. Just tell me when to pull the plug—I don't want to do it prematurely; I know you're still conducting your investigation. It could get dicey."

"Yeah, you could say that. Listen, I think we shouldn't be seen together. Not to sound paranoid, but the judge's tentacles reach far; I'm afraid he's out to discredit me and I'm sure you're already on his shit list."

Don pulled a piece of paper from his pocket and scribbled a number on it. "This is a secure cell number when you want to reach me, and maybe you want to call from a pay phone, if you can find one. Oh, and probably the best place to meet might be right under his nose, in the court house, which is perfectly legit for both of us. Catch you later."

Rory sat for a while, taking in the gravity of what she'd been discussing with two men she trusted and admired. It was both exhilarating and terrifying. But she could see no other way—for many reasons, it was the only course of action. In the meantime, she needed Sam and Sarah to keep digging in the archives to look for any irregularities associated with Judge Keller's hearings.

Looking at her watch, she figured she had time to go back to the office and check her messages, then decide the best action to take next. She didn't want her interns to know about the tape—the fewer people the better—there could be blow-back.

Blake was at his desk when she arrived at the office. "How was lunch with Charlie?"

"Oh, you know, he's so wise; he always makes me feel better. He agrees the judge is a sleaze, but doesn't think he's a murderer, which leaves me back at square one. I should just go on vacation with my family and give it a rest, but I can't do that, knowing Korbin is rotting in jail."

"You're right, you should go, but knowing you, you probably won't. Can you postpone the vacation?"

"I really doubt that Marc wants to entertain that idea. Any messages?"

"Yeah, there's one from Como, and, I can't believe it but it's really nice." He handed it to her.

She read it aloud, shaking her head, "Sorry about the hearing, Rory—honestly I knew nothing about the change of judges.' Well if that don't beat all—an apology from Como! Almost, but not quite, worth the price. Actually, he's been quite nice to me lately—I may have to change my opinion of him. Hate it when I rush to judgment. By the way, have I gotten any messages from Helen Yates? I called her and got Jeremy—asked him to have her call me. I'm concerned about her—she wasn't herself when I last saw her and I wanted to take her out to lunch."

"No, she hasn't called, and she sometimes calls me just to chat—nice lady. She might be upset over Kathie's death—they were pretty close."

"Hmmm…that's odd," reflected Rory.

"What's odd?" inquired Blake.

"Well, Jeremy said they weren't friends when I specifically asked if that was why Helen was upset."

"That's guys for you," Blake said dismissively. "Want me to give her a call?"

"Would you?"

"Sure thing." Blake dialed the number, then listened. "I got voicemail, but didn't leave a message; I'll try again later."

"Thanks, Blake, I'm going to head home now—my girls have a tough play-off game tonight, and I hope to get a little shut-eye before then."

"Good idea—tell them good luck from me. See you tomorrow."

Rory was really feeling her bruised hip as she walked to her car. It was going to feel so good to slip into a warm bath and try to forget how the case was going.

She tried to relax her shoulders as she left Media and got onto less traveled roads. More than once she caught herself gripping the steering wheel so tightly her knuckles were white. Looking in her rearview mirror before executing a left-hand turn, she thought she caught a blur of dark blue a few cars back. Now, she was on full alert again, and focusing her attention on her rear mirror instead of the road in front of her. She veered into the left lane, provoking a loud horn blare, from an on-coming vehicle, then slammed on her brakes, nearly causing a rear-end collision. Over-correcting, she ended up on the shoulder, amid flying gravel and a cacophony of angry calls and honks from drivers. A navy blue BMW blew by.

Shaking, Rory picked up her cell and called Roland.

Chapter 13

Trembling, Rory sat in her car alternating between crying and cursing; trying to pull herself together as best she could before Roland arrived.

Lights flashing, she saw his approach long before he arrived; she'd never been happier to see a State Trooper. He pulled up behind her and made it appear like a routine stop for anyone who may be watching. When she rolled down the window, he looked at her tear-stained face with concern.

"Rory—you ok to drive?" he asked gently through the open window.

She nodded. "It's not far to my house—if you can just follow me…"

"Just what I had in mind—go slow now."

As expected, no one was home when she arrived. She looked around, half hoping that the blue car would drive by now, *God damn him*! Roland helped her out of her car and then just held her.

"You're still shaking, Rory—let's go in and you can tell me what's been going on. Has to be something big to put you in such a state!"

Once inside, Rory collapsed onto the bench of her breakfast nook.

Peaches appeared from nowhere, jumped onto her lap and nestled in protectively.

"What's that, your guard cat?" Roland tried for and elicited a smile from Rory.

"Yeah, really, she's always there for me."

"You want me to put on some tea or something? I mean the Brits swear by it!"

He was happy to get a laugh this time. "What are you trying out for, stand-up? Thanks. But I don't need any tea. Unless you want some. Just sit down and I'll try to tell you about this mess from the beginning."

Rory started at the beginning and told the no holds barred version.

He was silent for a moment, rare for Roland, as he took it all in. He gave a low whistle, "You have stumbled into a hornet's nest, Sugar, maybe a few. I'm not sure they're all related, I mean the judge stuff and the stalker. You maybe have pissed off a couple of people here. What does Marc think?"

Rory's hesitation spoke volumes.

"Oh no, you mean you haven't told Marc, one of the best profilers around? Are you nuts?"

"Normally I would," Rory was defensive. "It's just that he's dead set against me taking on this case for some reason and I can't even talk to him about it."

"Doesn't sound like Marc—there has be more to it." Roland was shaking his head.

"Well, he knew Korbin in high school, says he had a fixation on Kathie, was very jealous…"

"Yeah, but still, doesn't sound like Marc…"

"I know, that's what I keep thinking but I can't come up with anything, other than it's taking up a lot of my time, and we're supposed to go on vacation. And now with Korbin not getting bail, I really can't afford to leave right now. I know he'll hit the ceiling; I dread telling him."

"Well, I'm not one to meddle in couples' business, but I do hope you can work it out; you're one of the best heterosexual couples I know!" He winked.

"Thanks, Roland—we've been through rough patches before and I'm sure we'll work it out, but there's lots of stress right now."

"Well, I've got your back—I'll help you any way I can. Your road is a state road, so I can patrol it legitimately, and I will. I'll also be on the lookout for a navy BMW. License number?"

"Never caught it," Rory answered unhappily.

"OK, please call on me for anything. Lock the door when I leave, and try to get some rest." He gave her a peck on the cheek. "Bye—Love you!"

"Love you, too, Roland, and thanks for everything."

Roland had made her feel so much better—he hadn't judged her, but he had made her wonder again why Marc was so angry about her involvement in this case. She felt as though she'd been treading on egg shells ever since she'd told him. And that wasn't like Marc. They'd had some good times in between, but she was relying more on other people for support than she was Marc, which was way outside the norm; Marc usually knew everything about the cases she was working on. Sighing, she looked at the clock—4:00 PM.. She had time for only a quick shower before heading out to the girls' playoff game. It was going to be a nail-biter, but then, it might take her mind off her other worries.

It was a long drive to Phoenixville, and the traffic was, as always in this area, incredibly heavy. What could've been a 45 minute drive took well over an hour. Anticipating this, Rory had left herself plenty of time. She'd been late to her share of games and knew how important this one was for the girls.

The drive also gave her time to reflect on Korbin's case and where she was going, or, as it seemed, where she was stuck. As several people had pointed out, the judge was, in all likelihood, not her stalker. Who was it then, and why was he—she assumed

100

it was a 'he'—after her? Who had she pissed off besides he judge? Did he have 'toadies' doing his dirty work? That seemed unlikely. Was she completely wrong to suspect the judge of involvement in Kathie's murder? It seemed she had nothing but questions. She needed to talk with Helen, and wondered again why Jeremy's secretary hadn't returned the call.

Perhaps Jeremy had forgotten to give her the message. Blake may have reached her after Rory had left the office; she hoped that was the case.

Reaching her destination, Rory searched for a parking space and then had to find the right playing field. Fortunately there were not many from which to choose. Ultimately, the school bus led her to the right field.

The girls were on the field practicing; they were too far away to see or hear her. She looked into the bleachers for Marc and saw only a sea of faces. She called him on his cell. He answered, obviously irritated.

"Hey, Marc, I'm here at the field and just wondered if you were too, it's so huge..."

"Oh, hi, Rory—I'm glad you're there. This fuckin' traffic—I'd forgotten how bad it is at rush hour. I'll be another 15 minutes, at least; just find a spot, and let me know what section you're in and I'll find you."

Rory allowed herself a small smile at having the tables reversed for a change. "Looks like there are some spots in section C," she answered, looking around, "so look for me there, and take it easy. Bye."

Finding two seats together in section C was no easy matter and they were not the best, but they would have to do. Rory sat and put her jacket on the adjacent seat to reserve it for Marc. The game started a few minutes later.

It was a very fast paced game; Rory soon realized with chagrin that the Suns were in a different league entirely. The Panthers fought back valiantly, but soon they were down by three runs. The Panthers were not a come from behind team, she'd understood from listening to Marc and the girls. Things did not usually work out this way for them. They were in over their heads, and they seemed to know it. But still, they played their hardest.

Rory hardly noticed when Marc made his way up the stands to his seat. When she did notice him, he was scowling. "Is this the best you could do?"

She bit back a sharp retort, taking into account his commute and the lopsided game, replying simply, "Yep, this is a huge game, and it was already packed when I got here."

He sat down abruptly, continuing to grouse about the seats.

"Be nice if I could actually see some of the action..."

Refusing to take the bait, although tempted, Rory said sweetly, "Why don't you look around and see if you find any open seats?"

To herself, she wondered if it was just the traffic that brought on his attitude.

That shut him up for the moment. They both focused on the game, which wasn't so great. The Panthers weren't making errors; they were simply being outplayed by a superior team. Rory felt bad for the girls, they'd worked so hard; and they'd come so far. After all, the winner of this game would go on to the state championship. Her ego didn't require that they go the whole way; she was proud of them anyway.

She heard Marc groan and put his head in his hands as the Panthers were struck out for the second time. That was disheartening, Rory got it.

Marc had followed this team much more closely than she had, and knew them all, their individual strengths and weaknesses. He was taking it harder than she was.

She put her hand on his arm to console him. He made no movement. In their last inning at bat, Alex slammed one over the fence with two runners on base, and that put them back by only three runs. Marc was up on his feet and screaming, pumping his fist in the air—"Way to go, Alex!"

His whole demeanor changed. He turned to Rory, "They still have a chance, you know!"

"Of course they do—Go Panthers!" she yelled. They had two outs, so their chances of winning this were statistically low, but it could happen. She was just happy they had rallied and that Alex had made it happen.

Kate was up next and got a base hit. The next batter also got to first, advancing Kate to second. At this point the Panthers' cheering section was standing and screaming. They actually had a chance to tie up the game! It was turning into a real competition. The third batter after being up for what seemed an eternity was walked, loading the bases.

Oh my God! thought Rory, *could it get any more exciting?*

The Suns, predictably, put in a new pitcher. She was big and intimidating; she was the closer.

The next batter stepped to the plate. Marc groaned; Rory assumed that she wasn't a hitter. He confirmed it by whispering to her, "She'll swing at anything." He was right. She did—one, two, three strikes—game over!

The Suns fans went wild, while the silence in section C was overwhelming. Then, Rory began to yell: "Way to go, Panthers!" And the crowd picked it up. Soon the stadium, at least half of it, was echoing with support for the Panthers, drowning out the victory cries. Rory was so proud of the effort they had put forth.

She grabbed Marc's hand and led the way down to the field. It wasn't easy to connect with the girls through the milling crowd, but finally Rory spotted the girls and the twins sped towards their parents. Grabbing both into a bear hug Rory and Marc exclaimed how proud they were at how close the team had come to winning this game. Surprisingly, the girls didn't seem upset by the loss; they were still pumped on adrenaline.

Kate spoke first, "The Panthers did so much better than expected—we didn't think our team had a snowball's chance in hell. It was *almost* as good as winning."

"Yeah, the Suns had to work for the win—and to think the Panthers came that close," Alex said holding her thumb and first finger an inch apart. "I mean, the Suns have to respect us, if nothing else. The team has never played better, we gave it all we had! Whew, I'm beat! Coach is taking us out for dinner, so see you at home later." Alex said.

"It is absolutely the best game the team ever played—you guys really rose to the occasion—couldn't be prouder if your team was going to the State finals." Marc had obviously gotten over his disappointment.

"Me, too!" Rory exclaimed. "Enjoy your dinner and we'll see you later."

Rory and Marc stood smiling as their daughters disappeared into the crowd. Marc ended the silence, by saying, "That was a good thing you did, Rory, starting that cheer. It made everyone, including me, realize we had to celebrate just how well they'd done and not focus on the loss. That's so *you!*"

"Thanks, I never thought about it, it just seemed the right thing to do. I really thought what they did was extraordinary, and Alex was a big part of rallying the team. I guess that's why she's co-captain."

"Yeah, you're right. Anyway, I'm starved, how about we catch a bite to eat out here? Then maybe the traffic will have dropped off a bit—I don't think I could take another drive like the one here."

"Sure, why not? Any ideas?"

"I remember passing a Panera—it's just down the road on the way home. You can follow me, ok?"

Within ten minutes they had their salads and were seated at Panera. They talked about the game for a bit and how pleased they were for the girls. Then Marc mentioned it was a good thing that vacation was coming up soon—the girls had been training so hard they needed a rest. "By the way, how's your case coming along?" he asked.

Instead of giving him a direct answer, she asked if it was possible to push the vacation ahead to later in the summer, cringing inwardly. No getting around it— it had to be discussed.

He didn't speak immediately but she could feel the heat. When he did speak, it was as if to an errant child. "You do realize Rory that the beach house was rented in January. If we renege now we will lose our deposit, which is a big hunk of change. And there's no guarantee, is there, that you will find yourself available in the next month or the month after, ad infinitum? So no—we can't change the dates. Sorry if you can't come, but that seems to be your choice."

Rory had lost her appetite. The now familiar lump in her stomach had rendered her food tasteless. Rising slowly, she took her tray to the bussing area, and threw away her uneaten food; she hated to waste—it made her feel guilty. On her way back to the table, she noticed that Marc was gone.

Sighing, she thought, once again, *I can't think about this tonight; I'll deal with it tomorrow.*

Chapter 14

Marc sped off from the restaurant as if pursued by demons. Actually, he was being driven by his own demons. He was angry, of that he was acutely aware. He had tried everything to get Rory off this case, and nothing had worked. He believed his anger was justified in that she seemed to be choosing Korbin over her family.

He glanced at the speedometer as he blew by every other car on the road— he was going 87, and that, finally, frightened him enough to slow down. His racing thoughts slowed down, too. As that happened, he had to face the truth behind the anger. It was a truth he'd been running from ever since Rory took this case; it was the fear that she would discover more about him than he wanted her to know. He'd had the opportunity to tell her, when he'd disclosed that he'd known Jeff in high school. That part was true. All of what he'd told her was true; his falsehood, which had taken up a haunting, guilty presence, was one of omission; there was so much he hadn't told her. He tried to rationalize it away. He was afraid of losing her, but was it really cowardice? He wondered. So, he'd been acting like a complete asshole for the past several weeks, almost causing it to happen. He was a psychologist, for Christ sakes; he was supposed to know what to do. He'd dug himself a big hole. And now he'd announced that he and the girls were going on vacation without her. Oh yeah, that would be fun—the girls would thank him for that! But he was too stubborn to back down now.

He stopped at a light and opened the sun roof and all the windows, letting in the cool, fragrant June breezes. It took him back 20 odd years, to when life was just starting and everything seemed fun and easy He remembered senior week in Sea Isle, after graduation, with all his buddies. And Kathie was there. She hadn't graduated, but she'd come with Brandon, who'd dumped her midweek. That's when Marc had a long awaited chance to connect with her. And he'd taken full advantage of the opportunity. Kathie was a beautiful, smart, funny girl. She was also uninhibited about sex, which was rare back then. She genuinely enjoyed sex and was unapologetic about it. Never considered promiscuous—she was too classy for that— most guys didn't talk about her afterward, they just counted themselves lucky. She was, however, discerning about whom she chose; she avoided the braggarts, who would've talked, and it drove them crazy.

Marc's affair with her was brief—it didn't last the summer— but he never forgot her and they remained friends. It was the kind of memory that would linger, part nostalgia, part desire, and always the question of 'what if' hanging in the balance.

Marc grieved when she'd been killed, and though he didn't believe that Jeff was guilty he knew he didn't want Rory messing around in this. He didn't want to see Jeff wrongly charged, but more than that, he didn't want Rory to know the fling with Kathie didn't really end that summer.

Chapter 15

Rory stared for a few seconds at the empty table, then shrugged and headed for the door, marveling at how quickly Marc had made his getaway. Well, *fuck him*, she thought. She'd done without him for the past several weeks, put up with his mercurial mood swings, and basically she was still standing. She missed the old Marc at a visceral level and hoped, once this trial was behind them, they could put things back together.

As she got into her car she realized that, although she was tired, she had no desire to go home—she needed to talk to someone who would understand and she thought of Don. She had his secret cell number—she didn't want to abuse it, but was feeling desperate. She called; he picked up after a few rings. "Rory, I'm just wrapping up my class—do you want to meet me at the Arby's on City Line?"

"I'm out in Phoenixville—just call me back when you're done—bye."

She felt badly taking him out of his way, and she'd forgotten to use a pay phone.

When he called back, they agreed to meet at a place closer to his home in Swarthmore, ironically, at another Panera.

He'd sounded curious, but not put out, so Rory was feeling less guilty.

When she arrived, he stood up to hug her, as was his way of greeting friends.

"So, what's going on? You sounded a bit strung out."

"You could say that...it's been one Hell of a day. Actually, it seems like several bad days strung together, And I should be exhausted, but, I'm evidently running on adrenaline."

"So, you want some coffee?" Don joked. "Sorry..."

Rory cracked a smile, "Don't apologize, I need a little levity. You will too, once you hear about my day!"

She started with facing Judge Keller instead of the scheduled Judge Campbell, went on to with Korbin still in jail, she was no closer to the culprit; instead, she seemed to be in increasing danger. And the family was going on vacation while she was hitting a blank wall.

"Fuck—now, I'm depressed! Just kidding. But, you really have had a bad day, bad week. Here's what I think: You're at a standstill for now; you need to back off. You could go on vacation, but knowing you, you'd probably be miserable. Is there anything else you can focus on while your interns are doing their digging? Hopefully, out of town?" Don asked.

Rory's brow furrowed, then she smiled. "Brilliant! Yes, I've been planning to handle an expungement hearing for my brother in Baltimore, provided he's done what he needed to do, and once it's set up it should take a few days. And I can visit my parents while I'm there, and the dastardly Judge Keller won't be on the bench!"

"That sounds very good," Don nodded his approval. "And in the meantime I'll scout around for anything I can find. I know there's not much. Do you have a best guess?"

"I've been trying to reach Helen Yates, she was working with Kathie —the last time I saw Helen, she wasn't herself, and I've heard she was friends with Kathie. I can leave Blake in charge of that—he knows her. But that's the best lead I have; that and the interns by chance finding anything in the archives."

"OK, well, it sounds like they can carry on, and you need to get away from it. Call me if you need to talk or if you think of something I can do. When do you think you'll leave?"

"Probably tomorrow after work. And thanks for your time, Don. Hope I didn't get you into hot water with your wife."

"No worries—she's always asleep when I get home, and I can't ever go straight to bed after teaching, so it worked out well all around. Take care and travel safely."

When Don left, Rory called Sean. He answered immediately, sounding elated. The thought flitted across her mind he might be in a manic phase. "What are you, like, psychic? I just got off the phone with Josh, who's agreed to testify on my behalf. In fact, he's happy to do it. Turns out he'd been feeling so guilty he was drinking too much and just recently got sober, so this is part of his making amends."

"Sean, that's great!" Rory sighed with relief. "I'm friends with a DA in Baltimore, went to law school with her, and she says it's no big deal to get it on the docket, so maybe within a few days... what do you think? You and Ginny want some company? "

"Sounds great—would the girls want to come? Are they out of school yet?"

"Yes, they are, and they just lost their playoff game—played their hearts out—so they may be up for a road trip. They haven't seen their grandparents and you guys since Christmas, so maybe. But, you never know with teenagers. I'll get back to you as soon as I know for sure. And, Sean, you sound great, I'm real happy—hugs to Ginny!"

Rory was happy for some good news, finally, to end an otherwise stressful day. She already knew Marc would be pissed off about her trip to Baltimore, but what was new? That act was getting old. He'd be especially put out if the girls went, but it was entirely up to them—she wouldn't pressure them one way or another.

She pulled into the drive just as the girls were getting home—they still seemed pumped from the game. Marc's car was in the garage, but there were no lights on in the house.

Rory and her girls headed into the house and went straight to the breakfast nook .

"You girls need anything, or you just want to talk?" Rory asked.

"I'd like some water," Kate said. "We've been talking and yelling—I'm dry."

"Yeah, me too," Alex put in.

Rory joined them at the table with water for all. "I just can't get over how   well you all played today—you gave it everything!"

"That we did," Alex agreed. "By the way, word has it that you're the one who started the cheer after we lost—that was, like, so cool! It changed everything for us!"

Rory didn't say anything, prompting Kate to urge—"It was you, wasn't it? That's just like something you would do."

" Yes, I led the cheer—I didn't even really think about it— it just seemed the right thing to do. Your team had no reason to slink away in shame."

"Anyway, we're tired of talking about the game—what have *you* been up to? And how come you're just getting home, and where's dad?"

"Whoa, what's this, the Inquisition? I doubt if I could get away with asking you two that many questions at once! But, I'll try to answer them, nonetheless. I met with a colleague after your dad and I had dinner in Phoenixville. I've been working, as you know, on a difficult murder case, and it's been smothering me. I'm planning to go to Baltimore to handle a legal matter for Sean, which should free him up to go after a teaching degree. And actually, since you two are out of school and finished with softball, you may want to come with me; Sean suggested it. We'd be gone for only a few days, and you'll get to see your aunt and uncle and your grand-parents. Entirely up to you."

Kate wanted to know, "Will we get to see you in court?"

"Sure, why not?" Rory answered.

The girls looked at each other and shrugged. "Why not, then?" Alex said.

Kate said, "You didn't say where Dad was."

"Well, his car's here, and I don't hear him moving about, so I assume he's in bed—it is, after all 11:00pm on a weekday."

"He won't be happy being here alone," Kate remarked.

"Well, he'll get to have you girls all to himself on vacation." Rory announced, immediately regretting it, as they looked at each other, crestfallen.

But, she'd worry about that tomorrow.

Chapter 16

Rory sat in the breakfast nook with her coffee, Peaches on her lap, waiting for Marc to come down for breakfast. He'd either been asleep or feigned it when she'd come to bed last night and had appeared to have been sleeping as she got ready for work. She wondered how long he'd play this out—she'd just as soon get it over with and get to work.

Just as she was finishing her coffee and ready to leave for work, he appeared.

"Good Morning, Marc—looks like you had a nice long sleep. Can you spare a moment to talk?" Rory inquired.

He looked at the clock, as if in a hurry, then said, "Sure, a minute or so."

"OK, I'll be as succinct as possible. I'm really sorry about the vacation, but it can't be helped. And while I know you're upset about that, I might as well tell you I have to go to Baltimore for a few days to handle a legal matter for Sean. If it turns out as expected, it will be a game-changer for him..."

"Just like Korbin's bail hearing? I think I've heard enough!" He spun on his heel, as if to leave.

"No, I don't think you have—the girls have opted to go with me. It will be for only a few days. It was their choice..."

"Yeah, sure!" He slammed the door as he left, reacting like the two-year old she'd come to expect lately.

This is becoming ridiculous, Rory thought; what was the point of discussing anything? Don was right— it was time to get out of town.

The slamming door had apparently awakened Alex, who stumbled sleepily into the kitchen. "Damn—that woke me up! The whole house shook. What gives?"

"Your dad closed the door a tad hard…" Rory was in a tough place here.

"Yes, and why?—look, I'm not a kid, Mom, I know you two aren't getting along." The normally unflappable Alex looked angry.

"All right, he's not happy that I'm going to Baltimore, and even less happy that you girls are going—I guess he thinks I coerced you. It really is your choice—I hope I made that clear. This isn't about choosing parents or taking sides. I know this is tough on you, but we'll get through it. We've had rough times before, but you were probably too young to know."

"Don't bet on that!" Alex said with feeling. "Kate and I always know, and it sucks!"

"Yeah, it does; for us, too ! Sorry, we're not perfect."

"Who is?" Alex asked, rhetorically. "I'm goin' back to bed."

"OK—see you after work—Bye."

That went well, Rory thought to herself. Now half the family was at odds with her. She felt self-pity creep in and she hated that, nor, did she have time for it.

Rory was a little late to work. She felt undone and exhausted, following the emotionally charged exchanges with both Marc and Alex. Still, she pondered what was with him, and it was somewhat alarming that she'd come to expect an outburst, at any time, even if it was an ordinary discussion. She began to wonder if this was men's equivalent of menopause, or if there was some other stress working on him. In any event, she was too engrossed in her work right now to delve into whatever it was.

Blake was on the phone when she arrived at work so she went straight through to her office. He came in a few minutes later with her coffee, shaking his head. "I was just trying to reach Helen again. I either get voice mail or, just now, I got Jeremy. He cut me off quickly, saying she's out sick and he's been swamped; I just don't get it."

"Well, maybe she is sick, and that's the reason we haven't been able to reach her and why she wasn't herself when I saw her. But, try again in a few days, please. Right now, I feel as if I need to get away from it all—I'm just too close to the case; it seems I'm drowning and I'm probably missing things. So, I'm going to Baltimore for a few days to clear up some legal matters for my brother. Getting away may give me a better perspective."

"That's probably a good idea, boss," Blake agreed. "You have been pretty stressed out lately. Sam and Sarah can continue to do their research in the archives—we'll call you if anything comes up."

"I'll go over to the archives later and tell them. And after lunch, I'll go out to the prison and talk with Korbin to see if he can come up with anything. I'll let him know I'll be away for a few days and to contact you if he needs anything."

Rory went straight to her overdue paper work. She called Como and thanked him for his call. He apologized again, to her surprise, and seemed a bit piqued that the president judge had taken over the hearing. He wondered aloud why he would do that. Rory said only, "He's not fond of me—I avoid going before him."

Next, she called the DA in Baltimore and set up the hearing for two days later. Then she called Sean and gave him the information, asking him to relay it to Josh. She and the girls would probably leave after dinner, arriving in the early evening.

She called Marc, although she was sure he wouldn't pick up when he saw her number. He didn't, so she left him a message that she and the girls would be leaving for Baltimore after dinner; she'd plan dinner for about six.

After a quick lunch at her desk, she left for the prison. As usual, she suffered panic, but told herself it was important to see Jeff before she left.

The unwelcoming presence of the prison rose up before Rory was quite ready deal with it. But, she had to. She thought about what she would say to Korbin, hoping to reassure him that she, and her interns, in her absence, were still engaged in his case. It also occurred to her that she'd never asked him the important question that Marc had suggested— why he'd hit Kathie.

Finding herself in the interview cell, awaiting Korbin's arrival, Rory was still wrestling with a way to approach the question diplomatically; she decided there was none.

Korbin arrived and took his seat. He was escorted by Gus, who smiled and nodded to Rory in greeting. The failed bail hearing had obviously taken its toll on Korbin and she felt a pang of compassion for the man.

"I'm sorry about the hearing, Jeff," she said, deliberately using his first name to be less formal. "I thought you'd be freed. In fact, the DA was surprised as well; I know that doesn't help as you sit in here day after day."

"Look, Ms. Chandler, I tried not to let myself hope and you never promised that I'd be out. It's just that, well, I guess I was hoping more than I realized. Thanks for coming today—I know you must be busy."

"Actually, it's your case I've been focusing most of my efforts on lately. But I came to tell you that I have to go out of state for a few days, my interns will keep working on their research, and you can call my office if you think of anything or have any questions."

"Thanks, Ms. Chandler, I appreciate you letting me know."

"I, uh, I've…" Rory began uncomfortably, "…never asked you this, and I think it's important. Why did you hit Kathie? And was it the first and only time?" Her words came out in a rush.

Korbin put his head in his hands, then pushed his hand through his hair and looked up, tears in his eyes. "You know, sometimes, there's a moment in life that you wish you could take back, that changes everything, forever. That was the moment." He sat silently for a few seconds. Then he took a deep breath and began, "Kathie was a beautiful woman, in every way—she was smart, sweet, fun and loving. I guess I would have to say she was flirty, too. I don't think she meant anything by it but it drove me crazy. I was insecure in our marriage, thinking that she might leave me, feeling that I didn't deserve her. One night, she came home after working late— she'd been working late all week—and I was getting suspicious that she was seeing someone. When I asked her, she dismissed it, saying, 'Don't be ridiculous!' For some reason, that really angered me; she showed no regard for my feelings—like they didn't matter—and I smacked her in the face. It was harder than I'd intended, and she fell and hit her head. I could see it was starting to swell. I felt awful and tried to help her. She just screamed at me 'Get out—Get out!' So, I left and went to my sister's, hoping we could talk the next day. Well… that never happened, at least for a while, until we started counseling." He sat still, looking drained.

Rory didn't know what to say. But she began thinking. "It would be helpful if we spoke with your sister; could you give me her phone number? Also, can you think of anyone, anyone at all who would wish to do Kathie harm?"

"I don't know, I just don't know. To be truthful, I don't even care if I am found guilty, because I blame myself—I started this whole thing by losing my temper and hitting her. If I'd been with her, this never would've happened."

"Jeff, look at me, and please listen. I know it must be incredibly tough to keep up your morale in this place. But, when we go to trial, if the jury sees a man who believes himself guilty, they'll be more than willing to convict. This isn't about winning a case for me; it's about not allowing the system to imprison an innocent man." She deliberately didn't mention the looming possibility of a death sentence. "Please try not to lose hope. And keep your mind occupied by thinking; thinking of anyone you believe might've been capable of murdering Kathie."

To her surprise and relief, her little speech had hit home—Korbin was looking much better, more purposeful. After giving her his sister's information, he thanked her again for coming and they said goodbye.

It was a longer visit than Rory had anticipated; she hoped that Sam and Sarah would still be working in the archives when she got to the courthouse.

When she arrived at the courthouse, it was after 4:00 p.m., but she hoped her interns would still be there. She hurried through the lobby and down the stairs to the archives. *Not a beehive of activity*, she noted to herself, with a pinch of anxiety. This was another of her less favorite places—dark, dusty, and windowless. She went to the area where she knew Sam and Sarah been working and found nothing and no one. Resigning herself to the fact that the interns had probably left, she was about to do the same when she heard the door close; heavy footsteps approached. Fear prickled up her spine, as she ducked out of sight. Soon the footsteps stopped near the area she'd just left. She heard heavy breathing and muttering. "Stupid kids... what're they looking for? None of their fucking business! Need to stop snooping... all of them!" He shuffled around a bit longer before stomping off and slamming the door behind him.

Rory remained immobile for a few seconds before exhaling. She thought, *Oh my God! Judge Keller, stalking my interns!* This was intolerable—it had to stop.

Recovering slowly, Rory stayed hidden, marveling to herself that she hadn't collapsed. When she thought it was safe, she ran for the door and scurried up the steps. *Thank God*, she saw no sign of the judge in the lobby.

Squaring her shoulders, she marched to the bank of public phones. She dialed Don's private cell number, and he answered quickly. Rory spoke urgently, "Details later—time to pull the plug!"

Chapter 17

Hurrying across the street, Rory reached her office in moments. She'd never been happier to see Blake and her interns sitting in the anteroom to her office.

They looked up in surprise; Sarah jumped up and ran to Rory's side. "What's wrong, Rory? It looks like you've seen a ghost!"

"I wish!" Rory replied, her voice shaking. Then she went on, "That Goddamn Judge Keller was in the archives, when I came looking for you—he was right where you'd been working—don't know how he knew. But he was there, muttering to himself about you being snoops. He just won't quit—he's got to have something to hide! Why else would he go to such great lengths to try to stop us?" she shivered involuntarily.

Sam and Sarah exchanged glances. Sam spoke, "Well, we found a few cases of his that were overturned by the State Supreme Court, quite an embarrassment to him; he may not want to repeat that experience again."

"They were PFA cases, right?" Rory asked. Sam nodded. "Then, why does he continue hearing these cases and making poor judgments? It doesn't make sense!"

"It does if you look at the scope of his political influence at this point in time," Blake commented. "You may not know, but he was a heavy backer, financially and politically in the last Pennsylvania Supreme Court selection. It was all under cover, but I follow these things. He's fixed himself quite well, and may feel that he's invincible."

"Well, if he's so secure, why does he bother with us—why do we threaten him?" Rory inquired.

"It's simple, Psychology 101—inferiority complex! Why do you think he set out to be king of the hill, President Judge, in the first place? It's an attempt to cover up his inadequacies!" Sarah beamed at her explanation.

The other three stared at her. Rory was first to recover, "Makes sense to me—I think that could be it. He's got to protect his position, no matter what. But, the real question is, does that include murder?"

"That, unfortunately, we don't know yet," Sam concluded.

"No, but listen, I came back to tell you that I'll be out of town for a few days, clearing up a legal matter for my brother. I don't want you going back to the archives, now that he knows where to find you. I met with Korbin today and got some more info. He told me why he'd hit Kathie and how she'd thrown him out. Anyway, he'd gone to his sister's. He gave me her phone number and permission to interview her. I think she may be another lead. So, while I'm gone, that's the direction I'd like you to go in. I'll be tough to reach, but call Blake if you have any questions. Sound good?"

"Yeah, that sounds good," Sam replied, and Sarah nodded.

"The archives were getting to me—a little creepy," Sarah concluded.

"I know what you mean," Rory concurred. "You two have probably gone as far as you can in that arena, but it was helpful. And I thank you for doing something I'm not sure I could've done."

"So," Blake said, puffing himself up, "did I hear you say that I'm in charge while you're gone?"

"But of course," said Rory, "everyone knows you're the go to guy!"

"Well thanks for confirming it," Blake said, lowering his eyes in mock humility.

"OK guys, I have to run—looks like takeout for this family again," Rory muttered ruefully as she looked at the clock.

Calling home as she walked to her car, she got Kate, "Hi Katie, sorry, I'm running late—what would you guys like me to get for dinner?"

"Oh, I dunno—let me ask Alex..." Rory heard her shouting for Alex. "Can't find her; she's been holed up in her room all day, in a mood. Just get whatever... we'll deal with it. OK, gotta run, getting a text."

"That was a big help!" Rory grumbled to herself. *Looks like pizza for them and a salad for m*e. She called in the order and got in her car.

When she arrived home with the food, the house looked abandoned, although it was obvious by the disarray that the girls were here, somewhere.

Putting the food on the table, she sat in the nook, with her head in her hands. The aroma must've wafted upstairs as both Kate and Alex appeared.

"Hi, Mom," Alex still seemed a bit miffed. "Pizza, again?"

"Well, you didn't answer, when mom called to ask, so I just told her to get whatever." Kate returned the fire.

"I'm getting a shower; go ahead and eat if you want. By the way, are you packed?" she asked.

Alex rolled her eyes in response, and Kate answered, "No, it'll only take a few minutes. I mean, who cares what we wear in Baltimore?"

"You know, you don't have to go if it's too much trouble." Rory was getting annoyed. She was wondering if it had been a mistake to ask them. She left the room abruptly and headed for the shower.

Feeling marginally better after a shower, Rory started packing. She cared what she wore in Baltimore; she had to appear in Court.

A few minutes later, Alex came into her room. "Mom, is it possible to do a load of wash before we leave?"

"Alex, you were home all day; you couldn't have a done a load then?" Rory was not in the mood for this.

"Ok, whatever... I'll just pack some crappy old dirty stuff..." Alex flounced out of the room.

"Teenagers!" Rory muttered to herself, momentarily regretting her offer to take them.

Almost finished with her packing, Rory went down to the kitchen. Marc had apparently just arrived home. He was examining what was left of the pizza, which was on the table, the box open. Partially eaten crusts were inside with the two remaining pieces.

"That looks really appetizing," Marc said with a look of disgust.

"Sorry," Rory replied. "The girls were hungry so they ate."

"Well, I was hungry, but..." Marc grimaced.

"There are some frozen dinners if you want to nuke one. Sorry, but I didn't get home in time to make dinner."

"Nothing unusual about that." Marc scowled.

"OK, you know what? Just take my salad; I'm not feeling very hungry now, and I've got packing to do." Her words were dripping with sarcasm and she felt like a stick of dynamite with a short fuse.

Venting her anger, Rory threw things into her suitcase, blinded by tears of rage, hurt, and defeat. She'd no idea what she'd packed, and didn't care. She left her suitcase on the bed, hoping to finish when she was calmer.

She went down to the kitchen because she was really hungry and wanted that salad.

Marc had nuked the pizza and was eating it. Her salad sat unopened on the table. Sitting down across from Marc, she took her time opening the salad. There was a gulf of silence between them. The nightly news was blaring on the TV, and Marc appeared to be totally engrossed in it. *No need to talk*, Rory thought.

She ate her salad in silence. When she'd finished, she spoke. "I'd like to talk with you. We don't usually part on an angry note, and I don't want to now. The girls are upset with the anger between us these past several weeks. I've felt they've been directing their anger towards me, and I'm feeling very isolated. I don't imagine you're happy about it either. What I'm attempting to do, with both Korbin's trial and the expungement hearing for Sean, is out of my own personal conviction that both of them are innocent and deserve a fair shot. This is in no way against you or the family—you seem to taking it personally."

"Hmm... I didn't know you were doing an expungement hearing for Sean—based on what?" He seemed confused.

"Yeah, well, we didn't discuss it. It's based on his former friend, Josh, recanting his testimony that he hadn't given Sean permission to stay at his neighbor's house on the night in question. In fact, Josh is willing to admit he was lying to stay out of trouble. I'd assumed that all along, but he's now man enough to own up to it."

"He's not afraid of perjury charges?"

"No, he's not, and that shouldn't happen—apparently it's beyond the statute of limitations, and besides, they were both eighteen when it happened over twenty years ago. I don't think the judge will have a problem with it, at least I hope not. I've spoken with the DA, who was a classmate of mine at Penn, and she seems to think it will go well. Anyway, with this burden gone, Sean can go on to get a teaching degree—his felony conviction prevented that—and hopefully he can get on with his life. He should have freedom of choice once the roadblocks are removed."

"That's pretty lofty, Rory, I hope it works out for both of you."

"And it can help us as well—I'll have less reason for concern about Sean, at least I'll feel as if I've done all I can."

"Well, that's good, then. Thanks for telling me."

"So," Rory continued, "can we leave as friends?"

Marc looked directly into Rory's eyes, "Rory, I…"

Just then the girls burst into the room with their bags, stopping short when they realized their parents seemed to be in the middle of something. Kate broke the silence, "We're just gonna put our stuff in the car, Mom. Ready when you are."

Rory looked back at Marc and realized the moment was lost.

Marc said—"I'll clean up the kitchen. Why don't you go and get your things?"

"Okay, then…" she said as she went up the stairs to gather her luggage.

When she came down, the kitchen was cleaned up and Marc wasn't there. She went through to the garage, and found him saying goodbye to the girls. She slid her luggage into the back of the Prius. Then she walked around the car to say goodbye to Marc.

Unexpectedly, he caught her up in a ferocious hug and gave her a real kiss—it took her breath away. When they parted, he had tears in his eyes. "I'll miss you, Rory" he said quietly. But it was the look on his face that would stay with her.

There was a mixture of regret and guilt etched into his face.

Chapter 18

Rory was once again driving on autopilot as the miles slipped away. The girls were both attached to their iPods, so the car was relatively quiet; traffic was sparse.

She couldn't get Marc's face out of her mind. Rory knew him so well, but lately she hadn't been able to read him; she just couldn't figure out what was driving his anger and why they were still unable to communicate. They'd never been at an impasse this serious or for this duration in the course of their entire relationship. The look he'd given her seemed based in guilt, and that was what she just couldn't fathom. Was he feeling guilty because he'd been overreacting to her absence from home, and if that was the case, why couldn't he talk to her about it?

He'd seemed on the verge of divulging something when the girls had come into the kitchen. But then, he'd quickly retreated, his face an unreadable mask.

They'd met as undergrads at Penn State. She was a mere freshman and he a sophomore when they'd taken the same Psychology class. He was taking an introductory course because he'd just decided to major in the subject. There was a group project, and she'd somehow managed to maneuver herself into his group. She'd had her eye on him from the beginning. It turned out that not only was he gorgeous, he was also smart, funny and kind. They'd bonded easily and it soon became their project, the other three students fading into the background. They were compatible in so many ways—it was inevitable they'd become a matched pair.

Throughout their undergrad years they were mostly inseparable, sometimes breaking up for a few days or more, but always realizing how empty their lives were without the other. As Rory thought back, she remembered a particularly long breakup, and when they'd reunited, he'd confessed to having had a sexual encounter. He claimed it'd meant nothing. Still, Rory was hurt deeply, even though they'd broken up.

A light went on in her head as she recalled the look on his face when he'd told her. It was very close to the look she'd just seen on his face when she was leaving. It shook her to her core. Had she been so busy with her work that she hadn't noticed Marc slipping away? Was he involved with someone else? But, if that were the case, why would he object so strenuously to her absence from home? She couldn't answer the question. It was so much easier to remember their carefree early love affair. She drifted back to her memories.

When Marc graduated, he'd stayed in State College, taking a menial job in the Psychology department so they could be together. She'd left her sorority suite, taken a part-time job, and they'd moved into a small apartment. In hindsight, she thought, with tears in her eyes, those may have been the happiest times. They'd had virtually nothing in the way of material goods, but they'd had each other, and that was really all that mattered. *How could they get back to that place*, she wondered—or was it even possible?

So deep in thought was Rory, that she would've missed her exit, had not Kate spoken up. "Hey, Mom, our exit's coming up, right?"

"Oh my God—thanks Kate, I would've missed it!" Rory was feeling guilty for having become so engrossed in the past. She'd have to shelve her doubts and fears for the time being. She'd need all of her faculties to finesse this expungement for Sean. She knew it wasn't a slam dunk, nothing ever was, she'd found. But she'd need to be firmly rooted in the present to pull it off.

Concentrating on her driving as she negotiated the winding roads to Sean and Ginny's house, she checked in with the girls. "We're almost there—it went pretty quickly, huh?"

Alex removed her ear buds, and seemed surprised. "Jeez, seems like we just left—were you speeding, Mom?"

Kate, in the front seat, answered. "A few times, maybe, but I was keeping an eye on the speedometer. Mom seemed to be sort of spaced out. No offense, Mom, your driving was fine."

"None taken, Katie. I was lost in thought; I've had a lot on my mind." She answered truthfully, if not completely. "But I'm glad you were looking out for us."

They soon arrived at her brother's house, a small, cozy looking cottage nestled in a grove of pines. The long driveway made it virtually invisible from the road.

As the trio got out of the car and began removing the luggage, Ginny, followed closely by Sean, emerged from the house to greet them with bear hugs. They'd obviously been awaiting their arrival with great anticipation.

When the hugs and welcomes were finished, Sean took everyone's luggage and led the way into the house. Rory was pleasantly surprised to see Sean looking healthier than when she'd last seen him. His color had been restored, and he seemed happier than he'd been in a long while. A whisper of anxiety crept into her thoughts, realizing Sean was pinning his hope for a better future on this hearing. Though she was confident they would win, Rory felt a huge responsibility to see the expungement would, in fact, come to fruition. She vowed to keep her misgivings to herself and tried to exude confidence.

Sean and Ginny were showing the girls to their room and pointing out renovations they'd done since the girls' last visit. Rory noted that Sean had made the same kind of magic in his own home that he'd done in hers. It was a small, but welcoming house with many of the special touches that were his hallmark. She particularly liked the wide bay windows with cushioned seating. She also admired the area around the fireplace, hand set with stones indigenous to the area. Some were smooth river stones, others contained granite. She was taking in these special touches when Sean came up quietly beside her.

He hugged her again, saying in her ear, "I love you so much, Sis, and thanks for believing in me."

Rory began tearing up. The emotion of the past several weeks caught up with her. When she'd regained her composure, she said, "Sean, I'm just trying to get you what you deserve— what you've always deserved—a second chance. I expect the expungement will go through, but I have to caution you, as I would any client, you never know how a hearing will turn out. Just before I left, I had a bail hearing for a man I believe innocent of murder. I was sure he would be granted bail, and then this prick of a judge, not the one scheduled to hear the case, refused to allow it. I had, of course, cautioned my client, but he'd hoped for freedom and then been devastated all over again."

Sean took Rory by the shoulders and looked into her eyes as he spoke. "Rory, I'm not the same man who tried to commit suicide weeks ago. That was a desperate act that in fact scared the shit out of me and has taught me a new perspective. I had to face that it was selfish and that I'm in charge of my life, whatever obstacles might deter me. I do have a new lease on life; I refuse to wallow in what could have been. I focus on what I can do now and have faith in the future. If the expungement goes through, I will treat it as the most loving gift from a wonderful sister, and if not, I still have you to thank for helping me through some awful times. So, please, don't worry about me—one way or another, I will pull through."

Relief flooded Rory's face. She was momentarily at a loss for words, so she just hugged him again.

Ginny came into the room, and Sean opened his arms to include her in the circle. "And this is the other woman in my life who has stood behind me no matter what, living up to our marriage vows, proving they were more than words." He looked lovingly at Ginny.

Sensing more tears on the way, Rory asked, "Mind if I trouble you for a glass of wine?"

Ginny said, "We got some just for you—let's go into the kitchen."

Feeling momentarily guilty, since Sean couldn't drink, and Ginny chose not to, Rory said, "I'm sorry, you didn't have to go to the trouble."

"It's not a problem, Ror, it really doesn't bother me to be around alcohol. That's something else I've had to face up to, and I've started going out socially when I know there will be drinking. Actually, it can be amusing to see people make asses of themselves, as I used to. Not that everyone drinks to excess," he was quick to add.

As they entered the kitchen, Rory headed for the breakfast nook, much like hers, in front of a window he'd enlarged. "You know, it's my favorite place in our house, and one where most of the family drama is played out, and yours is almost identical"

Ginny looked up at Sean and agreed, "It's my favorite place, too. But Sean has made so many improvements to this little house that it's tough to choose."

"You have a real gift, Sean," Rory agreed. "Seriously, almost every day I admire something you built in my house."

Sean nodded, "It's a gift of love to people I love. And when I'm working with my hands, my mind clears. It's one of the ways I've learned to heal myself. No matter what else I'm doing, I'll always be a carpenter. Who knows, I may open a small business someday."

Just then, the girls came into the room. "Aunt Ginny, we had dinner before we left, but we're hungry again—do you have any leftovers?" Kate inquired.

Ginny laughed and answered, "I'm so glad you feel free to ask for what you want, and of course, I anticipated we'd have some hungry teens around, so….Come with me to the fridge, and I'll show you your choices." She turned to Rory, "Are you hungry, too?"

"Well, maybe some cheese and crackers with the wine?"

"Coming right up, why don't we sit in the nook?"

They sat for nearly an hour, chatting, laughing and generally bonding. It was a wonderful, relaxing time for Rory. Even as she enjoyed the camaraderie, she missed Marc and wistfully hoped that soon he would bond with her brother. He'd never been close to Sean, probably because he felt Rory was too close. The Sean Rory had seen this night was a new man, who seemed to have finally come into his own. And regardless of what happened tomorrow, Sean had taken the burden off of Rory's shoulders.

Chapter 19

After Rory left the office, headed for Baltimore, Sam suggested to Sarah that they go out to dinner and toss around ideas for their interview with Korbin's sister. To his delight, she agreed.

Giving her the choice of a restaurant, she thought a bit and then said, "Let's try LA NA, it's a Thai/French place and I've heard it's good."

Momentarily regretful that he'd given her a choice—he had no idea what Thai food might be like—Sam decided to try something new. "Sounds like a plan," he said.

They walked the short distance from the office, and, since it was early, there were few diners.

After being seated, Sam looked at the menu; he had no idea what to order, so asked Sarah. "What do you think looks good? I don't know much about Thai food."

"I always get Pad-Thai, but if you want something spicier, you might want the Chicken Vindaloo. Do you like spicy?" Sarah inquired.

"Yeah, I do, I think I'll try that."

After their orders had been taken, Sarah said, "Well, what do you think about our interview?"

"I'm glad Rory gave us a chance to do this, but I'm a little anxious about doing it right. What are your thoughts?"

"Well, I think we have to be sensitive to how she must be feeling. Hopefully she won't be hostile towards us, you know, digging around."

"Right," Sam answered. "I think we need to proceed cautiously, but we also need information from her. We need to ask how Korbin was acting when he came to her place."

"And," Sarah added, "we need to know what Jeff and Kathie's relationship was like before he hit her; did he routinely abuse her?"

"Jeez," Sam said, "this could be really tough if we don't handle it right."

"It could be," Sarah agreed, "but I think we're up to it. I think between the two if us, we'll figure it out. We're a good team." She smiled.

For some reason, Sam felt himself blush; he hoped he wasn't reading too much into her comment.

The ringing of the other diner's cell phone got louder and louder, Sam turned to say something and instead rolled over to a face full of sunlight streaming into his bedroom. *Oh shit*, he thought, realizing he must've turned off his alarm and gone back to sleep. Smiling despite his tardiness, he remembered the evening he'd spent with Sarah. He decided to give her a call.

Sarah answered after 4 rings, just as Sam was beginning to get nervous. She sounded sleepy. "Oh, Hi Sam—sorry, I'm just getting up. I hope I don't make us late, I know we agreed…"

"That's fine, Sarah," Sam interrupted, "I was calling to say I was running late. I'll call Ms. Willis and try to arrange a later time; how much time do you need?"

"Oh, a half hour ought to do it; of course I may be a bit disheveled, so don't be frightened," she joked.

"You always look great—no worries!" Sam embarrassed himself with his forthright response; the usual filters weren't working. Then he thought, *Fuck it*—I'm not going to start worrying about saying what I mean.

Sarah's response confirmed his resolve. She sounded flustered as she replied, "Why thank you Sam, that's very sweet." And then joking again, she said, "To hell with makeup—see you in a half-hour."

"See you then—I'll call Ms. Willis. Bye"

Sam was feeling elated over their conversation, although he tried not to exaggerate its significance. If this relationship was going anywhere, then it would; he would just relax and enjoy the ride, a radical departure for him.

Calling Korbin's sister, he arranged to move the appointment to a later time, allowing them, it occurred to him, time to have breakfast. Smiling, he thought *gee, it's nice to be spontaneous.* This was new territory for him.

Pulling up to Sarah's a few minutes late, also atypical, he was pleased to see her waiting with her bulging briefcase. She got right in the car, smiling at him.

"We accomplished a lot last night," Sam said. "But I thought we could maybe tune it up a bit over breakfast—ok with you?"

"Great—I'm starving! We have time, then?"

"Yeah, we actually have 'til 10:30—that was a good time for Ms. Willis Seems as though she was running late today, too. Coincidence, huh?"

"Coincidence or no, I'll take it!"

"I agree—I don't do well without breakfast. I run out of steam by mid-morning. Then, I compound the mistake by having coffee and I get revved and cranky!'

"Can't say I've seen you cranky... well except for that one time." Sarah chuckled.

Sam had to laugh, too. "Oh, you mean my 'fuck it, we're lost' meltdown?"

"That would be the one," Sarah confirmed. "So, was it lack of breakfast that day?"

"I don't really remember, but I know I hate being lost. When I was a kid, my mom, who had no sense of direction, got us lost all the time, and for some reason she thought it was my job to get us found. So, learning to read maps became a necessity for me."

"By the way," Sarah asked innocently, "do you know how to get to Ms. Willis's house?"

"Yeah, I googled it, but right now I'm looking for... there it is, the Court Diner. I've had breakfast there; it's pretty good. And, despite its name, there aren't a lot of lawyer types here."

The diner was fairly quiet at this hour, so they found a seat in a back corner. After ordering breakfast, Sarah dug into her briefcase and got out last night's notes.

She looked over at Sam and inquired, "Do you carry a briefcase, ever? What do you do with your case notes?"

"I, um...well, I seem to have a photographic memory. I usually remember important details, sometimes even unimportant ones. If it's crucial, I'll write it down. But see, I don't have a great filing system, and notes are easy to lose. I do appreciate that you take notes, and I hope you know that I don't expect you to be my secretary, or anything..." Sam added hastily.

"Oh, no, nothing like that. It's just I seem to need the added step of writing things down to embed it in my mind; I don't really trust my memory." Sarah laughed. "I take so many notes in class that I might just as well tape the lectures. I've done that a few times, but writing it makes more of an impression."

"Yeah, I don't take notes in class. Some of my classmates are outright hostile about it; law school is so competitive, don't you think?"

"I do, but not so much at Widener; the Ivy's are probably worse. That's one of the reasons I chose Widener; my dad was lobbying hard for me to go to Yale, but the idea overwhelmed me, and I also thought he would probably have to pull strings to get me in; no way did I want that! Besides, 'George W' went there—yuck! And boy were some strings pulled to get him in, with his 'C' average and all!"

Sam laughed at that, then asked, "Does it challenge you enough? You're so smart, so intuitive…"

Sarah blushed, but answered, "I think Widener is underrated; it challenges me plenty, and I like the fact that some students are working part-time to get through. I always went to private schools, and feel I missed out on the diversity thing— you know? Sort of like a steady diet of white bread!"

"Every day a new surprise from you, another layer, as Shrek says. And here comes our breakfast!" Sam exclaimed.

Digging into their food, they ate in companionable silence for a while.

"What did you mean by that last remark, you know about another layer?" Sarah looked puzzled.

"I guess it's just that I'm getting to know you," Sam answered between mouthfuls, "and you're full of surprises."

She gave him a coy look, "Like Mata Hari? Seriously though, that goes both ways. Like, today I just learned that you have a photographic memory—you've never mentioned it— I think it's amazing. I guess I wonder what you've discovered about me."

"Since you ask," Sam plunged in without thinking, "I'll be honest. My first impression was wrong… I thought because you're so beautiful, you must be superficial. And, every day I realize just how wrong that was. And I have to say you're equally beautiful inside, and way smarter than I would've guessed. That's it, in a nutshell—I could go on, but that would probably take longer than we have."

Sarah was blushing to the roots of her hair, but she seemed pleased.

"Wow! Didn't see that coming! I… I don't know what to say. I'm flattered. And, coming from you, 'no bullshit Sam'— that's my private name for you—it means something. I've heard lots of flattery, and BS in my time. It's refreshing to hear compliments from someone as genuine as you. And it's hard for me to accept such lovely remarks graciously because I've heard too many that were phony. Thank you for that."

The waitress came over with their check, and Sarah grabbed it. "My treat—and not just because of what you said. You always drive, so I owe you one!"

That diffused what could've been embarrassing for Sam, who felt a flush rising up his face.

In the car, Sam thanked Sarah for breakfast, and consulted a map before they left the parking lot. He glanced at the dashboard clock. "It's 10:15, and we're going to Wallingford, which is, by the way, the next borough over from Rory's. It should take us under fifteen minutes, so we're cool."

Sam gave Sarah the map and told her what landmarks to look for. In less than ten minutes they were a block away from the Willis home. This was not the "millionaire/estate" part of Wallingford, it was a nice, comfortable, middle class neighborhood.

Sam pulled over and stopped. "I hate to show up ahead of time, so we can maybe just walk from here and get there on time. OK with you?"

"Splendid idea," Sarah agreed. "And thoughtful, too. I'm nervous, are you?"

"I am," Sam confessed. "But she probably is, too, so it's our job to get over it and put her at ease."

"You're right, Sam, but do you mind taking the lead? I think you'll do a better job."

"I don't agree, but I have no problem going first—then, feel free to jump in, ok?"

"Yep... here we are—it's just across the street." Sarah took a deep breath.

Jay Willis answered the door on the second knock. She resembled her brother to an astonishing degree.

Smilingly hesitantly, she watched as they showed their ID, then ushered them into a sunlit, comfortable living room and offered coffee or tea. They declined, citing their recent breakfast.

Sam added, "And you don't want to see me on another cup of coffee."

The remark, intended to put Ms. Willis at her ease, seemed to do just that.

As agreed, Sam opened the interview, telling Jay who they were and what they hoped to accomplish. He made it clear that the defense team believed in her brother's innocence and wanted to get all of the information they could for the trial.

Sam asked first about the night Korbin had hit Kathie, and had stayed with her.

"Honestly, I've never seen Jeff so upset. He's always had a temper, but I think I can say positively that he'd never hit Kathie before. They'd had their arguments, and I was close with both of them, so I was usually privy to both sides. The hitting, though, came out of the blue—I was shocked, and Jeff was more upset than I've ever seen him. And remorseful—he was so ashamed of himself. "

Sam nodded empathically. Sarah spoke up. "You said you were close to both of them. In the weeks before her death did Kathie seem particularly upset? Did she mention anyone who might want to harm her?"

Jay seemed thoughtful, then she spoke. "On the one hand, she and Jeff, who followed my suggestion for marriage counseling, seemed to be working things out. She was on the verge of having the PFA rescinded. So on that front things were looking up. But she did seem preoccupied, and maybe a little frightened. I thought maybe she was afraid to trust Jeff again, but I don't really think that was it."

"When was the last time you spoke with her?" Sam asked.

"She called me the night before she died. But I wasn't here—I'd taken my kids to a movie. I didn't check my messages until the next day…" The tears started to fall, and soon she was sobbing. Sarah went to her side and offered tissues. Through wracking sobs, she tried to talk. "I… feel so guilty, if only I'd been home. She did sound scared and asked if she could come over and spend the night… if only!" Jay put her head in her   hands as Sarah tried to comfort her.

"But Ms. Willis, she was killed the next day; it was during the day. You can't blame yourself." Sarah spoke with compassion.

"I think she might have told me who she was afraid of, if I'd been here!"

"Your brother said she'd called him, too; he feels equally guilty," Sam said. "Did you, by any chance, save the message?"

"Yes, I did—I felt that was all I had left of Kathie, even though it makes me sick when I hear it. Do you want me to play it?"

"Yes!" Sam said emphatically.

"Come to the kitchen with me," Jay led the way. She soon found the message and played it back.

"Jay, Jay, if you're there, please pick up! It's Kathie, and I'm sorta freaked out, it may be nothing. Living alone is maybe getting to me, but I swear I'm being followed, and I might know who it is, but if you get this tonight, can I come over to stay? I tried to reach Jeff, but he didn't answer. Call back! Love you- Bye."

Chapter 20

As the recorded message ended, there was silence, but for a gasp from Sarah. Predictably, a keening emanated from Jay, who, despite Sarah's best efforts to comfort her, was inconsolable. Sam lowered his eyes as if in prayer.

Sarah, for once, was clearly at a loss for words. She'd been shocked by the recorded evidence, and couldn't imagine the depth of Jay's grief. She tried to think of something to say, any distraction. She looked helplessly at Sam, whose face was grim.

As the sobbing subsided, Sam spoke quietly to Jay. "I can see how difficult it is for you to hear that message, but I'm glad you saved it. In fact, I think it might help Jeff. It seems clear that Jeff isn't the person she's afraid of."

Jay nodded and said again, "I had to save it, and even though it always ends in a melt-down, I think it's helping me get through the grieving process. Jeff doesn't have the luxury of grieving because he's fighting for his own life. I do worry about him, but he's seemed better since Rory and you two have taken on his case. Even though he didn't get bail, he's still coping better. I think you're doing a great job, and I thank you for that."

"Well, "Sarah said, "Rory's an exceptional lawyer; we were lucky to have an internship with her. She put us right on the case, first day. We all believe in his innocence. And as Sam said, the tape should really help him."

Sam nodded, then said, "I'm surprised the police haven't taken the tape for evidence; did they question you about it?"

Jay looked surprised, and said, "The police? They never questioned me."

Sam and Sarah traded looks. *Of course they didn't*; their look said.

A question occurred to Sarah, so she asked, "Did you think about offering the tape as evidence, even though they didn't come to you?"

"I thought long and hard about it, but I wasn't sure it would help his case. In fact, I called the lawyer's office where Kathie used to work, and asked his advice. He advised me not to."

"Hmm...." Sarah was thinking what to say. She looked pleadingly at Sam, who shrugged his shoulders.

"What, do you think I should've?" Jay asked, nervously.

"Honestly, Jay, I think Rory's the one to answer that. " It's a tough call." Sam concluded. "When she gets back, I think she needs to hear it."

"You said that you and Kathie were pretty close. Can you think of anyone else we should talk to, anyone close to her?" Sarah was grasping at straws.

"Kathie kept to herself a lot. Her parents are dead and her siblings live in different parts of the country; she didn't have much contact with them." Jay was pensive. Then she said, "She talked a lot about Helen; I don't know her last name, but she worked at the law office with Kathie. It seemed she was almost a surrogate mother to her. So I think it's a fair guess that she would know something."

"You know," Sam said, "Rory's been trying to reach her. She's either been sick or hasn't answered messages."

"You're right," Sarah answered. "I think she left Blake in charge of trying to reach Helen while she's away."

"Anyone else you can think of, anyone at all?" Sarah inquired.

Jay shook her head. "I can't, at the moment. But I will continue to think about anything she might've said to me that could help."

"Sometimes it's the smallest detail that ends up solving the case, so yeah, keep thinking of conversations she'd had with you close to the time of her death." Sam handed her a business card. "And call us with anything you think of, even something that seems unrelated could help."

"Thanks so much for you time," Sarah patted her arm. "You've been very helpful."

"Thank you for coming," Jay sounded grateful. "It's good to know you're on the case. And I look forward to meeting Rory."

They said their 'goodbyes' and left

Walking to the car, Sam and Sarah were silent, as if there were hidden mikes on the street.   As soon as the car door closed, they both started to talk at once.

"Nice lady…" Sarah started.

"Something's not right," Sam began.

"What do you mean, Sam? You didn't believe her?" Sarah was incredulous. "I think she was genuine!"

"Whoa, slow down, Sarah," Sam held up his hand. "Of course I believe her! But two irregularities occurred to me. First, the police never bothered to question her. And second, it's tough to believe that the lawyer, Katz, would advise her to withhold evidence from the police. Now, I haven't passed the bar yet, but common sense tells me the police should have it. I mean, it doesn't exactly exonerate him, but it corroborates his story about Kathie calling him. And the DA didn't give us any discovery regarding his cell. That's unconscionable; they may have even erased the message. I was on the verge of taking the tape, but really thought that was Rory's call."

"I agree," Sarah nodded. "I'm starting to feel we're maybe in over our heads, but I think Rory will be happy with what we've uncovered. Man, the police dropped the ball on this one. Or, perhaps it was on purpose."

"Something to remember—they're not infallible—they don't always get it right."

"I don't know, but I think you're right; we've already found evidence that they don't have. It's hard to believe that the force is overworked in this town. So, I think they've made up their mind and haven't gone any further. Lucky we're on the case, partner!"

Sarah laughed, but felt proud, too, that they'd uncovered some evidence that could be crucial. She wished Rory were here so they could discuss it at once. Impulsively, she pulled out her cell and dialed Rory's number. She didn't expect to be able to reach her, and when the beep came on she left a message: "Rory, it's Sarah, please call me as soon as you can."

"Good idea, Sarah, I was just thinking the same thing. But we could also run it by Blake when we get back."

"Not a bad idea—he's pretty smart, and he's been working with Rory for a long time and he knows how she works."

Arriving back at the office, they found it locked.

"Damn," Sarah exclaimed. "Now what?"

"I think I have a key in my car, so I'll hike back and get it."

"I'll wait here, if you don't mind, Sam, just in case Blake comes back—he's probably at lunch."

"OK, back soon." Sam took off jogging.

Ugh, thought Sarah—too hot to run today.

She was pleased that she and Sam had handled the interview with Korbin's sister well; she was fairly certain Rory would agree. She felt sorry for Jay. She was grieving for Kathie, and at the same time, unable to have any meaningful contact with her brother. The prison is hardly a place to share confidences. Sarah thought about how she would feel in the same situation and couldn't imagine it. She shivered, despite the heat.

Sam returned sooner than Sarah had expected, brandishing the key.

"Yea," Sarah enthused, "My hero! I was about to melt onto the sidewalk."

"I'm surprised Blake's not here, he usually has lunch at his desk," Sam mused as he unlocked the door.

"Ahhh, it's cool in here, wonder where he went?" Sarah looked around the office, searching for clues. She soon spotted a paper propped up on his desk. She grabbed it.

"Look Sam, this is for us. It says: 'I'm on Helen's trail— got tired of the run-around. See you tomorrow, hopefully with good news!' "

Chapter 21

Rory awoke as dawn broke, after a fitful night's sleep. Although she'd told herself repeatedly everything would be ok, and Sean had reassured her he'd be fine whatever the outcome, she was still uneasy. She'd been over the legal argument in her mind ad nauseam and found no weakness in it. She had to let it go. She rolled over and went back to sleep.

A few hours later, the aroma of coffee woke her gradually from her slumber. She looked at the clock. *Holy shit, it's 8 o'clock!* Then she relaxed and realized that she'd had more sleep, a bonus, and they didn't need to be at the courthouse until 11. And someone else was making breakfast.

Those few extra hours of sleep had done her good. She sat in bed for a moment savoring an unfamiliar sense of wellbeing.

A tap on her door startled her. "Mom—are you up?"

"I am, Alex, come in."

Alex was fully dressed and seemed surprised that her mother wasn't. "Are you OK?" she inquired. "I know I've been bitchy and I'm sorry."

"I'm fine—actually, I woke up at dawn, still tired, and went back to sleep. I just decided there was no point in worrying, although I'd fretted half the night over it. I think we'll be ok, and I've done all I can do…"

"Good for you, Mom—by the way, Dad called earlier to wish you luck, and I didn't want to wake you so just told him I'd pass on the message."

"Oh, that was nice of him, how'd he sound, Alex?"

"Oh, fine," Alex sounded insincere.

Rory wasn't fooled, but didn't feel like ruining her mood, so she let it go.

"Guess I should get up—do you know if the bathroom is free?"

"Yep, everyone else is done." Alex smiled indulgently.

"Oh my, imagine that! Well, don't wait breakfast for me. I shouldn't be too long. Josh is due here by nine or so."

"Josh is here—he's having breakfast with Sean, and everyone. But I'm waiting for you," Alex informed her.

"Why?" Rory asked.

"Oh yeah, I got the short straw, there are only four comfortable seats in the nook. Just kidding!"

"While you're here, check the clothes in the closet and see if you can put together something suitable for court I just threw stuff in. I'm off for the shower."

When Rory returned, she found an outfit she'd never have put together, assembled on the bed. Alex was sitting in the window seat thumbing through a fashion magazine.

"Hey, Alex, that works—never would've thought of it—but I like it," she hastened to add.

"Well, lawyers tend to dress so conservatively—I don't think you have to. You're not a guy, so you don't need to dress like one!"

"Hmm, never thought of that either. No, seriously, I think you're right. Men have dominated the profession for so long that when women started creeping in, well, we just dressed in dark suits like the men. I may start a whole new trend, who knows?"

"I just noticed you dress way cooler when you're not going to work. Not that you care about being cool at your age..."

"Yeah, like, why bother? Might as well pick out something for the casket, dontcha' think?" Rory turned and left the room abruptly.

Alex shrugged, put her magazine down and followed her mom.

As they arrived in the kitchen everyone appeared to be finishing up. Sean got up to hug Rory, and reintroduce her to Josh. She would never have recognized this man as the youth she'd known. He got up to shake her hand, smiled warmly and thanked her.

Ginny broke in to say, "Sit down, you guys, there's plenty of breakfast left. We have blueberry waffles, eggs any way you like, bacon, toast…"

"Whoa, I'm full just listening," Rory protested. "For me, two sunny side up and whole wheat toast, thanks. What a luxury this is!" She helped herself to coffee as Alex gave her order.

When she'd finished eating, Rory, Josh and Sean went into the den to discuss the hearing.

Rory first outlined how it would proceed. She explained Josh would have to take the stand and basically tell the Court he'd perjured himself at Sean's trial all those years ago. She would lead him through the testimony via a series of questions. Rory looked at Josh and asked if he was ready to do this.

His response startled Rory. Looking directly at her, he said, "You're giving me the chance for redemption I've wanted ever since that dreadful day in court, when I lied to save my skin. I haven't had a moment's real peace since then. I tried to find solace in drugs for a long time, and my family had disowned me. It was only when I went into recovery for good, a few years ago, that I did the 12 steps. When I got to the step of making amends, I knew I couldn't go further without making things up to Sean. But, I didn't know how to do that. I was afraid he would reject me. When I saw him at the reunion, I thought I had my chance, but I could tell he'd closed me out. Later, when he called, I felt my prayers had been answered. No matter what happens today, I'm doing the right thing. I just hope the judge does, too."

"Well," Rory replied, "you just made my job a hell of a lot easier! I can't think any judge would take issue with your sincerity. You've obviously thought it through. I'm blown away!"

Josh shook his head. "I knew when I testified, it wasn't the person I really was, but I took the coward's way out and paid for it."

Sean had tears in his eyes, as he said, "That wasn't the Josh I knew either and I won't lie, I did feel betrayed. But, then we were both so fucked up on drugs—we compromised so much. We didn't know up from down in those days. I've often wondered what I'd have done, had the situation been reversed. My parents were pretty tough on me—they threw me out all the time. But, I forgave them, and you, long ago. It just took me back when I saw you at the reunion; it brought up painful things long buried. But right now I agree with you, whatever happens, happens. I've been going to meetings, too, and I realize, to quote the wisdom of AA, that I'm the master of my life, to a point and I've learned to take one day at a time; I'll be fine either way. And Josh, it's good to have you back, man."

Rory felt like the fifth wheel as she watched the two men hug and clap each other on the back. The emotion in the room was palpable—it was a good, clean feeling.

Rory stood to leave the room. "You guys are good to go. Any judge ruling against you would have to be heartless. But, as I always say, nothing is a sure bet. We don't need to leave for another hour, so why don't you two just catch up."

She left the room smiling but there were tears in her eyes.

Rory found Ginny in the kitchen, cleaning up and went to work beside her.

"Why don't you just sit, Rory? You've already done so much for us—let me do for you for a change."

"Ginny, you did breakfast, which was marvelous, by the way. Anyhow, I get antsy before a hearing, so it's best for me to keep moving."

"Gosh," Ginny marveled, "you always seem so calm, so Zen. How do you do it?"

"You mean how do I fool everyone? It's part of being a lawyer. You have to appear confident; if not, the juries smell it. So, I just suffer on the inside. Not all the time, but often enough."

"Are you nervous about this hearing?" Ginny asked quietly.

"Yes, but only because I want so much for Sean's felony conviction to be erased. He deserves it! I think we have a really good chance, but I'm always afraid to be overly confident."

Ginny gave her a fierce hug. "You're the best, Rory! I don't know what we'd have done without you all these years."

"Oh, I don't know, Ginny, the two of you are pretty solid."

"Yes, we are, but you've always been my go-to gal when the going gets rough. So many people, including some of my best friends, just don't understand,"

"I know that. But, if you haven't been there, you can't imagine; that's what ALANON is for. The folks in the rooms understand, they've been there."

Kate and Alex strolled into the kitchen from outside. "Yuk," said Kate. "Baltimore's weather is even worse than Philly's!"

"Marginally, as I recall," Rory remarked drily. "So, why'd you go out?"

"Just checkin' out Uncle Sean's new pond; have you seen it? It's totally *Sick*!" Alex enthused.

"Sick? That's a good thing?" Rory shook her head, and raised an eyebrow.

"Mom, you're hopeless!" Alex said.

"I have seen it, but it should be calming to just gaze at the pond," Rory said.

After a trip to admire the pond, she decided it was time to round up the troops.

They arrived at the courthouse in plenty of time. Rory found the courtroom, and her DA friend, and they all waited anxiously in the anteroom until their case was called. Somehow, her friend, Lucy Thomas, had been assigned as the DA on the case. She didn't feel the need to recuse herself because she hadn't been involved in the original case, nor did she know either of the men involved.

Shortly after 11:00AM, the case was called. On the bench, Her Honor Jessica Short sat. She was a middle-aged African-American woman, with a world-weary demeanor. Rory could only guess what it'd taken for her to become a judge, given how difficult it was for women, let alone women of color, in the justice field.

The court crier called the hearing to order. The DA outlined the case, referring the judge to the case file. Josh Benson was called to the stand. He raised his right hand and took the standard oath to tell the truth.

Rory began the questioning. "Mr. Benson, I want to take you back to June 1989, 25 years ago, when you testified in a courtroom much like this one, in fact, in this same court house. Do you recall?"

"Yes, Ma'am."

"Do you recall that you testified that one Sean Morris, seated today in the body of the courtroom, entered your neighbor's home without your prior knowledge, and invitation?"

"Yes, Ma'am"

"The truth was, in fact, that you were planning to meet him there, and the two of you planned to spend the night, as you often did when you took care of their pets when the neighbors were away. You were grounded by your parents and couldn't meet Sean, is that correct?"

"That is correct."

"And you also knew that the neighbors had returned early?"

"Yes, I did." Josh looked down.

"So, in fact, Sean did assume he had permission, and you are admitting now that you committed perjury, rather than risk the consequences from your parents."

"Yes." Josh spoke with a hitch in his voice.

"As a result, Sean was found guilty of felony B&E and sentenced to six months in jail. Are you aware of this?"

"I didn't know it at the time, but I later learned it." Josh's face showed remorse.

"Mr. Benson, I understand that you are here today to ask the court to right the wrong you believe occurred as a result of your perjured testimony twenty-five years ago. Is that correct?"

"That is correct. May I address the Court?" Josh looked pleadingly at the judge.

"If the DA and defense are in agreement, I have no objection," the judge replied.

"No objection, Your Honor," was the reply of both attorneys.

Josh spoke in a clear voice, looking directly at Sean: "Sean and I were best friends in high school. We played sports together, and spent most of our time together. We made a bad choice, got into drugs in our senior year, and stopped our healthy activities. It was a downhill spiral for us. I'm not blaming drugs for what I did; there was no excuse for what I did to Sean. Addicts are selfish and I didn't want to get thrown out of my home as he'd been. But if I thought I'd taken the easy way out, I was wrong. I lived through a hell of my own creation. I was using drugs for many of those years to try and ease the pain. It didn't help. Only recovery has helped. And admitting my perjury today is the best thing I can do. I know whatever I went through, it was ten times worse for Sean. That he's even willing to forgive me and be my friend amazes me. I beg the Court to expunge Sean's record so he can make a new start in life. If the Court finds it necessary to punish me, I am ready to accept my fate. Thank you, Your Honor, for allowing me to speak." Josh lowered his head as the tears streamed down his face.

The courtroom was silent, as if respecting the metamorphosis that had taken place here.

Rory found her voice and asked the Judge. "Your Honor, I would ask The Court to expunge Sean Morris's felony record, which was, as we've heard today, based on perjured testimony."

"The State concurs," DA Thomas added.

The judge addressed Josh. "Mr. Benson, perjury is a very serious offense. It appears you have found that out in your own way over the last twenty-five years. I doubt there is any punishment I can impose that would accomplish the goal of repaying Mr. Morris. It took great courage to come before me today and admit your guilt. And I thank you for that."

The judge continued, looking in Sean's direction. "Mr. Morris, the Court owes you a huge apology; The Court is not infallible. There's no way we can give you back the time you lost; you've learned some lessons in life the hard way, no doubt. I wish you the best, with the rest of your new life, as a man with NO criminal history. Expungement granted. You are all free to go." The judge paused, "And thank you for giving me a glimpse at the best side of human nature. Court dismissed."

This time when the gavel banged, it was music to Rory's ears.

Chapter 22

Marc was miserable—Rory and the girls had been gone for two days. He'd followed his normal routine: breakfast, work, exercise, but his heart wasn't in it. He'd gone through the motions at work, and fortunately he didn't have any high profile cases.

His family was important to him, he loved Rory and ironically, the secret that was supposed to keep her by his side was actually pushing her away. How long, he wondered, could they keep going like this? He'd been on the verge of telling her when the girls had come into the room. Then, he'd lost his courage, just like he might lose Rory. He had to come clean, and the longer it took, the harder it would be. It was clear to him what he had to do—he just didn't know how. He wanted Rory back, but would the truth end the marriage? That was the problem.

The TV was on, but he wasn't watching it when the phone rang. His heart was pounding as he ran to answer it. The number was unfamiliar, but he picked it up anyway.

"Hey, Marc, it's Norm. If you're not busy, I'm wondering if you feel like meeting me for a drink?"

Marc was about to refuse the offer, but decided it beat wallowing in misery. "Sounds good, Norm, where and when?"

Having agreed upon the time and place, Marc decided to clean up and change his clothes. Showering, he reflected upon the fact he hadn't been out with a male friend for many years. Norm Brewer was probably his best friend at work, but they'd never been out together. Norm knew he was home alone, it occurred to him; that's why he'd called. Norm was recently divorced, a thought that jolted him, as he realized how lonely Norm must be. He'd never talked much about it at work, and Marc had never asked. But he was fairly certain he'd hear more about it tonight. And though he didn't relish it, he owed it to Norm. He began to feel bad he'd never offered to have him over to dinner or out for a drink after work.

It was Friday night at the Iron Hill Brewery, and the place was packed. Marc scanned the crowd, but couldn't pick out Norm. *Oh, crap*, he thought, feeling suddenly out of place, how would he find him? There were plenty of single women hanging out, apparently on the make. Some glanced at him admiringly. It made him nervous—they were obviously twenty-something's. He realized he was so not into the bar scene, and nearly left.

Just then, he spotted Norm, flagging him down from the bar. He walked over quickly to join his friend, noticing attention from nearby females. He had to admit he still liked it when women seemed interested, but at the same time, it made him feel guilty.

"Hey Norm, thanks for calling," Marc said over the din. "When Rory and the girls are away I feel sorry for myself, so I'm glad you called." He immediately regretted what must've seemed a callous remark, given Norm's situation.

Norm flinched for just a second, but Marc knew it had hit home. He tried another tack. "I haven't been very busy at work—how about you?" It sounded lame, but he didn't know what else to talk about.

"Actually, I've been pretty busy—been doing some overtime. I can use the money and it helps, you know, to stay busy."

Knowing he couldn't avoid the subject any longer, Marc asked, "So, how are *you* doing? I mean, with the breakup and all?"

"Not well, man, not at all. At least Nate is away at school; well, he's home for summer break now. He lives with Linda, but he's so busy with his friends he doesn't see much of either of us. I really miss him."

"Yeah, that must be tough. My girls are still in high school, but I feel them pulling away, too. It happens, but looks like you got hit with a double whammy. I'm really sorry."

"Thanks. Like I said, I'm not handling it well. I suggested to Linda that we go for counseling. She gave this sort of bitter laugh and said, 'So now you want to go, after all the years of begging you! Sorry, that train has left.' I didn't know what to say. But I blame myself..."

"Yeah, but you know, in any relationship, there's plenty of blame to go around." Marc countered.

"Yes, but I chose to work long hours, all at the expense of my family life, and I thought I was working for them. What I think now is I needed to feel successful. Though I hate to admit it, Linda went elsewhere for what I failed to give her."

Marc felt sucker punched; this hit too close to home and he didn't know what to say, but Norm's outpouring demanded a response. "I'm so sorry, Norm—I never knew why you'd divorced."

"Yeah, ironically, now I'm in therapy myself. Otherwise, I wouldn't be functioning at all. I know I can't change the past, but I sure as hell don't want to repeat my mistakes." Norm spoke with conviction.

"That's really smart, going into therapy. Even though we're psychologists, or maybe because, I think it's hard to own up to our shortcomings. And how many men do you see in therapy? I have to hand it to you—you're making the best of a bad situation— I'm impressed." Marc thought, *God, I'm sounding like Rory*, then squelched the thought.

"It's not easy, but it beats putting a .38 to your head." He grimaced.

You weren't..." Marc stifled a gasp.

"Oh yeah, I was. I had a gun in my hand when Nate walked into my study—he'd just gotten home from school. I don't think he saw the gun—I hid it pretty quickly—but it forced me to think of how he'd feel.

And for me, it would've been an act of anger against Linda. I knew then I needed help. Maybe someday Linda will join me in a session or two, just so we can have, you know, some closure."

"I'm really sorry," Marc said again. "I'm sorry I wasn't there for you—it must've been awful. I never knew..." His voice dropped.

"You didn't know because I tried to keep up a strong front—hid my feelings, or stuffed them, as my therapist says. I was arrogant enough to believe I could do it on my own. Hmm..., that was a huge mistake."

"Sounds like you've come a long way, man—good for you."

"Afraid no congratulations are in order yet, but..."

"You've put in a lot of effort, and it's sure to pay off." Marc finished the sentence for Norm, eager to end this discussion.

"True—I'm not out of the woods yet, but at least I've found a path."

"Good way to put it." Marc raised his beer: "Here's to better days!"

They stayed at the bar for another hour or so, staying away from emotionally charged subjects. Marc didn't feel it was the time to discuss his own concerns. And he realized he wasn't sure he'd ever be able to.

As the crowd thinned, Marc looked at his watch—it was later than he'd thought. He was feeling better, as he hoped Norm was, but he was tired.

Getting ready to leave, Marc said impulsively, "Hey, You want to go jogging tomorrow, you know, get those endorphins cranking?"

"That sounds great—call me in the morning; and thanks for meeting me."

Norm grabbed the check. "This is on me—thanks for listening."

"No problem—it was good seeing you. Call you tomorrow."

On his way to the car, Marc checked his cell—it had been too loud in the bar to hear any calls— he'd forgotten to look.

There were two messages from Rory—he cursed himself for not being available when she'd called. He played the messages.

The most recent message said, "Oh... you're still not there—I'm going to bed now—long day. Talk to you tomorrow." She'd sounded tired, Marc thought, and also disappointed.

He played the earlier message. "Hi, it's me—just wanted to talk with you about my day... we're staying through tomorrow—back Sunday." Then, a pause. "Listen, we're meeting my parents for lunch at Phillips to celebrate—why don't you join us?"

It was good to hear her voice, Marc thought. He knew it was too late to call. Even so, what would he say?

Marc had to admit to himself that while his conversation with Norm had been therapeutic, it'd also depressed the hell out of him. He was terrified he would find himself in the same boat soon. It was obvious Rory was offering an olive branch now, but could he take it?

Chapter 23

Rory was deep into a dream when her cell buzzed. She somehow incorporated it into her dream, but the incessant noise finally jolted her awake. She bolted up, looking for the source. Finding her cell, she mumbled "H'lo" without looking at the number.

"Sorry, Rory, I woke you up." Marc sounded amused.

"S'ok, wasn't asleep," she protested.

"Yeah, right—you want me to call back when you're fully awake?" Marc chuckled.

"No, no, I'm fine; I'm awake now—just got disoriented being in a different place. Hey, where were you last night?" She was awake now. "I called twice."

"Yeah, I know, I got your messages, but it was too late to call. I was at Iron Hill with Norm, a buddy from work. He called and asked me to meet him. He's gone through a tough divorce, needed someone to talk to."

"So, can you come down and join us for lunch at Phillips today?" Rory cut to the chase.

"Jeez, I asked Norm to go jogging with me, and it seemed to make him so happy—I'd hate to disappoint him. It's already ten, and we're going soon..."

"Oh well," Rory's voice registered disappointment and a trace of annoyance.. "It's just that we're celebrating Sean's victory in court..."

"You mean your victory—that's great Rory, I'm really pleased, for both of you! I'll make it up to you and Sean. When your case here is done, we'll go visit; it's time I got to know him better."

"OK, well, I'd best be getting ready since it's later than I thought. We'll be back tonight or tomorrow—I'll let you know. Bye"

Marc was left with the phone in his hand and a look close to self-loathing on his face.

Rory sprang up from bed. She was pissed! She began, in lawyer-like fashion, to poke holes in his story. Who the fuck was Norm? And why had she never heard Marc so much as mention his name before? It just did not ring true. All the doubts that had been accumulating of late rose to the surface. Then the self-doubt started to kick in. *What an ass I've been*, she thought. My husband has been stepping out on me, and I've been too busy to notice.

Rory grabbed her cell and was about to call Marc back to vent her fury. She noticed a message she hadn't seen. She listened; it was from Sarah, who'd called her yesterday. It didn't sound urgent, and Rory assumed it could wait until Monday.

Nixing the idea of calling Marc back, Rory allowed herself to wallow in the shower for a few minutes, then decided, to think about it tomorrow. She was determined not to ruin Sean's day, and she certainly didn't want her parents to be upset.

Hurrying from the bathroom, she went to her room to get dressed. She wanted to look her best for the occasion, but had no clue what to put on. She needed Alex's help. Just as she put her hand on the door knob, Alex knocked, and genie-like, appeared.

"Hey, I thought I heard you get up—you really slept in, again. You OK?" Alex asked with concern in her green eyes.

"I'm fine," Rory insisted. "Maybe I'm getting too much sleep. Anyway, I was just about to yell for you. I need your fashion assistance—please!"

"Sure, what look are you going for today?"

"Oh, I don't know, casual, but celebratory—how's that?"

"All right, let me see what you've brought." Alex proceeded to go through the closet and the drawers, pulling things out, matching them up.

"How about this?" Alex arranged the outfit on the bed: black capris, a bright blue tank top, with a sheer blue cardigan. "And your black espadrilles will put it all together—ok?"

"You're good, Alex. Have you thought about a career in fashion design?"

"You're kidding, right? You didn't raise me to do something so... superficial with my life; fashion is just a sideline."

"So, what do you think you might want to do?" Rory asked.

"I dunno, don't have a clue, really, but I don't need to decide today."

"Jeez, I wasn't pressuring you to decide today; it was just a question."

"Getting a little testy, Mom?" Alex flung back.

"God forbid I'd start acting like a teenager—that's your excuse!"

Just then, Kate entered. "Wondered where you went... what's up guys?"

"Mom's just a little touchy this morning." Alex answered quickly.

"Yeah right—whatever..." Rory felt herself getting ready to explode.

Kate and Alex gave each other a look, then Kate said, "See ya' at breakfast."

When the girls had left, Rory cried until she felt better. Then she mentally prepared herself to put on a good front and enjoy the day; she'd earned it, and so had Sean.

As Rory descended the stairs to the living room, she saw her parents had arrived and hurried to greet them with hugs; she found herself crying again.

"Rory, you look marvelous!" her mother exclaimed. "And rumor has it you have a hot new fashion consultant." She smiled indulgently at Rory and the twins.

"Indeed I do, Mom, but it's just a side line for her, nothing serious!" She winked at Alex, as if to say, *we're fine.* Then turning to her father, she said, "Sorry, Dad, you have no time for such frivolities! How are you? You both look great!" She hugged them again.

Sean came into the room with coffee for their parents. "Hey, Rory, can I get you a mug?"

"Thanks, but I'll go get some toast first—can't do coffee on an empty stomach. Have you told Mom and Dad?" she said quietly.

"Told us what?" demanded her father, who allegedly had a slight hearing loss.

Sean looked uneasily at Rory. "Go ahead," she urged. "It's your news."

They both sat down across from their parents. Sean started, "Well, Rory gave me the gift of a lifetime yesterday..." He almost broke down, then started again. "She gave me my life back—we went to court and she had my charges expunged, erased; I have no criminal record now, thanks to her!" His eyes were glistening.

There was a startled silence as their parents took it in, then all hell broke loose and everyone started talking at once. Bit by bit their parents heard the whole story.

Their father was obviously moved; they'd never seen him cry, but he did so now, unabashedly. He clapped Sean on the shoulder, but still couldn't find words.

"I just can't believe it—why it's the best news we've heard, in...well, forever." Mrs. Morris was flushed with excitement.

"I wish we could've been there to see it," their father finally said.

Rory and Sean traded glances. Sean said, "We wanted to—we talked about it—but Rory's practical. She was sure it would happen, but as she says, 'you never know what's going to happen in court.' We didn't want you to be disappointed, so we both agreed it was best to wait. We're sorry that you weren't there—it was a wonderful moment, and the judge was...well, she was almost as eloquent as Rory!"

"Josh gave a pretty nice speech, I thought; it impressed the judge," Rory said.

The conversation and camaraderie went on for the better part of an hour, until Ginny intervened and said, "I hate to break this up, but we have reservations in... fifteen minutes at Phillips, so..."

They arrived at the restaurant on the harbor a few minutes late, but their reservations had been held, although a line was forming outside.

Everyone was in high spirits on this jubilant occasion. Mr. Morris declared, "I'm paying, so order whatever you want! I couldn't be prouder of our two kids!" He and his wife shared a heartfelt smile. It had, indeed, been a very long time since they'd celebrated like this.

Later, they walked around the harbor, watching kids enjoying the paddle boats and taking in the life of the busy harbor. Rory's mother pulled her aside and suggested they sit for a bit; they found a shady spot outside of Phillips.

"Rory I'm very proud of you," she said, taking her hand. "But, something's troubling you. Can I lend an ear?"

Rory almost laughed, and then nearly cried. Her mother read her like an open book; she'd never been able to fool her, damn it! And it'd been years since she'd confided in her. She knew it was time now. She sighed.

"I should've known nothing gets by you—you're still sharp as a tack, and still working, I'll bet!"

"Just part-time, Rory, but let's not get off track…"

"Oh, Mom, I love you." She took a deep breath. "Things aren't going well between Marc and me. I'd say for the past month we've been at odds. He's not happy I took on this murder case, and now he's taking the girls on vacation without me because I can't leave right now, and shit!, it's just a big mess, Mom—now I'm thinking he may be having an affair. I called him twice last night and he didn't answer. Then he called this morning and gave me some bullshit about going out with some guy from work whom he's never so much as mentioned! And then, I asked him to come down and meet us for lunch, and he says he's going jogging with this guy." Rory ran out of words as the tears trickled down her face.

Her mother put her arm around her gently. "It just doesn't sound like the Marc we know and love."

"I know, I know, but maybe I'm just too involved in work, and too damn dumb to get the picture. I love him; what if, what if he's found someone else? You know, this mid-life shit… it could happen."

"It could, of course, but you're neither dumb, nor self-involved. And I've never known you to be obsessed with work—passionate about what you, do, yes, but you keep a good balance, I think."

"I've always believed that. But since I took on this case, and Marc hasn't been supportive of me, I seem to have lost my confidence. I think I might've been taking him for granted. I think it's my fault." Rory had finally admitted her biggest fear.

"You know, in any relationship it's never one person's fault. But, more to the point, fixing the relationship is number one. Blame, and the guilt that goes with it, are both unproductive—you can get stuck there."

"I know, Mom, but there's so much going on, and I'm just so tired, and… confused." She put her head in her hands.

"I know, dear, and I feel your pain. But you can't second guess yourself. You're involved in this case right now, and Marc and the girls are going on vacation. That should be a good time for you to take a breath, and take stock of the situation. Then, maybe you and Marc will decide you need to reconnect, maybe go to counseling." She was looking behind Rory's right shoulder as she said, with a smile, "If I were a betting woman, I'd put money on you and Marc surviving this."

Following her mother's gaze, Rory turned around just as Marc reached out to embrace her.

Chapter 24

The rest of the weekend flew by, on gossamer wings, Rory thought. It was the most fun Rory remembered ever having with all of her family. Marc and Sean had gotten reacquainted, engaging in long conversations. Marc took the time to inspect the improvements Sean had made to the house, and it seemed that after a long, dry spell, they'd bonded. It was time, Rory thought.

Rory's and Sean's parents were positively glowing. They were totally involved in what felt like a healing process. And they couldn't have been more generous. They took the twins shopping, which made them happy, and insisted on paying for all the meals.

It was a time they wished could go on forever. But work was looming on Monday. It was late when they finally were able to tear themselves away and they made promises to get together soon.

Kate offered to drive the Honda home with Alex so Rory and Marc could ride together. "I'll be careful, I promise; we'll stay behind you."

"OK Katie, I trust you," Marc said. "I know you'll drive responsibly." He handed over the keys.

Rory was happy to be driving home with Marc, and more than relieved that he was doing the driving.

They talked about what fun the last few days had been and Rory let Marc know how much it'd meant to her that he'd come.

Rory was so tired that she lapsed into sleep, mid-sentence. It was a deep, untroubled sleep, and she didn't wake up until they stopped in their driveway. She was disoriented at first, then said sleepily, "We're home. My God, it's midnight."

Marc smiled, "Well, you're already ahead on sleep; you'll be OK."

"I'm sorry I wasn't better company..."

"No problem, we'll have time to rehash the wonderful weekend. I'm really glad I went."

The girls pulled up behind them, cutting the conversation short.

"Guess we'd best get unpacked and off to bed." Rory got out of the car and went to help the girls, who'd stashed their luggage in the Prius. Marc joined her and took the lion's share.

They dumped their luggage and went straight to bed.

Rory fell asleep as soon as her head hit the pillow. But then she awoke much later with her mind abuzz. She was thinking about work, and about Marc and his mysterious friend, Norm. She got up to make herself some warm milk.

Sitting in the nook with her milk, Rory tried to stop her whirling mind. She knew she had to go back to work tomorrow, and wondered where that would lead.

Lost in reverie, she never heard Marc enter the room. "Trouble sleeping, Hon? I hate it when I wake up and you're not there." He reached across the table and took her hand. "I really missed you."

"Who's Norm?" she blurted without thinking. "And why have I never heard you mention him?"

"Jeez, is that what's keeping you up? Look, Norm is a really good guy; he's my best buddy at work."

"But, I don't understand why you never talk about him or go out with him..."

"I guess it's just a guy thing, but I feel badly now that I was never there for him when he was going through the divorce;

he's really hurting. But he's doing better, he says, since he got into therapy."

"Well, I hope you know it's fine with me if you want to spend time with your friends. Certainly I do, when work's not too taxing."

"Like it is now…" Marc commented ruefully. "I hoped you might reconsider the vacation. If I cancel, we'll lose the deposit, which is considerable."

Not this again, thought Rory. She couldn't bear dissension now, after such a perfect weekend. She wondered why Marc had this perverse need to put a damper on her spirits. What she said was, "I'll have to see if there were any big developments in my absence. I'll let you know."

She got up to leave, saying, "Goodnight, I'll try and get more sleep." In truth, she doubted it would happen.

When the alarm went off at six am she wasn't ready to get up, but was glad that she hadn't lain awake for the rest of the night as she'd feared. She could hear Marc in the shower so decided to stay in bed until he'd finished.

Marc came out of the bathroom, obviously in a rush. "Just remembered that I have an early case in Philly; thought it was later 'til I checked my calendar. Doubt if I'll have time for breakfast," he said, as he hurriedly dressed.

Rory got out of bed, and gave him a kiss. "I'll say bye now, in case you've left when I get out of the shower."

"OK, Bye—sorry I'm in such a hurry."

In the shower, Rory thought to herself that there was a bit of a chill between Marc and her—again. Damn! It was so upsetting after such a special weekend; all the warmth seemed to evaporate. She shook her head and realized that she couldn't afford self-pity—in fact, she despised it. She had a job to do, and was afraid that nothing had changed in her few days away. But she would soon find out.

Arriving at the office at her usual time, Rory was happy to see Blake and her interns in the outer office.

"What, no muffins? I guess absence didn't make the heart grow fonder this time! Just kidding," Rory broke into a smile. "I missed you guys, but was so busy, I hardly thought about the case. And, Sarah, I didn't see your message until Saturday, so figured it could wait..."

"We did miss you, Rory, and in fact couldn't go ahead until we consulted with you." Sam smiled at her.

"But first," Sarah interrupted, "tell us your news—how'd the expungement go?"

"It was beyond my wildest expectations!" Rory beamed. "I think I might move to Baltimore to practice law—it went so smoothly. The judge not only agreed to expunge, she went on to apologize to Sean for the time he'd lost in prison, and the impact on his life. She really made everyone feel good. "

"Congratulations, Rory—we were pulling for you, and betting on your success!" Blake was effusive.

Sam and Sarah chimed in with their words of praise.

"Thanks, all of you, and now let's retire to my office and discuss what went on while I was gone. You, too, Blake, after all you were in charge."

Once they'd settled, Blake started, "You might as well hear the bad news first; my goal was to find and speak with Helen. I went to the office; Helen wasn't there, and Jeremy, who seemed annoyed with me, said she'd been sick. So, I went to her house and she didn't answer the door. I peered through the garage window and saw an older model Camry there, but she may have another car..."

"No, that's the car I've seen her drive," Rory put in. "I don't think she has another. Damn! I want to talk to her."

"OK, I'm ready for the good news." Rory looked expectantly at Sam and   Sarah.

Sam nodded to Sarah, who was obviously bursting to tell Rory what they'd found out. She pulled out several pages of notes from her briefcase, and scanned them. "OK—we interviewed Jay; actually we learned a lot. Too bad the police never bothered, for whatever reason. Anyway, Jay confirmed that Jeff had stayed with her the night he'd hit Kathie, and for a while after that. She said he was beyond remorseful, very ashamed of what he'd done. But the most shocking news was that Kathie had called Jay the night before she died. Jay was out and didn't get home 'til late. She didn't even notice the message until the next day. She played it for us—it's still on her phone. You need to hear it, but the gist of it is that Kathie was afraid because she thought someone was following her. And Jay feels guilty. She sobbed when she played back the message. I really think you need to hear it, and talk to Jay in person."

"So, she never turned the tape over to the police?" Rory inquired. "This evidence could be really helpful, for Korbin, I'm thinking."

Sam and Sarah shared a look, then Sam said, "We asked— she'd thought about it and called Katz's office and was advised against it. We wondered what you'd think about that."

Rory appeared puzzled, saying "I really can't second guess his decision, but I will definitely take it up with him. I need to talk to him anyway about Helen."

"Oh," Sarah said, "I almost forgot to tell you—Jay said that Kathie may have confided in Helen. They were good friends."

That, of course, had been Rory's contention all along. She wondered again why Jeremy hadn't noticed. Was that just a guy thing too?

They spent a few more moments discussing different angles of the case. Rory decided it was time to take action. "I'm going over to Jeremy's office, and then to Jay's—by the way do you have directions to her place?"

Sam looked to Sarah, hoping she'd saved them, and sure enough, she had.

"Why don't you two go over to the Law library; there's not much to be done until I see these two. Oh, and thanks for doing a great job!"

Rory left the office and headed straight to Katz's office on foot. As she walked, she called Jay on her cell. Jay answered and seemed pleased to hear from her. She praised Rory's handling of Jeff's defense. They arranged to meet in a little over an hour.

She reached Jeremy's office within minutes; she knew he was in when she saw his red Mercedes. Having failed to call before she came over, Jeremy's face registered surprise when she entered. He was at Helen's desk and no one else appeared to be in the office.

"Sorry if I've caught you at a bad time. I've been trying to talk to Helen and no one seems to know where she is." Rory was very direct.

"Yeah, well, I told your guy that she's been sick. She might've gone to her daughter's... I don't really know." It sounded like whining to Rory. "I just know that with my partner and Helen both out sick, I've been swamped. By the way, do you have a minute? I've been wanting to talk with you, anyway."

Rory sat, then said, "Sure, I have some time—what's on your mind?"

Jeremy didn't answer at once. "This is delicate and I hope you won't think me callous, but, the truth is, I don't think Joe's getting any better; his illness may be terminal."

"Oh, I'm so sorry," Rory said sincerely.

"Yeah, thanks, me too. Anyway, this may be premature, but I was wondering if you would consider partnering with me, in the event...of Joe's demise. I'm finding that I have way more on my plate than I can handle. Just think about it, would you?"

Rory was flattered, and confused at the same time. But, of course, she'd consider the offer—should the occasion arise. "I will give it some consideration, but ideally the best outcome would be Joe's return."

"Of course." Jeremy said without conviction. "It's just that I've been overwhelmed lately. He does manage to come to the office a few times a week, but he doesn't look good, and he tires easily. Thanks for considering it; we'll talk later. And if I hear from Helen, I'll be sure to let you know. God, I hope she comes back soon!"

Rory thanked him and started to leave. She'd forgotten to ask the most important question. She turned toward him and said, Colombo-like, "Oh, by the way, I've been wondering why you advised Korbin's sister not to turn over the tape of Kathie's phone message to the police."

Jeremy looked confused, then he answered, "I, umm, really don't remember her calling. You sure she didn't talk with Joe? "

Chapter 25

Driving to Jay Willis's house, Rory mulled over her encounter with Jeremy. He was definitely having a hard time keeping things together. He had to be upset about the likely demise of his partner, and presumably close friend. Yet, it didn't seem so. Perhaps he was just overwhelmed by the workload, as he'd said.

Rory also thought about Jeremy's offer of partnership; it had taken her completely by surprise. After all, their styles were quite different. Jeremy, it seemed, ran the office like a business. He sought out and attracted primarily high income clients, didn't do pro bono work, and didn't represent reduced-fee clients. She couldn't really see herself fitting in there, considering their divergent philosophies; she certainly wasn't bringing in the big bucks.

Realizing that her mind had wandered, Rory pulled off the road to look at the map. Despite living in a nearby borough, this part of Wallingford was unfamiliar. But she soon found her way and arrived at Jay's house just about on time.

Jay answered the door as soon as Rory knocked. She was obviously related to Jeff, and though she was older, Jay appeared younger. No doubt the stress Jeff had been enduring had aged him considerably. She fervently hoped to free him soon.

"Ms.Willis, I'm Rory Chandler; thanks for seeing me."

"No, thank you for representing Jeff; I'm more thankful than you'll ever know!"

"I hope to earn your thanks by winning his freedom," Rory replied earnestly.

"Win or lose, you've restored his faith in people. And you've given him, and me, hope." Jay's face showed strong emotion. "Now please, come in and have a seat. Can I get you anything? Coffee? Tea?"

"Thanks, no, I'm fine. If you could just repeat what you told my interns, about the night Jeff hit Kathie and came to stay with you, I'd appreciate it."

Jay recounted basically the same story she'd told Sam and Sarah; there were no inconsistencies that Rory noticed. She reiterated that the police had never once interviewed her. When she talked about the taped phone message, Rory had a question.

"My interns said that you'd called Katz & Klein and asked if you should turn the tape over to the police." Rory paused, and Jay nodded. "OK, now I want you to think back to that call. Did you speak with Katz or Klein? And did you repeat what was on the tape?"

Jay became pensive; she looked confused. "You know, a man answered the phone and said, Katz and Klein. Then, I just stated my business, and asked the question. Honestly, I don't know who it was that I talked to. I just assumed it was Katz because that's who Kathie worked for. But I was really upset when I called; I just blurted out what I had to say to the person who answered the phone. I'm sorry, I just don't know. But, he seemed in a hurry, so I really didn't say what was on the tape."

Rory was disappointed, but said, "It's understandable that you'd be unsure of who exactly answered, but it's probably good that you didn't give details about the tape."

"Now, if you don't mind, I think I should hear the tape."

"Of course," Jay ushered her into the kitchen.

The message started: "Jay, Jay, if you're there, please pick up! It's Kathie and I'm sorta freaked out, it may be nothing. Living alone is maybe getting to me, but I swear I'm being followed. And I might know who it is, but if you get this tonight, can I come over to stay? I tried to reach Jeff, but he didn't answer. Call back! Love you-Bye." When the tape was over, Rory asked Jay to play it again.

Jay had remained reasonably controlled, and complied with Rory's request.

This time, Rory concentrated on every word. When it ended, she said, "Wow, that's very powerful! Her message virtually rules out Jeff as the person following her. If she'd thought it was Jeff, why would she have called him? And more to the point, why haven't the police turned over his cell phone to the DA as evidence? Let's hope they didn't erase it. That makes your message all the more crucial. Hang onto it while I check with the DA. Hmm..., she also mentioned that she might know who was following her." That struck a chord with Rory.

They spoke for a few minutes longer. Rory rose to take her leave, and said, "I'd best be getting back—I really need to talk with the DA. For now, keep the tape until you hear from me."

They said goodbye, and Jay opened the front door for Rory. Rory quickly stepped back and closed the door.

Addressing Jay's quizzical look, Rory composed herself and said, "Is there anyone you could stay with for a few days? I'm not trying to frighten you, but there's a navy BMW that's been trailing me for weeks. I just saw one go down your street, slowly. It may be nothing, but now that this person knows I spoke with you, I don't want to take any chances. Oh, and you'd best give me the tape; I'll take it to the DA for safekeeping. You stay safe! Here's my card; call me if you have the slightest worry."

Chapter 26

Rory scanned the street as she left Jay's house, clutching the briefcase with the tape tight to her body. She slid into her car and looked around again before pulling out. There was no traffic to be seen on the street, yet Rory was watchful. Even though she wasn't familiar with this neighborhood, she found a roundabout way back to the courthouse.

Parking in the lot across from the courthouse, she walked quickly to her destination. The DA's office was on the first floor so she didn't have far to go. Walking down the hall to Stan Como's office, she prayed she'd find him there. She greeted Janet, Stan's office manager, and asked, "Is he in?"

"He is, but he's due in court in about 20 minutes; I'll see if he has time to see you."

"Please tell him it's urgent."

"Go right in," Janet said after a quick exchange with Como.

"Thanks so much, Stan, I have something really important that I want you to hear."

"OK, what do you have?"

"First, some background. I just met with Korbin's sister, Jay. The night he hit Kathie and she threw him out, he went to stay with her. Anyway, that's why we visited her. FYI, the police never interviewed her. So, in the course of speaking with her it came out that Kathie had phoned her the night before she died and had left a message on her machine. That's what I have—the tape—and I want you to hear it."

Stan glanced at his watch, so Rory hastened to add, "It's short, but well worth your time."

"OK," Stan decided as he got the machine ready. "Let's hear it."

They both listened intently as Stan played it, and then replayed it.

"You realize, of course," Stan said matter-of-factly, "that it will have to be verified that this is, in fact Kathie's voice. That shouldn't be too hard. By the way, did she say why she hadn't turned this over to the police?"

"Of course I asked her, and apparently she'd called for legal advice and was advised against it."

"What?" he asked incredulously. "Who was it?"

"Katz or Klein, I can't say positively, because she wasn't sure. But, if this is genuine, as I'm sure it is, it confirms that Kathie called Jeff that same night. He told us she had, and that the police confiscated his cell phone. Yet, you never received any information about that. I'm sure you'll agree, that should've been included in their report."

"Let's not get ahead of ourselves, Rory. First we have to verify this tape. And then follow the usual procedure."

"Be my guest, but please put it in a safe place and can you sign a receipt for it? I'd like a copy of the tape as well. I came straight here from Jay's house, so I haven't even been back to my office."

Stan looked again at his watch, and then said, "I really need to be in court; I'll ask Janet to give you a receipt and make a copy. I'll get back to you. And thanks, I appreciate that you came here first."

Rory hoped fervently that she'd done the right thing. She wondered if she could trust Stan. She'd never really liked his style but he had a reputation for being fair and for ferreting out the truth. He was a formidable opponent in court; she had to trust that the truth was more important to him than winning a case.

Janet went efficiently about the business of writing a receipt of evidence form, and then copied the tape while Rory waited. She soon presented Rory with both.

"Thanks so much, Janet!" Rory said sincerely.

"No problem, good luck with the case. Look, I know you and Stan have had your differences, but he is a good guy."

"Yeah, I've been seeing more of that lately," Rory replied as she took her leave. She went directly to her office across the street.

Only Blake was in, since Sam and Sarah had gone to the Law Library. Rory's emotions were in turmoil. Blake didn't miss it.

"What's up, Rory? Sit down and spill it!"

Taking a deep breath Rory went through the whole story, then said, "Before we discuss any more, please open the safe so we can secure this tape."

"Sure thing, Rory," Blake said. "So , you're onto something really big, eh?"

"Yeah, I think so. The recording can go a long way towards establishing Korbin's credibility. I just hope I can trust Como. He says he has to verify the voice on the tape as Kathie's. And that's something he has to do. I hope Stan takes this as seriously as I do."

"Well, he's a tough prosecutor, everyone knows that, but he also has a reputation for being fair. Let's hope that's true."

"I'm banking on it; that's why I took the tape directly to him. So, I guess we'll see," Rory said nervously. "You know, the police could be in trouble for not reporting Korbin's cell phone messages, or for not turning the phone over to the DA. They surely won't be happy if they have to answer to Como."

"Well, he should let 'em have it, if they've withheld evidence. They did a sloppy job all around from what we've seen."

"I agree, but that often happens when the investigators are so sure the guilty party has been arrested. And from what little, circumstantial evidence there was, it looked like Korbin was the perp."

"By the way," Blake asked, "do you have any more news on Helen?"

"Oh, thank you for reminding me. I need to find her. Jeremy said Helen may be with Alicia, her daughter. Can you go on Facebook or wherever you go to find people and get Alicia's information? I need to get in touch with Helen today. I think her input will be invaluable. And I'm concerned about her. Something's not right."

"Sure, Boss; I'll do some digging and get you the info ASAP!"

"Great, I'll be in my office catching up on paperwork."

It was difficult for Rory to concentrate on anything other than finding Helen. She was staring at a document, with no clue what it was about when Blake entered.

"Here it is—everything I could find. Hope it helps to locate Helen."

"Thanks, Blake, you're a wiz; what would I do without you?"

He smiled and left the office.

Rory decided to compose an email she hoped wouldn't alarm Alicia, then looked at the rest of the paperwork, planning what to do next if the email didn't pan out.

She was still working on her plan when her email pinged. She retrieved the message; it was from Alicia. She confirmed her mother wasn't staying with her, and that Alicia had been trying to reach her for the last few days. Alicia also said she'd been home a few weeks before and her mother had been fine physically, but had seemed preoccupied.

Rory replied to Alicia's email, suggesting she should call her so they could discuss what to do next.

A few seconds later, the phone rang and Alicia, on the verge of tears, said, "Rory, I'm so glad you contacted me. I've been in the middle of finals, and haven't had much time, but Mom's been on my mind. She just doesn't lose touch with me for this long."

"OK, look Alicia; I'll just have to go over there. If your mom doesn't answer the door, is there any way I can get in?"

"There's a key to the back door in a magnetized container on the bottom of one of the wrought iron chairs out back. Shouldn't be hard to find."

"I'll leave now; by the way, can you give me your cell number? I'll give you mine." They exchanged numbers, and Rory said, "I'll get back to you as soon as I know something."

Rory went out to Blake's desk and said, "Alicia said Helen's not with her and hasn't been in contact with Alicia for the last few days. Alicia's obviously worried, and I am too. We need to go over to Helen's house; Alicia told me where the key's hidden in case Helen doesn't answer."

Blake jumped up and said, "Let's go! I'll drive."

They didn't talk much on the way over. Rory was trying not to imagine a worst case scenario, but a knot was forming in her stomach and her mouth was dry. Blake looked equally concerned as he gripped the wheel with white knuckles.

A few minutes later they pulled into Helen's drive. They went to the front door and knocked. They rang the bell. No response. They checked the garage and saw Helen's car inside.

"We'll have to go out back and find the key." Blake followed as Rory walked around to the back patio. She spotted the chairs, went over to them and ran her hand under the seat of one. The key wasn't under the first chair, but she found it under the second.

"Let's see if this opens the door." She handed the key to Blake and they walked up the steps to the back door. He put the key in the lock and jiggled it until the door opened.

As soon as they were in the kitchen, Rory called, "Helen, Helen; it's Rory—are you here?"

Walking towards the front of the house, Rory almost gagged. There was a horrific smell, which she recognized and it stopped her dead in her tracks.

"Oh my God, Rory, what is that stench?" Blake sounded horrified.

Rory found she couldn't answer, but knew with certainty what they would find.

Chapter 27

Alicia paced around her apartment, stopping every so often to call Rory. It had been over an hour now since she'd spoken with Rory, and Rory had promised to call back as soon as she knew anything. As each minute ticked by, Alicia's panic grew. She tried to will her mind not to conjure up scenes of disaster, but it becamemore difficult by the moment.

When her roommate, Vanessa, came home she noticed Alicia pacing and on the verge of tears. Going to Alicia, she hugged her, asking, "What happened, Ali? What's wrong?"

"I can't reach my mom, haven't heard from her in several days. Her friend, Rory contacted me; she'd been worried, too. I don't know what to do. I last spoke to Rory an hour ago and she said she'd call me as soon as she knew something. Rory was going to the house."

Vanessa made a quick decision, "We need to go to your mom's, now! The car's out front, come on."

Alicia followed obediently, like an automaton.

As she drove, Vanessa asked, "Is there anyone else you can call?"

"I could call Rory's office, see if anyone there can help."

"Good idea, why don't you?"

Finding Rory's office number in her phone, Alicia called. It was answered by a young woman, not Rory. "Hi, this is Alicia Yates, I spoke with Rory over an hour ago about my mom, Helen, and I haven't heard anything. Can you reach her?"

"Alicia, this is Sarah, I work with Rory. She left us a note before she left for your mom's house. We haven't heard from her either. Give us the address, we'll go over and check, then call you."

"Thanks so much, Sarah, we, my roommate and I, should be there in about forty-five minutes, we're on the way from Philly."

Luckily it was a bit before rush hour in the city, and they made reasonable time. Alicia felt better since they were actually doing something, she'd been beside herself with helplessness and panic.

The worry was still there in the pit of her stomach; she was holding it at bay for the moment. There was silence between them, as Vanessa concentrated on driving.

With a rush of affection for Vanessa, Alicia said , "You really saved me; I was losing it big-time! Thank God I have you, and thank God you came back when you did! By the way, didn't you have a final this afternoon?"

"Yeah, I did; I came back to the room to cram a bit more, but, no worries, the prof will understand. It's a Psych course; she'll know you have to put relationships first."

"I can't believe you missed your final to drive me home… I just don't know what to say…"

"Words aren't necessary—I just told you, it's relationships that matter. And you, my dear, matter. You've always been there for me, and your mom has always gone out of her way to make me welcome when we visit."

"I still feel blessed to have you."

Vanessa didn't answer. She was looking for the exit sign. She knew to get off at the Media exit. Then she said, "You'll have to direct me from here."

Soon they were approaching Edgemont, the Yates's street.

Alicia felt herself tense up. Neither Rory or Sarah hadn't called; that couldn't be good.

As they turned onto her street, Alicia gasped. The street was ablaze with flashing lights; rescue and police vehicles littered the lawn. There was yellow tape guarding the entrance, and people were milling about. Alicia slumped in her seat, overcome.

Chapter 28

Rory made a quick decision and told Vanessa the two could stay with her, since she knew Alicia had no other family, except a father from whom she'd been estranged. And Rory had known Alicia since birth; she'd played with her own girls when they were younger.

Hours later, Rory sat in her breakfast nook with Vanessa, who, as it turned out, was Alicia's partner. Rory thanked God that Vanessa had accompanied her. Their bond was helping Alicia attempt to make sense of this tragedy. Alicia was now asleep, under medical supervision. Rory's doctor, and friend, Paul Hunter, had come to the house to treat Alicia.

All was quiet at this hour; everyone had gone to bed, but Rory and Van found sleep impossible, so they sat up to talk. Vanessa was strikingly exotic looking, probably biracial, Rory thought. She was also compassionate and intelligent and she had questions for Rory. "So, I know everyone is calling this a terrible accident that Ms. Yates fell down the steps. I heard that lawyer, her boss; say she'd been having dizzy spells. But, there were police cars there, and the coroner's van… What do you really think happened?"

It was impossible for Rory to ignore Vanessa's direct look. She couldn't, and wouldn't lie to her. "I'm not sure where to start with this, but I guess at the beginning. I'd been trying to reach Helen for at least a week; I'd been to the law office, only to be told that Helen was sick, and might be staying with Alicia. That last bit, I heard just today, so I got in touch with Alicia. As soon as she told me that Helen wasn't there and that she'd been trying to reach her, Blake and I went straight over. I was dreading what we'd find and it turned out to be a worst case scenario. She'd obviously been dead for a while, and I'm really glad Alicia didn't see her crumpled at the bottom of the stairs; it's tough for me to get that picture out of my mind. We called the police immediately, and it just grew from there. Despite Jeremy's claim that she'd been having dizzy spells, the police view it as a suspicious death. We'll wait for the coroner's report, which may take a few days." Rory closed her eyes and shook her head, as if trying to obliterate the mental image.

Vanessa took some time before she spoke again. "Rory, I know you must be incredibly tired, and I hate to keep pressing you, but you mentioned that you'd been trying to reach Ms. Yates for about a week? Was there urgency, or were you just a concerned friend?"

"Well both, really. I'd been by the office to talk with Jeremy about Kathie Korbin's death; I'm representing her husband, who's been charged with the murder. Kathie was working with Helen in Jeremy's office at the time of her death. When I last saw Helen, she didn't seem to be herself. She's normally bubbly and chatty, and we've been friends for a long time; I've watched Alicia grow up. Anyway, she barely spoke to me that day, so I began to wonder if she and Kathie had become friends, and if that was the reason she'd seemed upset. It also occurred to me that Kathie might've confided in her and she might have some information useful in Korbin's defense. So... you can understand why I might be suspicious. We just have to wait for the coroner's report; I can't speculate."

"Either way it turns out, this is a huge blow to Alicia; she really has no other family. She and her father haven't been in touch," Vanessa added.

Rory patted her hand and said, "I'm so glad she has you; you've been such a balm for her. She'll need you even more as this goes forward."

Vanessa looked up gratefully, "Thanks, Rory, I just hope I have the strength to get Ali through this. We had just told her mom, you know, about us, the last time we visited. She was really nice, and...accepting. She made me feel welcome." Tears began to form in Vanessa's amber eyes.

"We'll do it, together. Now, why don't you try to get some sleep? The doc left mild tranquilizers for me to dispense, so if you want some..."

"Yeah, all of a sudden I feel very tired. I think I'll take one; what if Ali wakes up?"

"Her dose was stronger; she should sleep for a long time. It will help her cope. Dr. Hunter is coming back tomorrow to see her; he's a good friend and a great healer."

"Ok then, I think I'll turn in." Vanessa spontaneously gave Rory a hug, then buried her face in Rory's shoulder and sobbed. Rory held her until the sobbing subsided. Then she repeated what she'd said before, "We're all in this together. My girls are friends with Alicia; they've always idolized her, like an older sister. They'll help, too. They haven't seen her since she went to college, so Kate and Alex will be happy to see her, even though the occasion...is dreadful."

Having taken her medication, Vanessa said goodnight, and retired. Rory knew she needed sleep to deal with this horrific development, but her mind was buzzing. She also knew, with a deep certainty, that these two deaths—both murders, in her view—were connected. And she was sure that Helen had known something, or at least, had some suspicions. That would explain her atypical behavior when Rory had last seen her. How could she find out what Helen knew? Maybe she could get some information from Alicia. But it would be a few days before she'd even consider doing that. And it would have to wait for the coroner's report which Rory both anticipated and dreaded.

The magnitude of this was suddenly overwhelming. Rory decided to take some meds and try to sleep. She was surprised to see it was just midnight; this day had seemed to go on forever. She couldn't imagine how things could get worse.

She must have fallen into a deep, dreamless sleep. When Marc gently awakened her, she startled. "Oh my God, am I late? What's happening?"

Marc sat down next to her, taking her hands. "I'm sorry; I didn't mean to frighten you. I have an early case; why don't you try to go back to sleep. I wish I could be here to help you out..."

With sudden impact, Rory recalled the previous day, and felt immediately overwhelmed. "Oh, God!" Rory put her head in her hands. "It's almost as if yesterday was a nightmare..."

"I know," Marc said soothingly. "I'll try to get back as early as I can; the next few days will be tough for all of us." He kissed her and said, "Love you—Bye."

"Love you, too," Rory said automatically. She knew there was no more sleep for her, so she roused herself and got into the shower. The warm water massage was relaxing. But she had what felt like a rock in the pit of her stomach. She had so much to do. Today her focus would be on Alicia, and trying to help her cope.

Preparing to dress after her shower, Rory smelled the welcome aroma of coffee wafting up from the kitchen. God bless whoever made it, she thought gratefully.

She found her daughters in the kitchen, trying to decide what to make for breakfast. Rory suggested, " Why don't we wait for the others to get up. By the way, thanks so much for putting coffee on; it just makes me feel better somehow."

Alex and Kate embraced her. "Mom, this must be so awful for you, and for poor Alicia; I can't even imagine..." Kate's voice trailed off.

Alex said, "Her friend is really nice; it's so good that she came with her. They're a couple, aren't they?"

"Yes, they are; Vanessa told me last night, and Helen had told me not long ago. You're right, Van's pretty incredible, she just hopes to have the strength Alicia needs."

"We'll all try to help," Kate said.

"That's what I told her; I'm glad for your support."

"We still need to go to softball camp..." Alex sounded apologetic.

"Of course you do, that's your job right now," Rory said.

Vanessa entered the room, an uneasy look on her face. Rory went to her, hugged her and asked, "How'd you sleep?"

"Like a rock. I feel rested, but I'm worried that Alicia hasn't moved."

"The doc gave her a higher dose of tranquilizer because her whole system is in shock. She really needs to sleep. Doc Hunter will be over this morning to check on her. He'll likely give her daytime meds as well. She'll be in shock for a while. Her body needs to rest so her mind can heal as well."

"All the breakfast stuff is on the counter—help yourself, Vanessa," Kate said. "Mom, Alex and I are getting a ride to camp, so we'll see you later."

Vanessa helped herself to yogurt and coffee. Then she took a seat in the breakfast nook.

Rory kissed her girls goodbye and took her coffee into the nook to sit with Vanessa. They sat in companionable silence.

Without warning, a loud wail, followed by an intense keening came from the second floor.

Chapter 29

Blake was in the office alone. He hadn't slept well after the shocking discovery he and Rory had made the previous day. And it had been a long, tedious day. He found himself pacing, his thoughts muddled. He wanted to call Rory, see if there was anything useful he could do, but he knew she already had too much to deal with. He decided he'd have to wait for her call. He busied himself making coffee, an effort that might be unnecessary, since he'd no idea who'd be coming in today.

Just then, the door opened; it was Sarah. His happiness at seeing her turned to concern when he noticed her uncharacteristic disarray—she actually looked disheveled. It looked as though she hadn't had a good night's sleep either.

She plopped into the nearest chair, and said, "God, Blake, I feel so awful. I don't know if I can do anything, but I had to come in."

Blake brought her a cup of tea, handed it to her and sat down next to her.

"Yeah, yesterday was the worst. I'm really glad you came in; I was just wondering what we could do to help Rory. Maybe we can put our heads together and think of something; she must be feeling pretty awful herself. And she has to take care of poor Alicia. God, the whole thing stinks!"

They both looked up as Sam entered. Blake thought he looked better than they did. Sam said, "Hey guys, glad you're here; wasn't sure what to do, but I wanted to come in. Looks like you two didn't get much sleep."

Sarah yawned and Blake nodded.

"I knew I wouldn't be able to sleep, so I belted down a few beers; that did the trick." Sam helped himself to coffee and took a seat near the others.

Blake said, "Sarah and I were just wondering what we could possibly do to help Rory; we haven't come up with anything…."

"Good thought," Sam agreed. "Let's put aside our feelings for the moment and think about what Rory has to get done. She can't make funeral arrangements until the coroner releases the body. We probably can't search Helen's house, which I'm sure Rory would want, because the police are still there. I drove by on my way in and it's still a beehive of activity."

"So," Sarah put in, "maybe we can help her with more practical things, like getting meals in for the extra people staying there. Or, running errands that she doesn't have time for…"

"That sounds good," Blake agreed. "But, I didn't want to call Rory and distract her. Maybe if we could get in touch with one of her daughters…"

"Oh, good idea!" Sarah came alive. "I have Alex's cell number; Rory gave it to me last night. So I guess that means she wouldn't mind if I call. What do you guys think?"

"Why not?" Blake asked. Sam nodded.

"OK, here goes." Sarah dialed the number, then held her breath. After a few rings, Alex picked up.

"Hello?" she said uncertainly.

"Alex, Hi, it's Sarah. I'm sure you guys must be in over your heads. We—Blake, Sam and I—are trying to figure out how we could help you out. Can you think of anything practical that you need done? We're feeling quite helpless…"

"Oh, that's so sweet of you guys," Alex paused. "Well, Kate and I are at soccer camp. Alicia was still sleeping when we left. Ummm, I'm thinking, there's so much… You know, maybe you could do some grocery shopping for us? Not that anyone feels like eating, but it would be good to have some staples in. Like, milk, coffee, bread, cold cuts, that type of thing…"

"Ok," Sarah said briskly. "I think that gives us a starting point. By the way, where do you usually shop?"

"Trader Joe's, Giant, whatever is easier; thanks so much! I'd best go now; see you later." Alex hung up quickly.

"Alex isn't at home—she and Kate are at soccer camp. But she said they could use groceries, and Trader Joe's is a good place to go, and close by, so let's get on with it."

Blake offered his car, which was parked nearby, so they went off on their mission.

An hour or so later, they'd purchased several bags, some of which contained perishable items they needed to drop at Rory's right away.

"Maybe it's best if I take it in," Blake said. "We don't really want to overwhelm them. And if I get a chance to talk with Rory, I'll ask her if there's anything else we can do."

"That sounds good, Blake. You're right, we don't want to get in the way," Sarah said.

"We're almost there," Blake announced. "You guys haven't been here, have you?"

"No," Sam and Sarah answered simultaneously. "It's a nice neighborhood," Sarah noted.

"Here we are," Blake said as they stopped at big, cedar-shingled house. There were two unfamiliar cars in the drive. "I hope I'm not interrupting anything, but here goes."

Blake grabbed two bags of groceries and headed into the house.

Rory answered the door. "Wow, that was quick; Alex called and told me what you guys were doing; thanks so much, Blake," she said as she led him to the kitchen. As he put the groceries on the counter, he noticed Vanessa seated in the nook.

She was more stunning than he'd remembered, but then chastened himself for having thoughts like that during this tragedy. He nodded to her and she smiled.

"How's it going?" he asked Rory quietly.

"Much better, thanks… the doc is seeing to Alicia now; she was hysterical when she woke this morning. I think he'll want to keep her sedated. You can stay for a bit, if you like."

"Sounds good, but first I have more bags in the car—along with Sam and Sarah—be right back."

"Bring them in too, Blake," Rory said

Blake took a few more bags, and said to Sam and Sarah, "Rory wants us all to come in; Alicia is sleeping."

They all headed into the house with the groceries.

Rory greeted them warmly and thanked them for bringing the groceries. "How much do I owe you," she asked, reaching for her wallet.

"Nothing," Sarah said. "We wanted to do something, so please let us."

"That's so thoughtful of you; I can't begin to tell you…"

"We're just so sorry you all have to deal with this tragedy. Are you sure we won't be in the way?" Sarah asked.

Rory assured her, "Things are much better since the doc arrived. He has a nice bedside manner, and makes us all feel better." Rory took them to the kitchen, and offered coffee. Blake and Sam got coffee and went to sit in the nook with Vanessa.

Sarah joined them, offering her sympathies to Vanessa. "How long will you be staying?" Sarah asked Vanessa.

"Can't say for sure," Vanessa replied. "But, I'm here for the long haul. I'll probably go back to the apartment to get some more clothes for us."

"I'll be happy to drive you, "Blake offered. "We're here to do anything we can to help out."

"Really?" Vanessa looked surprised. "That would be so nice. Thank you for offering."

"No problem; I'll drop these two off and we can leave."

Sarah spoke to Rory, "Please let us know what else we can do. Otherwise we just feel useless."

"Well then, please stick around for a while; it's good to have company and to keep things as normal as possible."

"I'm going to drive Vanessa into the city," Blake said, "but Sam and Sarah can stay here if you want."

Vanessa went upstairs to get her things.

When Blake started towards the door, Sarah came over to him and whispered, "She is beautiful, but before you get your hopes up, just wanted to tell you she and Alicia are partners."

"Yeah, I knew that," Blake said, too quickly. The look of shock and dismay on his face belied his words. He hated being thought a user.

As she walked Blake to the door, Sarah noticed the paper had arrived. She went to retrieve it. Picking it up, she stared at the headlines: "PRESIDENT JUDGE BEING INVESTIGATED FOR INAPPROPRIATE CONDUCT; GRAND JURY IS CONVENED."

Chapter 30

Sarah pushed Blake out the door, gesturing frantically to the headlines. "This is not what Rory needs to see right now," Sarah hissed. "But, I think I need to find out more about it. Listen, I left my laptop at the office so please take me back so I can get on the internet."

"OK, sure," Blake agreed, "but what are you going to tell Rory?"

"I'll think of something—meet you at the car."

Sarah went back in as Vanessa was coming out. "Blake's dropping me at the office after all—be right out."

Rory was seated in the nook with Sam when Sarah reentered. "Hey Rory, I'm going back to the office; I'm way behind on my journaling. I'll be back later."

"OK, fine Sarah—see you later."

Ignoring Sam's astonished look, Sarah decided she'd text him later, when she knew more. She was fairly certain that Rory was too preoccupied to miss the morning paper.

Getting into the back seat, she said "Thanks for waiting; I really have to catch up on school work." Blake had left the paper on the floor of the back seat, she noticed.

"Jeez," Vanessa replied, "I know what you mean, but I just can't focus on that now. I've emailed Ali's and my professors and requested an incomplete until we can do our finals."

"They should understand, don't you think?" Sarah inquired.

"I don't think it will be a problem; I missed one final and Ali has a paper due. She's an honor student, always on the dean's list. And I've never been late with an assignment."

"Sounds like you have a good track record," Sarah agreed.

Arriving at the office, Blake asked, "Sarah, do you need me to unlock?"

"Yep, forgot my key again, sorry. See you later, Vanessa."

Sarah grabbed the newspaper and followed Blake into the office.

"Listen," he said, "I really didn't know Van was gay, and I feel like such a jerk, but I would never take advantage of her situation..."

"Blake, that's between us; I'd never tell anyone. I just wanted you to know. Any guy would be attracted to her. So, no worries."

"You're right, and thanks."

Sarah closed the door and set to work. First, she made herself more tea. Then she sat down with the paper and read the entire article. Apparently, the president judge was relieved of his judicial duties until the Grand Jury made a decision. That would be months, Sarah thought, given the time other cases had taken. *My, my, the shit has hit the fan,* Sarah thought.

Good, we're all well rid of him. She knew Rory would be pleased, but now wasn't the time for her to be distracted. She hoped she'd made the right decision to withhold it from her for the moment. Her indecision prompted her to text Sam; she'd been discussing difficult situations with him. The text said simply, "Excuse yourself from Rory and call me."

A few minutes passed before her cell rang. She picked up immediately.

"What's up?" Sam sounded confused.

"Here's the deal," Sarah replied, "When I went outside with Blake, I picked up the Delco Times, and the headlines were all about Judge Keller being investigated by the Grand

Jury! And while that's great, I didn't think Rory needed to hear that right now. Then, I started to have second thoughts, so I called you because you have better judgment than I do. So, what do you think? Did I do the right thing or was I too hasty?"

"Wow, that's some news! It's awesome, actually. Let me digest it a minute. I mean, how'd they find out about him?" Sam was incredulous.

"An anonymous, but reliable source, was all they'd reveal; you know, they have to protect their informants. I'm sure it wasn't Rory, but I'm betting she knows who it was. So that's why I didn't want her to have more to worry about.   Do   you agree?"

"Yeah, sure, I think you did the right thing, but how long do you think we can keep this from her? Right now, I agree, she's concerned about Alicia and has the funeral to plan…Jeez, I'd love to sit down and talk about this with you…"

"I know, me too, but for now I'm afraid you'll have to keep Rory busy, or occupied, or whatever…I'm trying to gather as much info as I can. So it looks like I'm stuck here for a while, anyway. Just sit tight, and when Blake gets back, he can drop you off here."

"Okay, of course I'll stay with Rory, and thanks for calling. I was confused about why you left in such a hurry. Bye for now."

Just talking with Sam had calmed Sarah; she tended to second guess herself a lot, and, she realized with a start, she'd come to rely on Sam's steady presence to ground her. He was quite a guy, when she thought about it. She mentally shook herself. This wasn't the time to be mooning over Sam, but it was worth storing away for later.

Sarah got back to work, reading the paper from cover to cover, every article about the breaking news. It was fascinating. And she felt privileged to have some insider info. One article in particular caught her attention. It alleged that several women had come forward with similar complaints of remarks of a sexual nature made by the President Judge. These women had been subpoenaed to testify before the Grand Jury.

Sarah went on the internet and was surprised to see many articles on the judge. *Hmm, I guess it's big news outside Media,* she thought. She looked up at the clock and realized she'd been at this for almost two hours. Time for a break.

Sarah got up, stretched and made some more tea. Walking around the room until her tea was ready, she cleared her head. Then she sat down, sipping her tea and renewing her search.

Without warning, she heard loud footfalls, and the front door burst open.

When her brain registered who it was she gasped and froze in her chair.

Judge Keller, his face crimson, walked towards her shouting, "You fucking assholes have ruined my reputation! It's all lies, and you know it—you'll pay, all of you! I will personally see that you're all disbarred—you'll be ruined, not me... I should waste the bunch of you!"

When he stopped to catch his breath, Sarah came to her senses and bolted for Rory's office, her mug of hot tea splattering the judge. He reacted with a surprised shriek, while Sarah slammed and locked the door behind her. Within seconds Judge Keller was pounding on the door, still raging. Sarah looked around frantically to see how she could secure the door and settled on a sturdy chair. Placing it under the knob, she was reaching for the phone when she heard a scuffle taking place on the other side of the door.

The familiar voices of Sam and Blake were music to her ears. Then she heard grunts and thuds, and the judge was still ranting. In her rush to move the chair, she slipped on an area rug, hitting her head on the side of the chair before she could catch herself.

The last thing she heard was Sam, "Sarah...you in there? Are you OK?"

Chapter 31

Sam was frantic. He and Blake had managed to overtake the judge and were awaiting the police. His main concern was for Sarah. He prayed she was safe in Rory's office, but so far no response from the other side of the door. He renewed his efforts, shouting, "Sarah, are you in there?" and pounding on the door.

Finally he heard what sounded like movement, and responded "Sarah, it's Sam. If you're in there, open up!"

More shuffling sounds, and then, a weak voice, "Sam... I hit my head—but I'm ok. Just don't know if I have the strength to move the chair..."

"Thank God you're ok; can you just unlock the door?" Sam's breathing slowed a bit and his heart rate decelerated.

He heard the lock snap open and tried the door; it was stuck. "Can you push the chair a bit, then I should be able to force it open."

Sam could hear Sarah trying to push; it seemed to be an effort. He pushed the door again and finally, it swung open.

Breathing a sigh of relief, he opened his arms for Sarah; she fell limply into his embrace, murmuring, "Sam, I was so scared... is he still here?"

"Yeah, he's here, Blake's got him covered; we're waiting for the police. They'll want to question you; are you up to it?"

"Well, yeah; I'll pull myself together—wouldn't miss it!"

"That's the spirit, Sarah. Now why don't you stay in here— I'll get you some tea—until the police arrive. Looking at her closely, Sam said, "Is your head ok? Looks like some bruising there; I'll get you some ice."

"Thanks, Sam, you showed up just in time. He was pounding on the door so hard the windows were rattling." She shivered, remembering it.

"Yeah, that's what he was doing when we arrived, and it was a bit of a struggle, but we got him down. He's big, but not very strong. OK, I'll be right back—you should sit until you get your strength back."

Sam went back to the outer office. The judge was still face down on the floor, muttering incoherently. Sam rolled his eyes at Blake, and asked, "Everything okay in here?"

"Oh just dandy—I've learned a few new curses, but now I can't understand a word he's saying." Then Blake whispered, "Guy's nuts—certifiable!"

Sam nodded and went to prepare Sarah's tea. "Well, at least Sarah's safe, and unharmed, although shaken. Good thing our timing was right." He looked in the freezer and found an ice pack.

"Yeah! Hate to think of what might've happened."

When the tea was prepared, Sam took it and the ice. He noted that Sarah's color was coming back and she seemed more herself. He bent over to hand her the tea, and she leaned up to kiss him. It was a sweet lingering kiss, one he wouldn't soon forget.

Nor would he forget the way she'd looked at him as she said, simply, "You saved me."

Sam couldn't control the blush moving up his face. "Here, put this ice on your bruise." He touched it tenderly. "Thank God you're safe," he said quietly.

He pulled a chair over and sat down next to her, finally handing her the tea. Her hands were shaking as she took it.

"Look at me," she chided herself, "still shaky. I thought I was over it."

"Give it some time; it must've been awful; that horrible man! He's lucky we didn't smack him around. It makes my blood boil to think of it." Now that Sarah was out of danger, Sam realized how angry he was.

"He's not worth it, Sam. He's on the way out and he knows it; he's desperate."

As if on cue, the judge started ranting again. "My lawyer will make mincemeat of you—you got nothing on me! Just you wait, you'll see how I can make your lives miserable, ruin your careers!" Then he seemed to just run out of steam.

Sarah whispered to Sam, "He's a real nut job, don't you think?"

"Oh, absolutely; sounded like he was speaking in tongues a while ago, and his eyes were all glazed over—Blake and I came to the same conclusion. He needs to be 302'd, I think."

"What's that mean?" Sarah asked.

"It's an involuntary commitment to a psych ward." Sam answered.

Just then, conversation was cut off by the scream of sirens close by.

"About time," Sam said. "Stay in here until they cart him off."

Sam came out to open the door for the police. The judge was wedged under a heavy chair on which Blake sat.

Officers Jamison and Gordon introduced themselves and showed their ID.

Officer Jamison surveyed the scene and said, "So, it looks like there was some kind of a scuffle, what happened?"

Blake summed up the situation and looked to Sam for confirmation.

"Sounds about right. But, Sarah, an intern of Rory's, is in the next room; she's the one you want to talk to. We came in while he was pounding on the door where Sarah had barricaded herself."

This seemed to enrage the judge. He started to rant again, "That bitch thinks she's going to ruin me, but I've got news for her..."

The police took charge of the situation here, "Sir, you need to calm down; I want you to get up and sit in the chair and refrain from making any comments—you're not helping yourself."

Officer Jamison, who knew the judge from his many years on the force, helped him up.

"You're damn straight I won't say anything—I need to call my lawyer. Do you know who I am? The nerve of these people trying to take me down—the Goddamn nerve!"

"Judge Keller," replied Officer Jamison, "Of course I know who you are, but that doesn't give you the right to keep shouting. We need to hear the facts. And if we decide to charge you, you may call your lawyer. Do you understand?"

"What do you think I am a fucking moron? Of course I understand! But if you think you're going to charge me with anything, I'll have your fuckin' badge!"

"George," Jamison nodded to his fellow officer, "It's time for the cuffs."

Officer Gordon walked towards the judge with the cuffs. Keller jumped from his seat, unexpectedly agile, with a threatening gesture towards the officer. Jamison quickly joined Gordon in restraining the judge and putting cuffs on him.

Keller kept screaming and fighting against the cuffs; he tried to run towards the door. Blake put out his foot and the judge went sprawling. He was down, but hadn't stopped cursing.

"I think he needs a psych evaluation; we may need to 302 him," Jamison said to Gordon. "Let's get him to the car." The two officers hauled him out of the office, while he continued to resist and shout insults, which lapsed into incoherence.

When Office Jamison returned, leaving the other officer to guard the judge, he said, "Well, you don't need to convince me that he was threatening someone; Whew! That was tough. I should probably speak with the person who was here when he first entered."

"That would be me," announced Sarah, emerging from Rory's office.

Officer Jamison extended his hand to Sarah and introduced himself.

"Nice to meet you, Officer; I'm Sarah Justice. I was alone in this room when the judge barged in."

Officer Jamison asked Sarah a number of questions, which she answered to the best of her recollection. She said that she'd felt threatened as the judge walked towards her, screaming and using threats like, "I should waste you all!" She also volunteered that this wasn't the first time he'd made threats. She told the Officer about the threats she and Sam had heard him make to Rory a few weeks prior.

"Do you have any idea why the judge would threaten you and Rory?"

"Yes, well, we—Sam and I—have been helping Rory with her defense of Jeff Korbin. Since an important part of the case involves the PFA order taken out by his late wife, we were looking into old PFA cases to see if we could find anything helpful to the case."

"And did you?" inquired Jamison.

"Well, we found it strange that Judge Keller heard a disproportionate number of these cases, and always ruled in favor of the plaintiff. We didn't understand why the President Judge would hear such minor cases."

"So, you think the judge knew what you were doing?" asked Jamison.

"Not sure," answered Sarah. "He knew Rory was sitting in on some of his recent PFA cases."

"What, if anything, do you know about the investigation just announced in the papers?" Jamison inquired.

"I saw the paper at Rory's house this morning and brought it here; she's caring for Helen Yates's daughter and I didn't want her to see the paper—she has enough to deal with. But, to answer your question, I knew nothing until today."

"And why would that upset Rory?"

"Well, I think since she's already had a run-in with him, she'd be afraid of what the judge might do now."

"If I might add something, Officer," Sam intervened. "I think the judge is seriously over the edge—I mean certifiable. Before you arrived, it sounded as if he were speaking in tongues. He's pretty scary."

"Thanks for the information; we may have to 302 him if he hasn't settled down. From what Sarah's said, and from what Officer Gordon and I observed firsthand, there are a number of charges we could bring against him. Certainly terroristic threats, and resisting arrest, to name a few."

"But I think we may try the 302 route—get him evaluated—before we bring formal charges. Who knows, he may not be competent to stand trial," Jamison speculated. "Anyway, thanks for your cooperation; we will, of course, need to speak with Ms. Chandler, but it can wait a few days. Here's my card if you think of anything else, and I would like your cell numbers, in case I need any more information."

The trio offered their cards to Officer Jamison. When he'd left, they sat down to try and figure out what to do next. They'd hardly begun, when the office phone startled them.

Blake went to answer, then held the phone away from his ear. Rory's voice, raised several octaves, and demanded, "Just what the hell is going on?"

Chapter 32

Later that afternoon, Rory gathered her staff; they sat in her breakfast nook with cool drinks, and waited for her to speak.

"OK, now that Alicia is sleeping and Van is with her, we can talk. In case you're wondering if I'm psychic, or psychotic, for that matter—that's a joke kids—I'm not. I do, however, have spies everywhere. OK, lighten up—that was a joke, too."

She almost laughed at the stricken looks on their faces.

The three relaxed marginally, still waiting.

"Look, I'm not angry. Not now, anyway. When I got the call from Anderson, whose office is next door, and he told me the police were there and it looked like Judge Keller was being taken away; well, you can imagine! I hate being out of the loop, so fill me in.

Sarah started, "I guess it was my doing. When I went outside with Blake this morning, I found the newspaper and, well, here it is—you can see for yourself."

Shock registered on Rory's face as she took it in, "Holy shit—he really did it!" She stopped abruptly, realizing what she'd revealed. "I mean, I mean, I can't believe they finally caught him."

"Look Rory," Blake broke in. "Right now, we know nothing about this; that's what we told the police, so it's probably best we keep it that way."

"You're right, Blake, I'm sorry." She put her head in her hands.

"Sorry about what?" Sarah quipped, "We didn't hear anything."

Rory gave a wan smile, then said, "OK, what happened next?"

Sarah continued, "I made a snap decision to keep it from you, at least for a while, because so much else is going on. So I made up an excuse to go back to the office, read the paper and go on the internet. I wanted to know just how big this thing was." She stopped to take a breath. "It's big; it even made the New York Times, although not front page. So, I got lost in my research, and didn't hear the front door open. Then I heard loud footsteps coming towards me, and was shocked to see the judge! I froze for a minute, then came to my senses and ran into your office, locked it, put a chair under the knob. He started pounding really hard on the door, then I heard voices—Sam and Blake—and I sort of hit my head on the chair and I don't know…"

"Oh my God, Sarah! Are you OK? Now I see you've got a bruise on your head."

"Yeah, I'm fine, thanks to these guys." Sarah smiled appreciatively at them.

"So," Blake went on, "we grabbed him and subdued him and called the cops."

"Sarah came to, after a brief scare, and I made sure she was all right—we put ice on her head—and she stayed in your office until the cops took him away," Sam clarified.

"But I'll tell you what, "Sarah put in, "that guy is seriously fucked in the head!"

"That's true," Blake confirmed, "he even threatened the cops. He was so over the top! Officer Jamison, he was the officer we dealt with, mentioned they had enough to at least charge him with Terroristic Threats, and Resisting Arrest. But he also said they might consider having him 302'd."

Rory nodded, "Maybe that's where he belongs for now, in a psych ward."

"Anyway, "Sarah continued, "Officer Jamison will get in touch with you in the next few days. I told him the judge had threatened you a few weeks ago. Of course, he wanted to know why and I said that you'd been sitting in on PFA hearings, for your murder case. Also told him we'd researched PFA hearings and found out Judge Keller heard the lion's share of those hearings."

"Ok, Ok, all true, what else?" Rory asked, feeling there was more.

"He asked me if I knew anything about the investigation that was in the papers today, and I said honestly it'd come as a shock to me. And I told him you were dealing with Helen's daughter, so you had enough to worry about—so I took the paper. Of course, he asked why you'd be upset and I told him because the judge had threatened you before, even though I'd already mentioned that."

"So, that's it? Is that everything?" Rory looked at each of them directly.

They all nodded somberly.

Rory took a deep breath, then said, "I can't fault any of you—I can see you were trying to protect me. And it did bring this to a head, in terms of the judge's outrageous behavior. I mean, now we're not the only ones who've seen him act bizarrely—he actually threatened the police? That's beyond the pale; it's on record now. And he was violent, as well…"

"Yeah," Sarah said, "I was wondering, with all of the media attention, what else might come to light. There are several women who've come forward to testify before the Grand Jury—I mean, this is really huge."

"I just don't know if it will help Korbin," Rory mused.

"We'll have to wait and see," Blake said. "At least there's a spotlight on the judge; that should help our case."

Just then, Vanessa entered the room, her eyes downcast. Rory got up and went to her. "Oh, Van, I'm sorry if we were making too much noise…"

"Not at all, Rory; she's sleeping quietly. I just felt a little isolated, wanted to be with you all..."

Blake moved over and patted the seat next to him. "Come on, have a seat; we've finished our business discussion, and would welcome a change. Not to minimize your distress..." Blake looked uncomfortable.

"Believe me, I could use some regular old chitchat—I need a break from doom and gloom." She smiled at Blake.

"Well," Sarah said, "no reason not to share with you the BIG news of the day. Not that it influences you, being in Philly, but it's real news around here!" Sarah pointed to the headlines.

Then they all started talking at once, each sharing a different perspective. And soon Vanessa was joining in.

*****

Rory excused herself and went to her office. She was dying to talk with Don, but couldn't call from her home or cell phones. She toyed with the idea of meeting him somewhere, but that was an emotional decision, not a practical one. So, that left only one option—calling his disposable phone from a pay phone. Looking at the clock, she realized that it was nearly time to pick up the girls from softball camp. If she left early, she'd have time to call Don before she picked the twins up from camp.

The group in the dining nook was still engaged in lively discussion, and hardly noticed when Rory left.

She got into her car and thought about the best pay phone location; there weren't many, she realized. She settled on one outside of a WAWA, which was on the way to the school.

Arriving there and finding the booth unoccupied, she dug around for change, hoping she had enough. With shaking hands, she dialed the number she'd committed to memory. Don answered and said abruptly, "I'm just leaving work; I'll call your number—assume you're in a booth—as soon as I get to my car."

Rory confirmed she was in a booth and he hung up. He sounded stressed; she was feeling guilty that she'd gotten him into this and hoped he wouldn't be hurt by it. It was certainly a bigger deal than he'd been involved in before, as far as she knew.

The ringing phone startled her, and she picked up immediately. It was Don.

"Mission accomplished, to quote one of my favorite Americans," he drawled. "Can you believe how this thing took off? Hot Damn! It's really hard to keep to myself, but of course, I know I have to." Don was elated.

"I'm glad you're not mad at me for dragging you into this..."

"Are you kidding? I'm delighted to be involved, and to help remove one serious scumbag from the bench!"

"Oh, I agree, I just hope you don't take any heat. And I need to tell you the latest, before you hear about it on the news. I mean, this is really up-to-the-minute news." And she went on to tell him of the afternoon's events at her office.

"Awesome! I'm glad he may be off the streets now. And I don't think he'll be quite so arrogant when he finds his legion of supporters have abandoned ship. I seriously doubt any of his cronies will want to represent him; he'll soon be a pariah." Don spoke dramatically.

"Listen," Rory said, "I've got to go pick up my girls—we'll find a way to talk later."

"Sounds good; talk to you later. Bye"

Rory was feeling so much better now that she'd spoken with Don. He seemed fine; he was just a natural risk taker, she concluded. As she was hanging up the phone, she saw movement out of the corner of her eye. The phone dropped from her hands as the navy blue BMW cruised by.

Chapter 33

Sarah had enjoyed the conversation; it seemed like it could go on longer, but she was beginning to feel the stress of the day. And it was nearly dinner time; she didn't want to put that burden on Rory. So she suggested, "Blake, do you mind dropping me back at my car? I'm running out of steam."

Sam was quick to add, "I'm ready to go, too, if that's okay, Blake."

"Sure thing," Blake answered. "I'm set."

Saying goodbye to everyone, the trio promised to check in with Rory the next day.

When they got into Blake's car, Sam asked Sarah, "Do you want me to drive you home? I think you may still be in shock…"

"That's a good idea if you don't mind picking me up tomorrow to get my car."

"Not at all," Sam answered. "Are you parked in a safe area?"

Sarah couldn't help but notice the smirk on Blake's face, but she chose to ignore it. Instead she said, "I think most of Media's pretty safe, but especially where I parked—across from the police station."

"It's pretty safe," Blake agreed, "but there was that unsolved murder several years ago—a young girl's body found burning in a trash heap."

"Hey, thanks for sharing, buddy," Sam replied sarcastically.

"I thought you should know...but yeah, Media is pretty safe."

Blake stopped next to Sam's car. The two got out and thanked him for the ride.

They got into Sam's car, and Sam asked, "Do you want to go out to eat? I hate the thought of you eating alone tonight."

"Why don't we get takeout and eat at my place? I'm not real hungry, but I could go for some Chinese—sound ok?"

"Yep—you got it! I'll drop you at your place and you can phone in an order to Peking while I go pick it up. I like chicken with black bean sauce. "

Stopping at Sarah's, she got out and Sam left for the restaurant.

Sarah had time for a quick shower and change of clothes before Sam was back.

They watched the news while they ate; it was riveting.

That is, until Sarah leaned over to get the remote, and somehow ended up in Sam's arms.

The news forgotten for the moment, they were both jolted by the buzzing of Sarah's cell.

"Hello," Sarah said somewhat breathlessly.

"Hey, Sarah, just wanted to make sure you were watching CNN; I think they have the best coverage," Rory said.

"We were just about to try that channel, thanks."

"OK, well, I won't keep you," Rory replied, with what sounded like a smirk. "Bye."

"She knows!" Sarah said, turning to Sam.

"So? No big deal, we're adults. Now, where were we?"

*****

Hours later, Sarah awoke, disoriented. She was in her bed but couldn't remember getting there. And Sam had been here; where was he?

Padding out to the living room, she found Sam, asleep on the couch, the sound on the TV turned down. With his hair flopping over his forehead, she'd never seen him looking so sexy. She bent down to kiss his forehead.

He awoke, sleepily rubbing his eyes and smiling.

"Thanks for tucking me in, Sam. But I hate to see you out here on the couch. My bed is much more comfortable," she said, leading the way to her room.

As they snuggled in her bed, Sam asked, "Are you sure this is what you want, Sarah?" He cupped her face and looked at her tenderly.

"It is; I really don't hook up with just anyone; you are very special."

Sam's smile said it all.

Chapter 34

Rory awoke early, her mind jumbled with so many different thoughts. She got up and showered, remembering vaguely hearing Marc leave a while ago. His work was keeping him busy as he prepared to go on vacation. Surely he understood why she'd be unable to join the family. But he didn't seem to understand that she was overwhelmed.

The navy blue BMW was her biggest concern right now. She'd been operating on the assumption the judge was involved in both murders. But if he was in a psych ward, as had been reported, who the hell was in the BMW? Did he have toadies doing his work? Somehow that didn't sound like his style. And besides, with the investigation heating up, in all likelihood, his cronies would distance themselves. *What am I missing?* She asked herself. No answers jumped out at her so she decided to have a no holds barred discussion with her staff when they showed up today. She smiled, knowing Sam and Sarah would be late.

But they surprised her when they knocked on her door a few moments later.

"Good morning," Sarah said. "Hope we're not too early."

"Nope, I'm ready to go. Looks like someone put coffee on before they left. Oh, and Alicia will probably be joining us for breakfast; she's doing better. She's open to talking about her mother, so don't feel constrained. After breakfast, she has an appointment with Dr. Grant, Korbin's therapist. Van will take her."

"Sounds as though you've been very busy taking care of other folks, how are you doing, Rory?" Sam's face showed concern.

"I'm doing ok, guys, and you've all been a big help. Just having you around makes things seem more normal, which I really need; I'm happy for your company."

Sam and Sarah smiled, and nodded. "It's been an incredible summer so far, despite the judge from hell," Sarah said.

Rory could feel love in the air; these two were radiant. Rory was a bit nostalgic as she remembered head-over-heels love with Marc. Nothing could compare with that. She hoped she and Marc could reclaim what she'd always thought was a solid marriage.

"You have a secret, Rory?" Sarah asked, teasing. "You've been smiling," she added.

"No secrets here, but I can tell you this—your secret is safe with me."

Sam and Sarah made no denials; they smiled, too. "Thanks, Rory—I told you, Sam, I told you she knew." Sarah said smugly.

Just then, Blake arrived at the door and came in to join them. "Sarah's car still at the police station? I noticed yours outside, Sam." He grinned, "I just noticed…"

"Blake, you want coffee?" Rory intervened. "And we can make more—what does everyone want?"

Sarah got up and joined Rory in the kitchen. "I was a short order cook one summer—I sucked—but I know how to fry an egg."

Vanessa and Alicia entered. "Just getting breakfast, put your orders in here," Sarah called out.

Eventually it was all sorted out and everyone got basically what he or she wanted. Rory was gratified to see that Alicia looked better; the daily doctoring had helped.

Conversation flowed as they ate. When it was time for Alicia and Van to leave, Rory leaned down to pick up Peaches, who'd been in hiding because of all the commotion and new, strange smells in the house. She settled in Rory's lap contentedly.

"Okay, we need to get to work. Blake, I assume you had my office phone rerouted here, and picked up any messages that arrived in the interim?"

"Yes, Boss, on both accounts. I screened your messages, and brought the ones that seemed most crucial." He handed her a stack of messages.

She leafed through them, commenting as she read. "Ok, Como got back to me about the tape from Jay's phone; they've verified that it was, in fact Kathie. That's good, I think!" She flipped through several, and stopped, looking stricken. "I need to call the coroner back. I need to do that now." She excused herself to use her office phone.

She was gone for over 15 minutes, and her staff was beginning to feel uncomfortable.

Rory came back looking drawn; the conclusion was obvious. She sat down, remaining quiet for a moment. "You know, I expected it to be ruled murder, but I still have trouble accepting it. I think I should call Dr. Grant and ask her advice before she sees Alicia." She pulled out her cell and punched in the number. Dr. Grant answered, and Rory identified herself, telling her the news she'd just received.

"I'm out of my depth here, Dr. Grant; I don't know if it should come from you or me."

Dr. Grant replied, "Now that I have that information, I'll have to decide based on my meeting with her, whether or not she's ready to hear it. In any case, I'll let you know the outcome, if Alicia gives permission."

"That sounds like a good idea—thanks so much. I know your appointment is soon, so I'll let you go. Bye now."

Rory was relieved and it showed on her face. "All right, let's talk about where we are with the case. As for me, I feel like I'm at a dead end, and I'll tell you why. For the past several weeks, ever since I took this case, a navy blue BMW has been showing up—I mean, a lot. I'd been assuming, since we've been looking into Keller, that it was him, or someone hired by him. But now that he's off the streets, I was surprised the BMW showed up yesterday when I went to pick up my girls. Once, when I was jogging near my house at dusk, he actually forced me off the road; I got a little banged up."

"Rory, who else have you told about this?" Blake seemed angry. "You could've been killed, and you never told us!"

"But, I wasn't, and I have confided in a friend of mine who's a State Trooper; he's been keeping an eye out." Rory spoke quietly.

"But, just yesterday, he followed you again; that's really creepy. He could hurt you!" Sarah was upset.

Sam said, "I'm really glad you've told us; maybe we could do some counter surveillance. You know, like if you call us and give your location when he's following you and we can follow him—it could work…"

Rory almost laughed, but realized he was serious. "I do appreciate your concerns, and it might work, but we can't focus too much on laying a trap for him—that could be a very dangerous game. My friend, Roland, the trooper, is always available and has already been helpful. I'll give you his cell number, and if you think it's necessary, you can call him."

That seemed to mollify the group and they wrote down the number.

"So," Rory began, "back to square one. Who are our suspects? Have we made too much of the appointment with JK? I don't think we can afford to wait until someone stumbles over something that implicates the judge. And I'm thinking that it's probably not him. Suggestions?"

She looked around at the group. Sam looked pensive, Sarah confused, and Blake, it appeared, was still angry. Silence reigned.

Sam spoke first. "I think we haven't fully explored other "JK" suspects. It seems to me that we have Jeremy Katz, and also his partner, Joe Klein. What do we know about them?"

Rory answered, "I've known Katz for years; not that we're buddies or anything. He's been acting somewhat strange lately, and I've attributed that to the loss of Kathie, and the fact that his partner's sick. Also, he drives a red Mercedes Benz.

As for Joe Klein, I think we can rule him out; he's been out battling cancer, and Jeremy thinks he may be terminal; he comes to the office only a few days a week."

Sarah spoke up, "It may be worth our while to do some investigating of Katz, anyway, just to rule him in or out. And he could have another car."

"Where would we even start with that?" Sam inquired.

Blake weighed in, "Well, I can tell you there's an informal network of legal assistants, like me, who know a lot of what's going on with attorneys and judges. I could tap into that and see where it leads."

"Sounds good," Rory answered. "I assume you never talk trash on me, Blake."

"Never!" Blake seemed insulted.

"Just kidding," Rory assured, "but if you want to get dirt, you have to give out something..."

"True," Blake said, "but, frankly, you're too clean."

"OK, enough about that," Rory was businesslike. "I really think our best bet is to look in Helen's house for anything that might give us an answer. There has to be a link between Kathie's and Helen's deaths. I think Helen knew something and maybe she's left something written..."

"Or maybe the killer took it," Sarah reasoned.

"Yeah," Rory sounded weary. "I'm not looking forward to the conversation I need to have with Alicia."

Just then, Rory's cell chirped. She answered immediately. "Hello?"

"Rory, this is Adele Grant, can you come right over?"

Chapter 35

Alicia sat next to Rory as they drove home from Dr. Grant's. She was overcome by a sense of relaxation and knew the sedative the doctor had given her was working. She could now view her meltdown at the doctor's office objectively.

Rory leaned over and patted her knee as she drove, asking "You feeling better, sweetie?"

"I am," she answered slowly. "I wish I could get rid of the damn pills," she said, clutching the prescription close to her chest. "But Rory, who would want to kill my mother and why? She was the sweetest, kindest person..." Tears streamed down Alicia's face. "Dr. Grant says I should cry, that it's part of the grieving process."

"She's absolutely right. And you must grieve; it's normal." Rory assured her. "And I can't imagine what kind of monster would kill your mother. But I'm almost certain it's the same person who killed Kathie Korbin. You might not know about that..."

"Yes... actually, I do. My mom mentioned last spring that a good friend who'd worked with her was killed. She was quite upset."

"That's one reason I was trying to contact your mom; she probably knew more about Kathie's last days than anyone. Also, I was concerned that the last time I'd seen your mom she hadn't been herself. When did *you* last see her?"

"Well, I came home for Mother's Day for a day or two. That's when she'd told me about Kathie. She was sad, but also seemed preoccupied. But she certainly wasn't having dizzy spells; I've no idea where that came from. She was fit, in fact, we'd been jogging together that weekend."

"That never rang true for me, either—the dizzy spells." Rory concurred. "There are so many things that don't add up; it's been a nightmare trying to solve this case. And I truly believe in Jeff Korbin's innocence."

"That's what my mom said, too." Alicia responded. "Now that I think about it, that was one of the things that'd upset her the most."

"Do you think your mom might've left anything in writing, if she'd had any suspicions as to who the killer was?" Rory inquired.

"She kept a journal, I know that. But would she have hidden it if she was frightened? I've no idea. But I know some of her hiding places. When can we get back into the house?" Alicia asked.

"Well, the police are still investigating, but we could probably get permission for you to go into the house to get clothes for your mother's funeral."

The comment predictably put a damper on the discussion. Alicia slumped in her seat and closed her eyes.

"I'm sorry to bring that up, Alicia. Why don't you rest; we're almost home."

Soon Rory pulled into her driveway.

Alicia jolted awake, disoriented.

Rory helped her out of the car and into the house. Vanessa had gotten home before them and was waiting at the door. Alicia fell into Van's embrace. Although tired, she spoke with determination. "Van, Rory and I will find out who killed my mom!"

Chapter 36

The killer sat in his BMW on a wooded lane not far from Rory's driveway. He could see anyone entering her place, but could not be seen by them. Today he'd seen her staff, a woman he wasn't familiar with, and, worst of all, Helen's daughter.

He was beginning to panic, fearing that Helen might have told her daughter about her suspicions. He'd regretted killing Helen, to an extent, but it really was her own fault for not minding her own business. It had been necessary, but now there was the daughter. How could he find out if she knew anything? And, of course, the more she talked to that meddling Rory, the more likely she was to remember something. This was getting out of hand. The first murder had been so easy; the cops helped out considerably. Of course, they always went for the husband. It was almost laughable how easy that setup was. And he'd have been home free if Rory hadn't taken Korbin's case. She was the bitch he really had to waste. So far she hadn't seemed intimidated by being followed. Well, except for that time the trooper had shown up.

What had she told the trooper? He was spiraling into desperation mode which would be his undoing. Rory was getting to him; she was too smart for her own good. Two cars entered Rory's drive. One was local police and the other was a trooper. *Oh my God*, he thought; *what did that mean?*

And then with a cold clarity he knew: they hadn't been fooled by Helen's fall. Her death must've been ruled a murder. It hadn't made the papers; he'd scanned them this morning. The news about the judge dominated the papers; that was to his benefit. But why wasn't it in the paper? Were the cops keeping it secret for some reason? Were they working with Rory to trap the perp? He'd have to lay low for a while. It was not safe for him to be parked so close; he felt vulnerable. Perhaps he should get out of town for a while, wait until things cooled down.

He couldn't be linked to Helen's death, unless of course she'd written something. He'd looked around her place for evidence that could be used against him for as long as was prudent, and tried not to disturb anything. He didn't think he'd left any prints, but he'd been pretty rattled; she'd put up quite a fight. There was probably nothing; maybe she hadn't known anything, but she'd looked at him speculatively and he'd assumed...

Oh well—too late now. There was only one thing to do — lay low.

Seeing no movement on the road or in the driveway, he inched out of his hiding place. Then he took off as fast as possible.

Chapter 37

Detective Hanover and Officer Jamison entered Rory's home and showed their ID. She ushered them to her office, where her staff had assembled and she offered coffee. Her friend, Trooper Johnson had come to see if he could be of assistance. Roland walked around the grounds of Rory's home before going in.

Alicia and Vanessa had gone to the Yates house to get clothes for the funeral. There was still a police presence there, but the investigation had concluded. Rory hoped Alicia had found her mother's journal, and had remembered to note if anything had been disturbed. Alicia was doing better every day, Rory thought. It seemed that focusing on finding her mother's murderer had given her purpose.

Now settled in her office, Rory was prepared to answer questions. She knew she'd be walking a fine line here, but was accustomed to that.

The detective began the questioning. "I understand you're under a lot of stress, what with knowing the victim and now taking care of her daughter. We appreciate your willingness to talk with us. Obviously the judge is being investigated on numerous levels, but our focus is on his threats towards Ms. Justice. We were also given information that he'd previously threatened you. Can you tell us more about that?"

"Certainly," Rory took a deep breath. "As you know, I'm representing Mr. Korbin who has been charged with murder. Having very little information, I decided to observe some Protection from Abuse hearings. As it turned out, the day I observed, Judge Keller was hearing PFA's. I sat for the morning hearings and came back just before the afternoon hearings started. When I realized that I'd left my briefcase in the courtroom, I went in to get it. I was startled to see Judge Keller on the bench and a young woman who'd been granted a PFA that morning, standing before him. But I gathered my briefcase and went back to the lobby. I'd barely taken a seat when the woman strode quickly out of the courtroom, with a look of utter disgust on her face. She left the building immediately." Rory paused for breath. "Of course, I wondered what had happened, and at the time I thought it unusual, perhaps unethical, for the judge to be speaking with her informally. "

"So, you're saying," Detective Hanover said, "that a judge seldom, if ever, speaks with a plaintiff personally, except during a hearing? Is that basically it?"

"I'm saying," Rory clarified, "that I've never known that type of exchange to take place. If a plaintiff wishes to speak with the judge outside of the courtroom, it would be arranged by his or her attorney, and would probably take place in the judge's chambers. What I saw was irregular, to say the least."

"So," the detective continued, "what were you thinking, and what did you do as a result of observing this encounter?"

"Well, it occurred to me immediately that Judge Keller had granted the PFA for Kathie Korbin. And I decided to have my interns, Sarah and Sam, research PFA cases in general, and to specifically look for any irregularities in Keller's cases. So, the next day, I think, they started their search in the archives."

"And the threats from Judge Keller to you, when did they take place?" Officer Jamison asked.

"I think it happened a day or two after I observed him. I actually have it on tape, which happened by accident because we'd just been reviewing a tape I'd made of an interview with Korbin. When the judge stormed in, I was ready to record my impressions. I have it here, so we can play it. Do you want to listen to it now?

Both officers indicated they did.

Blake set up the tape recorder and hit play. The judge's voice came across in a loud, angry tone: "How dare you spy on me! What do you think you're doing? Do you have any idea I can end your career like this?" A snap of fingers was audible. "Stop snooping!"

"That's it," Rory said. "Sam and Sarah had come back for something and were in the doorway to hear at least part of it. He nearly collided with them as he left."

"OK. So what did you make of this threat?" the detective asked.

"I thought he was angry that I'd seen him and the plaintiff in an unusual exchange. It made me wonder what he had to hide, so we felt we were justified to look into Judge Keller's affairs." Rory answered. "We didn't have much to go on in Korbin's defense, so anything unusual was fair game."

"Why do you think he went after your intern the other day?" Officer Jamison inquired.

"Somehow, Keller found out that Sam and Sarah were looking through cases in the archives. I learned that quite by accident, when I went looking for them there. They weren't where I knew they'd been working and I was about to leave, when I heard the door open and heard loud stomping coming in my direction. I ducked just in time. Then I heard Keller muttering something about 'stupid kids, need to mind their own f—ing business;' it was similar in tone to what he'd said to me."

"You're sure it was Keller? You said you heard him, but did you see him?" the detective inquired.

"I am sure it was Keller; his voice is etched into my brain, probably from the first encounter, and from listening to the tape. But, no, I didn't see him. I was hiding and I was terrified, so I didn't move. In fact, I waited a few minutes before I felt safe enough to leave." Rory shivered involuntarily at the memory.

"Have there been any other encounters with the judge?" Detective Hanover asked.

"Well, he heard Korbin's bail hearing. It was scheduled to go before another judge, but Keller showed up. Even the DA looked surprised. Of course, he refused to grant bail, and the look he gave me was chilling. So, I guess I'd have to say he has it in for me. And I wondered what we were getting close to."

"What did you think?" Officer Jamison asked.

"I guess it sounds nuts, but I was wondering what, if anything, he had to do with Kathie Korbin's death. After all, that's what I was investigating..."

"And do you still think that?" Jamison asked.

"I don't know what to think! It seems he's now being investigated for irregularities similar to what I saw. And Helen's death, which I think is connected to Kathie's murder, took place when he was in custody..."

"That's a separate case, but I'd be interested in your thoughts on the subject. I assume she was a friend of yours." The detective commented.

"She was a friend of mine, but also of Kathie's. I'd been trying to reach her for at least the last week to see if Kathie had revealed anything to her that would point to the killer. I never reached her." Rory's voice dropped. "Anyway, I do believe the two deaths are connected; I think Helen knew something, or at least the killer thought she knew something. But who the killer might be..."

"More coffee?" Rory asked, to break the tension. She excused herself to get it. Seeing peripheral movement, Rory looked out the kitchen window and was shocked to see Roland sprint across the lawn, jump into his cruiser and take off.

Chapter 38

Rory was deeply engaged in conversation with several people when Alicia and Vanessa returned. It was basically pandemonium. When Rory noticed them, she went straight to them.

"We have a bit of a situation here; my friend Roland, Trooper Johnson, was here while we were talking with the police. He said he just wanted to keep an eye on things. So, when I came out to the kitchen for more coffee, I saw Roland run to his cruiser and take off. We haven't heard from him since, so I don't know what happened."

"Wow!" Alicia responded, "What do you think happened?"

"Well, I assume he spotted the BMW, and took off after it, but not having had that confirmed, I don't know for sure." Changing the subject, Rory asked, "Did you find anything at the house, Alicia?"

"It didn't look as if anything had been disturbed, but I couldn't find my mother's journal, and I know where she normally kept it. So, either she'd hidden it very well, or the murderer took it."

"But if the murderer had taken it, I wonder why he's still following me? It doesn't add up. Jeez, I hope Roland has some answers for us—he's been gone what, a half-hour?" Rory was pensive, nervously chewing her lip. "He could've at least called. I hope he's ok."

"We could try to put out feelers, if you want, Rory," Officer Jamison offered.

"Thanks, but let's just give it a few more minutes; I'm sure he's ok."

Jamison went out, with Hanover trailing behind; they'd decided to see if there was any chatter on their radio.

The rest of them reassembled in the nook.

Ten minutes later, the officer and detective came in. "There's nothing, so far, on the radio, maybe that's good."

Waiting was always the most difficult part, Rory thought. She couldn't still her mind; her thoughts were racing. And she was concerned for Roland; he'd been doing her a favor. But, she consoled herself; he knew what he was doing.

Conversation was sporadic and inconsequential; everyone was just waiting.

Rory's cell rang, and she pounced on it as conversation stopped. "Oh, hi Marc," the disappointment in her voice was unmistakable.

"Gee, I'm sorry if I got you at a bad time," Marc's tone was sarcastic.

"Yeah, well, it's a long story, and we're waiting for Roland to get back and…"

"Gotcha," Marc said abruptly, "See you tonight. Bye"

Rory hung up, both disappointed and somewhat regretful at having cut Marc off. Everyone was on pins and needles. Sitting idly didn't help; it just increased the anxiety.

Rory suggested that Alicia, Vanessa and she retreat to her office to begin the unwelcome, but necessary, planning of the memorial service.

Alicia had brought clothes for her mother, although she was being cremated, as had been specified in Helen's will. They'd visit the funeral home this afternoon, Rory told Alicia. She knew Alicia wanted some time alone with her mother's body before the cremation. Rory understood this, but hoped the undertaker had restored Helen to some semblance of herself. Rory still had nightmares of Helen's crumpled and decomposing body at the bottom of the stairs; she awoke in terror often as the vivid images filled her dreams.

The three were wrapping up plans for Helen's memorial service when they heard loud voices from the kitchen. Rory virtually flew to the other room. Roland stood in the doorway; everyone was shouting questions at him.

Rory ran to him, exclaiming, "Roland, thank God you're ok—what happened?"

Roland appeared dejected. "I lost him Rory, I lost the son-of-a-bitch!"

Chapter 39

Roland sat in Rory's nook, with his head in his hands. The crowd had dispersed. He wasn't sure where everyone had gone, but, like magic they'd all disappeared. He was left with Rory, who came to sit with him.

She just sat quietly for a moment sipping her tea; his sat untouched. He looked over at her and tried for a smile. He knew he'd have to tell the story again; in all the commotion, he was sure she'd heard only bits and pieces.

"OK, Rory," Roland took a deep breath, "maybe it'll help to tell it again; perhaps I'll remember an important detail or something…"

"In your own time, Roland," Rory answered. "It's just good to have some quiet around here; it's been a circus."

"Now's as good a time as any," he sighed. "As I was walking around your property, I saw something glinting in the sun, across the road, hidden by trees. I was walking back to my car for some binoculars, when the car, a blue BMW, took off from that spot and raced past your house. I didn't think he'd seen me, so I ran to my car and took off behind him. Actually, I kept my distance, hoping to follow him home. I knew I had no legit reason to stop him. I got close enough to read his plate, 'JK', imagine that! I must've slowed a bit as I called the license in, because when I looked up, he was tearing down the road. I decided not to use my siren, hoping he'd be lulled into thinking I wasn't pursuing him. Turns out, I was wrong; when I crested a hill, I didn't see him anywhere. There was a four-way intersection, and I looked down each road, but saw nothing."

"He's always pulled the disappearing act with me, too, but I never tried to follow him. So, did you hear back about the plate? That's the part I missed before," Rory added.

"Yes, I did, and I thought I was onto something. The plate is registered to a corporation, for God's sake! 'Jonas Kapital' is the name, and the address was on Morton St. in Chester, down by the old ship yard. So, wanting to come back with something, I went straight there. It took a while to find—you know what a rabbit warren those streets are—probably because I was looking for a business, but instead found a vacant storefront; looked like no one had been there in years. There was a rental sign on it with a phone number, and I called it, but, no surprise, the phone had been disconnected. So, I was at a dead end with nothing. I'm really sorry, Rory, I'd hoped we might finally conclude this business."

"Interesting, that all this time I'd thought of 'JK' as a person, well, I guess it still could be. I can't believe a corporation is after me. At least it ties 'JK' to the case, whoever that might be. I'm guessing I won't be followed by that car any time soon!"

"Maybe not," Roland agreed. "Of course, I never got a look at the driver. I'm thinking if I were him, I'd leave town for a while, until things cool off. But, who knows, maybe he's desperate. At the very least, I think I put a scare in him; he'll be more careful. And you won't have to look over your shoulder as you go to the funeral; I doubt he'll be there. But, I will; I'll be scanning the crowd and I won't be in uniform. And I'll be driving an unmarked car."

"That's a good idea, I appreciate you coming."

"Well, I'm in it now, Rory! I'll see it to the end with you, and hopefully that will be soon." Looking at his watch, Roland said, "Time for me to be off; I'll be in touch. The service is tomorrow, right—10:00 AM?"

"Right—I'll see you then."

Rory spent the rest of the afternoon putting the house back in order. She enjoyed having everyone around, but it took a toll on her. She realized how much she'd missed talking the case over with Marc; he'd always helped her see it more clearly. She sighed, knowing their road back wouldn't be easy. She took a pile of what she considered junk, to the attic, among the items was Marc's high school yearbook; interesting, she'd never looked at it, and didn't have the time now.

When she finally looked at her watch, she saw it was time to get the girls from camp—*where had this day gone?* she wondered. She hadn't given a moment's thought to dinner. Well, there was only so much she could do; she'd worry about that later.

As she drove the short distance to the field, she found herself looking for the BMW. She knew it was foolish, but she couldn't shake it. Agreeing with Roland, she thought that, unless he was certifiable, her stalker would lay low for a while.

The girls chatted incessantly on the way home; that was fine with Rory, because she was still thinking about the day's events. Her cell chirped, but she wouldn't answer while she was driving. She saw the call was from her former partner, Charlie. That made her smile—she'd definitely call him back.

Arriving home, the girls got out while Rory stayed in the car to call Charlie.

"Hey, Rory thanks for getting back to me!" Charlie boomed.

"Can't resist, Charlie—what's up?"

"Well, I just wanted to gossip about the judge—not that you have any inside knowledge…"

"Oh, a fishing expedition, eh?" Rory smiled. "I don't know nuthin' about it; that's my story and I'm sticking to it!"

"That's what I figured. But have you heard that he's been released from the hospital? My sources tell me he's now wearing an ankle bracelet, and got out on an obscene amount of bail."

"Oh, shit! One more thing to worry about," Rory complained. "I truly haven't been following the case, because

Helen's daughter Alicia is staying here with her roommate. That's another nightmare, Helen's death, I mean."

"That is sad about Helen's fall..."

"Oh, you're outta the loop on that one. But you can't say a word—promise?"

"Of course, but I'm not liking the sound of this," Charlie replied.

"Well, the coroner's report calls it murder; that hasn't been made public yet, and I don't think it's leaked. As for me, I'm almost certain that her death is connected to Kathie Korbin's. I just haven't found the link. But, I'm working on it, and after the memorial service, I'll have more time to devote to it. Oh—have to go—Alicia and her friend have just returned; we'll do lunch again, soon. Bye"

Getting out of her car, Rory met the girls in the driveway. They were each carrying a huge bag, and the smell wafting towards her was heavenly.

"What do we have *here*? Something smells mighty good!" Rory exclaimed.

Alicia and Vanessa both smiled. Van said, "We thought it was time that someone besides you got dinner."

"And neither of us is especially good at creating gourmet delights, so...."

"If that's what I think it is, mmmm!" Rory was salivating.

"Well, your daughters said you liked Indian, so we were lucky to find one so close—in Media." Alicia remarked.

"Oh, let me guess—'Sheri Punjab;' I love the place. And they have a $10 lunch buffet to die for!"

They continued talking as they entered the house. Alex was in the kitchen, bemoaning the fact there was no food. She quickly changed her tune, as she smelled the aroma of Indian food. "Oh, my God, is that what I think it is?"

Alicia put the bag under Alex's nose, playfully, saying, "What does it smell like?"

"Heaven! I'm so hungry!" Alex exclaimed.

Rory said, "That was so nice of you girls—I really appreciate it; I had no plan for dinner, but for sure, I couldn't have chosen better. If you girls are all as hungry as Alex, you can go ahead and eat—just leave some for Marc and me. Not sure when he'll be home."

The smell of food had brought Kate into the room, so the four of them tucked into it.

Rory went to her office to review the final arrangements and make sure all was in order. It would be a pretty straightforward service. The minister from the Unitarian church Helen attended would officiate. She looked over the readings she'd do and thought about what she wanted to say.

She was so engrossed in her thoughts, that the phone startled her. She answered immediately, assuming it was Marc. It wasn't.

"Don't think you'll get away with this!" rasped the now-familiar voice of the judge. "I know you're behind this, this travesty, and there will be payback!"

Chapter 40

"God Damn! That bastard is *still* after me!" Rory's wail was heard throughout the house.

After exchanging looks of alarm around the table, her daughters, followed by Alicia and Van ran towards Rory's office.

Rory was standing stock still, holding the phone, her face drained of all color. "What more can the crazy fuck do to me?"

Kate and Alex embraced their mother, hung up the phone and led her to a chair. "What happened, Mom? Who was on the phone?" Alex asked, her face mirroring the concern of her twins.

Rory just sat, facing ahead and didn't answer at once. Van and Alicia had left the doorway to give Rory privacy with her girls. "The judge, it was the judge. Threatening me again." Her voice was emotionless.

"Well, at least you have some recourse now; he's been arrested. How'd he get out, by the way?" Kate was trying to get a response from Rory.

"Charlie called me earlier today to tell me he'd been released from the psych ward, posted an outrageous sum of bail. He's also got an ankle bracelet, courtesy of the state. So, he can't stalk me in person; now he's calling me! The nerve! The unmitigated gall!" Rory finally got angry.

"Like Kate said, you can fight back; that was really stupid of him. You need to call the DA or the police, or whoever..." Alex was glad to see Rory recover.

Alicia and Van approached the doorway cautiously. Alicia was carrying a cup of tea.

"Come in—sorry for the outburst. Thanks for the tea, Alicia." Rory accepted the cup gratefully. After taking a sip, she put the cup down, and said, "As you no doubt heard, the judge has now threatened me by phone, basically saying he will pay me back. He thinks I brought about his downfall—ha! The girls are right, though, I do need to report this. I mean, he's already been charged with Terroristic Threats, how stupid, or maybe *nuts*, can he be?"

"Who can you call, Mom?" Kate asked.

"I'm calling the head DA; I think he's prosecuting the case, at least he should be. I need to collect myself and approach this logically. In fact, I need to meet with him in person; I wonder if he's left for the day. I'll call now and at least leave a message." Rory was feeling stronger, acting more decisively.

She knew the number cold and dialed it. The call was picked up by the DA's secretary, Leigh. "Hi, Leigh, it's Rory Chandler, is Conner in by any chance?"

"Yes, he's still here; sort of enmeshed in the Keller case. What can I do for you?"

"Well, I wanted to set up an appointment to meet with him, about that very case; it's urgent," Rory added.

"Let me just buzz him, Rory."

A moment later, Conner McClain was on the phone, "Rory, you have something urgent about Judge Keller?"

"Yes, yes, I do, and I'd prefer not to talk on the phone."

"OK, can you come right over? God knows, I'll be here for a while."

"I can," Rory answered. "I'll be right there."

"He wants to see me right away," Rory announced. "Do I need to change?"

"No, Mom, you look fine. Do you want us to drive you?" Alex asked.

"I'm fine now, really. Just stay here and tell your dad what happened, and maybe leave me some food?"

"Sure, Mom, no worries. Just take care." Kate said.

Rory left hurriedly, shouting over her shoulder, "Don't answer the phone or let anyone in unless you know who it is!"

She was facing rush hour traffic, which to be sure, wasn't much of a challenge here in the suburbs. She used the time to think how to be most effective. She knew the head DA, Conner McClain, fairly well. She liked his no-nonsense approach to the law. And he was fair. Best of all, he didn't appear to use his office for political gain.

Parking near the courthouse was not difficult, as most were leaving at this hour.

Walking up the three flights to McClain's office, Rory was winded; she stopped to catch her breath, and regain her composure. Having done both, she entered the office.

Leigh was still at her desk. "He's ready for you, go right in," she smiled at Rory.

Rory returned the smile, "Thanks, Leigh."

Conner looked up as she entered. She was surprised to see another person there. Conner got up to shake Rory's hand, "You know, Stan Como, he's working with me on this."

"Sure do, we're on opposite sides of the Korbin case." Rory nodded to Stan, and they all sat down.

Conner led off the conversation; "This is going to be a real bitch, this case. We have to proceed carefully; really, this is big news everywhere." Rory and Stan nodded in agreement.

"So," the DA said, "what do you have on the judge?"

"To give you a brief history, since I'm representing Jeff Korbin, my interns have been reviewing PFA cases, and I've observed some hearings. I watched Keller presiding over a few. He came to my office to threaten me shortly after I observed him in court. Somehow, he also found out my interns were reviewing PFA cases—many of which were his—and I was in the archives near where my interns had been working when he came down looking for them. I hid and heard him muttering about 'those kids snooping.' They had, in fact, found some interesting trends; Judge Keller presided over the largest number of PFA cases. Also, some of his rulings have been overturned by the State Supreme Court. In a nutshell, that's why he's targeted me and my interns."

"So," Conner prompted, "when's the last time you heard from him?"

Rory looked at her watch, "About a half hour ago, just before I called you."

"He came to your office?" McClain was incredulous.

"No, he called me at home, said he knew I was behind what was happening to him, and promised 'paybacks.' That's the latest."

"And are you responsible for sending the tape to the AG and press?" McClain asked.

"No," Rory replied honestly. "But I can't say I'm sorry about it."

"He's pissed off a lot of people—lawyers, clients, judges," Como added. "The list of possible suspects could stretch around this courthouse. I doubt we'll ever know, or care, for that matter, who did it. It took brass ones, and I take my hat off to whoever it was." He winked at Rory, which she pretended not to notice. "He's not getting much of a sympathy vote in the legal community, and frankly, most of us are relieved that he's no longer the President Judge; he gave the court a bad name. So I guess, or hope, that the next President Judge will be selected on merit."

"Wouldn't that be nice?" Rory commented.

"Okay, so what to do about Rory's latest encounter with the judge?" Conner asked.

"I think he's violated the terms of his bail; it should be revoked. He might learn some humility in prison," Stan said emphatically.

"He might deserve that, but I honestly think he's psychotic; I'm not sure why they released him," Rory weighed in.

"You're probably right, Rory, but, our mental health system is broken. And I'm thinking he may have sociopathic tendencies, so it's easy to fool the professionals." Stan countered.

"True," Rory agreed.

"So," Conner got back on track, "I'll see about setting up a review of bail hearing; the State will ask for his incarceration. You'll need to be there Rory."

"Sure, by the way, who's defending him?" Rory asked, out of curiosity.

"Well, the usual suspects—his cronies—have fled the scene. Jeremy Katz is representing him."

Chapter 41

The day of the memorial service promised to be as gloomy as the affair itself. The weather did nothing to lift Rory's spirits. It was humid, with dark, foreboding clouds, and rain predicted later in the day. She'd slept fitfully, even after taking pills; she just wanted the day to be over.

Knowing she had to get herself together for Alicia, Rory showered and dressed early. She made coffee, and got out cereal, bagels and muffins for an easy, quick breakfast, aware that no one might be hungry. She knew she wasn't.

Marc came downstairs, dressed and ready to go. "How are you holding up?" Marc caught Rory up in a hug.

"I just need to get through today," Rory answered.

"I'm here for you, Rory." Marc assured her.

Before long everyone but Alicia was in the kitchen getting breakfast. There wasn't much talking. No one felt the need or desire to keep up conversation. Blake arrived, looking dignified and somber in a dark blue suit. He greeted everyone, and Rory offered him breakfast; he took only coffee.

Alicia entered the kitchen looking flushed, "My dad called last night—it was quite a shock; I haven't seen him since he remarried and moved to California two years ago. Apparently the police notified him and questioned him. He's coming for the service today." She gulped and had tears in her eyes. "He sounded pretty broken up; I was surprised and I'm a little nervous," she confessed.

"Sure, that's understandable," Rory said. "But I'm glad he's coming."

Alicia joined the others for a quick breakfast, and finished just in time for the arrival of the funeral director. They all proceeded to the stretch limo.

After a short drive, they arrived. Rory was surprised and touched at the number of people gathered outside already. The crowd moved aside respectfully as the seven of them walked into the funeral home.

Rory and her family along with Alicia stood in front of the altar with the urn of Helen's ashes on display. The door was opened to the public and people began to stream in. Sam and Sarah were near the front of the line; Sarah had tears in her eyes, and Sam had his arm around her. Looking towards the front door, Rory thought it seemed like a never-ending line; she knew nearly everyone. Jeremy Katz was accompanied by his wife, Cary. Tears were staining his face as he whispered his condolences to Alicia. "Your mother was the best..." he managed. He hugged Rory, and thanked her for taking care of Alicia.

Alicia gasped. Rory followed her gaze and saw Alicia's father, whom Rory hadn't seen since the divorce. Rory went to him and ushered him to the front so he could stand with Alicia. There was a long and tearful embrace before other mourners came to the front.

Rory saw regret and grief etched into Jim Yates's face. He stood with his arm around Alicia protectively, as if he could somehow take away her pain. Alicia appeared to welcome his presence, and leaned into him.

The crowd kept coming; Rory was surprised at the number of judges present. This was truly a fitting accolade for a wonderful person; Helen had touched many people's lives with her grace and humor, and they were all paying their respects.

By 10:30, the service was ready to begin; the funeral director and his staff instructed people to take their seats. Some of the mourners had left, but many more chose to stay.

The service was simple but eloquent. Given the opportunity, several people stood to praise Helen. Jeremy tried to say a few words, but soon gave over to his emotions; Rory had never seen him so broken up. His reaction appeared to be genuine.

By 11:30, the service ended. Friends and family were invited to the luncheon. Alicia and her father stood by the urn, arms around each other. Alicia slumped in her father's arms, sobbing.

Then, seeming to gather strength, Alicia lifted the urn and took it with her.

Rory, her family, Vanessa, and Blake stood respectfully at the front door, waiting for Alicia and her father to join them, her tears falling. "You did well by your friend, Rory; you planned an amazing sendoff." Marc tightened his arm around Rory; she put her head on his shoulder. "So many people came to honor her."

Rory was too choked up to answer, so she just nodded. She glanced outside and saw Roland, but he got lost in the crowd before she could talk to him. She hoped to see him at the luncheon.

*****

After the luncheon, Rory invited some people back to her house. She was surprised when Jeremy and his wife entered. Jeremy had collected himself, and indicated he wanted to speak with her. Rory took him aside, curious. He said, "I called Joe as soon as I found out about Helen, but he didn't answer his cell. I've left several messages, but he never got back. I don't know what's going on, but I don't really like to call his home—you know, in case he's in the hospital or something. Anyway, I'm sorry he's not here, and I'm hoping it's not because he's too sick or something."

"Well, let's be optimistic, unless we hear something," Rory replied, wanting to move on and speak with other people.

"Oh, and Rory, sorry about defending the judge; frankly, I need the money…"

"What can I say, Jeremy? That's business." And she excused herself.

She went to the kitchen and helped the girls and Marc put out desserts and drinks.

Later she noticed Sarah and Alicia, with their heads together, tears on both their faces. It looked to Rory as though they were sharing the grief of losing their mothers.

Jim Yates was conversing with Vanessa. Blake and Sam were keeping each other company.

Rory looked up as a tall figure stood in the doorway. She immediately went to Roland. "Glad you could come..." There was an odd look on Roland's face that silenced her.

He spoke tersely, "BMW showed up at the funeral home. He took off real quick. The bastard's still here."

Chapter 42

The day following the funeral Rory forced herself to go back to the office; she had so much catching up to do. Many other cases needed her attention. Sam and Sarah could work on some of them; others, she'd have to manage by herself. Everyone was busy in the office.

One of her priorities was to visit Korbin; she wasn't sure how much outside news got through to the inmates, but she was certain he'd heard about the judge and probably Helen as well. She needed to catch up with him, and felt she owed him a face-to-face visit.

Much of her work was repetitive drudgery and she had a hard time keeping focused. She thought about the previous day's funeral; she'd been pleased that Alicia's father had come and it seemed to be helping Alicia immeasurably. Her father had, in fact, postponed his return trip to spend some time with her. Although Rory had offered Jim Yates a room in her home, Alicia wanted them to stay at her mother's house. Van had gone back to the apartment in the city, which left Rory's home feeling empty.

Rory was dying to get into Helen's house and thoroughly search it. That couldn't happen until Saturday, when Jim Yates left. Rory's family was leaving for vacation then, too. She'd have more time to focus on finding the link, whatever and whomever that was.

When she finally looked at the clock, it was lunch time. On impulse, she called Don at his office and he agreed to meet her for lunch. Though they felt the heat was off, they decided to lunch outside of Media. She told Blake she'd probably be out for the rest of the day, since she was visiting Korbin after lunch. He'd nodded, hardly looking up from his work; she'd left a lot for him to do.

Arriving at The Flying Pig, in Malvern, quite a hike from Media, Rory found Don already seated. He was drinking a beer, but got up to hug her. "Want one?" he asked, pointing to the beer.

Rory screwed up her face, "At lunch? No not really." She sat down and glanced at the menu, looking for and finding the salad offerings. She decided quickly and put the menu down.

"What're you having?" she asked.

"Not rabbit food, like you'll get," Don teased. "Real men..."

"I know, I know, eat meat!" she interrupted.

They were laughing when the wait staff came to take their orders. Then they got down to the business at hand. Rory said, "I spoke with McClain the other day..."

"As in the DA?" Don interrupted.

"Yep, I called for an appointment and went straight over two days ago. I think it was two days, but things have been so nuts with the funeral and all..."

"Yeah, sorry not to have been there, but I thought it best..."

"You're probably right," Rory agreed. "Anyway, it was when Keller was released from the psych ward, and then posted a very large bail. He's also got an ankle bracelet, did you know?"

"Yes, I heard all that from my sources, and I heard about him threatening your intern, and resisting arrest..."

"I'm impressed. But I bet you don't know why I went to the DA, do you?"

"I actually don't, but I know you'll enlighten me," Don said drily.

"I'll be happy to. Charlie called to tell me the judge got out on bail. I didn't think much about it; I was planning Helen's funeral when the phone rang. Expecting it to be Marc, I answered right away. It was the judge. He told me he knew I was the one ruining his life and said there'd be 'payback.'"

"Holy Shit! He's either a dumb fuck or way over the edge," Don replied.

"He's probably both," Rory answered. "Anyway, I was, like, in total shock. I decided to take it to the top, and I did. McClain said they're going to revoke his bail and put him in the slammer until his hearing. And, get this; you know who's defending him?" Don shook his head. "Jeremy Katz; he was at the funeral yesterday and wanted to apologize to me for that. I just cut him off and said something like, 'that's business.' He said he needed the money, but he's always looked pretty affluent to me."

"Well, he is pretty choosy about his clientele, until now, that is." Don chuckled. "You're really in the loop now, aren't you? I guess I can't divulge any of this…"

"No, please don't. But, oh, I almost forgot the best part. When I was telling McClain about what the judge said Como was in the room. The DA had just asked me if it was true that I'd contacted the AG and news media. I said 'no,' and Como gave me this sly wink, and then went on to say they'd probably never find out who it was because the judge had pissed off so many people. I think it was his way of telling me they weren't going to pursue it. But," Rory warned, "We still have to swear ourselves to secrecy on this, agreed?"

"Yes," Don said reluctantly, "But it really was my best work, so far."

"It was awesome!" Rory agreed. "But I'm sure you'll have more battles…"

"Yeah, there are a few things waiting in the wings. And you're right, it's best for me to maintain my anonymity, like other superheroes!" Don laughed.

They'd concluded their secretive discussion when their lunch arrived. The rest of their conversation was gossipy and banal. When they'd finished, Rory grabbed the check, saying, "I owe you big for this one; I'll be buying you lunches for quite a while."

Don smiled, saying, "Yet another perk of my job; thanks!"

They parted ways in the parking lot, and Rory headed to the prison, which was more or less, on the way back.

Arriving at the prison, Rory was surprised that she felt no anxiety. She wondered if maybe the scare she'd survived in the archives had cured her claustrophobia. It was ironic to think the judge could've had any kind of positive impact on her life.

She soon found herself in the usual stark interview room.

Korbin came into the room looking better than she'd seen him recently. Smiling, he thanked her for coming.

She apologized for not coming sooner, and he cut her off.

"Look, I know you've been under a lot of stress; we do get news in here. I heard about Helen; that was awful. I think I told you she and Kathie were good friends, but actually, Helen was more like a mother to her. You knew her, too, right?"

"Yes, I was very fond of Helen; her daughter's been staying with me." Rory felt she shouldn't tell Korbin the truth about Helen's death.

As if reading her mind, Korbin said, "Word around here is that it wasn't an accident, but you can't believe everything you hear."

"No, you can't," Rory said without emotion. "Anyway, I wanted to tell you I met with your sister, Jay…"

"She told me last time she visited; she said she really likes you," Korbin interrupted. "She also said you seemed pretty excited about the tape, you know… for evidence."

"Yes, I took it straight to the DA, and I just found out that they were able to confirm that it was Kathie's voice, so they'll enter it into evidence. I requested they get your cell phone from the police, but I haven't heard about that yet. All in all, I'm pleased with the case we're building."

"I am, too, but I learned from the last hearing not to get my hopes up too high." Korbin spoke without rancor.

"That's always a good idea, because you never know…"

"…What's going to happen in court," Korbin answered for her.

"You've been paying attention," Rory smiled. "I'd best be going, but I'll be back if anything crops up. You take care, now."

Leaving the prison, her cell rang just as Rory was getting into the car. The number was unfamiliar to her, but she answered anyway.

"Rory, it's Jay—I listened to you and went to my friend's house with the kids. Thank God I took your advice! My home has been ransacked!"

Chapter 43

"Don't touch anything!" Rory advised Jay. "Call your local police; I'll call the DA's office and come right over. Is anyone with you? Are you okay?"

"My neighbor Robin is with me; I called to ask her if she'd heard anything…"

"And, did she?" Rory asked.

"She thought maybe a few nights ago she'd heard some noise, but assumed it was raccoons getting into the garbage." Jay answered.

"OK, I'm glad you have someone with you; just stay put and I'll be there. And don't forget to call the police."

She quickly placed a call to the DA's office. She was able to get through to McClain more quickly than she'd expected. "Hi Connor, it's Rory. I'm calling about the Korbin case now…"

"Como's handling that, right?" he asked.

"Yes, he is. I'm not trying to bypass him, it's just that what I'm asking has to be approved by you. A week or so ago, I gave him the tape from Korbin's sister's answering machine. On it was Kathie Korbin's last call. Como's confirmed that it was Kathie. I just spoke with Korbin's sister, Jay, and learned that her house has been ransacked. I have a gut feeling it's related to the tape I gave Como. Since your office is already working on that case, I was hoping maybe you could send someone to have a look. Jay's calling the local police, but I'd like to have an expert from your office to be there, too. I'm heading to Jay's now."

"I hear, you, Rory, that's a good idea; I'll send someone; just give me the address."

After giving Jay's address, she said, "Thanks so much! Oh, and please tell Como what's up; I don't want him to think I went over his head," Rory added.

"Sure thing; thanks for letting me know." Connor rang off.

Rory was so anxious to get to Jay's she almost forgot that her girls were waiting to be picked up from camp; a quick call to Alex solved the problem; she assured Rory they could get a ride.

"Oh, and Alex, please tell your dad I'm running late."

"Okaaaay," she sighed.

Rory chose to ignore the reproach in her daughter's voice. This couldn't be easy for the girls, or Marc. But she'd had that thought too often of late, so she pushed the now familiar guilt away.

Jumping into her car she contemplated the latest development in her case. She was relieved she'd had the foresight to give the tape to Como, but she wouldn't have done it if she hadn't seen the BMW. And the logical conclusion was that Jay's house wouldn't have been ransacked if the killer hadn't seen Rory there. The next question was how did the killer know Jay had the tape, or even that there was a tape? Perhaps he was just looking for any evidence that might incriminate him. The more she thought, it seemed, the less sure she was of anything. She'd have to hope they were able to find prints at Jay's.

Arriving at Jay's, she saw the police were there and had already cordoned off the house; she wondered when this nightmare would end, but at least no one had been killed this time.

Since she knew the policeman at the door, it wasn't a problem getting in. She waved to Jay, who was seated in her living room answering questions. Rory didn't know the detective who was asking the questions. She went back to talk with Officer Hudson, at the front door.

"So, Rory, what's your interest in this?" the officer asked.

"I think it's related to the Korbin case; Jeff Korbin's her brother, and I'm defending him. By the way, the DA's office will be here to look it over; they have a tape that was in Jay's possession. Whoever broke in may have been looking for it."

"Well, whoever it was, has a huge anger problem; his destruction went beyond the usual crime scene of a burglary. And she doesn't even think he took anything!" Hudson shook his head.

Rory noticed the detective had finished with Jay, so she thanked Officer Hudson and went to Jay. Jay introduced her to Detective Carla March, and they shook hands. Rory told Detective March about the DA's involvement, and added they would be sending someone over.

"That's good," Detective March said, looking pleased. "It benefits everyone when we collaborate."

"I agree," Rory answered. "Good to meet you, Detective."

As the detective left, Rory turned to Jay. "How are you doing?"

"I'm better, thanks. The police came quickly and they've been very helpful. They questioned my neighbor, Robin first and let her leave. It's still hard for me to believe it—I must be in shock— I just can't fathom why someone would do this."

"Yeah, they really turned the place inside out. Yet they took nothing, right?" Jay nodded.

"My theory is that it has something to do with your brother's case. I think the real killer is getting scared and is trying to cover his tracks. I'm afraid he targeted you because he saw me enter your house. He may even somehow know about the tape. But since your entire house was overturned, who knows what he was looking for."

"I wonder how long it will be before I can clean up." Jay looked around her house sadly.

"It may be some time; we want them to be thorough. The officer said it looked like the perp seemed angry or frustrated, judging by the total upheaval of your home. He may be getting desperate because he thinks we're onto him. God, I hope we're getting close." Rory said. "Oh, by the way, you obviously can't move back here now; can you stay with your friend longer?"

"That's no problem. In fact a lot of my stuff is still there; I just came back today to get some things for the kids and me."

"Oh, good." Rory was relieved. "Is this the first time you've been back?"

"No, I came a few days after I'd left. The house was fine then. I told the police. That narrows down the time frame, they said. And that was probably the noise Robin heard two nights ago," Jay answered.

"It probably was, "Rory agreed. "Just please keep alert, especially for anyone following you. And call me immediately if you notice a blue BMW anywhere near you."

"I've been cautious, without getting completely freaked out; I don't want to upset my kids. Actually, they're keeping me sane; I'm focused on protecting them. It's been tough enough with their aunt being murdered and then their uncle being jailed." Jay's voice was filled with emotion.

"How old are your kids?" Rory asked.

"Jenna is 10 and Rob's 13. They really loved their aunt, and they love Jeff, too. I've been as honest as I can with them; I think they need to talk about it. But I don't think they need to hear about the break-in, but of course no matter what I do, they probably will sooner or later." Jay looked overwhelmed.

"Well, it sounds like you're doing a good job; it's true, kids do ground us. Hey, I think you're coping pretty well." Rory tried to lift her spirits. "Listen, I should run now, do you need a ride or anything?"

"No, I'm good, thanks; Robin's going to follow me back. The police were very good about letting me get some of our things."

"Great; so call me if you need anything, and I'll bring over some troops to clean up your house when you can get back in." Rory gave Jay a hug and said quietly, "I have a feeling this will be over soon—keep the faith!"

Driving home, Rory wondered if she could take her own advice. She had looked at this case from so many different angles, and felt she was close to an answer. But, for some reason, it was still eluding her. Perhaps what she needed to do was stop over-thinking and let the facts gel. That would be hard to do; she was getting impatient and frustrated.

It was past dinner time when Rory arrived home. Marc's car wasn't there and the house looked deserted; Rory assumed they'd probably gone out for dinner. Putting her key in the lock, Rory noticed it was open already. So, the girls might be home, she reasoned.

She entered and dropped her briefcase on the bench in the foyer, calling out, "Hey, I'm home! Alex, Kate?" Hearing nothing, she went upstairs looking for the girls. She looked in all the rooms, confused because the girls never left the house unlocked. She seemed to be the only one here. Even Peaches, who always greeted her, wasn't around. Fear prickled at the back of her neck, as she turned to edge down the back stairs. Midway down, she heard footfalls and then the click of the front door closing.

Chapter 44

Marc, Kate and Alex were having dinner at Ruby Tuesday's. Marc had been trying to keep up a conversation with the girls, asking about softball camp, and things he thought would interest them. It had been like pulling teeth; he'd been getting one word answers and was feeling frustrated.

Finally he said, "OK, what's up with you two? I know I'm a boring old fart, but can you humor me?"

That at least got half a smile from them. They didn't say anything right away. Alex broke first, "You sure you want the truth, Dad?" She sounded aggressive.

He wasn't sure he did, but he said, "Yes…"

"Well," she looked at Kate for support, "we're not happy with you and mom sniping at each other. One day you're fine, the next day you're not; it's a pain in the ass for us. We've got stuff to do; we don't have time to worry about you and Mom getting a divorce…"

"Whoa, who ever said anything about a divorce?" Marc was appalled and his stomach lurched.

"Nobody said anything—it's just the way you're acting. You think we don't notice?" Kate joined the fray.

Marc found himself wishing Rory were here; she always helped to diffuse these discussions. He knew he was in over his head, but he had to say something. "Uh, I'm sorry. I guess we never realized how our arguments were affecting you. We're going through a tough time…Well, when your mom is less busy at work, maybe we can work it out. I'm upset that she works such long hours and that she can't go on vacation with us."

"So this is Mom's fault?" Alex crossed her arms over her chest.

"Don't put words in my mouth, young lady—I didn't blame your mom."

"Sounded like that to me," Kate weighed in.

"Look," Marc said in exasperation, "we shouldn't be having this discussion without your mother, so let's drop it for now. And really it's between Mom and me." Marc suddenly remembered that he was the adult and didn't owe them an explanation.

"OK, so let's talk with mom as soon as we get home." Alex suggested.

"If Mom agrees." Marc felt as if he'd been granted a stay of execution. These were tough debaters, he thought. Then he began to feel resentful. He'd been to all their games, taken them out for breakfast and dinner when Rory was too busy and he felt, martyr-like, that he'd been the better parent lately. And they were taking Rory's side.

There was little else to be said, so the rest of dinner passed in stony silence. Marc reflected ruefully that teenaged girls had an incredibly well-developed ability to give off attitude. His girls had it in spades.

When they'd finished their dinner, the girls decided they wanted dessert. So, Marc thought, they were willing to keep up the agony longer. He ordered a dessert, too—something he virtually never did. The girls seemed amused by that.

Finally the dessert plates were cleared away and he asked for the check, half afraid they'd all of a sudden developed a fondness for coffee.

The drive home was equally uncomfortable for Marc. The girls seemed unfazed; they continued to talk about their friends, and who said what on Facebook, completely ignoring him. He stifled the urge remind them of all he'd done for them. Then he almost smiled as he realized he was sounding like his parents— *Oh God!* But he did appreciate his parents a bit more.

"Oh, Dad," Kate said, "could we stop by CVS, for girl stuff—it's on the way home."

What could he say? Now they were trying, successfully, to embarrass him.

"Of course," he said shortly. In the rearview mirror he could see them exchange conspiratorial looks. Man, he thought, they sure knew what buttons to push. But that was fine, he was in no hurry for the discussion looming ahead when they got home.

Pulling into the CVS parking lot he asked, "How much do you need?"

"Oh, you're not coming in?" Kate asked innocently, no trace of humor on her face.

"Naw," he said, "I don't really need anything. Is ten dollars enough?" He fumbled in his wallet but could come up with only a twenty, so he handed it over.

"Thanks, Dad," Kate said as the two of them ran into the store.

Was it his imagination or did he hear them giggling? He chose to let it drop. This evening had been a nightmare. He began to have second thoughts about taking them on vacation.

Predictably, they took their time in the store, but he'd been entertaining himself answering emails on his phone. Still, when he looked at his watch and realized it had been fifteen minutes since they'd gone into the store; he toyed with the idea of going in after them, or worse, leaving. Fortunately, he saw them emerge from the store before he could act on that very bad impulse.

In a few minutes, they were home. A State Trooper's cruiser was in the driveway. Marc's stomach knotted, as he realized that dinner probably hadn't been the worst part of the evening.

Chapter 45

Rory was sitting on the front step with her head in her hands. In the dusk, Marc almost tripped over her in his haste to get to the house. The girls were right behind him, stunned into silence.

Rory looked up, grateful to see Marc. But she had a look of defeat on her face.

"My God, Rory!" Marc exclaimed, "What happened? Are you okay?" He bent down to be at face level with her and took her hands in his.

"It's a very long story, Marc, but what happened tonight..." She took a deep breath and began again. "Someone was in the house when I got home. The front door was unlocked, so I assumed the girls were home. I dropped my briefcase in the hall and went looking for them. I couldn't find them, or Peaches. I got scared and crept down the back stairs. I heard footsteps and then I heard the front door click closed. Whoever it was took my briefcase on the way out. I called Roland and he just got here. He's dusting for prints."

"Jeez, I'm sure we locked the front door..." Marc began.

"We definitely did, because, remember, I asked if Mom had her key." Kate spoke up.

"Right, right," Marc said. "But who would do this; do you have any idea?"

"I can't give you a name, but I'm sure it was the same person who killed Kathie and Helen." Rory said with conviction.

The girls had regained their composure and took seats on either side of Rory, putting their arms around her.

"But you don't know who it is, right?" Marc asked.

"Not for certain, but I'm working on it; I think the guy's getting desperate; he'll show his hand soon." Rory replied.

Just then, Roland came out of the house. He greeted Marc and the girls. Then he said, "Looks like he picked the lock on the front door—see those fine scratches? Nothing seems to have been disturbed, so I think you surprised him soon after he'd come in. There was a blurred print on the front door; it may pan out. You were lucky, Rory. He's been getting closer. And he's getting panicky."

"How do you know this?" Marc asked.

Instead of answering him, Rory suggested they go inside to talk. They all trooped in and took seats in the breakfast nook.

"Mom, I'm making you some tea, anyone else want some?" Alex asked.

"Thanks," Rory murmured. No one else took her up on the offer.

Rory said, "I'm really tired, on the verge of exhaustion. I don't feel like talking; Roland, you know the storyline, do you mind?"

Surprise, then pain showed on Marc's face. Rory noticed it and thought she knew how he was feeling—left out. It couldn't be helped, she rationalized; he hadn't been available to her through most of this ordeal. Still, she felt the familiar guilt.

Peaches emerged from wherever she'd hidden and jumped into Rory's lap. "There you are my sweet thing!" Rory exclaimed, hugging her close.

Looking to Rory for the go ahead, Roland began to tell what had been happening for the last month. He included the BMW stalking Rory, intimidations by the judge, Helen's death, and, most recently, the ransacking of Jay Willis's house.

"And," Rory reminded Roland, "the recent office encounter between the judge and Sarah. Oh, and then the phone call here from the judge, threatening me again. The DA has asked for revocation of bail and the judge has already been picked up. The revocation of bail hearing is tomorrow, and I have to testify. That's about it, minus small details."

It took Marc some time to recover. Then he said, "My God, Rory I had no idea what you'd been going through…I don't even know what to say. I'm completely floored." His face showed confusion, guilt, and shame. And, more than a little anger.

Rory realized belatedly that she wished she had brought Marc into the picture, but he had seemed so unapproachable lately. That was no excuse, she knew. "Marc, I'm really sorry, I guess I was afraid you'd try harder to get me off this case. Do you have an opinion of our suspect, a rough idea of the kind of person we're looking for?"

It seemed to give Marc a chance to regain his standing. "Well, this is off the cuff, I'll need more details to make a strong profile. But I would say what jumps out is a sociopath, a smart, even arrogant guy. I'm pretty sure he knew the victims; there was no forced entry in either case. But he could've broken in, as he did tonight. He also seems to have some time on his hands, as he was able to follow you at odd hours, Rory. That's a rough outline; does it ring a bell for either of you?"

Rory said, "Yes, it does. At first, I was looking at the judge, but he was out of circulation when Helen was killed. And I've wondered about Jeremy Katz, but he's been very busy at the office. Whoever it is, he's definitely been a step or two ahead of us, but I think we're getting close because he's becoming more erratic, acting on impulse."

"And, possibly more dangerous?" Marc asked. "Thank God he didn't hurt you tonight," Marc said with barely controlled emotion.

"You know, I've been thinking about that. He's been looking for something, maybe he's not even sure what, but I think when he saw my briefcase, he took it thinking he'd hit gold." She smiled here. "Lucky for me I'd just cleaned it out today, and I rarely bring sensitive material home with me. But, I just had a thought; the tape of the phone message is in the safe at the office, and also some notes the killer might find useful."

Roland grabbed his cell and called the Media police, suggesting they keep Rory's office under surveillance.

"Good move, Roland, thanks." Rory thought about whom else might be vulnerable, and she thought immediately of Alicia. She asked Roland, "What do you think about Alicia; I mean, her dad's with her, but there may be something the killer wants at Helen's house."

"I'm not sure Media has the staff to keep two places under watch, but I can try…" He sounded doubtful, then said, "Why don't I stop there on my way to the barracks and warn them to call the police if they hear anything suspicious."

"That sounds good," Rory said. "Her dad is staying there until Saturday."

Kate and Alex were still looking shocked. Finally, Kate spoke up, "Mom, I'm really scared for you; what will you do when we leave on vacation?"

"Oh, I think I'll have adequate protection. I think Alicia and I will stick together. I also think the killer is more likely to make a move and tip his hand if he thinks I'm home alone. He seems to know my every move."

"Yeah, well, I know at least one of his hiding places; he was hidden on a path in the woods across from your house and down the road a bit when I chased him," Roland replied. "Not sure if he's put the BMW away for now, but he must have another car…"

"Aw, gee," Rory tried for humor, "and I was getting so attached to the BMW! At least I knew what to look for."

"Well, as you may recall, he was still driving it the day of the funeral," Roland added. "Maybe he is that arrogant! He's bound to make a mistake soon."

Marc, who'd been listening intently with a look of near-panic on his face said, "I don't like this, Rory—I'm not at all comfortable with you being the bait. You got lucky tonight, but you said the guy was getting desperate. We can't leave you here and blithely go on vacation—we'd all be a mess!"

Kate and Alex nodded. Alex said, "I know how important it is for you to solve this case and free the guy, but, we can't risk losing you."

Roland broke in, "I think there's a solution everyone can live with. I think Marc, you and the girls should appear to pack up and leave on vacation, and just drive away, trying to be sure not to be followed. Maybe even go as far as I-95; it'd be easy to lose someone on a four-lane highway. Then, double back and maybe go to Rory's office and wait."

"Saturday's also the day Alicia's father is leaving; I can plan to go to her place when she gets home from the airport. Then both of us can be under surveillance. It may be a bit risky, but with the two of us together…"

"And what about a weapon for you, Rory?" Marc asked.

"You know how I feel about guns, Marc." Rory said.

"And, I hope you know how I feel about you. You know where my gun is, and I'll teach you how to use it."

"Sorry, but I have to disagree; a novice with a gun is far more dangerous, and besides, I'm not doing it!"

Roland stepped in, as it looked like a standoff. "Look, Marc, we can't force Rory to use a gun, but I'm thinking she might come over to the barracks tomorrow and I can teach her defensive moves. I think that's our best compromise."

"I like that, Roland; I've had several sessions of self-defense training, but could use a refresher," Rory said with relief.

"I guess that's the best I'll get," Marc said with resignation. "I'll have to trust you on this one, but I'm not happy…"

Roland got up to leave, saying to Rory, "I'll call you at work tomorrow and plan a time, ok?"

Rory rose to give Roland a hug. "Thanks for everything, my friend; talk with you tomorrow. By the way, I have to be in court in the morning for the bail hearing, so it'll have to be later."

"Ok, sounds good. In the meantime, I think everyone should go on as usual; just be extra alert and call me if anything unusual happens." As he was about to go out the door, his cell rang. He answered, "What? Oh, I guess that's good—take it to the barracks and we'll dust it for prints." He looked at Rory, "A motorist saw something being flung from a car and called the police. They found what is probably your briefcase not far from here."

Chapter 46

The next morning, Rory was meeting with her staff at the office. She'd checked everything, and all seemed in order. She'd rounded up anything important that was related to the case and had put it in the safe.

Leaving Marc this morning had been difficult. He was very clingy, and reluctant to let her go. She was touched by his concern; it felt good to have him back in her camp. But she wondered how he'd be able to even pretend to leave tomorrow. Oh well, she thought that was tomorrow. Today she had the bail hearing to occupy her.

Blake was the first one in. "Morning Rory," he said, noticing the brewing coffee. "Hmm, must've been a coffee fairy here! You trying to take away some of my responsibilities?" He smiled and said, "Thanks! You okay? You look a little... frazzled."

"That about sums it up, Blake; observant as ever! There's a story, of course, but it'll have to wait until the other two get here; I can't possibly go through it more than once." Rory sat down, staring straight ahead.

"Sounds ominous..." Blake said gravely. "Coffee's done, let's have some while we wait." Blake poured her coffee and brought it to her. "You know, you've been a real trooper through all of this; I just hope it's over soon." He sat down next to her and they drank their coffee in silence.

A few minutes later Sam and Sarah entered. Sarah's face fell when she looked at Rory, prompting her to blurt out, "What happened?"

Rory looked up. "Good morning, kids," she said, trying to rev herself up. "As I told Blake earlier, there's a story, but I wanted to wait until everyone was here."

They looked at her expectantly. She said, "Get your coffee and tea first, then I'll start."

Sam and Sarah got their drinks, then pulled up chairs next to Rory.

"It's really not a huge deal, just another chapter in a series of unpleasant events. But after a while, they do take a toll." She paused and took a breath. "Well, as I was leaving the prison, Jay called me. Her house had been broken into and ransacked while she was staying with a friend. I called McClain and asked him to send someone over, and Jay called the police. I went over, talked to her and the police. Her house is an awful mess, like the killer didn't know what he was looking for. The cop said it indicated the guy was angry, frustrated. Anyway, she was going back to her friend's house. It was late when I left." She paused here to take a sip of coffee.

Sarah's blue eyes widened. "Wow!" she said, "that's awful; Jay's such a nice person. We should help her clean up the mess."

"Actually, I told her I'd get her some help, as soon as the police are done. It may take a while; every room was turned over. And I'm hoping the DA's office might be of some help in finding prints."

Blake commented, "It's probably a good thing that you and Como are getting along better now."

"It's been very good, and I'm ashamed to admit I was wrong about him. He is a tough adversary, but he's been quite helpful. It's always good to stay open...I'm learning," she admitted.

"So, that was a rough ending to a long day," Sam commented.

"Yeah, if only it had ended there," Rory said. Noticing their surprised expressions, she continued. "Yes, there's more. So, it was nearly dark when I got home. Marc's car wasn't there; I assumed that he'd taken the girls out for dinner. When I put the key in the front door, it was already open..."

"Oh, God!" Sarah exclaimed, "What did you do?"

"Well, I thought the girls might be home, but I couldn't find anyone. As I was creeping down the back steps, I heard quick steps and then the click of the front door closing. Of course, I freaked—locked the door, looked out the windows—then called Roland. He came right over; dusted for prints. Oh, and the guy took my briefcase; fortunately nothing important was in it—he ditched it later and Roland took it to the barracks. Any questions?" Rory slumped in her chair, exhausted.

There was a moment of shocked silence.

Blake said, "Jeez, Rory, is that all?"

That was the icebreaker everyone needed; laughter rang through the office and, finally, broke the tension. Then they all began asking questions at once.

When the subject had been discussed ad nauseum, Rory said, "Well, now we have the pleasure of testifying against our good friend, Judge Keller. And I think we'd best leave for the courthouse and get it over with. Any questions before we leave?"

"We just tell it like it happened, I guess..." Sarah sounded unsure.

"That's right," Rory said crisply. "And don't elaborate, just answer the question—sometimes it requires only a yes or no answer. You guys might not even be called to the stand. But I need you for moral support, anyway."

They left together and walked the short distance to the courthouse. The news media was there in force; the four of them hurried past before they could be recognized.

They saw Como in the hall, and he showed them to the courtroom, saying, "McClain and I are handling the case, and, of course, requesting revocation of bail."

They entered the courtroom and sat in the front row, behind the DA. Rory was unaccustomed to sitting on this side of the court. It felt strange to her, but it would be a learning experience, she decided.

Soon, Judge Keller was brought in by the sheriffs. It was difficult to see him as the same man who'd been so threatening. He looked disoriented and somehow diminished in his orange jumpsuit. Rory felt a momentary stab of compassion for this man, realizing again that he was not well.

Rory stood up and whispered to Como, "I don't think he'll make it in jail; he looks dreadful. Maybe he needs to be hospitalized."

Como looked surprised, then shrugged, "I'll see what I can do." Then he added, with a smile, "I know why you're a defense attorney."

It didn't sound like an insult, so Rory smiled back.

The hearing got underway. Judge Hanover, a senior judge, was presiding; a good choice, Rory thought. He was dignified and highly regarded, also having the distinction that none of his decisions had been overturned by a higher court. And with all of the media attention on this case, he wouldn't allow it to turn into a circus.

McClain stated his request for revocation of bail, citing a further allegation of Terroristic Threats, against Rory, while he was on the electronic monitor. He summarized the content of the call to Rory and asked if the judge would like to question her on the stand.

The judge demurred, but asked Katz if he wished to question Ms. Chandler.

Jeremy, appearing torn, said, "Yes Your Honor. I believe it is in my client's best interest." He looked apologetically in Rory's direction as she took the stand and was sworn in.

Following protocol, the DA led the questioning.

"Ms. Chandler, would you please tell the court about the phone call in question."

Rory spoke clearly and without hesitation. "The judge said, 'Don't think you'll get away with this…travesty. There will be payback.'"

"And are you positive it was Judge Keller?" McClain asked.

"Yes, I'm positive." Rory answered the question asked.

"Can you tell the court why you are so positive?" McClain inquired.

"Yes, well, the judge had threatened me before, in my office, while my tape recorder was on, so, after the phone call I listened to the tape again. There's no mistaking his voice."

Having finished questioning Rory, McClain nodded to Katz.

Jeremy began tentatively, "Ms. Chandler, do you have any idea what the judge was referring to; was he perhaps holding you accountable for the recent, and as yet unproved accusations?"

McClain and Como were on their feet simultaneously. McClain erupted with, "Objection—leading the witness!"

"Sustained," Judge Hanover agreed.

Before Katz could continue his questioning, Judge Keller, who'd been glaring at Rory for the entire hearing, stood and began to yell: "That's right, you tried to ruin me, but it's not over yet—you'll see—I'll get you!"

"Bailiff, please subdue the defendant," Judge Hanover ordered calmly.

Two sheriffs came forward and attempted to get the judge under control. He was still vocalizing, but the words had become incoherent. The sheriffs held him, looking expectantly at Judge Hanover.

"Under the circumstances, the defendant will be ordered to the psychiatric wing of the prison to undergo further testing. We need to know if he's competent to stand trial. Mr. Katz, Mr. McClain, any objections?"

"No, Your Honor," they said, nearly in unison.

"This hearing is concluded; bail is revoked and the defendant is remanded to the psychiatric wing of the prison, pending establishment of competency," Judge Hanover declared, banging the gavel.

Chapter 47

Stan Como caught Rory before she left the courtroom. "Hey, I just wanted to tell you that our evidence expert found some prints at the Willis house that don't match anyone in her family. We haven't found a match through the database either. But, if we find that we have a suspect, it'll be easy to verify print-wise."

"Thanks," Rory said, "That was fast work. I'll let you know if any of my suspicions pan out."

He gave her a speculative look, and said, "Don't put yourself in harm's way, Rory. There are regular channels you can use." His concern seemed genuine.

"Yeah, they haven't worked so well. My client is still sitting in jail thanks to the regular channels. By the way, have you asked the police for Korbin's cell phone?"

"Yes," Como answered, grimacing. "The police checked it in as evidence, but it's gone missing. They're investigating," he said.

"Hmmm, well, I guess it's good we have Ms. Willis's tape. I need to get back to the office, so I'll talk to you later."

Rory found her staff in the corridor, and suggested they leave by a side door to avoid the press.

Skirting the huge crowd of reporters and news vans, they quickly made their way back to the office.

"Whew!" Rory exclaimed when they were inside. "I'm so glad that's over. I don't know how the rest of you felt, but I actually felt sorry for Keller. I predict he'll be found not competent to stand trial."

"I think Blake and I concluded that the day he stormed the office," Sam replied. "He did look pathetic in court, and his outburst only made it worse."

"I'm just glad he's off the street," Sarah weighed in. "I'm still having nightmares and I'm afraid to be alone."

"And, fortunately, you don't have to be alone," Blake smirked.

"Yes, I am lucky," she gave it back to Blake. Her blush, however, revealed her discomfort.

"OK, kids, enough!" Rory reminded them. "We have some serious business to discuss."

They looked at her expectantly. She said, "Tomorrow—I know it's Saturday—we may have the opportunity to flush out our culprit."

"Do you know who it is, then?" Blake was incredulous.

"I'm not sure, but I do know that he's still dogging me. For God's sake, he was at my house last night!" Rory exclaimed.

"Too bad you don't have surveillance cameras," Sam speculated.

"Yeah, might be a good investment," Rory said. "But, as I was saying, this guy is watching me. We're hoping to turn the tables, tomorrow."

"What?" Sarah asked. "Rory you're not going to put yourself in danger are you?"

"Hey, I've been in danger since I took this case. This time, when I put myself out for bait, it will be orchestrated. And, hopefully, it will work without anyone getting hurt, except maybe the perp."

"Exactly what are we talking about here?" Sam asked.

"OK, tomorrow my family is scheduled to leave on vacation, without me. When Marc was clued into the situation, after the break-in at our house, he refused to leave me home alone."

"So, how will that work?" Blake asked.

"So, my family will pretend to leave; that is, there will be a great fanfare of them packing up the car, and driving off. Roland's in on this, so he'll be in a position to see if anyone's following them. "

"I don't know," Sarah commented. "Is Roland the only officer?"

"At the moment, yes, but he has access to back up pretty quickly." Rory assured them. "So the plan is for me to look vulnerable. When Alicia gets home from the airport, I'll go over to her house, where we will be actively looking for evidence that Helen may have left, like her journal."

"Unless the killer took it," Sarah added, looking pensive and twirling her hair.

"Yes, but if the killer had found the evidence, would he have trashed Jay's house, or Rory's?" Sam was quick to point out.

"Bingo!" Rory said. "That's my thinking exactly. Alicia's had her dad there at the house for a few days; he leaves tomorrow. Our plan is to thoroughly search her house; it's almost a sure thing that he'll be interested in both of us. And he's bound to show himself."

"Meanwhile," Blake added, "where will your family be, that is if you can actually get Marc to leave?"

"They may come to the office and wait—you guys are welcome to be here as well—until something happens. They can provide back up. Roland will stay in contact with all of us."

"Besides Roland, does anyone have a weapon?" Sarah asked. "I'm just saying…"

"I hate guns," Rory said, "Marc has one, but I refuse to use it. I'm meeting Roland later to get a quick refresher in self-defense…"

"I have a gun," Sarah admitted, "although— I agree with Rory—I don't like them! But my dad wouldn't let me go to school so far away without it."

Blake and Sam exchanged glances. Sam said, "So, I guess we'll have to be sure and stay near the women!" He chuckled as he said, "Armed and dangerous!"

"Let's just hope that none of us needs a gun," Rory said adamantly.

"Here, here!" Sarah said. "Carrying a gun gives me the creeps."

Blake said, "The plan has some holes, Rory, it's a bit scary for you and Alicia....Have you thought of the 'what if' scenarios?"

"Yeah, I mean, I guess so. But we're trying to keep it simple; if it gets too complicated, there's more of a chance for it to go south. At least, that's what I think."

"What can we do if we're here in the office?" Sarah asked.

"Looks like it might get crowded in here if everyone comes," Blake noted.

"It might, "Rory conceded. "You don't all have to come; I just wanted you to be aware of what's going on. And the office might be a target, because the killer is still looking for something. Also, please be aware of anyone who might be following you."

They decided to go to lunch together; something they'd not done in a while.

"Does everyone like Mexican?" Sarah asked. "Because Diego's looks like a nice place and I hear it's good."

They enjoyed a convivial and delicious lunch. After lunch, Rory said to the others, "Why don't you take the afternoon off? I've got to go meet Roland, after I go back to the office to make sure it's secure."

"I planned to go back, Rory," said Blake. "What do you need done?"

"You know, I just want to make sure there's nothing left out that shouldn't be. Thanks, Blake."

They went their separate ways. Rory had a few items to pick up while she was in Media; her parents' 45th anniversary was coming up and she wanted to look for something special at Earth and State, where she shopped for unique gifts.

Having concluded her shopping, Rory's cell rang as she was walking to her car. It was Blake.

"Rory—you won't believe this, but just as I got to the office, I saw a guy trying to get in the door," he said breathlessly. "I yelled, 'Hey, can I help you?' He ducked his head and ran off—never saw his face. I'm going after him…"

Chapter 48

Blake took off running after the guy as he was ending the call with Rory. He believed himself athletic, so thought there was a good chance of catching the would-be intruder; at least he'd give it his best shot.

The suspect, wearing jeans, a dark tee shirt and Phillies baseball cap, was dressed like half the teen population. He didn't look like a teen, but he was fast. Blake watched as the guy bolted across Orange Street, disregarding traffic, but kept him in sight, even as he paused before crossing. He was running full-out down Front Street; Blake was gaining on him, but the guy seemed to know he was being chased. He zigzagged through a parking lot as Blake struggled to keep up. It was hot; sweat was pouring down his back and face, blurring his vision.

On the other side of the parking lot, Blake looked both ways, deciding in a split second to go to the right, towards the park. Taking off in high gear, he hoped his instincts were on target. When Blake reached the stone wall of Glen Providence Park, he looked over it, and saw his suspect running down the hill. Yes! He thought, *I was right.*

The guy was still in sight, but gaining ground as he ran down the steep hill. Blake ran after him, finding it easier to go with gravity. He could see the runner near the pond at the bottom, and he sped up, hoping to reach him. In his haste, Blake tripped over the root of one of the massive oak trees. He tumbled the rest of the way down the hill, hitting rocks and branches on the way. At the bottom, he got up, disoriented and limping. The man was nowhere in sight and Blake was in no condition to pursue him further. "Fuck!" he yelled. Probably the perp was laughing as he heard it, Blake thought bitterly. He was disgusted with himself; he'd thought he was in good shape. Apparently he was delusional.

Just then he heard his cell go off, but it wasn't in his pocket; it was coming from up the hill. He went in the direction of the noise and found it on the ground; at least it still worked. He saw it was Rory on the phone.

"Blake, where are you? I've been waiting at the office and got worried."

"I chased the guy," he answered breathlessly. "I'm at Glen Providence Park. I lost him, Rory. I tripped running down the hill and he got away. I'm sorry," he said morosely.

"He's eluded everyone; he's slippery," Rory said. "Why the hell did you do it? Never mind, just stay there—I'll come get you."

He felt like such a wuss; Sam probably would've been able to catch him, he thought, successfully making himself feel worse. He really wanted to help Rory solve this case, and he'd been so close to getting the guy. He'd lost his focus, he decided, and made a mental note to avoid that mistake again.

He was leaning on the stone wall, when Rory drove up. He limped to the car and got in. He was dirty, disheveled, bruised and dispirited.

"My God, Blake!" Rory exclaimed, taking in his appearance. "Well, you sure gave it hell trying. We need to have that ankle looked at. Fortunately, Penn Care is nearby. I'll see if I can pull some strings and get you seen."

"No, don't bother," Blake said, resignation in his voice.

"Yes, bother; it happened on the job and I'm your employer. We're getting it taken care of." There was no arguing with Rory.

"What about your self-defense lessons?" Blake asked, lamely.

"There's time for that; I'm a quick study," she joked.

Arriving at the medical center, Rory helped Blake out of the car, a gesture he resisted, but needed. They entered the building and she put Blake in the elevator, saying, "I'll meet you upstairs." He smiled in spite of himself, remembering her aversion to closed in spaces.

Rory was at the desk speaking with a receptionist when Blake got off the slow, clunky elevator. She'd already arranged for him to be seen, telling the receptionist to bill her office.

Blake took a seat in the half-full waiting room. Rory walked over to him with her cell at her ear; that reminded him to turn his off.

"That was Sam; he'll come get you. Just give him a call when you're finished. And, for God's sake, follow the doctor's orders!"

He sat there sullenly, looking straight ahead. Rory bent down, kissed his forehead and said, "I'm really proud of how hard you tried to catch the guy. Call me when you get home and let me know how you're doing. I don't think he'll try to break into the office again, but I did notify the Media police. They may call you for a description."

Blake smiled, nodded and said "Bye, and thanks," as Rory left.

He was seething inside and had already decided that as soon as he was patched up, he was going back to where he'd last seen the guy to try and pick up his trail.

Chapter 49

The killer, hiding in the dense underbrush by the pond, didn't move a muscle as he heard his pursuer go down. He was relieved; he'd planned to tackle him from his hiding spot, and was glad he didn't have to because it posed a risk. So far, he didn't think the guy—he was pretty sure it was Blake, from Rory's office—had seen him, but the killer had seen his pursuer. His temper rose as he thought of Rory, the bitch who was making all of this treachery necessary. But for her, he'd have been home free. He had to stop her, and then leave without a trace. He'd already transferred the money from his dummy corporation to the Caymans, but he had to tie up this loose end before he left. He had to.

Peering out through the brush, he watched as Blake limped up the hill, cursing.

He struggled to keep from laughing out loud. He'd done pretty well for a middle-aged "sick" guy against this young, strapping twenty-something.

He continued to watch from his shelter as Blake struggled up the hill, having been unable to bag his quarry. It was quite funny, actually; he stifled another laugh. He tried to rein himself in; he had serious work to do before he could enjoy the rest of his life in comfort.

His hatred of Rory was visceral, but it was really his wife, his cheating whore of a wife who had started him on this path. If he'd known where she was, he'd have done her in. After all, it was to satisfy her needs, for more money, a better house, a luxury car, that he'd begun to steal. And then she'd just up and left him anyway. He'd no idea where she'd gone; she took only their joint savings with her and disappeared.

He smiled, thinking money was no issue now; he'd stashed plenty, far from her clutches. Although her departure had come as a surprise to him, he supposed he'd been planning for it all along, at least he wanted to think that.

But it really bugged him that he couldn't find her; he'd tried in vain to have her tracked down, but she'd been more clever than he'd thought. That really pissed him off, to think she'd outsmarted him; that stuck in his craw like a bad meal. He'd never told anyone that she'd left, not that he had any friends to speak of. But he'd decided to take care of himself for a change, and he found he liked amassing money, loved it, in fact. People could be so stupid. Except for Rory, but she'd soon find out where her cleverness would get her!

Chapter 50

About an hour after Rory had dropped him off, Blake was bandaged, given pain pills and sent on his way. He had strained his ankle, and it was hurting less since he'd taken the pills; he found he could put weight on it.

He spent a few minutes outside the clinic debating what to do. He knew Sam was waiting for his call, but he was so close to the park. He made a snap decision to check out the park before calling Sam; he could always call him later if he needed help. He really wanted to find the guy who'd killed two women and was still stalking Rory.

It took only a few minutes to get to the park. As before, he looked over the wall and down into the park. A mother and two children were walking slowly up the hill; he didn't see anyone else.

He waited until the family was at the top of the hill before he went down the steps and into the park. He picked his way through the tree roots and rocks, watchful, so as to avoid a repeat of his earlier disaster. He stopped a few times to rest his foot, but it was feeling better. The doc had said to ice it. He'd do that—later.

Blake continued to stay alert, looking around for people and avoiding tree roots. It really bugged him that he'd been so careless, when he'd had the killer in his sights. The police hadn't called him to get a description, but then, how could he describe the guy? There was nothing distinguishing about him: he was slim, with a medium build, about 5'8" tall. Blake hadn't noticed any tattoos; he was wearing a Phillies baseball cap, concealing both his hair and face, and he'd never turned around; Blake could pass him on the street and not even know it.

Finally reaching the pond area, his last sighting of the killer, he stopped. He was next to the pond, looking for anything that might give a clue. Not far from where he'd ended up after his fall, he saw a disturbance in the underbrush. He examined it closely; branches were broken, grass was tamped down, and he saw a partial footprint, apparently made by a sneaker. He was careful to touch nothing. So he'd been that close to catching him, or perhaps the killer had planned an ambush; maybe the fall had been a blessing. After all, the murderer had shown no mercy to his other victims. The thought chilled Blake, but he was driven to push forward.

There was a path through the underbrush and Blake thought his suspect had probably taken it, to minimize the chances of being seen. So he continued on the path, finding partial footprints matching the one he'd seen by the pond. This path led all the way out of the park, and ended at the Third St. Bridge, which had been closed to vehicles for several years. It was, however, open to pedestrian traffic.

He stood in the street trying to decide which way the killer had gone. If he'd gone to the right, he'd be very close to the courthouse plaza. The road to the left led to wooded areas, fewer houses, and in general a less populated area. Trusting his instincts, he chose to go to the left. Looking up at the hill he'd have to climb, he had second thoughts. He decided to give his ankle a rest, as he contemplated his situation. Momentarily distracted by the noise and activity of the children playing, he looked over at the swim club across the street. It was a pleasant diversion, as he recalled spending a few summers at this very club.

Looking again at the hill, he decided it was time. He climbed slowly; although the sun was going down, it was still hot. It took about twenty minutes and most of his strength to get there. Recognizing this area, he remembered there was a smaller, lesser known park at the summit of the hill. It was actually a wildlife preserve, frequented by birders. There were trails, but it was left more or less wild.

He came to a small parking lot. The chain across the entrance was down, apparently broken. Blake decided it was worth the effort to at least walk around and see if anything caught his eye, but he was getting thirsty and didn't feel motivated to continue much longer. He'd gone a few hundred yards when he saw something glinting in the sun. Curious, he walked towards it; *who would leave an abandoned car in a park*, he wondered, growing uneasy. He soon realized, with a jolt, the car was a dark BMW.

Chapter 51

Sam was at Sarah's, waiting to hear from Blake so they could go out for dinner. Feeling impatient, Sam said, "It's been almost two hours since Rory called us, right? Don't you think we should've heard from Blake by now? I've left several messages."

Sarah responded, "Why don't we just swing by the medical center; he's got to be finished soon."

"Good idea!" Sam went to get his keys when his cell rang. He answered immediately, "Hey, Blake…"

"You need to get over here; I'm at Delco Park on Third Street, and…"

"Blake! Blake!" Sam heard a scuffling sound, then a thud and the phone went dead.

Sam called the local police, got Officer Jamison, told him about the call and said he'd meet them at the Third Street Park. "It's urgent!" he added.

Sarah, looking bewildered, asked, "What happened to Blake?"

"I'll tell you on the way there—let's go!"

When they got in the car, Sam said, "Damn, where's the Third Street Park?"

"I know where it is, I'll direct you; make a left out of my parking lot. Now tell me what's going on!"

"Blake just called me from there; sounded like he was in trouble, said we needed to get over there, then the line went dead. My guess is, he couldn't leave it alone after he lost the guy; I think he went back to follow his trail. He doesn't give up easily." Sam said.

Sarah continued to direct Sam to the park.

"You're sure?" Sam asked.

"I'm positive; the park will be on your left, past the Stop sign," Sarah replied.

As they were nearing the park, they heard the scream of sirens.

"We must be getting close; sounds like the police are, too," Sam was hoping.

Arriving at the park, they saw two local police cars, a Delco cop and one State Trooper, Roland.

Walking up to the officers, Sam acknowledged Officer Jamison and Trooper Johnson, telling them about the phone call. A few other officers were combing the area inside the gate. One of the officers was examining the chain that went across the entrance. He called to Jamison, "Looks like this was broken, and there are tire tracks…"

Sam and Sarah ran through the entrance, "He must be in here somewhere…" Sarah said, looking around.

Roland put a hand on Sarah's shoulder and said, "This park belongs to the county; I don't want to step on their toes, so let's ask first. "

"But, Blake may be hurt…" Sarah protested.

Roland asked the Delco cop, "Hey, Joe, okay if we walk back a ways; they're concerned about their friend; he called from here."

"Sure, go ahead," was the reply.

As they followed the tire tracks, Sam asked Roland, "How'd you happen to be here? You seem to show up everywhere!"

Roland chuckled, "Actually Rory called and asked me to check for Blake at Glen Providence, and then I heard the sirens…"

The tire tracks ended abruptly in a stand of trees. There was no car. Roland reasoned, "He must've left the way he came in. But, did he take Blake with him?"

Panicked by the thought, Sarah started calling, "Blake! Blake! Can you hear us?"

Not far from where the tracks ended, Roland pointed, "Look! The grass is trampled, like maybe something was dragged…" He started jogging down the path.

Sam and Sarah followed, calling for Blake as they went.

The path they were following ended. "Now what?" Sarah asked frantically. "What if he did take Blake?"

Roland said calmly, "Let's just have a look around here."

The area was thick with brambles and underbrush, some of which looked impenetrable. Roland was systematically checking the area.

"What's that noise?" Sarah asked, cocking her head to one side.

The others stopped walking and listened.

"I heard it from over there!" Sarah pointed to an area of heavily entangled brambles, and ran towards it, calling, "Blake!"

As they got closer, Sam heard a quiet rustling and then a hand emerged from the brush.

Sarah stifled a scream; motioning for silence, Roland put on his leather gloves and began disentangling the brambles.

Sam soon heard what sounded like a moan, and Roland called out to the other officers nearby, "Hey guys, over here; I need some help!"

Three officers came quickly, and waded into the brambles, following Roland.

"Can you see what's happening?" Sarah asked Sam.

"There's someone in there, let's just hope it's Blake and that he's ok.

The Delco cops radioed for an ambulance, and soon Roland, Jamison, and a third officer emerged with a limp body. Sarah said. "It's Blake! That's what he was wearing today."

As the men passed Sam and Sarah, Roland said, "He took a beating, but his vitals are good— I think he'll be OK."

Sarah buried her head in Sam's chest; she couldn't look. Sam bit back a gag reflex, relieved that Sarah hadn't seen the worst.

As they were leaving the area, Sarah asked, "Sam—do you hear that ring? Actually, it sounds like Blake's ring tone!"

Sarah, whose hearing was acute, led the way. "Jeez, Sam, how will we find it in these brambles?" Just then the ringing stopped.

"Shit! Oh, wait, I'll just call his number." she reasoned.

As she was pulling out her cell, she heard the ringing again; they redoubled their efforts. "It sounds like it's right here!" Sarah exclaimed, pointing.

Sam took a chance and plunged his hand into the brambles. He winced as he came away with a bloody hand, and the phone. "Hello?" Sam said uncertainly; he was having trouble hearing with the ambulance sirens blaring in the background. "Hello?" Sam said louder, with a finger in his other ear.

"Sam? Where the bloody hell is Blake and why am I hearing sirens?" demanded a familiar voice.

Chapter 52

Rory awoke on Saturday with sun streaming in the window. It had been a restless night, although she'd fallen asleep as soon as her head hit the pillow. Her dreams had been bizarre, mirroring her fears and her arduous day.

She'd stayed at the hospital until Blake had awakened and she'd spoken with the doctor, who'd assured her he would recover and be fine. But he looked awful.

Blake had told her about his contact with the presumed killer; she'd been horrified to learn that he'd come so close to being—what, kidnapped? Or worse; she didn't want to venture down that path. Still, he'd been unable to give a description of his attacker, other than a generic one; he'd assumed it was the same guy he'd chased earlier, and he'd seen him only from behind as they were running.

Just as he'd found the BMW in the trees, he'd been hit from behind; he faintly remembered hearing sirens. Then, nothing until he'd awakened in the hospital. The sirens, Rory mused, had probably saved his life. And Thank God for that.

Her thoughts were interrupted as she heard Marc finishing his shower, and a wave of nausea swept over her. It was Saturday, time to get her game face on. She dreaded how this day might play out. At the same time, she was eager to get it over with. Then, maybe nothing would happen today; maybe the killer had left town, but she had a part to play in this drama so she forced herself out of bed.

Marc emerged from the bathroom, an anxious look on his face. "Honey," he said sitting down on the bed, "we don't have to do this. There must be another way to catch this son of a bitch!" That he was angry, and frightened, Rory could see.

"I know, Marc, it's scary," Rory acknowledged. "And maybe nothing will come of it, but we have to try and draw him out, giving us the upper hand for a change. So far he's been calling all the shots and we're left to play catch-up! I'd like to see if we can orchestrate this to our advantage; we're in too far to give up now," she said with a conviction she didn't quite feel.

"I get that, Rory, I do," he said solemnly, "I just want to be sure you don't get hurt."

"That's not my intention either; I just want to get this monster!"

"I know, I know…" Marc was tearing up as he clutched her hand.

"Look, Roland and I have discussed this plan ad nauseam. He has guys on back up. Sam and Sarah will be at the office, if they're needed. You and the girls have to go somewhere safe, so I'm not worried about you."

"Sarah offered her place, which is close to everything in Media, so I think we'll go there," Marc decided. "I'll call her to verify and double check where she's leaving the key."

"So, we'll all be within a short distance of each other. I will either be here, with Roland nearby in an unmarked car, or I'll be at Alicia's, once she gets home from the airport. Roland will let everyone know where I am," Rory concluded. "If you get a 911 on your cell, assume it's me and send in the troops. What could go wrong?"

Marc wasn't smiling; he was looking at her with such longing that it made her uncomfortable. She didn't want to think about it, so she suggested, "Why don't you go to the attic and get luggage for everyone?"

Giving him something to do seemed to break the somber mood. "Okay, sure, as soon as I'm dressed." Marc assured her.

By the time she'd finished showering, Marc had left the room. The aroma of freshly brewed coffee wafted up the back

285

stairs from the kitchen; it never failed to make her feel better, even today. As she dressed, she tried to put a positive spin on the day and to ignore the panicky feeling rising from her core.

As she trolled her closet for an outfit, she toyed with the idea of asking Alex to find an outfit to catch a killer. She doubted Alex would find it amusing. Humor had always been one of Rory's most powerful weapons against fear; it seemed to have deserted her now, temporarily, she hoped.

Losing patience, she grabbed her standby black pants and a light blue V-neck, dressed and went downstairs to get breakfast.

Alex and Kate were sitting in the breakfast nook, apparently having an argument. They stopped talking abruptly when she came into the room.

"Morning, girls, is there a problem?" Rory asked, not expecting the truth.

They sat sullenly, as Rory thought resentfully; *of course their problems are bigger than mine.*

She was pretty close to the mark. Kate spoke, as Alex glared at her.

"I just think it's unfair that we have to sit around all day doing nothing, when we could be with our friends."

"Speak for yourself, you thoughtless cow!" Alex flung at her.

"You bitch!" Kate yelled back. "At least I'm honest about it; you don't want to do it either!"

Marc entered the room, laden with luggage. "Enough!" he shouted. "Your mother is putting herself at great risk to catch a killer and you're worried about being bored? I... I'm speechless!"

"I'm taking some luggage to the car," Marc told Rory. And to the girls, "Get off your butts and bring some of this stuff out to the car," he yelled over his shoulder as he slammed the door.

This is going well, Rory thought, as she looked at the girls, still glaring at each other.

"You heard your father!" she said more forcefully than she'd planned.

They took their time getting up and then fought over which suitcase they'd each take.

It would've been funny, Rory thought, if this weren't a serious situation. As Rory reflected, she felt sure this was their way of showing fear, but still, she didn't need the aggravation. She'd long ago stopped trying to predict teen-aged behavior. But sometimes it really sucked.

Marc came in, still looking annoyed. His expression changed when he sat down across from Rory. She was drinking coffee and looking out the window.

"Can I put on some toast for you, or anything? You don't usually drink coffee without food."

Rory looked up, touched by his offer, but preoccupied. "That would be lovely, Marc—just toast would be fine."

He got up to put on toast as the girls flounced through the kitchen and stomped upstairs. "What's that about?" Marc asked angrily.

"Marc, if I could interpret teen behavior, I'd be a millionaire. But today, I think they're scared and don't know how to express it. Then again, I could be way off."

"Yeah, they're like Jekyll and Hyde; never know which one's showing up!" Marc commented.

"True," Rory said with a small laugh, "even on their good days."

Finishing their toast and coffee, they just sat for a minute, looking out the window, enjoying the blooming roses and the sunlit day and gathering strength.

Marc looked at his watch, then said, "Well, I guess this can't be prolonged any longer; it's nearly ten." He shouted up the stairwell for the girls to come down.

"In a minute!" Kate responded.

Alex came down the steps with her iPod around her neck and some magazines. "I don't know what's keeping her," she cocked her head toward the stairs. "Can I sit in the back, Dad?" she asked, knowing it would infuriate Kate.

"Sure," he said. "You called it first." He knew the rules. Alex gave a mischievous smile and hurried out to the car to stake her claim.

Rory rolled her eyes, sorry that Marc would have to put up with their nonsense.

Kate came down the steps as slowly as if she were carrying a hundred pound weight. "She went out to take my seat, didn't she?"

"Didn't know they were assigned," Rory said drily.

Kate wasn't smiling as she marched out.

"Well, I'd best get this circus on the road." Marc looked at her intensely, saying, "Be careful, Rory—I love you!"

"I love you back!" she replied. "I think the script calls for me to escort you to the car and wave you off. " She tried to lighten the mood.

She and Marc walked out with their arms around each other. They kissed, then she went to the windows to kiss her daughters.

Alex rolled her window down, "Sorry, Mom, didn't mean to upset you." There was concern in her clear green eyes, and a sheen that could be the beginning of tears.

She went to Kate's window and bent in to kiss her. Kate said quietly, "Take good care of yourself, Mom. I love you."

"I love you all! Have a good trip," Rory said as they pulled out.

She continued waving until they were out of sight; then she went into the house, which suddenly felt quiet and empty.

She'd brought the morning paper in with her, and sat down in the nook with another cup of coffee. The Judge was still big news in the Delco Times, with new allegations and victims coming out every day.

She tried to interest herself in it, but it seemed as though it had happened ages ago.

Feeling restless, she got up, walked around putting the house back together; the girls had strewn their belongings all over. She almost cried as she picked up each article— an unmatched pair of socks, one soccer shoe, crusted with mud, a ripped tee shirt—she missed them already and thought with sadness that they'd left on a bad note. But at least Marc was with her, after a very long time…She still wondered about that, but certainly couldn't think about it now.

Walking upstairs to put the items in their rooms, Rory heard a muted sound. She stopped and listened, going cold with fear. She'd locked and bolted all the doors. The sound came again, muffled.

She laughed, then almost cried with relief as she realized it was Peaches. She called for her, and received a plaintive "Mrow" in return.

She looked in all the rooms on the second floor, then realized that the sound was coming from above. *Of course*, she thought. Peaches must be trapped in the attic; Marc probably hadn't noticed that she'd followed him up.

Rory pulled the stairs down to climb to the attic. She turned on the light and Peaches ran to her. "There you are my sweet— you do get yourself into a jam sometimes," she crooned as Peaches purred.

She hadn't really looked around up here for quite a while, Rory thought. She actually loved attics, and had since she was a little girl. She saw things she hadn't seen for years—an old rotary phone, Alex's first teddy bear, missing an eye, a Barbie, with a shaved head—when she and Marc decided to clean house, the clutter ended up here.

She was looking through a stack of books, making sure there was nothing here she hadn't read. At the bottom of the stack was Marc's yearbook she'd recently brought up. Curious, she picked it up. "Nether Providence HS Class of '90," she said out loud. She'd never really looked at it. *This could be very interesting*, she thought to herself.

She looked for Marc's picture and found it; even as a teen, he'd been hot. She noticed that many girls had signed his book, some suggestively. It occurred to her that Korbin was in this book; she found his picture. He'd been quite a hunk. She remembered that Kathie would also be in the yearbook, though not in the senior class. She didn't know her maiden name, but it wasn't difficult to find the most beautiful "Kathie".

She'd been a sophomore and was a real knockout. She'd signed Marc's book: "Never forget senior week at Sea Isle; I won't." It was signed with a heart. *Interesting*, Rory grimaced.

Perusing the page, she noticed a picture of someone vaguely familiar. It was Jeremy Katz—another surprise. .

Still turning pages, something jumped out at her; she turned back, scanning the page. There it was, the initials "JK." She read everything; he was voted "most likely to succeed," and next to that Marc had scribbled, "By any means." With a look of horror, Rory dropped the book as if it were a poisonous snake.

Chapter 53

Alicia arrived home from the airport, sad and happy at the same time; she would miss her dad, but he'd given her so much in the short time they'd had together. Even though he'd left, something of him was with her; she'd felt his love more strongly than ever before, and he'd made it clear that he'd loved her mother; he regretted the divorce and blamed himself.

Demonstrating that he wanted a relationship with her, he'd invited her to come to Santa Barbara any time to visit him and had thoughtfully extended the invitation to Vanessa as well, though Alicia thought it best to go alone for the first visit. She would definitely take him up on the offer.

Looking around, she decided the house needed tidying. But first, she had to call Rory; the plan was for the two of them to search for her mother's journal, as yet, still missing.

Alicia dialed Rory's cell; it rang through to the message. Alarmed that Rory didn't answer, she thought to call the house number. Again, no answer. Heart pounding, fear beginning to knot her stomach, she wondered, *why isn't Rory answering?* This time she left a message, "Rory, it's Alicia—please call me right back when you get this!"

To keep her mind occupied, Alicia began attacking the clutter that had accumulated during her father's visit; she half smiled, knowing she'd inherited this cleaning compulsion from her mother. The thought of her mother comforted her.

At the same time, she couldn't help wondering what could've gone wrong with their plan. Maybe Rory was on her way over and didn't answer her cell while she was driving. She couldn't bear to think that anything bad had happened to Rory.

Although she'd locked the doors, she double-checked. All but the back door had a deadbolt—too late to worry about that, she thought. She propped a chair under the knob, unsure whether it would help at all.

Unable to stop herself, she called Rory, and got the message once again. She knew she was close to panicking so she forced herself to sit down and breathe deeply. Who could she call? She didn't have Roland's number, which, she realized belatedly, was a mistake. Their plan, which had seemed foolproof, was unraveling already; she was horrified at the thought.

Again, forcing herself to breathe, she accepted she'd just have to wait, feeling sure Rory would be along soon. In the meantime, she decided to finish cleaning. She picked up dirty dishes and stowed them in the dishwasher. Cleaning up the kitchen, she moved to the living room, picking up clothes, shoes and books to take upstairs.

Having put things away in her room, she wandered into her mom's room. She hadn't really spent any time in here since the funeral, and suddenly felt her mother's presence in this room. She sat on the bed and cried, sobbing until she was gasping for air and the tears seemed to have dried up.

A sense of calm came over her, and without realizing it, she'd gotten up and walked to her mother's closet. She felt a stab of sadness as she took in the smells that evoked memories of her mother. She looked at her clothes, knowing that soon she'd have to box them up. Later, she thought, not now.

The shelf above the hanging clothes appeared cluttered with winter attire, haphazardly thrown together; this was not like her mother. Grabbing a chair, she pulled it over to the closet so she could check out the mess; her mother would want it to be orderly. She wondered, momentarily, if her mother had left this as a sign. Alicia wasted no time throwing things out onto the floor, amassing a large pile. With everything off the shelf, she took one last look to make sure she'd gotten it all. In the back corner, she saw something that appeared different from the rest of the shelf, but she needed more light to see. Retrieving a flashlight from her mom's bedside table, she got back on the chair.

She directed the beam into the corner, concerned that it might be water damage, but it wasn't. The shelf, which was made of drywall covered with contact paper, appeared to have a rectangular indentation. She stretched her arm until she could run her finger over the surface; it was indented! She needed something sharp to see what was underneath.

Running down to the kitchen, she grabbed the first sharp object she found, a butcher knife. Then she returned to the closet. Heart pounding, sweating from exertion, she slit the concave area, peeled back the paper and removed a book.

She knew what it was before she even looked at it. It was her mother's journal.

Chapter 54

Grabbing the yearbook and Peaches, Rory tumbled down the stairs in her haste to get out of the attic, gaining a foothold when she reached the bottom. As the staircase slammed shut behind her, she heard a scraping noise that sounded like furniture being moved, coming from the attic she'd just vacated.

Frantic to escape, she ran for her car, picking up her purse on the run. As the sounds from the attic grew louder, she was prompted to speed up, too frightened to turn around. In her haste, she didn't notice the blinking red light on her answering machine or her cell phone plugged in next to it.

The Prius was in the drive and she bolted for it, driving off as fast as she could. She drove straight to the spot where Roland had said he'd be; he wasn't there! Rory dug in her purse to get her cell, and remembered with a gasp that she'd left it in the kitchen charging. She couldn't go back for it.

Cursing herself for forgetting her cell, she made a snap decision to go to Alicia's; she might as well go with the plan, feeling sure Roland would come there when he couldn't reach her.

Taking deep breaths to calm herself, Rory realized she was running on adrenaline. Her heart was racing and she was sweating, even in the air conditioned car. Checking the rearview mirror as she drove, she accelerated, driving over the speed limit.

She knew Media would be clogged with traffic, as always on a Saturday, so she decided to take a circuitous route which might save time in the end. Peaches, still clinging to Rory, began panting. "It's okay baby, we'll be fine. We're not going to the vet." Rory saw her ears go back at the mention of the vet. *Smart cat.* She was glad she'd gotten Peaches out of the house. The thought made her feel better and Peaches was a comforting presence. Turning onto Alicia's street, Rory quickly surveyed the area. Seeing nothing, she parked quickly, gathered up Peaches, her purse and the yearbook. She ran for the house as if her life depended on it, and pounded on the front door, looking furtively around her.

It seemed forever before Alicia peered out the front window and opened the door.

"Thank God you're safe…"

"Thank God you're home…"

Both spoke at the same time. Alicia made sure the front door was bolted after Rory.

"What've you got there, besides the cat?" Alicia asked.

"It's Marc's high school yearbook; I think I've found the killer," Rory said breathlessly.

"Come on upstairs, I just found Mom's journal; we can compare notes."

"Wow, Alicia; just what we'd hoped to find!" Rory allowed herself to feel a small sense of relief.

"I was starting to read it when you banged on the door. I've got to admit I was scared to death when I couldn't reach you; why didn't you call me?"

"Oh, well, I found this yearbook up in the attic—Peaches had gotten locked up there—saw this," she pointed to the picture in the book. "And then I ran like hell when I heard footsteps in the attic. I left my cell at home," she added ruefully.

Alicia was staring at the picture, "JK; I don't think I've ever seen him. So you think he's the one?" Then, she noticed his name, and said, "Ohhhh…"

"Yeah, he's got to be our guy, but your mom's journal might give us the proof we need, so let's look through it." Just then a thought occurred to her. "I really need to call Roland, but shit, I don't know his number. It's in my cell—in fact all my numbers are in it, damn!"

"You mean Roland didn't follow you?" Alicia asked nervously.

"No, he wasn't where he said he'd be, so I just came straight here. I'm sure he'll come here when he can't reach me." Rory tried to sound more confident than she felt.

"We should call someone," Alicia said, biting her lip.

"I'll call Sam and Sarah; they can get in touch with him!" Rory said with relief.

She dialed her office number and got the answering machine. Looking exasperated, she blurted, "What the fuck—I can't reach anyone today!" She left a message, anyway. "Sam, Sarah, jeez, I hope you get this. I'm with Alicia, at her house; I ran out without my cell, so can't contact anyone. Please let Roland know where I am."

Alicia looked anxious, Rory was fighting panic; but that wouldn't help the situation, Rory knew.

"We could call the State Police barracks," Alicia suggested.

"Yeah, but Roland's off today; he's doing this on his own time." Rory added.

"I'm sure he'll be here soon; we might as well look through the journal… I'm thinking sometime around April, a month before Kathie's death," Rory said briskly.

Alicia scanned the pages as Rory read over her shoulder. Rory pointed to a page; April 17th Alicia read, "I'm concerned about Kathie; there's something furtive about her, almost as if she has a dark secret. She won't acknowledge it, when I ask, but I don't think it has to do with Jeff because she's said the counseling is going well." Rory and Alicia traded a look, then continued paging.

"Here's something; on April 25th she writes: 'Took Kathie out for lunch today and flat out asked her what was wrong. She tried making excuses at first, then finally leveled with me. She'd been trying to balance the books, and said she'd discovered huge sums of money couldn't be accounted for. She didn't know what to do, and wanted to be sure that she hadn't missed anything. That was all she'd say. She seemed real upset.'" Alicia's voice rose with excitement.

Rory said, "Let's look at something closer to Kathie's death—May 15th."

Alicia turned pages until they came to the second week of May. "Oh, here's one on the 14th." They both read the passage: "Kathie was really nervous today. I took her aside and asked what was up. She said, 'Wish me luck, I'm meeting with the person I think is cooking the books.' I told her 'good luck.' She seemed terrified, but refused to say any more. I'm really worried."

"That's the day she met with JK," Rory said, "Of course!"

Alicia continued to leaf through the book. "Wow, mom didn't write in the book until a few weeks after Kathie died. The next one is May 30th. Oh, this is sad, I can't read it out loud—can you read it Rory?"

"Sure," Rory said, and began to read: "'I still can't believe that Kathie's gone. I miss her every day, and I'm very upset that they've arrested Jeff; I just don't believe he killed her. I can't help thinking it had something to do with the office, and I wish to God she'd told me who she suspected. I'm a nervous wreck at work, always looking over my shoulder. I have to find another job.'"

Rory flipped through the pages and looked at the passage for June 6th. She read: "'Even though it scares me to death, I've been looking through the books, trying to find out who stole the money. I have to do it when no one else is there, and I'm not nearly as good at it as Kathie was. But I need to find out what she knew before I take action.'"

They were looking for more passages, when they heard a noise downstairs; it sounded like a chair toppling over. Turning towards each other, their faces mirrored frozen terror. Rory pushed the book under the covers. Peaches, who'd been sitting happily on the bed, ducked under it. Alicia grabbed the knife, sliding it under a pillow.

The killer stood in the doorway, grinning. "Well, well, ladies, I'm guessing you found what I've been looking for."

Chapter 55

Roland had watched Marc and the girls leave. The first part of the plan was set in motion. He settled back for what might be a long wait. Then, he sat bolt upright, as a black car, a late model Audi, turned at the intersection by Rory's house and began to follow Marc's Honda. The killer could've dumped the BMW; it'd been seen too often.

Shit! What to do? Roland decided quickly that he had to follow the Audi. When the car had passed him, he'd seen only a guy in a baseball cap and sunglasses.

That was only the second car that'd passed in the 15 minutes he'd been at his post.

Better safe than sorry, Roland thought, as he pulled out of his hiding spot and slowly tailed the black car with tinted windows.

After a few minutes, Marc had made three turns and the Audi had done the same—coincidence? Roland thought not. The black car was still trailing by some distance, as was Roland. He was getting edgy. Should he warn Marc, tell him to pull over? No, he decided; that was too risky, so he stayed with the caravan.

Close to ten minutes had elapsed, when suddenly, the black car signaled for a right turn, and pulled into a gas station. The driver got out, took off her cap, shook out her long blond hair, and began to put gas in her car.

"Jesus Christ!" Roland wheeled around and sped back toward Rory's house, thinking he'd best call Rory to let her know what had happened.

He dialed the home phone first and left a message when Rory didn't pick up. Dialing her cell, he again got her recording. He left a message on it as well, beginning to panic.

How could he have screwed up the plan so soon? He tried not to think of all the 'what ifs,' because it would make him crazy. He'd been entrusted with her safety, and he'd botched it already! Banging his fist on the steering wheel, he asked himself, *was that the right move?* Breathing deeply, he tried to regain control; he needed to think this through.

Meanwhile, he was racing down the back roads to her house; if only he wasn't too late! He pictured sitting in the breakfast nook with Rory later, laughing over this, but it was hardly a laughing matter now.

The plan hadn't included him stopping at her house, but all that had changed; he had to check her house and make sure she was safe. He'd made good time; in a few minutes he'd be there. He'd been gone, what? A total of fifteen minutes; not bad.

Slowing as he arrived at her house, the first thing he noticed was that Rory's car wasn't in the driveway; and second, the front door was partially open. *This could not be good.*

He checked for his gun, took the safety off and approached the house with caution. Nudging the front door open with his foot, he quickly entered. He listened, but heard nothing. Noticing the answering machine light was blinking, he realized she hadn't gotten his call. Worse yet, her cell was charging on the counter! That explained why she hadn't called, but where was she?

All of his instincts told him that she'd fled in a hurry, but he had to check the house all the same. He quickly checked the downstairs. Finding nothing, he crept up the back stairs to the second floor. He immediately noticed the stairs to the attic were down and the light in the attic was on. He hurried up the steps, sure by now that he was alone in the house.

Reaching the top step, he noticed the attic in disarray; furniture was askew, books were scattered and he saw broken glass on the floor below the attic window.

Stumbling down the rickety steps, he raced out of the house and back to his car, piecing together what'd probably happened. The killer had climbed a tree to the roof and broken the window. He'd entered and waited in the attic. At some point, Rory must've heard him and run for her life, forgetting her phone. He prayed she was okay.

Roland called the Media Police and asked for back-up, giving Alicia's address.

Instinctively, he headed for Alicia's, but on the way he called Rory's office. Sam answered the phone; "Sam, it's Roland, I'll make this quick. Have you guys heard from Rory?"

"No, what's up?" Sam asked anxiously.

"She's not at home; I think the killer was at her house and she fled; I'm on the way to Alicia's now! I alerted the police."

"Meet you there!" Sam flung the phone down. "Sarah, we've got to get over to Alicia's—I'll explain on the way. And you'd best call Marc!"

Roland felt better having talked with Sam, and he was glad for some back up, but he still prayed to God he wasn't too late. How much of a head start did the killer have on him? And had he taken Rory, or had Rory left on her own? If she'd run from the killer she'd have gone to Alicia's; he was sure of that. Of course, he thought guiltily, she'd probably come looking for him first.

Roland arrived at Alicia's just as Sam and Sarah got there. He spotted Rory's car out front, with relief. He didn't see the BMW, but that didn't mean the bastard wasn't here. He motioned for Sam and Sarah to join him, signaling silence.

Crouching near the front hedge, they whispered. Roland said, "Rory's obviously here, but the killer may be also. She fled her home, leaving the door open. We need to find a way into the house without making noise."

Just then, Marc pulled up, saw the three of them and ran over. "Jesus Christ, what happened to our plan?" He crouched down, whispering frantically.

"There was a car following you, so I followed it; turned out to be nothing—I thought it was legit, but that wasted valuable time. Anyway," Roland continued, "Rory's here and the killer may be as well; we need to find a way in."

Sam spoke up, "When Blake and Rory came here, they went in through the back; there's a key hidden under a chair."

"OK, good," Roland said, "here's the plan; I'll go in the back. Marc, you cover the back entrance, asking, "You have your gun?" Marc nodded.

"Sam and Sarah—you cover the front; either of you have a weapon?"

"I do," Sarah said. "I'm trained, don't worry," she answered, noticing Roland's surprised look.

"OK, then, be safe everyone!" Roland and Marc kept crept around to the back, staying close to the house.

As they reached the back door, they looked at each other in horror; the killer had preceded them; the back door stood open, a chair overturned inside. Roland motioned for Marc to stay, and put his finger to his lips.

He entered the house and soon was out of sight.

Chapter 56

The killer pointed a revolver in their direction and said, "OK, hand it over and I'll be on my way. You've put me through enough trouble already, so make it quick!"

Something seemed to snap in Alicia's head; she ran toward him, brandishing her butcher knife. "You killed my mother!" she screamed in a loud wail, knife poised to stab him.

She managed to slice his shoulder as he struggled with her, the knife clattering to the floor.

Before Rory could even react, he had his revolver at Alicia's head and had her in a choke hold. Blood trickled from his shoulder, but he managed to kick the knife aside.

Appealing to his over blown ego, Rory engaged him, "Why, Joe, why'd you do it? Did you need money for the cancer treatment?"

His laugh was maniacal; "Cancer treatment?" he asked, smiling. "Yeah, I guess everybody bought that; brilliant, huh? Just had to lose some weight, shave my head."

"So, why?" Rory asked, fighting for time.

"Why? Ask my bitch wife why! She needed more money, more things, more, more, more! And then she left without a trace—faithless whore!"

"She left, or you killed her?" Rory asked boldly.

"Oh, believe me, I'd have killed her in a heartbeat, but I couldn't find her. She wiped out our savings and left." He laughed again, nearly out of control. "By then, I had more than enough stashed elsewhere. You want to know where? But if I tell you, I'll have to kill you!" He laughed again, uncontrollably. Then he seemed to jolt back to reality.

In that moment, Rory realized how far he'd gone over the edge, and needed to keep him talking.

"But why Kathie and Helen?" Rory persisted.

"Why? The nosey bitches were on to me! They would've ruined my whole plan! Kathie was checking the books. She had the nerve, or stupidity, rather, to question me about the missing money. She wasn't sure if it was me or Jeremy. I had to put a stop to that before she told Jeremy."

"And Helen?" Rory knew she was pushing it a bit here.

"No more questions, and no more answers! " Joe exploded. "Give me what I came for or it will be a slaughterhouse in here!"

At that moment, Alicia gave him a vicious elbow shot to the ribs and he stumbled backwards. As soon as he released his grip, she dove for the floor and scuttled away from him. He fired, but she was already under the bed.

The gunshot spooked Peaches, who flew out from under the bed, surprising Klein, and knocking him off balance. Rory saw her opportunity, and swung into action, her self-defense training fresh in her mind.

With a swift kick to his gun hand Rory followed up with a knee to his groin. He buckled, but still held the gun, and began firing wildly. Rory ducked as a bullet whizzed by her head and hit the dresser.

Soundlessly, Alicia slithered out from under the bed and grabbed for his feet. Again, he stumbled, and realizing he was out of bullets, turned to retreat.

Behind him, Roland blocked his way—"Drop the gun— it's over!" He wheeled on the trooper; it looked like a standoff, but Klein ducked and ran for it. Surprised, Roland took aim and fired, but Klein was too fast and the shot missed him.

He ran into Marc, coming up the stairs, gun drawn, and gave him a vicious shove, toppling him over.

Marc recovered quickly and ran after Roland, in hot pursuit, as Klein darted through back yards and alleyways. The scream of sirens diverted their attention and then Klein was just gone, nowhere to be seen.

Marc and Roland hunkered down, catching their breath, and looked around. Roland must've seen movement; he motioned for Marc to go one way, and he went the other.

Marc was closest when Klein made his move to dart out from under a bush. Marc tackled him, knocking the gun from Klein's hand. Though smaller than Marc, Klein was strong and almost escaped from Marc's grasp. But Roland was there, and put a gun to Klein's head.

Sam and Sarah arrived, breathless, just as the Media Police pulled up.

Officer Jamison got out of the car. He nodded to Roland, asking, "This our guy?" Roland nodded, breathless.

Then Officer Jamison got a good look at the suspect, asking in surprise, "Joe Klein?" and shaking his head. Giving the man his Miranda warnings, he put him in the back of the car.

Klein was yelling, "I know my fuckin' rights, I'm a lawyer, for Christ sakes!"

Jamison looked at Roland and asked, "Who'd have thought?" Then he said to Roland, "This what you do on your day off?"

"Only for friends," he answered. "Good friends," he clarified, clapping Marc on the shoulder. "Hey, nice job, man, tackling the perp!"

"He almost killed my wife!" Marc said, dead serious.

Chapter 57

In the wake of the arrest, Rory was swamped with details. She knew she was running on empty, but had to keep going. Sam and Sarah were helpful, doing anything that was required.

She and Alicia had finally finished reading Helen's journal. Her last entry named Klein as the probable embezzler; she was planning to tell Jeremy.

Rory had turned the journal over to Como, who believed he had a strong enough case against Klein to drop the charges against Korbin. Elated, Rory urged him to expedite the paperwork so Korbin could be released today, not Monday. To her surprise, he'd agreed. She knew he'd have to find a judge to sign the order, but that wasn't a big deal. She took a deep breath, congratulating herself, but she knew she couldn't have done it without everyone else's help and support.

She'd called Jeremy, who was completely confounded. When he thought about it, he said, "Well, at least I know I'm not going crazy; I was busting my ass, taking more and more cases, and yet there was less money. At first I thought it was because Joe was sick, but then I began to question everything…"

Rory had a few questions, which honestly had made her look at Jeremy as a suspect. "So, did Helen really have fainting spells at work?" she asked.

"That's what Joe said—I believed him. And, frankly, I was overwhelmed with work and didn't question it." Jeremy replied. "Damn stupid of me!"

"Well, he had everyone buffaloed, with the cancer thing. No one would've thought to question him. When things got hot, he just had a relapse. He told me it was a brilliant plan, and he was right. But he's also nuts!" Rory said emphatically.

"You're probably right. He must've also told Korbin's sister not to release the phone message tape. When you asked me about that, it really bothered me. I didn't remember her calling, and couldn't imagine that I'd have given that advice. But, like I said, so much was going on I didn't know which end was up. I really dropped the ball, Rory." He sounded defeated.

"Well, under the circumstances, I think it could happen to anybody. By the way, Klein hinted at having stashed the money elsewhere, so the authorities shouldn't have trouble tracking his dummy corporation and figuring out where the money ended up. You should get most of it back, eventually."

"Yeah, well, that somehow seems much less important now; two wonderful women died for his greed, and if you hadn't ..." Jeremy's voice shook.

"It's ok, Jeremy, take some time off—you deserve it." Rory said and hung up.

The phone rang as soon as Rory had hung up. It was Stan, assuring her he'd done everything to secure Korbin's release; he'd be free within the hour.

"Stan, that's music to my ears—thanks so much!" Rory sat still, not quite believing.

Rory's call to Korbin's sister caught her totally unawares. "Jay, it's Rory. So, you have maybe an hour or so free today?"

"For you, Rory, of course! What's up?"

"Are you sitting?" Rory asked.

"No, why?" Jay asked, uneasily.

"You might just want to. Wait for it—Jeff is being released today! How soon can you get over there to pick him up?"

"I know you wouldn't kid about this Rory...."

"Hell, no!" Rory said unequivocally. "Get your ass over there!"

"Oh My God!" Jay shrieked.

Chapter 58

Rory was the last one in the office, having sent Sam and Sarah off hours ago. They were planning to visit Blake in the hospital and fill him in on the latest. She'd spoken with Blake by phone and he understood she was sorry she couldn't see him until the next day.

When she was overcome with exhaustion, Rory called it a day, looking forward to a quiet evening with Marc and the girls, assuming the girls hadn't gone out.

Rory was bone weary when she pulled into the driveway. There were very few lights on in the house and it seemed eerily quiet on her approach to the front door.

The door wasn't locked, so someone must be home. Rory had a déjà vu moment recalling the incident of a few days ago and shivered. Slowly opening the front door, the lights flashed on, and Rory heard a chorus of "For she's a jolly good fellow!" followed by cheers of, "Way to go!" "You did it!" "You're our hero!" and applause; lots of applause.

Rory was stunned. Marc and the girls came forward to embrace her. Still in shock, Rory looked around at the banners, balloons, and streamers, not to mention a huge buffet table. Heading for the food, Rory realized she hadn't eaten since that one piece of toast this morning. Was it possible that all of this had happened in one day? It all felt surreal.

Before making it to the food, more people came over to congratulate Rory; Charlie and his wife were the first to approach. "Always believed in you, Rory!" Charlie said with tears in his eyes. Then he whispered, "And you got the Judge good, too!"

"I'm not taking credit for that," Rory winked.

Alicia and Vanessa came forward, as did Jeremy and his wife. Officer Jamison was there, along with Stan Como, and McClain. *My, my,* Rory thought to herself.

Looking around for Sam and Sarah, she spotted them just entering. They came right over to her, and Sarah reported, "Blake is doing well; we even got to talk to his doc, who said he may be home in a few days. Blake sends his love, but he's pissed to miss the party, so you know he's feeling better! But I think he's sweet on one of his nurses, so he doesn't really mind staying."

"That's great news!" Rory said. "But now, I must eat, haven't eaten since breakfast." She took a plate and filled it with all of her favorites.

"Who did the catering?" she asked Alex, as she passed by.

"What, you don't think we did it?" Alex asked dramatically, pausing before answering, "It's from 'On a Roll'—I'd use them again. What do you think?"

Rory's mouth was full so she gave her a 'thumbs up.' Everything was delicious and she finished it quickly—too quickly— she had to sit. People were still seeking her out; Rory enjoyed talking with them all. She was talking to Don, when the place went silent. Rory looked up to see what was happening.

Jeff and Jay were standing in the doorway looking awkward. Rory jumped up and ran to them. The three embraced, all of them tearful. The gathering broke out in applause. Rory thought, *how quickly the tide can change.* But she was grateful she'd helped to bring about the change.

Rory brought Jeff and his sister into the room; introducing them to people they didn't know. Sam and Sarah stayed with Jeff and Jay, trying to put them at ease.

Como and McClain sought Rory out for some shop talk. Como said, "Well, now that we have Klein's prints, we know he was the one who trashed Ms. Willis's house. And he left a few prints at Helen's house, too. Of course, the journal is another good piece of evidence, and he did, in fact, confess to you. It's all circumstantial, of course, but we're pretty sure Klein will plead out, if he doesn't want to be looking at death row."

McClain added, "He'd better come up with the money, too; Jeremy needs restitution."

Como and McClain chatted a bit more with Rory before taking their leave. Other guests seemed to take the cue and came over to say goodbye; everyone knew it had been a long day for Rory.

When the last farewell had been said, Alex and Kate put all the food away, and then went out with friends. For them, the evening began at 10:00 p.m.

Rory was beat, but happy. She and Marc were sitting together on the couch. Looking up at Marc, Rory noticed something uneasy in his demeanor. She needed to know now what had been going on with him this past month.

"OK, Marc, I solved the big mystery, thank God. But now I need to know what's been going on with you, with us, for the past month.

"Rory…" he began, tears starting to well in his eyes. "I almost lost you today; I had to face what my life would be like without you. It would be pretty grim…"

"Yes?' Rory was waiting for more; even though she wasn't sure she wanted to hear it.

"I'm not finished, and I have to say this before I lose courage… if our relationship can't be based on honesty and trust, then it will fail."

Rory looked bewildered.

Marc continued, "This is about Kathie; I was smitten by Kathie in high school, and we had a little fling during senior week. But that ended, and I went off to school…"

"Yeah, I wondered about what she wrote in your yearbook..."

It was Marc's turn to look confused.

"I forgot to tell you; I found your yearbook in the attic; it helped me solve the 'JK' mystery—you know, that was Klein's nickname, in high school."

"Oh...I forgot that; never liked the guy!" Marc replied. Then he sighed and continued. "Anyway, I never quite got Kathie out of my head. It was a sophomoric kind of crush."

"So, what does that have to do with us?" Rory asked, impatient and uneasy.

"I hadn't seen her or thought of her in years, until I ran into her about two years ago. She was working for the same law firm I was doing some work for."

He hesitated, looking at the floor, not making eye contact. Rory tensed.

Marc continued, "If you recall, we were going through a rough patch at the time, not that it's an excuse. Anyway, Kathie and I went out for a drink, which became two, and... then... I slept with her. I realized my mistake immediately; there was nothing between Kathie and me. I knew with certainty that you were the only one for me. I never told you for fear of losing you. I've been wanting to tell you but never found the courage. Real bad timing, I know."

Rory had gone motionless; she was sitting there as still as a mannequin, her mind reeling, her body heavy and numb. She felt sucker-punched.

"I'm weak and foolish, but I love you. I've been acting like a total jackass for the last month, when you needed my support. I was so afraid you'd find out, afraid she'd told Jeff, that I pushed you away. I realize that now. I pray it's not too late. Believe me, whatever you decide..." Marc put his head in his hands.

Rory looked at her watch, expressionless. She said, "It's late, and I'm tired. I can't think about this tonight—maybe tomorrow…"

Epilogue

Martha's Vineyard- August

Rory, slathered with sunscreen and sporting a broad-brimmed hat, lay on a comfortable chaise by the pool. It was a perfect late-August day, with brilliant blue skies and not a hint of humidity. She felt her body settle into the chair as the tension melted away. Clearing her mind, she heard only twittering birds and the soft chirping of crickets. The buzzing drone of cicadas was fading, as was the hot weather.

Then, slowly, thoughts began to intrude. As she looked back over the past summer, Rory realized just how much tension she'd been holding onto. There was a certain satisfaction to having solved the mystery of the murder of two women. She flinched as she thought of Helen and of her horrific death.

The other mystery, the question of Marc's atypical behavior, had been answered. Rory wasn't always pleased she'd pushed for the answer. Of course, she'd needed to know, that was her nature. But how to deal with it was another matter entirely, one Rory could no longer put off until tomorrow.

Rory and Marc had struggled through July, with the twins waiting anxiously for their parents to get back to normal. Rory grimaced at the thought, *what was normal?* She understood now what people meant when they spoke of the "new normal". And that was what she and Marc would have to find. They'd both been changed.

Rory and Marc had begun marriage counseling, ironically with Adele Grant, Kathie and Jeff Korbin's therapist. As Korbin had told Rory, Dr. Grant was a skilled therapist. It was she who'd suggested that Rory spend a week of vacation, the long-postponed vacation, by herself. And that Marc and the girls join her for the second week, when she'd had time to clear her mind.

As was typical of Rory, she was just now beginning to sort out her thoughts. It was nearing the end of her week, and she could no longer put it off. Beginning to feel the familiar guilt, Rory shook it off, knowing it was unproductive.

Impulsively, Rory jumped from her chair, tossing hat and sunglasses and dove into the pool. The cold water shocked her senses and gave her clarity.

The first thought that came to her mind was a memory of the day the family were celebrating Sean's court victory. Rory's mother, sensing an unspoken sadness in Rory, had suggested they talk. That simple invitation released a flood of feelings as Rory poured out her agony to her mother. Rory remembered clearly what she'd told her mother. She was afraid Marc was cheating on her and she loved him so much.

As Rory swam fluidly back and forth in the pool, that thought stayed with her. It was really quite simple, with all the other "stuff" pushed out of the way. She loved Marc; they had built a solid, if not perfect, marriage and Rory wanted to improve on it. She'd been miserable this summer and had yearned for Marc's support. Both of them had been too stubborn to give in.

Swimming one last lap, Rory had decided to call Marc as soon as she got out of the pool, and tell him to come now; she needed him.

Pulling herself up at the deep end, Rory saw a pair of legs. Looking up, there was Marc, smiling and holding the towel open for her, waiting to enfold her in warmth and love. Rory didn't hesitate.

Enjoy this excerpt from Jacki Bishop's new book: Sarah's Gone Missing

Chapter 1

Daylight had begun to seep in under the blinds when the incessant buzzing of her cell phone awakened Rory Chandler. Reaching blindly for it, she nearly knocked it to the floor. Glancing at the clock she saw it was 6:00 AM; this could not be good news.

Taking a deep breath, she answered with an uncertain "Hello..."

"Rory, it's Sam. I'm sorry to call you so early, but I just couldn't wait any longer; it's Sarah—she's gone!"

Shaking her head, as if to clear her brain, Rory noticed that Marc was awake and looking at her quizzically. She gave a helpless shrug, and tried to concentrate on Sam.

"Uh, Sam, I'm not sure I follow; you knew she was going to the Hamptons to visit friends, right?"

"Yes, yes, of course! She'd been there a few days; they just called me, well, that is they called around 3 AM, to tell me she went out for a walk along the beach, and she hasn't come back!"

She could feel Sam's pain through the phone; Rory tried to soothe him. "I'm sure there must be some mix-up; it's just not like Sarah to go off and not tell anyone."

"I know, I know; that's the thing, it's not like her. She went out after dinner, Lisa and Rob went to bed early and left the light on for her. When Lisa woke up during the night, she noticed the light was still on and checked Sarah's room; she wasn't there!"

Marc was fully awake now and looking concerned. She handed him the phone and mouthed "It's Sam, not good."

"Sam, this is Marc; I gather there's a problem with Sarah. Rory just handed me the phone and from what I heard, it sounds serious."

Sam sighed audibly, "Yes, I'm afraid it is serious, you see Sarah was staying with friends in the Hamptons and went out for a walk on the beach after dinner; she never came back!"

"And did her friends go out searching for her?"

"They did, as soon as they realized she was missing, but that was in the middle of the night. It was dark out so they couldn't see too much, but…they saw tire tracks on the beach, which in itself isn't unusual; people drive down there to fish or park, or whatever…"

Rory walked into the room with two cups of coffee and handed one to Marc. He spoke to Sam again. "Hang on, Sam, Rory just came back with coffee. Look, why not just come over here; it's best we talk in person and put our heads together, ok?"

"Sure, thanks so much, I'll be right there." Sam said.

"Hey, Sam, drive carefully." Marc advised.

Disengaging the phone, Marc handed it to Rory, shaking his head. "Man, he sounds bad."

"I know," Rory replied, sitting down on the bed close to Marc, "not at all like the logical, calm guy we know. Sorry I dumped the phone on you; I just didn't know what to say. Good idea, inviting him over; we obviously need more info if we can find a way to help." Rory shuddered involuntarily, and a tear slipped down her face. "God, where could she be? She's become like a third daughter to me, and Sam, well, I can't imagine what he's going through. Mind if I shower first? It helps to clear my mind."

Marc nodded. "No problem." His face was grim.

In the shower, Rory gave in to her tears, letting the warm water wash them away. She'd known Sarah for, what? Five months? She and Sam had been interns in Rory's law office over the summer. Together, they'd solved a crime and saved a man from a possible death sentence. They'd grown very close in a short period of time. Sam and Sarah had become an "item", and now they were living together, both in their last year of law school, at different schools. It felt like they were part of her family. She couldn't fathom losing Sarah.

Getting out of the shower, Rory mentally shook herself. She was no good to Sam if she lost it, and they had to find Sarah.

Reentering the bedroom, she found Marc sitting in the same spot; he seemed in a daze. "Your turn," Rory said, gesturing toward the bathroom, "It helped me to focus, I need to get dressed before Sam gets here."

"Yeah, I hope..." Marc wandered into the bathroom, his sentence dangling.

Rory threw on some jeans and a tee shirt. They'd been enjoying beautiful Fall weather; Rory loved October and typically felt invigorated by the cooler weather. Right now, it felt as if she was moving through heavy sand.

Without drying her hair or putting on makeup, Rory went down the back stairs to the kitchen. The sun was up now, lending a cheery note to her well-appointed kitchen. Sitting in the breakfast nook, her favorite spot in the house, was comforting. She looked out the window and took in the gorgeous array of foliage.

The knock on the front door jolted her; Rory hurried to let Sam in before her daughters awoke. It was Saturday, and still before seven.

Rory wasn't prepared for the Sam Logan who appeared at her door. He looked gaunt, was unshaven, and his longish brown hair was flopping in his face. Typically handsome with a boyish smile and warm brown eyes, he'd lost his best friend and his appearance reflected that.

Opening her arms to give him a hug, Sam clung to her like a child and began sobbing.

Keeping her own tears at bay, Rory patted him on the back and assured him, "We'll find her, I know it!" She hoped her words, which sounded implausible to her ear, would comfort Sam.

Marc came down the front stairs as Sam was pulling away from Rory and wiping his face.

"Hey man," Marc clapped him on the shoulder, "rough situation; we need to talk and put our brain power to work. Come get some coffee."

Rory, already in the kitchen, asked Sam and Marc, "You guys hungry? We should probably eat something…"

Marc answered for both of them, "Let's just have eggs and toast; give our brains a boost."

Sam nodded, as he took the cup of coffee Rory handed him.

Marc and Sam sat in the breakfast nook while Rory prepared breakfast.

She could hear Marc talking quietly to Sam. He was asking Sam to think back over the past week with Sarah, before she left to visit her friends. Marc wanted to know if he could think of anything unusual that might have happened. Was there anything atypical in Sarah's behavior? Why did she decide she wanted to visit her friends at this time, and why hadn't he gone with her?

Rory was feeling reassured by the questions Marc was asking. She was so glad to have him in her corner. Thinking back over the past, difficult, summer when Marc had been angry with her much of the time, ostensibly for taking on a tough case that might interfere with their vacation plans, Rory was relieved. Of course, that had been just the tip of the iceberg, she found out as the case was being resolved. Yes, it had been a difficult summer, but she and Marc were back on track. Her feelings of betrayal were there, beneath the surface, but she and Marc were in counseling and they had a good, solid history; quite simply, they loved each other. Recently, their communication had improved immensely, and in Rory's mind that was key.

Glancing at the nook where Marc and Sam were still deep in conversation, Rory noticed that Sam looked better. Marc knew what he was doing; as a forensic psychologist, he was well equipped to ask the right questions. He had certainly put Sam at ease.

She brought the plates of food over and sat down to eat and join in the discussion.

Sam picked at his food as he talked. He'd listened to Marc's questions and began to answer them.

"Looking back, I think it was after Sarah's visit to her father a few weeks ago that she started behaving differently. She was quiet a lot, and when I asked her what was on her mind, she blamed it on school. I'd never known her to brood before. I know Sarah and her dad haven't exactly gotten along famously, but she'd never been this…distant after a visit with him. By the way, I've never met him; she hasn't seemed to want me to." Sam sighed and started to eat again.

"How were things between you and Sarah?" Rory asked, immediately regretting it.

Sam's face fell. Then he answered, "You know, I asked her several times if I'd done something to upset her; I was beginning to take it personally. She always denied there was a problem with us, but I felt she was slipping away. Definitely, there was something weighing on her. So when her friend Lisa called to invite us to come visit, I suggested that she go alone, that, maybe she needed time away to work things out. Oh God! If only I'd gone..." Sam put his head in his hands.

Marc patted his shoulder, while Rory sat stricken and mute.

The silence was broken by a muffled ringing, apparently from Sam's pocket. He came to life, tearing the phone out .

After a quick glance, he said, "It's from Lisa." He listened, nodding, then said, "Thanks, Lisa, appreciate it. I'll be in touch." The color had drained from his face. He sat down, mute.

Rory and Marc were anxiously awaiting his response.

Finally, he turned to them and said, "They found a sandal at the end of the beach...just one, they think it was Sarah's."

About the Author

Jacquelyn Bishop has lived in Media, Pennsylvania, a small town less than a half hour from Philadelphia (the end of the trolley line), for all of her adult life.

A veteran of the juvenile justice system, she brings a rich knowledge of the court's complexities to her first novel.

After leaving the justice system, and a brief stint of teaching, she took up her life-long love of writing.

She has two grown sons and lives with her husband, Hank (not forgetting her cats, Allie and Mitzi.)

When she's not writing, she loves to hike in the park, care for her orchids (inherited from son, Andrew) and other plants. Spending time playing with granddaughter Lilia, age five, occupies an important, if exhausting, place in her life.

Ordering Information

To order additional copies of this and future books by Jacki Bishop, please use the contact information below:

Early Riser Publishing
P.O. Box 711
101 E. Baltimore Ave.
Media, PA 19063
www.JackiBishop.com
jaxstir@comcast.net

Thank you for reading this book. I would appreciate any and all reviews online. ~Jacki

CPSIA information can be obtained at www.ICGtesting.com
Printed in the USA
BVOW08s1233051015

420493BV00001B/2/P